THE ZONE

a novel

by: Ed Kennedy

Connie,
We will always be connected by that very emotional time in our lives. I cherish your friendship.

This is a work of fiction. All characters, organizations, and scientific events portrayed in this novel are either products of the author's imagination or are used fictitiously. All federal and state laws cited are contrived to fit the story. The story transcends time. The Zone did not exist.

ISBN 978-1-312-27378-8

To Mom and Dad

Acknowledgments

This is an acknowledgment of gratitude not only for those who helped me with this book but to those friends and family who have so positively affected my life.

To my wonderful sisters, Roberta Douglas and Sandy Delaney, who encouraged and supported me through all the years. There has never been a harsh word spoken between us. I thank them for marrying so well; I couldn't ask for better brothers-in-law than Bob Douglas and Bob Delaney. My sisters were my early readers and they cut me no slack because I was their brother. It was needed and appreciated.

My lifetime friends are so important to me and I tried to honor them in my own way throughout the book. Thank you Henry Kopek, Bob Brown, Mike Uhes, Ian Griggs, John Sesney, Fred Howell, Bob Hayes, and Wayne Stoker for your contributions to the book and for your friendship.

There are others - a thanks to Cathy Griggs for introducing me to the Celtic Woman's version of 'You Raise Me Up' and to early readers and dear friends, Brenda Stewart and Victoria Fugit. It was Vicky who, many years ago, first awakened in me any artistic talents I may have. I will always be grateful.

To my secretary of many years, Flo Ruppert, who forever challenged me, a special thanks. The same to my good friends Lois Zabor, Jane Kennedy, Nan Kreher, and Sue Howell.

Longtime friend, John Intelisano, was my very first reader and most outspoken supporter. It came at a crucial time and motivated me to move forward and complete the book.

Rick Fiore was extremely helpful in sharing with me his own experience when self-publishing his book, The Premonition Code.

A special thanks to another old and dear friend, Barry Zimmerman. Barry immediately read everything that I sent to him and reported back to me in record time. He championed my work and was the most insistent of all that I publish. He and his wife Louisa's encouragement and praise was greatly appreciated.

The Zone would never have been started, completed, edited or published without the support and efforts of my wife and editor, Mary Beth McCleary. Her corrections, re-writes and additions were absolutely essential in writing this rather large novel. This is her book, too.

About The Author

Edward J. Kennedy, was born in Detroit, Michigan on July 7, 1940.

Unlike the protagonists of The Zone, he grew up in the suburbs of Ferndale and Southfield.

After attending Western Michigan University, the University of Detroit, the University of Miami (Florida), Utah State University, Michigan State University and the Detroit College of Law he emerged with a couple of undergraduate degrees and a Juris Doctorate.

Ed became bored with the practice of law and in 1980 took a 10 year sabbatical to travel, hike, run rivers and photograph wildlife in the great American West.
Economic reality set in and he returned to the business of law, retiring in 2005.

Ed currently resides in the beachside town of New Smyrna Beach, Florida, with his wife, Mary Beth, and their dog, Chip.

Introduction

I had not intended to render this story to the printed word let alone publish it. An interesting set of circumstances dictated otherwise.

Retiring from the practice of law, I rewarded myself with a trip to the Pacific Rim in 2005. After crossing many time zones and the international date line, I returned to the U.S. in December of that year. My body time clock never got the message that I had returned and for the next five years I stared at the ceiling during normal sleep time.

I tried all the usual remedies for insomnia, to no avail. I just lay there with my mind awhirl. I entertained myself by drifting into the world of fantasy. At first it was a return to my boyhood dreams: the star baseball player, slayer of dragons, and even the leader of the free world.

Then, for whatever reason, I decided to create a fictional story about children growing up in the ghettos of the city where I was born, Detroit, Michigan. Thus the genesis of The Zone. It is the only book that I ever wrote or probably ever will.

But back in my early stages of sleepless nights, it wasn't a book - merely another fantasy stored in my head. All my other fantasies lasted only one night, then off to another adventure. However, this one was different. It had evolved into a continuation of the previous night's episodes.
At first, I was interested in the developing story line; then I became fascinated by it. I used to dread going to bed because I knew that I would just lie there wide awake, frustrated by not being able to sleep. But now I couldn't wait to adjourn to my bedroom so I could 'read' the next chapter. I had no idea what it might contain or where I was taking it. That's because it was taking me. I never took notes.

As unbelievable as it might sound, I would resume this fictional story every night for five years. Sometimes I would spend several nights playing with only one character. When reduced to print, amazingly, this time spent would only amount to maybe one or two paragraphs. I didn't know it at the time but, stored in my head, was a novel of more than four hundred pages.

And there it stayed dormant. I had come to the end of this fictional story with no plans to take it out of storage.

In 2011, I attended a high school class reunion and reconnected with a classmate, Mary Beth McCleary. I hadn't seen Mary Beth in over fifty years; she was a retired school teacher, librarian, writer and avid reader. In our chats I told her about the book in my head... Well, I think you know where this is going.

Mary Beth, always the school teacher, became a persistent pest, insisting that I get the work out of my head into print. Then she became my editor, and finally my wife, all in that order. Three years later we self published The Zone.

The book's cover has an interesting story also. I took the photograph of the deserted street in Detroit long before I fantasized the book. I was standing on the corner of Woodward Ave. and Elizabeth street, looking East. What is interesting is the white building on the right, the old home of The Detroit College of Law where I attended law school. All of those structures in the photo have been bulldozed and the area is now the home of Tiger Stadium and Ford Field.

When I attended school there, the neighborhood *was* a ghetto, home to prostitutes and drug users. The entire section served as my mental picture for the fictional Zone.

Well, there you have it. All the characters are fictional and I haven't the slightest idea where they came from. I'm still amazed that I remembered the story exactly as how I fantasized it.

The Zone

Part One

Chapter 1: Nettie

"THE GIFT. THE GIFT! She has the gift!" Nettie's grandmother had shouted. She was referring to the extraordinary ability some of their ancestors had possessed. They had been able to remember and then repeat, verbatim, anything they had ever read or heard.

Nettie had certainly been blessed with those ancestral powers. She could listen to words spoken in German, French or any other language and repeat them word for word. She could look at a musical score one time and jot the notes down exactly as written. She could read a book and remember every word regardless of the language. Once the information was encoded, she never forgot it. Her abilities, however, went far beyond photographic memory skills.

Nettie's most remarkable ability, one that her ancestors did not have, was that she could not only remember words spoken in a foreign tongue, but immediately interpret them and converse freely in that language! She could hear music being played on a piano, watch the artist's finger movements and know exactly what key to press to make the same sound. She never had a lesson. How was all this possible?

OUR STORY begins in Brooklyn, N.Y.

If you closed your eyes, you would think you were in Russia, Italy, Germany, Israel, or dozens of other places around the world. The multiple languages, music, and food smells were all there. Brooklyn was a city of diverse cultures and ethnic neighborhoods and it was alive and crowded and vibrant.

Into this world was born Antoinette Jeanette Ferrari. 'Nettie' lived with her mother and grandmother on Cobble Hill, the Italian section of Brooklyn. Nettie's mother worked in a pasta making shop owned by

Mendel Kaplan. Nobody questioned why a Russian Jew would run a pasta shop; that's just how it was in Brooklyn.

Hundreds of people stopped in every day, dodging the dangling pumpkin spaghetti and squid-blackened linguine strands hanging from the rafters. The shop was a polyglot meeting place.

It was Kaplan who first noticed. Nettie, who would often go to work with her mother, was sitting at a small table in the back room with Kaplan's two children and he overheard the three of them talking. They were all speaking perfect Russian - Nettie, too! She was four years old.

Kaplan was astounded.

"Mrs. Ferrari, I didn't know your child could speak Russian!"

"What are you talking about, Mendel? She only speaks English and a little Italian."

"Go, go back there and listen to her talking to my children if you don't believe me!"

She did. After listening for a few minutes to their lively Russian conversation, she put her hands to her mouth and cried, "Oh no, she has the gift!"

"What gift? You mean she's never done that before?"

"No, she hasn't."

"Mrs. Ferrari, you must have your child studied by professionals!"

He pestered until she relented and agreed to have Nettie examined by doctors and psychologists in an attempt to explain the phenomena. The experts spent months working with the little girl. They could confirm her skills but never explain them. They soon wrote her off as an unexplainable freak of nature. This was just fine with Nettie; she went back to being a little girl.

Eventually Nettie's skills were taken for granted and she was left to enjoy a normal childhood. However, as she got older, she found her Catholic school boring and unchallenging and dropped out at the age of sixteen, taking a job in a day care center.

She loved children and had a natural ability to teach. 'Miss Nettie' sang to the little ones in their first language and told them folk stories from around the world. This is where she belonged.

Nettie was unimpressed by her powers - any computer could translate words, display musical notes and store information. She did understand, however, that few people, if any, could do what she did *without* the use of a computer. She couldn't explain these abilities, but suspected that it might have something to do with her constant exposure to the high energy, multi-lingual people who lived in Brooklyn.

With her brilliant green eyes and elegant tall figure, Nettie was striking but she had few dates. She was more interested in spending her idle hours in the city library devouring and retaining everything she read than in making small talk with potential suiters.

After both her mother and grandmother died of cancer, Nettie moved into a small flat in Cobble Hill a few blocks from the downtown area. She was now in her early twenties and was still working with children. Government agencies needed a linguist to help immigrant children as they integrated into American society. It was the perfect job for her as she could quickly become fluent in any language and use her gift to communicate with these young people.

Nettie's skills made it easy for her to succeed at whatever she attempted. Music, however, was her greatest frustration. She could play the notes and teach, but she could not play the music. On her way home from the Brooklyn Public library, Nettie often lingered outside Irish Pubs listening to the lilting music as it drifted into the street. These Irish musicians could naturally play the music and not just the notes. She never went inside but sat on a street bench near the door.

She was sitting on the bench in front of O'Toole's one early summer evening waiting for the music to begin when she felt the presence of someone near her. That presence spoke to her in a heavy Irish brogue.

"Aye lass, you be awaiting for the music to begin are ye?"

Nettie looked up and, standing in the entrance to the pub, was the most beautiful human being she had ever seen. He was tall and muscular with wavy black hair, pale green eyes and a perfect smile directed at her.

"I've been a seein' ya here before, I have, but ye never be a comin' in?"

Quickly gathering herself, Nettie said, "I dinna like ye pubs, I only like ye music."

He hesitated, then with a wide smile, said, "Ye be an Irish lass are ye? I should be a knowin' - ye with the eyes of a shamrock!"

She couldn't help but laugh, "Sorry Murphy, but I'm I-tal-li-a-no."

He looked at her inquisitively, "You be a trickin' me, you have, and my name be not Murphy, it be Sean. And what be yours?"

She stood up and still chuckling said, "I'm sorry, Sean. I rarely get to practice my Irish brogue and I couldn't resist. My name is Antoinette but everybody calls me Nettie."

She extended her hand. He took it and with a warm smile said, "Well, Nettie might be passing for Irish." They laughed.

Nettie noticed that Sean was holding a flute-like instrument in his hand and she said, "That's a strange looking flute."

"That not bein' a flute, Nettie; that be me penny whistle. A flute you be a blowin' across, me whistle you blow from the top." He demonstrated the technique, creating a beautiful soprano sound. Nettie sighed, in just a few bars she knew that he could play the music and not just the notes.

"We be about to start, Nettie, you be a comin' in now and I'll be buyin' ye a pint and I be a playin' ye favorite Irish tune."

"Oh, I don't think so, Sean," she said as he gently led her into the pub. She offered no further resistance. "Sean, what's a pint?"

A not so-cold-glass of dark liquid was placed on her table. She sipped it. Not too bad, she thought, if you like burnt coffee.

"Now, what be ye favorite tune, lass?"

Without hesitation, she said, "The Isle of Innisfree."

"Aye, lass, aye."

She knew and loved the melody but had never heard the words before. If she had, she never would have requested this haunting lyric about an Irishman far from home dreaming about his beautiful lost island. It never failed to make Sean homesick and the tune was best played on the penny whistle.

Sean's playing of the song was enchanting. Indeed, Nettie was right; he could play the music. As Sean played, the other musicians sang the melancholic words. Nettie retained every word of the song and recorded Sean's finger movements on his whistle and the length of every breath he took.

She stayed through all the sets, slowly sipping on the pint.

As she was thanking Sean and getting ready to head out into the dark, he said, "You would not be walking home by yourself would ye?"

"I just live a few blocks away. I'll be fine."

"You shall do no such thing! I'll be walkin' with ye!"

He extended his arm to her and she took it as naturally as could be. On the way home she first started to hum 'Isle of Innisfree'. Then, totally forgetting herself, she softly, and slightly out of tune, sang the song exactly as it was written finishing just as they got to her flat. He turned and looked at her, "You be knowin' the words?"

Nettie recovered nicely, "Oh yes, I've been singing it for years; it's my favorite Irish ballad."

"You'll be a comin' to the pub in the morrow. I'll be a waitin' for ye!"

"Good night, Sean, I'll be a comin'." She couldn't hide her smile.

Once inside her lonely flat, she stood peeking out the window as he strolled down the busy sidewalk. It had been an enjoyable evening with all the singing and the laughter. It made her realize that she had no real social life to speak of.

Chapter 2: Leaving

NETTIE DID RETURN the next night and the night after that. Sean only played three nights a week. She stopped in to hear him play whenever she could and he would walk her home when he finished.

As they chatted during their walks, Nettie learned that he was Sean McCleary from Belfast, Ireland. In Belfast, Sean was a highly skilled welder working for an American company that made robotics used to build cars. The parent company was located in Detroit, Michigan; its corporate headquarters was in New York.

Sean had accepted a transfer to Detroit and was routed through New York to complete paper work and visa processing. While there he was advised that his position in the Detroit plant had not cleared and that he was to stand by and wait for a call. He was allowed to remain in the country as long as a job was guaranteed. He had now been in the United States for two months and his work visa would expire one year from date of entry if he was not actively working for the company.

Sean played his music at the pub just for something to do. He had been playing the penny whistle all his life; the instrument had been passed down from his father. Sean had an excellent baritone voice and loved to sing. Like Nettie, he had no family and knew of no living relatives.

Sean began to meet Nettie every day for lunch. As an independent contractor, she was on call and worked all over the city. The lunches gave her a chance to introduce Sean to Italian food beyond pizza and spaghetti.

After pub nights, Sean and Nettie walked hand in hand to her flat. Sean would delay at the door, talking and laughing, sometimes singing, until she shushed him. They both longed for more than a goodnight kiss.

One night Nettie pulled him inside with her, closing the door behind them. He never left. It was that easy.

IT WAS A SATURDAY morning and Nettie was sleeping in after a hard week's work. Sean was off running errands. Suddenly her eyes snapped open and she sat straight up! She thought she had awakened from a heavy dream but her powerful mind would not shut down and her dream was now playing out in her conscious state. It was at once a kaleidoscope of movement, a grainy filmy scene, and then an image. A distinct image! It was an embryo, a tiny embryo! She thought she was dreaming, but no, she was awake. It was clear, so clear, and it was real - in real time - and now she felt it inside her.

Nettie was terrified. She instinctively knew that she was once again doing something with her mind that no one else could do; but this was different. Then it hit her! My god, am I looking at the inside of my own body?

She told herself that she was imagining it. But no, there it was recorded in her mind, just as always, and it was alive and real. She could recall the image in an instant and nothing would change.

She was frightened. Nettie, who rarely cried, was crying now and didn't hear Sean come in. When he saw her on the bed shaking and sobbing, he rushed over, "What is it, Nettie? What is it?"

Sean looked at her tear-filled face and he held her tightly.

"It's all right, Sean. I just had a bad dream. That's all." She looked up and was shocked to see Sean with tears running down his face!

"Why are you crying? I'm the one who had the bad dream."

"Aye, it always happens. When someone I love cries, I cry with them! It runs in me family, it does, always been so."

NETTIE WAS DETERMINED to find an explanation for what had happened to her. She spent hours in the library but there were no studies of any other such incidents. There was plenty of material on people who could control with their minds certain body functions - weight loss, muscle building, headache relief - but no reports on the mind's eye actually viewing the process. She also researched electromagnetic fields as it related to humans. She suspected that the answer might be there, but could find no conclusive studies.

Nettie knew she was pregnant long before the test results were in and knew it was going to be a son as soon as the embryo was developed enough for her mind to record it. She never disclosed any of this to Sean but simply handed him the results of the medical reports. He was overjoyed. Nettie never told Sean that he was going to have a son but, for some reason, he assumed the child would be a boy.

They planned an immediate marriage, which would also serve to give Sean a permanent resident status. They made an appointment with the Immigration office to review the procedures for filing and to pick up the necessary papers. That day would change Nettie's life forever!

Sean inquired if it was possible for their child to have dual citizenship status. It was important to him that his son could also claim Irish citizenship. The immigration agent told them that the U.S. would not have a problem with recognizing the child's dual status but it would be up to Ireland to grant the Irish citizenry.

They checked with the Irish Embassy and were informed that this would only be possible if the child were born out of wedlock. The father had to sign a statement affirming that he was a citizen of Ireland, supported by his immigration papers. Both parents would undergo blood testing and the baby's blood had to match. The child would then be granted an Irish citizenship. The couple could marry after the baby was born and it would not affect the child's dual status. Sean was elated; it meant so much to him for his son to be an Irish citizen. Nettie's Catholic upbringing was making her hesitant but she could see a real advantage in his dual citizenship, so she relented. They would not be married until after the birth of the child.

They filed the necessary papers with the Irish Embassy establishing Nettie's pregnancy. Sean declared that he was the father and their blood types were placed on record. They merely had to contact the Embassy when the child was born and send in the required documents. There was one problem. The baby was due after Sean's work visa expired which meant that he had to be called to work or be forced to leave the country before the child's birth. In that event, they would marry.

The matter resolved itself. Sean was called to work when Nettie was seven months pregnant. They made their plans to leave for Detroit. It would be an easy move. Nettie was renting a furnished flat on a month-to-month basis and she had few personal items. Sean had his whistle and some clothes. They could put all their possessions in three duffel bags and hop on a bus.

Sean had previously made arrangements for a place to stay in Detroit, anticipating a quick move. Through the company, he had made friends with a black man from Detroit whose cousin owned a boarding house close to the plant.

Sean's friend contacted his cousin who confirmed that she had a room available. The boarding house was within walking distance from the bus station. It would provide easy temporary quarters and give the couple time to get settled.

When Sean asked his friend for his cousin's name and address, the man laughed and said, "Just ask the bus station attendant to direct you to the Zone; he will know where it is. Oh, when you get there, ask anyone where 'Ma' lives. Everyone knows her."

It was time to go. Sean and Nettie boarded the Detroit-bound bus and left Brooklyn behind.

Chapter 3: The Zone

IT WAS MID AFTERNOON when their bus pulled into the Detroit station. The attendant indeed knew where the Zone was located. The man looked at them curiously as he gave them directions.

The neighborhood deteriorated as they entered the two-lane street into the Zone. Garbage was left uncollected. There were vacant buildings, abandoned vehicles and boarded-up stores. Theirs were the only white faces. This would have unnerved many white women, but Nettie had grown up a few blocks from Bedford Stuyvesant - at that time the largest Black ghetto in the United States. So the Zone was a familiar scene to her. As a matter of fact, she had had many work assignments in Bed-Stuy and was not intimidated by these new, but similar, surroundings.

The neighborhood was comprised mainly of single family houses. There were a few three story apartment buildings and a number of stores with rooms above them. Shaggy trees struggled to grow in the thin soil and there was no regard for urban planning. Nettie observed that many of the small deteriorating houses were apparently abandoned. She noticed a cluster of shops at the end of the block. Traffic was light and the only real activity centered around small children scurrying about in the heat of early summer.

Four or five blocks into the Zone, they stopped at an intersection where two shabbily dressed black men stood. The men glared at the white couple, but when Sean asked where he might find 'Ma', they seemed to soften and nodded in the direction of a small two story house across the street.

They thanked the men, crossed the street and approached the front steps to Ma's house. Sean whispered to Nettie, "Don't you be a worryin' now, we will only be here for a few days."

"I'm not worried, Sean."

They climbed the two small steps onto the porch and were greeted at the door by a pretty, caramel-skinned, hugely pregnant woman.

"You must be Sam's friends. People call me 'Ma' though I never had no children," she laughed.

"I'm Nettie and this is Sean." Ma looked Nettie over and said,

"Looks like you and me have something in common. How far along are you?"

"Seven and a half months."

"Well lordy be, I'm just about the same. If you stick around, we will keep Meg mighty busy. Oh... she's a midwife - delivers all the babies."

Nettie just smiled; she immediately liked the slightly older woman.

They were pleasantly surprised to see that the interior of Ma's home was in much better condition than the outside; Ma evidently ran a tight ship. She explained that there were four units, two up and two down, each with a combined kitchen-living room, a small bedroom, and a bathroom. The staircase was in the middle of the house. Their unit would be on the first floor. They could pay by the day, week, or month. They chose to pay daily.

"Here, sit and relax while I find a set of keys for you." Nettie gratefully plunked herself down on an overstuffed wing chair as she heard rustling at the door. A beautiful wide eyed little girl was staring at her. She was barefoot, wearing a grubby tee shirt and oversized shorts.

Ma looked over and said, "Well, don't just stand there, child. Come in and say hello to these folks."

The little three year old crept over to Nettie and looked into her eyes. Nettie smiled and said, "Hi, I'm Nettie, and who are you?"

"Skeeter," she blurted out.

Skeeter slowly raised her hand toward Nettie's eyes; this had happened many times. Small children were immediately attracted to the brilliant jewel green color. They wanted to touch them to see if they were real. Nettie took Skeeter's tiny hand and gently placed it on her closed eye.

"See, they're real eyes."

"They're green!" Skeeter exclaimed.

"Yes they are, Skeeter, and your eyes are brown and beautiful."

"If that child is bothering you, Nettie, I'll just shoo her away."

"Oh no, Ma, she reminds me of the children I teach."

Nettie gave Skeeter a little hug. Skeeter pulled away and asked, "Are you going to be our teacher?"

Nettie, surprised by the toddler's clear diction and the directness of the question, answered, "Ah sure, while I'm here, Skeeter, I'd be glad to sit with you." And with that Skeeter twirled like a ballerina and bounded out of the room.

"Is she one of the neighborhood children?" asked Nettie.

"Oh no, Skeet lives upstairs with her mother, whenever she's here." Ma didn't go into any details and Nettie didn't ask.

Sean asked Ma if there was a store nearby where they could pick up a few items and she nodded in the direction of the shops that Nettie had noticed earlier.

"There's a general store just down the block; they have a bit of everything. Uh, oh, Teach, I think your class just arrived."

They moved to the porch. Skeeter and a band of seven urchins, none of them appearing to be over five years old, were marching up the path to the front porch. Some of them had pencil and paper in hand and they stopped in front of Nettie who was standing on the lower step.

"I see," laughed Nettie. "So I guess this means that school is in session?" Nettie sat down on the step to be at eye level with her

persuasive students and Skeeter proceeded to make introductions.
"This is Miss Nettie and she is our teacher."
Ma was chuckling. "Skeeter, I swear..."
Within seconds she knew all their names and the children circled around her. Nettie was delighted.

"My, those youngun's took a shine to you, girl, and how did you remember their names so quickly?"
"She be doing it all the time, Ma," said Sean. "I'll be off to the store now, you're a might busy lass." Sean leaned to give Nettie a kiss and headed down the sidewalk, "I shan't be long."
Nettie waved to him as the children all tried to sit on her lap at once.

Sean strolled down the street and as he approached the store, he noticed faded letters on another building's window. He could make out the word 'Tavern'. Curious, he went closer and, sure enough, although barely legible, appeared the words 'Clancy's Tavern'. "Why, I found me an Irish pub," he said to no one and he opened the door and walked in.

It was not like any pub that Sean had ever seen. The one-room bar was dark and dirty and damp. The bartender dozed behind the bar. Two patrons sat at a corner table and a young boy shifted filthy dust around with a broom.

Sean walked up to the bar thinking about ordering a pint, thought better of it and turned around to leave. A large and angry looking black man blocked his way.

"Where the hell ya been, Whitey? We don't like to be kept waitin'!"
"You be a mistaken me for someone, mate..."
"Shut up, asshole, and give me the fucking MONEY!"
"You'll get no such thing," Sean said, thinking that he was about to be robbed, not grasping the real situation.
The black man, without warning, kneed him in the groin and Sean doubled over in pain. Sean, a Catholic, had been in many brawls in the tough protestant Belfast neighborhood where he grew up and knew that, despite the pain, he had to defend himself.

"I said where's the..." and that's as far as his assailant got as Sean hit him hard in the face.

Sean had forgotten about the other man and never saw it coming. The ice pick entered just below the backside of his left shoulder on a downward trajectory. He barely flinched as he crumbled to the floor. The six inch long weapon pierced his heart and he lay motionless.

Both assailants immediately tore through Sean's clothing and did not find what they were looking for. "Those lying sons-a-bitches. You tell his friends when they come after him that nobody cheats us. NOBODY!" one of them shouted as they bolted out the back door.

"Jesus Christ! Go get Meg," the bartender yelled at the young boy sweeping the floor. "You better get Papa Joe too!"

The boy raced down the block and as he was passing by Ma's, she yelled out after him, "Hold it! Hold it, Jimmy. What's wrong?"
"Somebody got knifed at Clancy's, I'm getting Meg!"
"Who was it?" cried Ma.
"Dunno. Big white guy, never saw him before!"
Ma and Nettie looked blankly at one another. Then Nettie jumped to her feet, shouting, "Sean! SEAN!"
"You stay here, honey! I'll go see what's happening. It might not be him." Ma was running down the steps.
"NO, NO, I'm coming too!"
They raced to Clancy's and burst through the door. Ma saw him first. She rushed to him, Nettie right behind her. He lay face up on the floor. Ma stopped in front of Sean's motionless body and whispered, "Oh no."
Nettie slid to her knees, put her hands on Sean's chest and peered down at his face. One eye was closed and the other was half open. She knew he was dead.
"No, no, no," she uttered. Disbelief. Shock.
Ma knelt next to Nettie holding her tightly. Nettie never moved. She was transfixed looking at Sean and her powerful mind took her someplace else. Time was suspended as her subconscious recorded everything, as it always did.
Through the door burst a wispy late middle aged black woman. She rushed over to them, knelt down and checked Sean for signs of life. She leaned over and closed his other eye.
"I'm sorry," she said compassionately to Nettie. "He's gone." Then she slowly stood up and her kind face turned into stone. She ferociously charged over to the bartender, "Who did this, Jackson, you son-of-a-bitch? WHO DID THIS?" She grabbed him by his hair and shook him.
"I don't know, Meg. I swear, I never saw the guys before!"
"You lying bastard!"
Meg wheeled away and charged out the door almost knocking another man over as he was coming in. "Meg, what's going on?"
"Over there, Papa Joe. I'm going to get Billy!"
He saw Ma kneeling next to Sean's body, holding on to Nettie. Ma looked up and said, "He's gone, Papa Joe. This is his wife."
The white man wore a black shirt, Roman collar and a cross which he held as he silently prayed over Sean.
Nettie was barely breathing and Ma feared that she was going into shock, not knowing where Nettie had really gone. Papa Joe took Nettie by both hands and simply said, "I'm sorry." There was nothing spiritual spoken, but she understood as her mind was taking it all in.
Everything was a blur to Nettie's conscious state as a huge black man in uniform came running into the bar, followed closely by Meg. He stopped for a second, looked at the body, put his hand lightly on Nettie's

shoulder then turned to the bartender.
"I don't know nothin', Billy. Honest!" cried the frightened Jackson.
Billy moved behind the bar, grabbed Jackson and threw him into the corner like a rag doll.
"Your fucking head is coming off in TWO SECONDS! Now tell me what you know!"
"These guys are traffickers, Billy. They're not from the Zone. I never saw 'em before! They took this white dude for their payoff guy and when he didn't have the cash, they iced him."
"Whad they look like?"
Jackson described them and Billy turned to Meg: "You'll deal with the coroner?"
"Of course, Billy."
Billy walked over to Nettie, knelt down on one knee, and said, "I'll find 'em Ma'am. I'm sorry."

The paramedics arrived and, when they finished their work, Ma gently ushered Nettie away.
"Don't you worry none. Papa Joe will stay with Sean for now and Meg will be by in the morning to tell you where they took him."

Back at Ma's, the tears finally came as Nettie slowly moved back to her conscious state. She was unconsolable and Ma never left her side. Nettie finally dozed off on the couch and Ma stretched out on the floor and every time Nettie woke, Ma was there.

Morning came at last and Ma put some coffee on. Nettie wanted to be outdoors and sat down on the porch's front step. Ma sat beside her.
"Is there anybody you want to call?" asked Ma.
"No, we have no one."
Ma took her hand and said, "You're not alone. You are welcome here."
Nettie looked at her. "I've known you for less than a day and I think you're the best friend I've ever had."
They hugged each other as Nettie quietly sobbed.

They were still sitting on the steps when Meg arrived. She walked up, knelt down and held both of Nettie's hands.
"We haven't been properly introduced; my name is Meg." Nettie looked at her and recalled Meg at the bar. Meg was no longer the ferocious tigress as she smiled warmly.

"I'm Nettie, and thank you for all your help."
"Your husband is at the coroner's and they need some information. I'll take it to them for you."
"We were not married, Meg. My last name is Ferrari and Sean's last name was McCleary. He was a citizen of Ireland and has no family."
"Is there anybody you want to contact?"
"No, Meg, I don't have a family either."
Meg glanced at Ma and said, "Well Nettie, you've got one now."

Nettie looked at the two women and thought, Who are these people, these wonderful people?

Meg collected the information she needed and went back to the coroner's office. They would prepare the body.

Ma and Nettie were still sitting on the steps when Papa Joe came up the path. He, too, knelt down on the lower step and said to Nettie, "I just talked to Meg and she thought that I could help with any service arrangements that you decide. My name is Father Joseph, but Skeeter associated Father with Papa and she couldn't pronounce Joseph so I became Papa Joe. That was fine with me. Everybody has a nickname in the Zone; you can call me by either name."

"I like Papa Joe," and Nettie smiled for the first time.

"Then Papa Joe it is. Meg told me your name and I should think that Nettie is a nickname also?"

"Yes it is, short for Antoinette."

"Look Nettie, I don't want you to think that you're alone. We are all here for you and will help you in every way."

"I've never had so many friends, Papa Joe," she sobbed.

"We have a cemetery in the Zone, but no white folks are buried there. I have a little office-chapel in the cemetery and if you like we can place Sean in a space by the chapel; there are no designated gravesites but we can make room."

"Thank you, Papa Joe, I'd like that. Can we not have a service and just hold prayers at the grave after he's been buried?"

"Yes, of course. With a name like Sean McCleary, I would assume he was Catholic?"

"Yes, Papa Joe."

No sooner had Papa Joe left then Billy showed up, "Ma'am..."

"Please call me Nettie," she interrupted.

"OK, Nettie, I'm Billy. We got those two guys and they won't hurt nobody no more."

Ma, gave Billy a knowing glance and patted Nettie on the arm.

"We've got everybody looking out for you and I just want you to feel safe and you come to me if you need anything."

"Thank you Billy," and again she thought, who are these people?

Nettie sat alone on the step as Ma left her for the first time. Her head was bowed and she was fighting back tears. When she looked up, there was Skeeter holding something behind her back. Before Nettie could speak, Skeeter presented her with a beautiful single red rose and climbed onto her lap. "Don't be sad," she says, stroking Nettie's face. As they hugged and rocked each other, the healing began.

One by one they came - seven of them, all bringing gifts: a bouquet of dandelions, some unidentifiable weeds, a coloring book. The oldest, Sammy, was the last in line. He extended his hand and Nettie held out hers. He put a very used but clean pacifier in her hand and said, “It’s for the baby.”

The healing power of children was the perfect tonic for Nettie’s broken heart. How did they know? She did not feel alone. She had found a family.

Chapter 4: History

THE CEREMONY was brief. Only Ma, Meg, and Papa Joe were present. Papa Joe's office-chapel was in the back of the cemetery and Sean was laid to rest in a corner plot close to the chapel. A service road separated the chapel and Sean's site from the other graves. The road encircled those graves.

A numbered peg was driven into the ground at the head of the grave. Sean's name appeared in a book alongside the corresponding number on the peg. The records were kept by Papa Joe. The peg would be replaced by a marker that bore the name of the deceased if it was properly ordered and paid for.

Sean, a foreigner with no known relatives, was declared to be indigent so all funeral expenses were paid by the county. Nettie made a small donation to Papa Joe whose parish was responsible for maintaining the cemetery.

Nettie placed Skeeter's rose on the grave and they all left the cemetery together. On the way out, Meg noticed that Billy was attending to two fresh graves. Zone justice had been served.

NETTIE AND MA sat on the front porch sipping coffee. Nettie was quizzing Ma about the Zone.

"Ma, why is this place called the Zone? Isn't it part of Detroit?"

"Yup. You see, the police refer to their areas of patrol as a zone followed by a number. This was such a dangerous place that they called it 'the Zone' and everybody knew exactly what area they were talking about."

"Wow! Just how big is the Zone?"

"It's really small - only about twelve city blocks long if you don't count in the cemetery. Center Street runs right through the center; it's the only one that intersects all the other streets. But there ain't been street signs for years," she laughed. "This house is about half way up Center."

"How can you tell where the Zone begins and ends?" Nettie was fascinated.

"Easy. We're surrounded on all sides by four-lane boulevards - cutting us off from the rest of the city," continued Ma. "Most of the blocks empty into one of the big streets."

Nettie took a sip from her mug and looked at Ma. "Where are the schools, the churches?... On Center Street?"

"There's NO schools, NO churches, NO banks here. And don't go lookin' for medical facilities or mail deliveries here in the Zone. We got no services whatsoever except garbage pick-up and that's only cuz the rats here run wild and get into other neighborhoods. Except for a couple a bars that serve food that ain't fit to eat and a few mom-and-pop stores, you have to go outside the Zone to get anything. Welcome to the Zone, Nettie."

"Thanks Ma. And to think this might be my new home!"

"Yeah. This is just a neighborhood where folks move in and out all the time. There could be eight hundred living here one week and four-hundred the next. I'm not kiddin'. Don't you be gettin' too close to your students. Most of 'em will be outta here by next week."

"I don't understand. You make it sound like some forgotten island and why is it so notorious?"

"Well, the authorities would like to forget that we exist and it was crime that made us notorious. *Everything* went on here - prostitution, drug dealing, murder... There were killings every week and it was open warfare between the druggies and the cops. The bad guys were winning! They moved in and out of the Zone and killed any cop they couldn't bribe. I don't know the details but some kinda peace happened about a year ago and things quieten'd down. Some sorta agreement, I s'pose. It was either that or the entire city would have turned into a combat zone. Billy could explain it better than me."

"An agreement?" asked Nettie.

"Yeah, an agreement! The hookers and dealers, ya see? *All* the lawbreakers are allowed to live here without being hassled so long as they don't bring their crime into the Zone," added Ma. "The cops like it cuz they no longer have to mess with the highest crime spot in the city. They let the dealers do the policing inside the Zone. Understand? This ain't no safe haven for criminals; there's plenty of arrests here. But it did stop the cops from shakin' down folks for no good reason."

"Jesus, Ma! Are you telling me that these twelve blocks are entirely inhabited by lawless criminals?"

"It's more like twenty-four blocks, with Center Street running down the, uh... center... the middle. And no, hon, not only 'lawless criminals' live here. Look at me! And there are a few others like me who call this place home. But most Zonies are folks who operate outside the law or are drifters and they move in and out for who knows what reasons. The hookers, like Skeeter's mom, have children who are pretty much left to look after themselves. At some point the mamas leave the Zone and take their kids with them. It's rare that the daddies of the children are known even if their mamas ain't Ho's. Zone kids never attend school; they ain't here long enough and the authorities don't give a shit."

"Ah," said Nettie. "That explains..."

"You got it, Girl! That's why Skeeter's gang globbed on to you. Some of us keep an eye on the kiddies when their mothers are not around. That's why they call me 'Ma'. My real name is Libby Munoz. I'm legally married to my Mr. Munoz, but he flew the coop when I got pregnant."

"You're doing a wonderful job here..." Nettie interrupted.
"Well, this here shaky truce seems to work and when something screws up..." Ma rested a hand on Nettie's arm and looked into her eyes. "Ya know, hon, like what happened to your Sean. Well, it's taken real seriously, 'specially in Sean's case cuz he was white. Actually, it's safer here than in some parts of the city cuz the bad guys take their crime elsewhere and, if they didn't, Billy or Meg would break their heads! It's the ones who don't live here that cause the trouble and they are dealt with real quick. Like Sean's... uh... you know, killers were."

"Tell me about the people who call this place home like Billy and Meg and Papa Joe. And you!"
"Well, lemme see," replied Ma. "Billy is the only one I know born and raised here. He's been a cop ever since he was grown. He was the logical choice to be the official law here. He lives in the Zone in an apartment above a garage that he uses for his office. His bosses pretty much leave him alone but he calls for backup when he needs it. Billy's as gentle as he is tough and he meant it when he said he'd look after you, Nettie. You won't find a better friend.

Now, Meg. Oooooooo. What can I say about Meg? Her name is Margaret Brown and she just walked in here one day some years ago and never left. She was a godsend. She knows more about medicine than any doctor I've ever met and acts as the midwife. She treats the injured and deals with gunshot and stabbing wounds better than the paramedics. The authorities trust her and accept her medical reports on any problems here in the Zone. She's smart and fearless and she does not back down from nobody! Meg has a heart as big as this house and she's my best friend. You'll love her as much as I do. And she likes you already."

"I know what you're talking about. I sensed all these things from Meg. She's special. Who else...?"

Ma continued like she was reading a 'Who's Who' of the Zone.
"Papa Joe. Let me see. Well, he's a Jesuit. He teaches at the University of Detroit. He talked his bosses into letting him start a little chapel here. Everybody respects him and a kinder man you will never meet. He performs all the religious services - marriages, baptisms, funerals - whatever is needed for the Catholics and non-Catholics alike. He is always here for everybody, Nettie."

"He teaches at U. of D.? Hmmm. What about you?"
"Me, I was left this house by my first husband about ten years ago. He was killed here in the Zone. Like your man. I had nowhere else to go so I stayed and turned my place into a boarding house to survive. I never fell into the Zone crime pit. I don't know why, I just never did."

Ma looked at Nettie and held her hand for a moment. They sipped the rest of their coffees and watched a group of youths pass by jiving to the blare of music they carried with them. Skeeter came out and sat next to Ma. “Hey,” she said. Ma smiled at her and began to braid her hair.

“I can’t imagine why you would want to stay here, Nettie, and raise your child in these surroundings, but you would be welcome and, boy, do we need someone like you.”

Chapter 5: Home

NETTIE AND MA were near their delivery dates and after long discussions with Meg, Nettie decided to forego seeing a doctor and put herself into Meg's hands. There was really nothing left to do anyway except to give birth and Nettie had wanted the birth to be natural. She felt comfortable with Meg and the confidence that Ma had in her.

Nettie had only ventured as far as the cemetery, where she visited every day. She wanted to become more familiar with the Zone and asked Meg to go on walks with her to explore the neighborhood. The Zone was much more active than she had first realized.

There were people moving about constantly, most of them walking to the four-lane intersections to catch a bus or hire a cab. Meg pointed out that many of them were into the drug trafficking business and were heading to other parts of the city to ply their trade. Some of the women were dressed in mini skirts and thigh-high boots - obvious prostitutes. Many of the residents waved to Meg and acknowledged Nettie. Billy had most certainly put the word out that there was a white woman living in the Zone who should be respected and looked after. Nettie felt strangely at ease in her new surroundings and was slowly recognizing that, indeed, she was needed here and, just as important, she needed a place like the Zone.

As they were returning to the house, a woman stepped off the porch. She was dressed like the other women Nettie had identified as prostitutes. The woman stopped as Nettie and Meg approached.

"Hey Meg..., this must be my new neighbor that Skeet can't stop talking about. My name is Sandy and you are Miss Nettie?"

"I am," replied Nettie. "You're Skeeter's mother?"

"Yeah. Thanks for teaching Skeeter. Gotta run." And she was off.

"That's about the most you will ever get out of her," said Meg. "And it might be the only time you see her sober. She shares the upstairs with her half-sister, Roberta but you'll hardly ever find one of them at home. Ma looks after Skeeter."

"What is Skeeter's real name?" asked Nettie. Meg looked at her strangely and said, "I really don't know. Most children born in the Zone have made-up names. In fact it's true bout most of the people who live here. Assumed names are the custom; no one wants to be identified. Take Sandy, for instance, she uses the last name of Devane but Skeeter's last name is Charles, Abrianna Charles. Sandy's last name is not Devane; I have no idea what it might be.

Ya see, they're scam artists! Here's what they do: Sandy and her sister find pregnant women all over the city who can't identify the baby daddy. When a woman gives birth, the father is listed as 'unknown' on the birth certificate and the mother's alleged maiden name is used as the surname for the baby. This all has to be verified by a midwife or a doctor, ya know. Now, the new mothers can qualify for government aid."

"That's not a scam, Meg. They deserve help raising a child alone."

"Ah, but then the two sisters check the morgue's register for the names of deceased men. Then they sell those names to the same new mothers who have just qualified for government aid. As part of their service, Sandy and Roberta provide a licensed but unscrupulous midwife who falsely prepares an application for another birth certificate for the same baby. But this time they identify the deceased men as the fathers. They also change the name of the mother, her address, and the date and time of the birth. The alleged fathers are obviously not around to contest the allegation.

This is exactly what Sandy did with Skeeter. So Skeeter is now saddled with the poor deceased Mr. Charles' name even though he is not her father. Skeeter has two birth certificates on record and she will never know that. Further, she will never know who her father is because I'm sure that Sandy doesn't have the slightest idea who that might be. Sandy could have used any last name on the legitimate birth certificate. There's no way of telling."

The two women went into the house. Ma was in the kitchen stirring a bean soup. "Did you two have a good walk?"

"Yeah. Meg was giving me a lesson about the multiple names of Zone children. Go on, Meg, this is just getting interesting."

"Well, Nettie - Ma knows all about this, too - the county has another fund to pay unwed mothers in need who have identified the father and have given the child the deceased father's name. This way they double dip on the aid. No one has any social security cards for cross checking and both Sandy and Roberta exchange favors with the agents in the Department to advert any investigations. They take a percentage of the aid money for their efforts, give a token fee to the midwife and use scary looking runners to collect their money."

"Wow," exclaimed Nettie. "I've seen a lot of scams involving illegitimate children back in Brooklyn, but this ranks right up there with the best of them."

"Yeah. I've found that it was best not to question things and just go about my business," replied Meg.

"I was not the midwife for Sandy. Skeeter was born before Sandy came here and just presented us with Abrianna Charles. As a favor to Ma, I verified Abrianna Charles's birth certificate. It was legit. It was impossible to find the truthful one that contained Skeeter's real name.

Ma nick-named her Skeeter because she seemed to be constantly swarmed upon by those pests and the name stuck. Nobody, not even Skeeter knows her name is Abrianna! That's the way it is all over the

Zone. Everybody is called something other than their real name. You will fit right in, Nettie," Meg smiled.

"Meg, that brings up something that I want to talk to you about." Nettie told Meg about the plan she and Sean had made for establishing their baby's dual citizenship. If Nettie were to decide to make the Zone her home, she wanted the birth certificate to list Sean as the father but did not want the people in the Zone to think that her son was illegitimate. She knew from experience how cruel children could be to their peers when it came to this subject. She asked Meg if she had any suggestions.

"Oh, that's easy Nettie. No one needs to know what name appears on the birth certificate, just the people you tell. You will not be registering your baby's name anyplace here in the Zone. Remember, there are no schools or nosy social workers to deal with. You can educate your child at home along with all the others you choose to teach and when the time comes for a formal education, you can then use his or her real name. Nettie, you can call your child by any name that you wish here in the Zone. Only you and I will know what name is on the birth certificate. Billy did not make an official report on Sean's murder. He doesn't know Sean's last name and I guarantee you he does not want to know. That leaves Ma and Papa Joe and they would never violate your confidence. No one else gives a damn; that's the way it works in the Zone."

"Yeah Meg, that does sound easy, maybe too easy."

"Nettie, this happens a lot. For instance, on the midwife verification form I have to sign, there's a place to insert the name that the mother prefers her child to be called. This preferred name is used to provide a tracking record of a child born out of wedlock who is not using the name that appears on the birth certificate which is usually the case. It is not part of the public record. All you have to do is to give me the child's preferred name and the real name that will appear on the birth certificate. Simple enough, huh?"

"Yes, simple enough Meg, and thanks." She paused and said, "I know what I want my son to be known as here in the Zone: 'Sean Ferrari'. I will think about the birth certificate name in the days to come."

"A son, Nettie?"

"Yes. It will be a boy."

Chapter 6: Two New Residents

"AFTER LOOKING at your medical reports, Nettie..." Meg poured herself a cup of tea at Ma's kitchen table, "It's quite probable that you and Ma could deliver within a few days of each other. Soon. Next week or even before!"

"The first one to deliver buys the other a beer!" laughed Nettie. "Make it a Henny," countered Ma. "Seriously, I'm feeling a little more pressure lower in my hip area. How about you?"

"No, just about the same."

Nettie didn't tell them that she knew exactly where the baby was in her body and that Meg was right on target in her timing predictions. Nettie was determined to let the birth take its natural course and would only use her powerful mind to help expedite the process if she found it necessary.

Three days later Ma walked into Nettie's apartment while she was helping Skeeter with her letters.

"Nettie, I felt my first contraction about ten minutes ago. It only lasted about thirty seconds or so... Holy Jesus, here comes another one!"

"Skeeter, run and get Meg."

"Just relax, Ma. I think this is just the first stage, it could take a while."

When Meg arrived, she confirmed that Ma was in the early stages of labor. They went to Ma's apartment to prepare her room for the imminent birth.

Ma was now well into her labor and the contractions were coming more frequently and lasting longer. She was beginning to experience considerable pain with each contraction and Meg was about to direct her to her bed when suddenly Nettie exclaimed, "I hate to steal your thunder, Ma, but I just had my third contraction in the last fifteen minutes and they aren't lasting very long!"

"How come hers came so fast?" cried Ma. "And look, she's not even breathin' hard!"

"It's not unusual, Ma," explained Meg. "There's never a way of predicting these things. Come on Nettie, lets get you set up in your room."

As they were getting Nettie settled, Ma appeared in the doorway and said, "I'm leaking, Meg, and these contractions are coming faster and hurt like hell."

"I hate to tell you this, Meg," added Nettie as she sat down on the bed, "but my water just burst!"

"Speaking of water, there goes mine," said Ma as she grabbed her stomach and winced in pain.

"Holy shit! Don't you two do this to me! This is coming way too fast! Skeeter, run and get Papa Joe; I'm going to need some help!"

A wide eyed Skeeter took off running as fast as she could.

"Nettie, move over. Ma, jump in here. I can't possibly run between two rooms to make these deliveries!
Look, you two, this could take an hour or even sooner. It's the first time around for the both of you and so it should not happen in the next few minutes. Just do me a favor and give me some time in between, okay?"

"You gotta be kidding," exhorted Ma after a painful contraction,
"Like I can control this?"

"Just say the word, Meg, and he's all yours," laughed Nettie.
"Can you believe her! Like she's out for an afternoon walk. Jesus Christ, Nettie, don't you feel any pain?"
"No, no pain, but I'm starting to feel something. I can't explain it."

"Just keep up the bantering, you two, it's really helping," encouraged Meg.

Ma now felt the urge to push with each contraction, and she did. Nettie let the natural contractions of her uterus do the pushing along with the force of her abdominal muscles.
The cervix on both women were now completely dilated and, with a grunt from Ma, her baby's scalp could be seen.

"You're on your way, Ma. I can see the top of the baby's head." Meg turned toward Nettie.
Not to be outdone, it was Nettie's turn and, slowly, her baby's head began to emerge also.

"What the hell is this, the fifth race at Belmont?" said an astonished Meg.
At that moment Papa Joe came strolling into the room.
"Hey, if that's the case, I've got five bucks on the lady to my left," Papa Joe joked nodding at Ma. Then he realized what he was looking at and fell to his knees genuflecting as fast as he could. "Jesus, Mother of God! Oh my, oh my!"

"Get off your knees, Padre, and go wash your hands. I need you!" exhorted Meg. "Move, Papa Joe, they're in the far turn coming down the home stretch!"

"Mother of God, Mother of God, I've never done...I, I've never seen...oh mercy, mercy!"

Ma's baby's head was crowning; the nose appeared, then the mouth.
"Your fiver looks good Padre. It's Ma by a nose so far. Hold the baby's head while I suction out the mucous. The baby is going to start to turn its head - just help direct it."

"Meg, my hands are shaking, what if I do something wrong?"
"Don't."
"Ma, you're doing fine; just try to stay relaxed."
Ma was sweating, gritting her teeth and clenching the bedsheets.

Nettie was different - moaning softly, not in pain but making sounds that a person who was experiencing extreme pleasure would make.

A confused Papa Joe looked at her and asked Meg, "Is Nettie all right?"
"She is fine Padre, Nettie is just, um..., it happens."
"What?" yelled Ma. "I'm in agony here, and she's having an orgasm?"
At that moment, Nettie's baby's head crowned and Meg gently turned it and the shoulder appeared and then the other and then the whole body emerged and the baby slowly dropped into Meg's hands. She quietly said to Nettie, "Hey lady, little Sean is here."
Papa Joe was completely transfixed with the look on Nettie's face and the soft sounds she was making.
"Papa Joe," snapped Meg. "You've got a baby in your hands; get to work!"
"I, I, I'm sorry Meg, It's just that I never seen a… I mean I've never heard a woman..."
"Too late to renounce your vows, Papa Joe," chortled Meg.
With that, Ma's baby's shoulder appeared, then the other and Papa Joe was soon holding a beautiful baby girl in his hands.
"Well, is somebody going to tell me what happened?" said an exhausted Ma.
"It's a girl, Ma, and she's beautiful. Just ask the proud Papa here," Meg chuckled.
Both babies were cleaned up and placed on their mother's bellies to keep warm. The placentas were passed, the cords were cut and the mothers were beaming at their babies and holding each other's hands. Baby Sean whimpered a bit and the little girl was howling. They both settled down when they were placed on their mothers' breast for feeding.
"Well," said Meg, "Nettie won the race by a minute, but I don't think that little girl liked being second one bit judging by all the racket she was making."
Once the feeding stopped, the babies were put in the same crib. The little girl was placed first and she came kicking and screaming.
"Oh Lady," stated Meg. "You are going to have your hands full with this wildcat."
Sean, the quieter baby, was settled next to the baby girl and miraculously she started to calm down. Both babies' eyes were fluttering and Meg gently turned them so they would be facing each other when their eyes were completely open. Within seconds they were staring at one another and they were the very first thing that either of them saw in their new world.
"Boy, this is giving a whole new meaning to love at first sight!" Meg said grinning.
"What's their names?" They all turned and looked at Skeeter who asked the question.

Chapter 7: The First Year

"MARTHA JEAN. You can put that down on your form, Meg," said Ma. "That's what I'm going to call her. I once saw a movie with this refined and classy lady in it and her name was Martha Jean. I said then if I ever had a daughter, I would name her Martha Jean."

"You're kidding! Naming that banshee after a sophisticated movie star?"

"Meg, she will quiet down!"

"Ma, the only time that child is quiet is when Sean's with her," replied Meg. "You better go relieve Nettie so I can complete her papers. And tell her to leave Sean with Martha Jean; I forgot my ear plugs!"

"Oh for god's sake, she's just a rambunctious baby full of spirit," defended Ma as she made her way to the room where Nettie was sitting with the newborns.

Nettie entered laughing, "That wild little thing just smacked Sean right in the face with all her flailing; I've never seen such a child!"

"Are you referring to sweet little Martha Jean?"

"Oh, so we finally have a name! I know, she's named after Ma's favorite female kick boxer," joked Nettie.

"You don't want to know," exclaimed Meg.

"Okay, I need a name for Sean's birth certificate, have you decided?"

"Yes, I have. His last name will be McCleary, of course, but I want him to carry a remembrance of me with his first name. Antoinette Jeanette won't do, so I'm just going to give him my initials, A. J. That's it Meg, A. J. McCleary. That's what I want."

A FEW DAYS later Nettie picked up the birth certificate at the Bureau of Vital Statistics, establishing the baby's automatic U.S. citizenship, and then checked with the Department of Immigration in the same building. Sure enough, the agents were able to retrieve their records from New York, and assigned her a case worker. The case worker confirmed what they had been told in New York. She instructed Nettie on how to fill out the proper forms that would allow the U.S. to acknowledge the baby's Irish citizenry.

She would first have to clear that with the Irish Embassy. The case worker directed her to the accepted medical facility to proceed with the blood testing. She did so and forwarded the required documentation to the Embassy.

She then filed her petition to establish A. J.'s dual citizenship with the U.S. and was told that it would take a few months before the certificate would be issued. It depended on how prompt the Irish Embassy would be in handling their end but it would be done.

Carrying her baby, Nettie paid Papa Joe a visit and set up a time to have her son baptized. Papa Joe looked at the birth certificate, smiled at Nettie and said, "Okay, we will baptize little A. J. McCleary..." and then he whispered, 'Sean Ferrari', "tomorrow at 10:00 A.M. Bring a godparent."

Nettie left Papa Joe's little chapel and walked the short distance over to Sean's grave.

"Say hello to your son, Sean. His name is A. J. McCleary. I've completed everything you wanted. He will have his Irish citizenship in a few months and will be baptized a Catholic tomorrow. The service will take place just a few yards from here. He will be able to see your resting place. We promise to make you proud, Sean. We miss you. I miss you."

NETTIE WAS BUSY changing Sean's diaper when Skeeter walked in with her crayons and drawing paper. She had drawn a picture of what appeared to be two babies, one lying down, the other standing up with stick hands in the air.

"This one's Martha Jean," she said, pointing at the standing baby.

"Can you show me the letters in her name?"

"Of course. Just give me a second with Sean here."

Nettie sat down at the kitchen table where Skeeter had set up shop and printed out Martha Jean's name underneath her stick figure.

"Here Skeeter, remember how we did this the other day? The big letter is what we call a capital and it's an 'M' - the first letter in Martha's name. The other big letter is 'J' - the first letter in her middle name, Jean." Then she showed her all the lower case letters.

"Here, now you write them down."

Skeeter picked up the crayon and promptly copied the letters M and J.

"What about the other letters?" asked Nettie.

"That takes too long," answered Skeeter. She grabbed her drawing and headed for Ma's.

"Look, Ma. I made a picture of M. J. and that's her name," pointing at the two wobbly letters.

"You mean Martha Jean," corrected Ma.

"No, that's too long. She's M. J."

Meg had just walked in and asked Skeeter if she could see her drawing. She examined it and said, "Did I hear you right, Skeeter? You're going to call your baby sister M. J.?"

"Yes, that's her name," replied Skeeter.

"You know something, Ma, it fits!"

"Now, just a minute here!" exclaimed Ma. "You know how these nick-names have a way of sticking and I want my child to have a real proper name."

Nettie came into the room holding Sean and asked Ma,

"Did Skeeter show you her drawing of M. J.?"
"Forget it, Ma," laughed Meg. "M. J. it is!"

IT WAS A BUSY time for Nettie: nursing Sean, helping Ma with M. J. and schooling Skeeter along with any of her little friends who showed up for class. As satisfying as this was, she knew that her limited finances made it necessary for her to find a job. Ma would never force her to leave but Nettie was determined to pay rent on time and put food on the table. Her exceptional abilities, she believed, would allow her to find employment. She would be able to provide for herself and her son.

Sean's eyes started to turn the same shade of green as his mother's and his hair was black like his father's. So far, he was a perfect baby in every way, sleeping through the night and hardly fussing during the day. Both babies were beginning to crawl and sit up. Sean had a way of seeming to focus on his surroundings like he was trying to reason things out.

Nettie was nervously looking for any sign that Sean may have inherited her extraordinary gift. She wasn't sure she wanted that for him but if indeed he possessed those powers she knew exactly how she was going to deal with it.

M. J. was another story. She inherited the best from both her parents. She was developing her father's Galician Spaniard features and combining that with her mother's hazel eyes, chestnut brown wavy hair, and light brown skin, she was an absolutely beautiful child. She was, however, anything but a perfect baby. M. J. was constantly clamoring for attention and only seemed content when Sean was placed next to her. Skeeter was fascinated by the babies and enjoyed playing the role of big sister. The three of them communicated on a level only known to children.

Time passed and It was almost a year since the babies were born and both of them were now shakily standing and repeating words.

Nettie reluctantly began experimenting with Sean's language skills. She would say a few words in English, wait for a response, then repeat the words in different languages, holding up a blank but different colored cue card for each of the languages she spoke. Sean caught on fast and soon he was speaking the correct foreign words when prompted by the cue cards. Nettie was stunned as he remembered more and more words. Sean was less than a year old and was demonstrating the skills of her ancestral gift. The training would now begin.

Chapter 8: The Gift

SKEETER STOOD GUARD outside the door of the abandoned house as the two four year olds scurried up the stairs to the top floor. They found an open window overlooking the alley below and peered out.

"How come those kids get to play there and we can't?"

"I don't know, M. J., but we will get into trouble if we do," answered Sean.

"But how are we going to throw rocks at the rats if we can't go down there?"

"We'll just have to wait for them to come running out and then get 'em."

"Look Sean! Those men are dragging something out the back door of that bar!"

The two children were saucer eyed as two lifeless bodies were deposited in the middle of the alley.

"Do you think they're dead?"

"M. J. we better get out of here right now!"

They ran down the steps and met Skeeter at the bottom.

"Somebody's coming!" cried Skeeter. "We have to go out back!"

"Skeeter, that means we will be in the alley," exclaimed Sean.

"No choice, we've got to make a run for it!"

"You don't understand, Skeet, there's two dead guys out there!"

"What?"

They heard someone climbing the front steps and all three children dashed into the alley. Their avenue of escape forced them to run directly at the two bodies lying in their path.

Skeeter and M. J. easily jumped over the first body and then the second one. Sean cleared the first but caught his foot on the second body and went sprawling onto the hard concrete. He jumped up and joined the other two as they headed for home.

Nettie was at work and Ma was in her kitchen when they arrived. Hearing them rushing into the house, Ma walked out, looked at the puffing and panting kids and said,

"What have you three been up to now?"

"Just playing," M. J. blurted.

"Well, get cleaned up. Nettie will be home soon and dinner's in the oven."

They went into Sean's apartment to wash their hands. Sean sat down on a chair and was bent over holding his arm.

"What's wrong Sean?"

"I don't know, Skeet; my arm really hurts." He was near tears.

"Don't you go crying," exclaimed M. J. "You'll get us all in trouble!"

"Trouble for what?" It was Nettie as she entered the room carrying a load of books. She noticed Sean holding his arm and said,

"What's wrong with your arm, Sean?"

"He fell down while we were playing," offered M. J.
"Let me see. Uh, oh, that doesn't look good. M. J., go get Meg."

Nettie tended to Sean who was clutching his arm and rocking back and forth in obvious pain. While gingerly cleaning up his arm she turned to Skeeter and said,

"Okay, Skeet, you've got that look on your face. Lets have it."

It was impossible for Skeeter to lie. "It wasn't Sean's fault, he tried to jump over them but didn't make it, and we had to go into the alley or we would have been caught... We just wanted to throw some rocks at the rats...and..and..."

"Slow down Skeet. Who was Sean jumping over?"

"Two dead guys were laying in the alley and we had to jump over them...and..."

"Okay, Okay, calm down."

"What's this about two dead guys?" Meg didn't wait for an answer as she hurried over to look at Sean's arm. She took one look at it and said, "It's broken."

Skeeter then burst into tears and when he saw her crying, Sean also started to cry.

"It's okay Skeeter, it wasn't your fault," sobbed Sean.

"Jesus, the kid's got a broken arm and he doesn't start crying until he sees his pal cry."

"Yeah, I know Meg. I knew someone else like that," sighed Nettie.

"That arm's got to be set, Nettie. I can do it but I don't have the drugs to put him under so we better get him to emergency."

"Meg, I need to be alone with Sean; just give us a few minutes."

Meg, who had been curiously observing some of the teaching techniques Nettie had been using on Sean for the past few years, hesitated before she left the room and said, "Be careful, Nettie. Make sure you're right."

"All right, Sean, you know what we have to do."

"It hurts, Mom. I don't know if I can find it."

"Sure you can. Just go inside now and follow it right to where it hurts."

Sean closed his eyes and using the technique taught to him by his mother, directed his mind's eye to locate the distressed area of his body.

"I can see it, Mom, I can see it!"

"Describe it to me Sean."

"It's... it's like a track with a hole in it and little trains are pulling away from it. They're... they're going really really fast."

Instinctively Nettie knew what she had to do, but she didn't understand why it would work.

"Stop the trains, Sean! Stand in front of them and stop the trains!"

He did. The electrical message of pain was no longer being carried to the brain.

"It doesn't hurt anymore, Mom."
"Just stay in front of the trains, Sean. We're going to let Meg fix your arm."

Sean felt no pain or discomfort as Meg set his arm. He fell asleep and his sub-conscious mind took over and continued to block the trains.

"You're not going to tell me how you did that are you?"
"I don't know myself, Meg. I just know that I have certain powers and Sean has inherited them. But he is much more advanced than I am, Meg, much more advanced."

Nettie still had no idea how her mind and now Sean's could accomplish these remarkable feats. She was confused by how her mind's eye could view the interactions of her body's functions but she suspected that somehow it was connected with her interpretive language skills.

Nettie had developed a technique wherein she could put herself into a sub-conscious state and do things with her mind. She was able to watch the blood flow through her veins and the beating of her heart. She slowly and cautiously trained Sean in the exercise. He had to actually see the process and not just imagine it.

As fascinating as this was, Nettie didn't realize its practical value until Sean broke his arm. However, her interest was only in raising her son and to fully develop in him the gift that she had passed on. It would be up to Sean to take it to the next level and introduce its potential to the following generations.

As part of his early training, Nettie had constantly conversed in many languages with Sean when he was old enough to repeat words. When he got older and could carry on conversations in complete sentences, Nettie started her experiments. She was trying to determine if, like herself, Sean could interpret and converse in any language and not merely remember the words. She accomplished this by asking him a question in one language and requesting him to answer in another, but not in English. He was slow in his responses but he could do it. That erased all doubt, Sean had indeed inherited the gift.

Nettie was excited but cautious and she couldn't wait to introduce him to English literature, music, and the sciences. She knew that he would excel by using his retention abilities alone.

Nettie started to take Sean with her to multilingual parts of the city - Hamtramck, Greektown... Mother and son went to butcher shops, and markets where foreign languages were spoken. Nettie noticed that Sean carried on conversations more easily in these places than he did with her on a one to one basis. Why? Why was that? These were questions that she could not answer.

When Sean was two, Nettie took a job. Taking advantage of her linguistic skills, she walked into the head of the language department at Wayne State University, located just a few short blocks across from the

Zone, and introduced herself as a linguist. She had no academic credentials and was told by the head of the department, Dr. John Telasantos, that she couldn't work for the University. Undaunted, she said that she didn't want to work for the University but thought that the professors could use her skills in helping them with their students' projects and papers. She added that she could be of service as a tutor. She proceeded to demonstrate her remarkable talent as a linguist in both speaking and writing. She was able to converse in most of the languages taught at the University. The Department head was sufficiently impressed and told her to check back from time to time. She did and was able to get all the part time work she wanted.

A SITUATION at the University brought Nettie closer to understanding the powers that apparently only she, and now Sean, possessed. The school had a very large Arab population and she was needed to help tutor those students who were struggling with the English language. Arabic was one of the languages that Nettie had not yet learned but needed to know in order to communicate with the students. She grabbed all the Arabic recordings she could find and took them home to study. Nettie, in the presence of Sean, played the recordings on a player borrowed from the school. They would learn the language together.

Neither one of them were having any difficulty remembering the foreign words, but Nettie could not automatically interpret the words into English or converse in the language as she had many times before. This was a mystery to her, but after reflecting on it she realized that she and Sean had never learned a language from recordings or print.

Nettie knew that she and her son could store and then recall anything they read, heard, or obtained electronically. This included foreign languages. She was discovering, however, when it came to interpreting or conversing in languages stored in that fashion, they couldn't do it! That ability seemed to only manifest itself when they received the words from direct human contact.

In an attempt to confirm her suspicions, Nettie went to the University's student union as soon as she could. She sat next to a group of Arab students and intently eavesdropped on their conversation. They spoke Arabic and she understood every word spoken and interpreted it into English as always. Nettie took another step towards understanding her powers.

She postulated that when she or Sean heard a foreign language spoken in their presence a dynamic was triggered enabling them to understand and converse in that language. Her research on electromagnetic fields led her to theorize that when they tuned into the sound waves, they also somehow connected to other frequencies that contained the interpretation of those foreign sounds.

It was then logical to believe that their abilities to retain and remember volumes of information exactly as it was presented to them were also connected in some way with human energy fields.

Nettie asked herself: if their powerful minds could receive such information, why couldn't their minds visually observe its electronic routes as the information passed into their bodies and on to their brains? She was grasping for an explanation as to how she and her son could see into their own bodies. She was getting closer to understanding her powers, but there were many mysteries and questions.

It was impossible for Nettie to completely understand their powers but she would, however, be prepared to reasonably answer Sean's questions that were sure to come. This was all she cared about.

Chapter 9: Birthdays

IT WAS JULY 7. M. J. and Sean were celebrating their fifth birthdays. Nettie and Ma were in the kitchen decorating a chocolate cake with fudge icing when Skeeter came bursting through the door.

"M. J. and Sean are at it again! You better come! Right away!"

"Now what are they fussing over?" asked Ma.

"They're playing that stupid riddle game and M. J. couldn't guess it and Sean wouldn't tell her so she belted him and he just laughed and that made her madder and now they're wrestling and rolling all over the place and..."

"Stay with the cake, Ma, I'll go," sighed Nettie. "It's time to get them cleaned up for the party anyway."

She found M. J. sitting on top of a laughing Sean threatening him with his life.

"You tell me where the key is, Sean, or I won't let you up!"

Nettie took charge. "All right - enough!"

M. J. released Sean and they scrambled to their feet.

"Can't you two just once settle things without clobbering each other?"

"He won't tell me where the key is, Nettie, and I need it to solve the puzzle!"

"You have to guess! Look for the hints!"

"Well, here's a hint for the birthday boy and the birthday girl. Get into that tub and get cleaned up or there won't BE a party."

They got it and happily bounded off, "Last one in is a sissy," chided M. J.

The children tumbled into the tub and were engaged in a fierce water fight when Skeeter came in.

"I'm supposed to make sure you guys get clean," she said, brandishing a wash cloth.

"Sure Skeet," M. J. giggled as she held up her arms to be washed. Skeeter fell for it and when she leaned over to do the scrubbing, they pulled her into the tub, clothes and all. The two birthday kids were now laughing hysterically, enjoying their special day.

Ma, hearing the ruckus, poked her head into the bathroom, took one look, turned around closing the door behind her and returned to the kitchen.

"How's everything in there?" inquired Nettie.

"Oh, just fine; the three of them are getting as clean as can be expected," chuckled Ma.

"The three of them?"

Ma bit her tongue in concentration; it was between her teeth as she squeezed a tube of white icing. She was spelling out Happy Birthday in cursive letters when Sean walked in. He asked if he could draw something on the cake. Ma was a little hesitant, not wanting her handiwork to be damaged, but she agreed and gave Sean the pastry bag and tip. He carefully etched out something that resembled a key, with a little arrow pointing towards the Happy Birthday salutation.

Unfamiliar kids were showing up at the door. Ma raised her eyebrows. "Who are they, Skeeter?" she whispered.

"Um, some are friends of M. J. and Sean's, I don't know about the others. M. J. just wandered around the neighborhood telling everybody she ran into about the party. And she ran into a lot of kids!"

They were all congregating in the front yard. This was no 'pin the tail on the donkey' crowd. These Zonie kids had their own games, learned on the mean streets and alleys of their neighborhood. They didn't have to be entertained. The party was on.

It didn't take long for M. J. to get into a brawl with a little boy about her age. He managed to wrestle her to the ground and was sitting on top of her.

"Get OFF me you SHITHEAD!" she bellowed.

Sean, who was playing a form of marbles using pebbles, heard M. J. screeching and zoomed off in her direction. He slammed into the little boy knocking him off M. J. And the fun started!

Billy and Meg were just coming up the path when the commotion began. They immediately put an end to the scuffle and restored peace. Most of the unidentifiable kids left. That was a good thing; they didn't have enough cake to go around.

Billy looked for Skeeter. She was his little girl. As a toddler she would come down to the station and put on his police hat and sit in his big chair. Skeeter always gave her 'Uncle Billy' a big hug.

"Let me guess," said Billy. "M. J. got into a fight and it was Sean to the rescue."

"Yup," said Skeeter. "Those two can kill each other but don't let anyone else try it!"

Ma corralled M. J. "How many fights are you going to get into today and where did you learn to talk like that?"

Papa Joe saved M. J.; as soon as he got into the room, she jumped into his arms wrapping her arms and legs around him. These two had bonded the day Papa Joe helped deliver her. She was his baby. He would protect her. Ma knew she had lost this attempt at discipline.

Things were peaceful as the children were busy playing and enjoying their pop and hotdogs and burgers. It was time to blow out the candles on the cake and sing Happy Birthday. There were ten candles, five for each of them and, of course, they had a race to see who could blow out their candles first.

As she blew out her candles, M. J. spotted the key on the cake. She jumped up and looked at Sean, "The key, the key to the puzzle! You're wishing me a Happy Birthday!" She gave him a sloppy kiss on the cheek and said, "OK, let's cut the cake!"

BRINGING UP CHILDREN in the Zone was not easy. The children, the transients and those who grew up there would be exposed to experiences unheard of in a normal environment - like needing to jump over dead bodies that were tossed out like garbage in a dark alley.

The lack of governmental scrutiny was both a blessing and a danger. The self policing policy kept crime in abeyance inside the Zone. Nevertheless the children would always be exposed to the criminal lifestyle of its residents. You couldn't shelter them from observing the drunks or strung-out dopers that hung out on the corners of the streets. There were open fist fights, and the constant presence of women they would soon identify as prostitutes. Zone children would be witnessing the results of self policing by the drug dealers. They were also subjected to a constant barrage of foul language.

All of the children that Skeeter, M. J. and Sean came in contact with were products of this transient and low life society. Further, the Zone was growing and becoming more active.

However, Nettie saw that children with this exposure were more advanced in their early development than those who had conventional home lives. She compared them to others of the same age she had worked with. Children from the Zone were more confident in expressing themselves even as toddlers. As they grew older, their environment would also make them tougher.

Nettie had given up on any thoughts of establishing a makeshift classroom for children of the Zone. Ma was right; most of the kids that Skeet or M. J. brought to the house would soon leave the Zone and never return. She decided instead to concentrate her efforts on those she considered 'her' children - Sean, M. J. and Skeeter.

Sean was way ahead of the other two. Because of his retentive abilities and one-to-one time with Nettie, he could read and write when he was three years old.

He met many Hispanics who lived in the Zone and he easily learned their language. Sean's favorite place outside the Zone was an Italian deli where his mother bought their olive oil and tomato sauce. Nettie and Sean only spoke Italian when they were in the shop and he learned that language also. He could speak and write fluently in three languages by the time he turned five. Nettie moved slowly and was not overwhelming him with stored language information.

Skeeter was her prize student. It was easy for Sean to learn but Skeeter had to work at it. And work she did! Completing every

assignment Nettie gave her and asking for more. Sean's prodigious learning abilities amazed her but it was frustrating that she couldn't learn as quickly as he did.
Skeeter's interests were reading and writing. She demonstrated a real talent in this area and could write and produce little books that delighted Nettie and entertained the other children. Nettie was quick to recognize this excellence and encouraged her. She brought books home for Skeeter to read as she knew that this was the best way for her to learn how to write.

Then there was M. J. - so different from the other two! She was bright and enjoyed numbers and puzzles, but had no interest in the other studies. She couldn't sit still for a minute. Reading bored her and the family had no television or computer. M. J.'s enormous energy needed to be channeled into something.

Nettie taught Sean how to play his father's penny whistle but he showed little enthusiasm for it. M. J. loved to hear the sound of the peculiar instrument when Sean played it. He was playing a little Irish tune for Nettie one day, and upon hearing the lilting music, M. J. burst into the room. She listened for a moment then excitedly said,
"I want to learn how to make those pretty sounds too! Can you guys show me how to play?"
"Of course we can, honey," Nettie smiled. "Sean will show you; he's better than I am."

Nettie stood back and watched M. J. clumsily attack the penny whistle with her characteristic exuberance. She was elated to see that M. J. was at last showing a real passion for something - music! This was the opening that Nettie was hoping for. She gradually introduced M. J. to various forms of music and, to her surprise, M. J., was most fascinated with the classical pieces. It was no surprise that she would juke and jive to the kids' music of the day, and she wasn't afraid to show off her dance movements. This little girl was going to bring fun into everybody's lives - all who met her.

Nettie and Ma knew that an academic education was essential, but with the influences of the Zone all around, keeping the children morally straight was the bigger challenge. In response to that, both mothers made enormous efforts to teach their children right from wrong. Meg, Billy and Papa Joe supported them in every way.

Nettie was not a certified teacher and she was not interested in home school diplomas; they were irrelevant. She just wanted the children to learn and earn the high scores on the ACT's or SAT's that would open college doors.

Chapter 10: Little Bit

THE COLD MONTHS of winter had little effect on people living in the Zone. They did move a bit faster to make their bus connections just to keep themselves warm. And patrons did stay longer inside the bars and shops instead of hanging around street corners, but other than that it was business as usual.

Communication was a major problem throughout the year. Rats were constantly gnawing the phone lines and only drug dealers and prostitutes could afford cell phones. Billy, because of his job, had the only reliable land line that he shared in an emergency.

Luxury items - televisions, cameras, DVD players, cars - were financially out of reach for most of the people who called the Zone their home. If they could afford these items, they wouldn't be living in the Zone. Full-time residents had learned that if they owned expensive personal properties, they wouldn't own them for long. Theft was not considered a crime but an entitlement. That's why the children never owned bicycles or brand-name shoes. The one so-called luxury Nettie longed for was a computer for the children; it would be used as a learning device. She was working on getting one for her family classroom.

Skeeter epitomized what they meant when they referred to each other as 'family'. With Ma, Meg and Nettie all taking care of her, she felt that she had three moms - four if she counted Sandy. Billy and Papa Joe filled the paternal role. M. J. and Sean were her siblings. Skeeter could be found sleeping with Nettie, Ma, her brother or sister, or curled up on the couch in either apartment. She rarely went upstairs to Sandy's place; her birth mother was never there.

IT WAS AN UNUSUAL DAY; nobody was home at Ma's. Nettie was at work. Ma and Skeeter were scouting thrift stores for winter coats and Papa Joe had taken M. J. to a theater on the U. of D. campus to watch a children's Christmas play. He only had one extra ticket and M. J. was unanimously selected to attend.

Sean had accompanied Meg on a house call as her interpreter for a Spanish speaking family. When they returned they went over to Meg's to wait for the others to get back. There was a knock on the door and when Meg opened it, Sandy was standing there. Meg hadn't seen Sandy in months. She looked awful - haggard and pale. What Meg couldn't see, because of Sandy's big overcoat, was that she was pregnant.

"Meg, I need your help. I just stopped by the apartment to pick up a few things. I think I'm sick. I'm pregnant, Meg, and the baby's not due for a

couple of weeks but I think it's coming now!"
"For god's sake, get out of the cold, Sandy, and let me have a look at you."

Sandy was sober; she always stopped drinking when pregnant. She was definitely having contractions and was in considerable pain. Meg laid her down on the bed and examined her.

She let out a low whistle, "Sandy, you're about to deliver but we've got a problem. The baby is sideways in your uterus and its shoulder is blocking the birth canal. I'm limited in what I can see but I suspect that the umbilical cord is trapped underneath the baby's shoulder. This could cut off the air supply to the brain causing permanent damage, or worse... the baby could suffocate! It puts you at risk, too. You need a C-section but we don't have time. I'm going to have to deliver this here baby."

Meg had no choice; she had to go internally and turn the baby and then try to deliver feet first. She had never done that before. She washed up and went to work. The unborn child was small. Sandy was big. They had a chance. Sandy was tough and she courageously endured the pain.

Meg was having trouble. As she suspected, the umbilical cord was trapped under the baby's shoulder. She had to lift the baby off the cord, holding and turning the infant at the same time. She didn't have enough hands, she needed help. She had forgotten about Sean. He was there, standing motionless. He's only five years old, for god's sake, I can't ask him to do this, Meg thought. But she was out of options.

"Sean, I need your help, son; go scrub your hands and arms. And hurry!"
He did. His little hands were exactly what she needed.

"Sean, do you see where I've put my hands? He nodded yes. I want you to tell me if you see two little feet beginning to come out of the place where I've reached into. If you do, I'm going to ask you to reach in and gently grab the baby above the ankles. Do you think you can do that?"
"Yes."

Meg was tiring. She was holding the baby off the umbilical cord with one hand and trying to straighten the baby with the other. With Sean's help and the fact this infant was really small she believed that she just might pull it off.

Meg had turned the unborn child and was gently directing it into the birth canal feet first.
"I see something Meg!"
"Good, it's the feet! Now go in and grab above the ankles and pull gently with both hands, straight towards you!"

He followed Meg's orders. His small hands were making this possible. They still had a chance. Sandy was in agony but she was gutting it out.
"I think It's coming, Meg!"

"Thank god. Keep pulling Sean. I'll keep the baby straight." The baby slowly dropped out and Sean instinctively grabbed it.

Meg removed the mucous from the tiny girl's mouth. She was breathing - a miracle! Then she attended to Sandy who was conscious with a rapidly beating, but slowing, heart. Meg cut the umbilical cord and the placenta discharged normally.

"You're going to make it, Sandy, and your baby is breathing on her own and has good color. I'll clean you both up and place her on your stomach."

"NO! Just let me rest!"

Meg, agitated, cleaned Sandy the best she could and did let her rest. Meg looked over and smiled at Sean; he was still holding the little girl and was not about to give her up.

"Look how little she is Meg!"

"Boy, she is a little bit, isn't she?"

"Can I keep holding Little Bit, Meg? I won't hurt her."

"Bless your heart, you sure can! You've earned it. Is 'Little Bit' going to be her Zonie name, Sean?"

"Yeah, I'm going to name her that. I've never delivered a baby before!"

That was all Meg needed to release her tension and she burst into laughter. Meg hugged Sean and they both forgot about Sandy.

After awhile Sandy tried to get up and was reaching for her clothes.

"Where do you think you're going?" asked Meg.

"I've got to meet Roberta at the apartment."

"Jesus, lady, you just had a very difficult delivery. You're in no shape to be going anywhere!"

"I'll be fine," groaned Sandy as she shakily pulled herself out of bed.

"Damn it, Sandy! At least let me make sure you're not bleeding!"

Sandy saw the wisdom in that and allowed Meg to examine her.

"I don't see how, but there's not too much blood."

Sandy got dressed, put on her coat and headed for the door.

"Just a minute!" exclaimed Meg. "What about your baby? I've got to fill out the birth verification form."

"Come over to my apartment. Roberta will tell you how it's gonna be filled out. And you can keep the baby."

Meg was gobsmacked! She had seen it many times before with all the illegitimate children that she had delivered, but it never ceased to amaze her how mothers could just walk away from their babies. Keeping the child was not the issue. Of course they would do that; she was Skeet's sister. Yes, she thought, I'm sure Roberta will tell me exactly how she wants the form to read. Meg was filled with simmering indignation.

Meg saw Nettie coming up her walkway and opened the door for her.

"I just ran into Sandy. She looked like hell! She told me Sean was here and she asked me to tell you that they're waiting for you. What's up, Meg?"

"Come see for yourself."
Meg led her into the bedroom where Sean was cradling the baby.
Nettie did a double take, "Sean, whose baby is that?"
"Mine," he stated proudly.
"Take your coat off and get comfortable, Nettie," Meg chuckled.
"It's a long story."
Nettie was dumbfounded.
"You mean she just walked in here..and..and... Sean delivered the baby?"
"He sure did, just pulled her out as slick as could be!"
Nettie walked slowly over to her son, shaking her head in disbelief.
"Is it all right if I hold Little Bit, Sean?"
Meg collected her notary seal and verification forms as she was leaving for Sandy's. "If I see the others I'll send them over. Start figuring out how we're going to feed this new addition."
Ma, Papa Joe, Skeeter and M. J. were at Ma's when Meg got there.
"Hey," grinned Meg. "There's a Christmas present for you guys at my place. Nettie and Sean are already there waiting for you. I'll be right over when I'm finished here." Then she went upstairs where Sandy and Roberta were waiting for her.
Meg was fighting to hold her temper. She didn't want to confront them by revealing that she knew all about their scam. Sandy, exhausted, had folded herself into a chair. Roberta was doing the talking.
"Look Meg, we want your form to state that the mother's maiden name is Gloria Watson and the father is unknown."
"You can stop right there, Roberta, I won't falsify a verification form!" Meg exclaimed.
"We're ain't askin' you to falsify nuthin'! You're just gonna write down the information given to you by the mother. You do it all the time, Meg. Ya don't have to conduct an investigation if it's true or not. You're just notarizing her signature that she's the one giving it. For Christ's sake, Meg, you know that people here in the Zone go by a lotta names!"
Meg knew she was right, these two were real pros.
"Go on," said a seething Meg.
"Gloria here is stating that she lives at 124 Elm Street, Detroit, Michigan, and the baby's name is Jessica. Jessica Watson. I doubt that anybody official will come around here to Center Street," declared Roberta, "but if they do, it might be a good idea if you and Ma claim that little Eboni belongs to Sharon Jackson who lives in the other apartment."
So that's it, thought Meg, the other birth certificate. They're renting this apartment as a cover and Sandy Devane already has a place here. They need an actual permanent place of residence for Sharon to complete their scam. They need me, the attending midwife, to legitimize the real birth of Jessica. Very clever.

“Of course, if you don’t agree with that, Meg, we can always work ‘round you.” Meg knew that if she didn’t cooperate they would simply take Skeet and Little Bit and move them to another location. That was unacceptable; they were family. She paused looking at Roberta coldly, and said,

“OK, I’ll play along, but if you even think about removing the children, WE GO TO WAR!”

“Easy, Meg. I think we understand each other.”

Sean was proudly introducing Little Bit to everyone when Meg returned. Ma and Papa Joe had their turns holding the baby and now it was Skeeter’s turn. Skeeter was beside herself with joy.

“Is she really my sister?”

“You bet, honey,” said Meg, “and I know you will share her with us.”

M. J. couldn’t wait for her turn and was jumping up and down in anticipation. “Skeet, I’m going to teach Little Bit how to dance!”

What a sad difference, thought Meg. Everybody in this room was overjoyed, but as far as the mother and aunt were concerned, it was just business.

Chapter 11: Computers

NETTIE HAD INTRODUCED all three children to the Detroit library system before the younger two were five.
Skeeter had exclaimed, "Sean, look at all those books! Wow!"
Sean became enthralled by the computers, "Skeet I think we can read them here on these televisions. Look, come see!"

M. J. never got past the picture books and went rifling through them focusing on all the princesses and unicorns.

They went often. Sean and Skeeter could spend all day there, completely absorbed. M. J. got bored in about fifteen minutes and became a distraction for the other two. Nettie was going to have to treat M. J. differently. M. J. needed to be entertained and the library wasn't going to work for her.

Nettie continued taking Sean and Skeeter to the library and, while they were enjoying the wonders on the book shelves, she and M. J. wandered down Woodward Avenue gazing into the display windows of fancy stores.

Now M. J. was interested! She wanted to go into every building and was overwhelmed by the big department stores.
"Can we ride those steps?... How come they dress up those ladies?... Who can wear that many rings?... What's over there?"
Her exuberance made Nettie smile; she just loved M. J.

The children's room at the library was equipped with computers. Although Nettie was computer literate, she asked the librarian's assistant to introduce the basics to Sean and Skeeter. This would give her more time to spend with M. J. She left Skeeter in charge of Sean and was being tugged out the door. "Bye, Skeeter! Bye, Sean...
Okay, okay, M. J. I'm coming!"

Sean's aptitude for the computer dazzled the assistant and astonished his mother. Nettie knew she had to get a computer for the children; it would be their library.

DR. JOHN AT THE UNIVERSITY introduced Nettie to the head of the Computer Science department, Dr. Michael Hughes. Nettie asked him to put her on his buyer's auction list. They were always turning computers over and they would periodically conduct a silent auction for the sale of used computers. She was placed on the list and, a few months later, was notified of an auction. Nettie put in her bid; she got lucky and became the owner of a well used but workable device.

Nettie wrapped up the computer as a Christmas present for all of them. No gift could have been more appropriate or exciting for the kids. They were absolutely thrilled; after all, they didn't even have a television set.

Not only did they have a new baby sister to play with, but they had the ultimate toy, a 'new' computer!

Nettie was doing well with her part time college work and she could afford the hookup. Now if they could just take the phone lines away from the rats' dinner menu...

The children took turns on the computer and it did become their library. Sean found the search engines and with the power of his gift there was nothing he couldn't figure out; he even found a site on how to dismantle and rebuild them. This could be dangerous for their tired old machine.

Skeeter was determined to learn how to type and Sean located a site for her. Her writing immediately went to the next level. M. J. was not the least bit interested in learning how to run the computer. Whenever she wanted to see a new dance, look at girly fashions, or locate a new tune, she just had Sean pull them up for her.

M. J. was a hands-on learner. After seeing the Christmas play with Papa Joe, she was hooked. She wanted to be the performer, not the audience. M. J. watched the dancers, singers, and musicians on You Tube and tried to imitate them. She discovered that she had no talent for singing. She even tried once again to learn how to play the penny whistle. She gave up, finding no talent there either.

But, boy, could she dance!

Ma took M. J. downtown with her when it was time to pay the utility bills. It was M. J.'s favorite thing to do. She never tired of looking into storefront windows. The J.L. Hudson Co. displayed an exhibit for children in one of their windows. It featured a hand puppet show and M. J. was mesmerized:

"Look Ma, what are they?" asked an excited M. J.

"They're called hand puppets, honey. Hands are making them move," explained Ma. "Whose hands?"

"People's hands. They're called puppeteers. They bring the puppets to life."

"Oh wow, can they talk too?"

"The puppeteers talk for them. Come on, lets go see how they do it."

She took M. J. inside to watch the show.

M. J. would never forget that performance and she immediately put her young mind to work figuring out how to produce her own puppet show. Who needs a computer?

THE COMPUTER LASTED for over a year and a half, but it slowly went down. It was never stolen - too old for thieves to bother with. Sean was determined to save its life and decided to perform an emergency operation.

"Sean, what on earth are you doing?" cried Skeeter as she walked into

the kitchen that was serving as an operating room. Sean had the computer completely disassembled with all of its parts scattered on the table. "Don't worry, Skeet, I know where every part goes and I can put it back together but I'm afraid that it is beyond repair - too many worn parts."
"Well, put it back together, I have to research something," exclaimed Skeeter. "Ah, I guess I should have told you. The patient died on the operating table; I was performing an autopsy. BUT, I am going to put it back together just to show you, and ME, that I can do it." He did just that and it was perfectly reassembled, but he was right, the patient had gone to microchip heaven.

Chapter 12: Kiddie Corps

M. J. AND SEAN were inseparable. The two seven year olds prowled all over the Zone. M. J., with her unkempt hair and golden eyes, was adorable. She was always laughing, skipping and dancing and her high energy was infectious. M. J. chatted with everybody and was fast becoming the darling of the Zone. Sean was pretty much considered the white boy who tagged along with her.

Skeet would usually join up with them somewhere along the way - Little Bit clinging tightly to her legs. They never considered Little Bit a burden or a pest. In fact, both Sean and M. J. insisted that Little Bit be included in whatever caper they were planning, much to the delight of Skeet. Sean, when spotting his baby, would immediately hoist her on his shoulders and she would go along for the ride, grinning and waving.

Children grew up fast in the Zone because of their early weaning from parental controls. Baby talk was never in the vocabulary of the adults helping to raise these four kids. They talked to them on an adult level and had little patience for whiners. When the children were old enough to know right from wrong, they were trusted and allowed to roam freely about the neighborhood. Billy, Meg, Ma or Nettie were always just a few blocks away.

The Zone was changing. Many vacant houses were becoming occupied and some previously boarded-up stores were now open for business. The new additions included a couple of beer joints, and a few establishments that sold newspapers, beer, wine, cigarettes, and porn magazines. There was a barber shop and a pawn shop. Some of the new stores were located on Center Street, but not all of them. More cars were parked in driveways, too. The dealers' houses were easy to spot; they had the BMW's and Cadillacs.

But to everyone's surprise, a Jewish deli opened up on the far end of Center Street, not far from Clancy's Tavern. The proprietors did not live in the Zone but, nevertheless, this was a welcome addition.

The kids would never cross the four-lane boulevards but they did duck in and out of selected streets inside the Zone, enjoying the barbecue chicken smells emanating from grills located on the front porches of the run down houses. They loved to hear the sounds of rap and soul music filling the air. Fascinated, M. J. would always stop and ask who the singers were and the names of the tunes being played.

In the summer, Detroit Tiger day baseball games could be heard blaring from the radios. Billy was a Tigers fan and it didn't take Skeet long to become one too. Many times Skeet would steer the kids to Billy's police station to watch the game on TV.

M. J.'s outgoing personalty and quick temper often got her into scraps and then Sean would be dragged in. Most of it was harmless wrestling matches but, when riled, M. J. started to throw punches. The problem was, they were getting older and the tough Zonie kids would fire back and more than once both children came home with bloody noses and black eyes. They were learning the ways of the street: be cautious, but never, never, never back down. If you did, you would be run over.

There were also more interlopers of all ages: a concern for everybody, particularly for Billy. This concern proved to be a legitimate one. M. J. and Sean were confronted one day by some slightly older boys from outside the Zone.

"Hey, you little Ho! Whatcha doin' hangin' with this here white boy?" taunted one of them. M. J. wasn't sure she knew the meaning of the word 'Ho', but she knew that she didn't like it.

"Who you calling a Ho, you dickhead?" and she lit into the heckler. Sean knew that this was the real thing and there were three of them.

M. J. was as big as they were but Sean was not. M.J. totally surprised them with her attack as she went in kicking and swinging. She quickly routed her protagonist and Sean seized their advantage throwing one of the remaining two boys to the ground and was wrestling with the other. Then it happened. The young boy got off the ground and with Sean's back to him he pulled out a small open bladed jackknife and jammed it into Sean's side. Sean reacted immediately and jumped back holding his side as the blood trickled out.

The three boys realized that this was trouble; they turned and ran. M. J. took one look and said, "We better go find Meg."

They found her at home and after a quick examination with her experienced eye, she knew immediately that it was a knife wound.

"Meg, it missed the bone and only went in a little bit," said Sean.

"OK, I know you know that, but it's still a puncture wound with a dirty knife and you're going to need a tetanus shot."

"How do you know it didn't hit the bone Sean?" asked M. J.

Not sure how he knew, he simply said, "I just know."

Meg was not licensed to administer the shot and took him to the emergency room for treatment. Nettie was at work. His name had to be placed on the record and it was recorded as Sean Ferrari, Age Seven, Puncture Wound, Blood Type-O Positive. It was his first trip to any medical facility; it wouldn't be his last.

Nettie was outraged when informed and was confronting both Sean and M. J. "You say these kids were from outside the Zone? You know you're supposed to avoid outsiders. What did you do to provoke them for god's sake?" She was directing her question to Sean.

"They called me a Ho and I went after them," blurted M. J.

"So, because you lost your temper, Sean gets stabbed!" exclaimed Nettie.

“I’m sorry Nettie, I didn’t know they would do that,” and M. J. started to cry. That was all Sean had to see and he started to cry too; he always did when someone close to him wept.

“All right, all right,” sighed Nettie. “But there’s a lesson learned here. You two are getting older and fighting will no longer be a form of play. There are some dangerous kids in the Zone. I don’t expect you to run away from trouble but I do expect you to use better judgment. Come here now,” and she hugged both of them.

Nettie had just reported the incident to Billy.

“I know you’re all by yourself, Billy, and you can’t be everywhere, but I’m beginning to see some bad characters hanging out in the Zone and I don’t think they’re from here. Can’t you get some help?”

“You’re right, Nettie, and there’s nobody more pissed off than I am about Sean. You know how much I love those kids.”

“I know you do, Billy. Is there anything I can do to help?”

A chill went through Billy, the last thing he needed was for a civilian with good intentions like Nettie, getting involved with police work.

“Thanks. I’ll report this and some other stuff and maybe, just maybe, they will assign me a deputy.”

Nettie returned home and was repeating to Ma the conversation she had with Billy. Skeet, reading in Ma’s living room, overheard them and was concerned when she heard that her Uncle Billy needed help. If he needs help then he should have it, she reasoned to herself. She mused on it for awhile and then determined that she had to do something.

Skeeter quickly corralled M. J. and Sean and told them about Billy’s situation.

“How many kids do you know that can keep a secret?” she asked.

“None,” they replied.

“OK, how many do you know who would want to play secret agent but would be thrown out of the game if they told anybody?”

“Lot’s of ‘em!”

“Good, here’s how we are going to help Billy! ...”

Skeeter was sitting in Billy’s chair when he walked into his office the following morning. “Uh, oh, you got that look, Skeet, what are you up to?”

“What look? Why does everyone think I’m up to something just because I look like I am?”

“I think you just answered your own question Skeeter,” laughed Billy.

“OK, maybe so, but here’s what we are going to do! You need help and we’ve decided to help you.”

“Whoa, young lady, what kinda help? and who’s *we*?”

“Just listen. Us kids know who belongs in the Zone and who doesn’t. I’m talking about other kids, like the ones who attacked Sean, not grownups. We’ve assigned two kids per block, one on each side of Center Street. Two more kids will be on duty on Center Street, one on each end. We will only work from 11:00 in the morning to 6:00 at night, then you're on your own; but most of us kids will be off the streets by then anyway. When we see someone who doesn't belong here, we go into action. We've worked out signals and will relay the warning to the kid closest to your office and they will run in and tell you! Here's your map of the blocks, we numbered them for you."

"Skeeter, I appreciate the help," said an amused Billy, "but I can't have a 'Kiddie Corps' doing police surveillance work!"

"Kiddie Corps! I like it, and you don't have a say-so. It's already in the mill!"

"Skeet!" Too late, she was heading for her troops.

Billy may not have liked it, but the 'Kiddie Corps' stood guard for almost three years. Billy never got his deputy; he didn't need one.

Chapter 13: That's No Repair Shop

THE COMPUTER FUNERAL had taken place a few weeks after Sean's stabbing. The children missed it but were kept busy with Kiddie Corps duty and other activities.

Skeeter had just relieved Sean who was patrolling one of the streets. Their assignment for the day was to observe the block that ran alongside their house.

Sean casually sauntered down the block, heading home and doing his best detective impersonation. He noticed a Hispanic man, sporting a bushy mustache, throwing used computer parts into the trash. Thinking that some of these bits could be used to resurrect the dead computer, he asked,

"If you don't want those pieces, I could sure use them."

"What for? They're no good," answered the man.

"Well, if they're not too worn out, they might be fixable," replied Sean.

"Help yourself, kid." He started to walk away, paused and said:

"Hey kid, can you take computers apart?"

"Sure. I just tore one up the other day."

"Hang on a second, I'll be right back."

Sean saw him talk to someone inside and come back out.

"Look, I got a garage full of parts that you might be interested in and some computers that need to be put back together. You wanna take a look?"

"Sure." Sean followed him into the garage.

There were hundreds of loose parts neatly stacked and dozens of new, but empty, computer cases.

"Wow," said Sean, looking around, amazed at the display.

"We own a computer store downtown but do repairs here. We put shiny new cases on them as part of the deal." He nodded at the stacked parts and added, "Do you think you can put those parts back into those cases?"

Surveying the inventory, Sean said, "Yeah, I can do it. If all the parts are here, it's just a matter of reassembling."

"Tell you what, kid, put one or two back together and then we'll talk. All the tools you need are on this bench."

Sean had no idea what the man was talking about but loved the opportunity to build a computer from scratch. He could easily recall everything he had learned about assembling and disassembling computers.

The parts were well organized and the tools were better than what he was used to working with. Sean had one computer assembled in no time. When he finished, he looked around and the mustache man and another much taller man were standing behind him observing his work.

"All done," said Sean, and he fired up the computer.

Sean moved over to let the taller man operate it.

"How old are you kid?" he asked.

"Just turned seven."

"Where do you live?" asked Mustache.

"Right around the corner."

"You come by tomorrow, kid, and for every computer you put together, we'll give you some money," said the taller man.

Sean thought about it and said, "I don't want the money but if I put ten computers together for you, can I keep one for myself?"

The two men looked at each other and shrugged. The tall guy said, "Sure, but you'll have to use one of the old cases."

Sean raced home and excitedly told M. J. what he had been doing.

"Cool," she said sewing a button onto a sock puppet.

"But, M. J., listen. We'll have a computer again!"

"Cool. Do you like this red button for the nose?"

Sean headed for the computer garage first thing the next morning. M. J. would cover for him. He checked in at home for a couple of hours around noon and then went back to complete his end of the bargain. By late afternoon he was finished and came home with a rebuilt computer.

He was beaming. "Look Skeeter, M. J. Look what I got!"

They immediately hooked it up and were checking it out when Ma walked in holding Little Bit.

"Where did you get that? Nettie didn't tell me she bought you guys another computer."

"She didn't Ma," explained Sean. "I built it."

"Do I want to know about this?" quizzed Ma.

"Nope," said M. J.

"Well, I know somebody who's going to want to know about it."

"Yeah, and I can't wait to surprise her!" cried Sean.

"Ahh-huh, I can't wait either," chortled Ma. "I can't wait."

Little Bit squirmed free and jumped on Sean's back as he got down on all fours. "Giddy-up horsey," she ordered, as he galloped around the apartment. He tipped her over and wrestled and tickled her until she was about to wet her pants from laughing so hard.

"I never get tired of watching them do that." It was Nettie just returning from a tutoring assignment.

"Mom, Mom, wait 'til you see what I got!" bragged Sean as he jumped up, grabbed her by the hand and led her to the kitchen table.

"I built it myself! What do you think?" He grinned proudly.

She took a long look and sat down pulling Sean close to her, "I think you should tell me all about it, son." Sean did, leaving out nothing and Nettie listened intently. Finally she said, "Where is this house?" He told her again and she looked at the computer saying, "You did a great job, Sean, a great job."

He hugged her hard, kissed her on the cheek and said, "Thanks Mom."

As the kids played with the computer, Nettie turned to Ma and said, "Well, should I go see Billy?"

"Like right now, Nettie, right now."

As Nettie walked into Billy's little station, Meg was just leaving.

"He tried to arrest me but I talked my way out of it," laughed Meg.

"Hey Billy, you got another customer; this must be your day." She waved some papers at Nettie. "Medical reports."

"Meg, stop by the house. Ask Ma to show you the new addition."

Nettie plunked herself down in the chair previously occupied by Meg and said, "What do you know about some dudes that live a block from us and run a computer repair shop?"

Billy drew a long breath and said, "That's no repair shop.
What's your interest, Nettie?"

Nettie told him Sean's story and after she finished Billy leaned forward and said, "Here's what they do: they buy stolen computers on the black market, get new cases - usually an Apple or a Dell - take out the parts from the used ones and install them in the new cases. Then they sell them on the open market as new Macs or Dells."

"It looks like our Sean is working as their new technician. Their old one musta quit."

"WAS working, Billy. Was."

"Good, cuz there's more. The operation's controlled by a guy named Marcos, Carlos Marcos. He's from South America and he's one of the biggest drug dealers in the city. He doesn't run his computer scam out of the Zone; no, he just does his technical work here. That keeps him safe under our stupid truce. He's big time and I'm not s'posed to hassle him. It's better if Sean never goes near that place. Marcos will get the message. But if he bothers Sean, you let me know and I'll pay him a visit."

"He won't bother Sean, Billy," she said as she got up to leave. Billy wasn't sure how to take that.

Nettie was furious. If she turned Billy lose on him she would make a bad enemy. If she did nothing, as Billy suggested, Marcos or his cronies might still come looking for Sean. And what about the computer? It was made from stolen parts. She knew what she had to do.

That night she told Sean what he had stumbled into. In the morning, she explained they would take the computer back. By doing it this way, she reasoned, Marcos wouldn't suspect that she blew the whistle on him. However, she would let him know that she knew what he was up to.

Nettie and Sean walked up the path to Marcos' house the next morning, carrying the computer with them. A new BMW sparkled in the driveway.

"Carlos, you've got visitors. That techie kid and some babe." Carlos looked out the window and drew a short breath, "My god, where did she come from? She's gorgeous!"

Carlos greeted her at he door before Nettie could knock. "Good morning. What can I do for you? I'm Carlos Marcos."

"Good morning," she said frostily. "I'm Mrs. Ferrari and I think you know my son, Sean." Sean did a double take; he had never heard his mom describe herself as Mrs. Ferrari before.

"Why, yes I do..."

Nettie quickly interrupted him, "I believe this is your computer."

"Well, we gave..."

Nettie interrupted him again, "Thanks for letting him borrow it and allowing him to play with your computers. He won't be back. You will have to get someone else to do your work for you. Do we understand each other, Mr. Marcos?" she asked staring him straight in the eye.

"I believe we do, Mrs. Ferrari. I'm sure we can find someone else to help us," he said smiling pleasantly.

"Thank you," she replied. Then Nettie really looked at him for the first time. He was handsome - tall with jet black hair. He was extraordinarily handsome. Nettie felt a stirring that she hadn't felt in years and became completely annoyed with herself. She turned around and left.

"Now, that was some lady and did you see those spectacular green eyes?"

"What I saw was trouble, Carlos. She should be watched," said Enrico, his associate.

"Maybe. But for now she is off limits to everyone. GOT IT?"

"Yeah, yeah, sure, Carlos, sure!"

A few days later, a UPS man came knocking at the door. Ma opened it.

"I've got a delivery for a Mrs. Ferrari. That you?"

"No, but I'll sign for it," said Ma.

She put the box in Nettie's apartment and returned to her cleaning.

When Nettie got home she spotted the package.

"Where did this come from, Ma? I wasn't expecting anything."

"UPS delivered it about an hour ago. I don't know how he found you without a street number."

Curious, she went back to her place and opened it. There was a message inside.

Mrs. Ferrari,
This is for Sean. It comes straight from the manufacturer direct to you.
Please accept this, not as payment for work performed, but as a gift making up for my bad judgment.
My apologies to you, Carlos

"Well, I'll be," she broke open the strong packing and discovered a brand new top-of-the-line Mac laptop. Another package inside the box contained small, but powerful, Bose speakers. "Wow!"
Now what to do? She quickly re-wrapped everything and hid it before the kids came charging in.

Ma gasped when Nettie told her what was in the package,
"Man, are you going to keep it?"
"Don't talk to me, I'm confused," said a truly confused Nettie.
"I don't want to be indebted to the guy but I don't want to offend him, either. Sean didn't know he was working with stolen goods and we did take the other computer back... and this is a gift not a payment... and...and... Boy, is that thing beautiful!"

She was off to Billy's.

"Under the circumstances, Nettie, I'd say keep it. You did everything right and his note gets you off the hook. Besides, ya got me to confirm your story."

"Hmmm, how long do you think this fancy machine will last in the Zone?" questioned Nettie.
"I've got a feeling it's going to be quite safe here."
"I don't want him to get the wrong idea, Billy."
"You can avoid him and still keep the computer. He won't bother you, I'll see to that. Sometimes, you just gotta make a pact with the Devil," sighed Billy.

While Nettie was mulling that over, one of the children's friends came running into Billy's office.
"Hi Miss Nettie!"
"Well hello, Pauly, what are you up to?"
"I'm just here to warn Billy." He shuffled from foot to foot.
"Number 4A," he shouted. "And if you hurry, Billy, you can catch 'em. Four of 'em... older boys! Bye Miss Nettie!" And he was gone.

"What was that all about?"
"Sometimes you gotta make a pact with the Angels too. I better git going," chuckled Billy.

As he opened the door for Nettie, he said, "By the way - you seen any bad characters around here lately?"
"Well, come to think of it, no!"
"You might wanna check with the Head Angel," and he hurried off.

Nettie was puzzled, check with... Then her eye's widened, "Uh, oh!"

Chapter 14: Fights and Rat Bites

NETTIE WAS RECALLING some of the papers that Skeet and Sean had strewn around and she seemed to remember a list with children's names on it. She hadn't paid any attention to it then but now she realized that it was probably the work of the 'Head Angel'. She gave it considerable thought and decided that whatever the kids were up to was between them and Billy. She was sure that Billy would never let *his* kids get involved in something that was dangerous. And besides, what a perfect way to keep them on the right side of the law. She stayed out of it.

Nettie decided that if she was going to keep the computer, it would be appropriate to at least send a thank you note to Carlos. She wrote a simple message, sealed it into a small envelope, and gave it to Sean to deliver. Sean made the delivery, handing the envelope to Enrico. Carlos wasn't home.

The Mac opened up new and exciting avenues of exploration that totally justified Nettie's decision to keep it. The broken old computer had been deficient in many ways and it slowed down the learning process.

The children were amazed at the Mac's endless capacities and they took turns using it. With the help of the tutorials, the search engines, and just plain trial and error, Sean was learning all of its secrets. Skeet focused on the things she needed to know and, when she got stuck, she called on Sean. He could always figure it out. M. J. was learning by just watching the other two while waiting for her turn.

Everybody immediately knew when it was M. J.'s turn and they all agreed that it might have been better if the speakers were not part of the deal. That problem was resolved when Nettie came home with a head set for M. J.

There was no stopping her now; she became 'the performer' as she danced and mimed to her tunes, whatever they were.

M. J. WAS READY for the big stage by fall of the following year.

"Ma, when are you going to help me make more puppets for my show?" demanded M. J.

"What show, honey?"

"Papa Joe said that when I was ready we can entertain the sick kids!"

"Well, go ask Papa Joe for some specific dates and we'll all start working with you. Just tell us what you want us to do."

"Papa Joe, Papa Joe! Ma says they're ready to help with the show; you just have to tell us when." M. J. had dashed over to the chapel and was sitting on Papa Joe's desk.

"Okay, little girl, why don't we shoot for Christmas week? That's when I tour the children's hospitals. Do you think you can be ready by then? It's only a couple of months away, you know."

"Yes, yes. I can't wait," she said, as she threw her arms around her Papa and gave him a big hug. Then off she danced, holding her arms up like they had little puppets on them while she carried on a dialogue.

"Are you going to be ready, Shorty?"

"You bet, Spud!"

"Jingle bells, Jingle bells..."

Papa Joe just shook his head. "That's my girl," he said proudly.

M. J. put the whole family to work. She had Ma, Meg, and Nettie going through their belongings in search of socks, buttons and yarn. She knew what she wanted the puppets to look like but didn't have the slightest idea what she wanted them to say.

When Ma asked her about it, M. J. just shrugged, "Beats me."

"Why don't you go and ask Skeet? She wants to be a writer," suggested Ma.

"Does she know anything about puppets?"

"I don't know," laughed Ma. "Why don't you ask her?"

Skeeter was on the computer when M. J. found her.

"Skeet, can you write a story for my puppet show? Ma thinks you can."

"Gee, I don't know M. J., but I'll try. Tell me a little bit about your puppets."

That was the beginning of the team: M. J. the producer-director and Skeeter the playwright. It would be the first of many plays and productions Skeeter would write in her lifetime.

It was a team effort. The adult women made the puppet costumes. Sean was in charge of sets and music; they made him play the penny whistle. Little Bit was going to make the introductions. Skeet wrote the dialogue. Papa Joe was the booking agent and M. J. told everybody what to do. Oh yeah, Billy was in charge of transportation and security. The kids took turns at being puppeteers.

They were a smash! The young patients at the children's hospitals loved it. M. J. wasn't satisfied, however; she had Skeet change the script once Christmas was over. She put on shows all through the spring and summer, playing at birthday parties and bringing her show to anybody in the Zone who was sick or housebound. She and most of her troupe were available if Papa Joe asked them to perform outside the Zone. She never forgot her hospital kids, though, and frequently visited them, sometimes doing solos when the others were busy. Sean was usually with her, playing his penny whistle.

"That little girl is bringing joy to a lot of people," Papa Joe told her mother. "We should be very proud of her."

In addition to puppeteering, the children were busy. Nettie was constantly schooling them. They were spending a lot of time on the Mac.

They had Kiddie Corps duties. And they still found time to just be kids.

For a treat, the family sometimes went to the Jewish deli for borsht or pastrami sandwiches. Sean, M. J. and Skeet became friends with Joey Goldstein, the boy whose parents owned the Deli. The Goldsteins spoke Yiddish to each other, many times in the presence of the children. They were flabbergasted one day when Sean joined the conversation speaking perfect Yiddish! No one was more shocked than M. J. and Skeeter.

"Were you just making up words?" they asked Sean.

"No, I just listen and learn," he replied. The two girls looked at each other not knowing what to believe.

Sean and M. J. still had occasional run ins with the transient kids of the Zone, but for the most part M. J. was more circumspect on who she took on. She had nothing to do with the fight at the deli.

Once again it was outsiders and this time their target was Joey Goldstein.

Sean was at home working on the computer when M. J. popped in. "I'm heading for Papa Joe's to look at his new schedule. I know I can talk him into buying me a sandwich at the deli. Why don't you meet us there?"

"Sure, I'll leave here in about ten minutes - I'm hungry," replied Sean.

As he was walking towards the deli, he spotted a Kiddie Corp member frantically giving a signal to her counterpart stationed on the opposite end of Center Street only a block away from Billy's. Following the strict rule Skeeter had laid down of not conversing with a fellow Corps member while on duty, Sean kept walking towards the deli wondering where the interlopers were.

Joey had just taken the trash to the containers in the alley, when they jumped him.

"You Jew pig," shouted two very scruffy boys about Sean's age. "You're the one that needs to be stuffed in the garbage can!" They were in the process of trying to do just that as Sean approached the Deli.

Joey, smaller but wiry, was fighting back. "Get out of here you ghetto SHITS," he bellowed as they crashed into the cans. Sean heard the fracas and peered into the alley. He rushed to Joey's aid when he saw what was happening.

This was no kid's wrestling match. It was a real fight, like the ones Sean and M. J. had witnessed many times before in the Zone. They were trading punches furiously.

Billy, alerted by the ever present watchful eye of the Kiddie Corps, pulled up in his patrol car. Hearing the sounds of battle, he darted into the alley just in time to see one of the troublemakers pull a knife and slash wildly at Sean who was bettering him. Sean jumped back, but not in time, as the knife cut across his chest opening up a four inch gash.

Furious, Billy grabbed the assailant in an attempt to dislodge the knife from his hand and threw him into the other boy, knocking them both into the garbage cans. These tough kids scurried to their feet and took off running, shouting as they ran, "We'll get both of you pale-ass whiteys next time!"

Billy took one look at Sean's wound and said, "Let's go, Sean, this is a nasty one!"

As they were about to get into Billy's patrol car, M. J. and Papa Joe arrived.

When M. J. saw the blood, she screeched, "WHAT HAPPENED?"

"Two kids jumped me and Sean came from nowhere. They cut him with a knife." It was Joey speaking while wiping a bloody nose with his hand.

"WHERE DID THEY GO?" M. J. demanded.

Joey nodded toward the alley.

Sean, knowing what she was about to do, cried out, "NO, M. J. NO!" Too late - she was in hot pursuit!

Sean started to go after her but Billy shoved him into the patrol car and, sirens blaring, headed for the emergency room. Sean wheeled around just in time to see Papa Joe chasing furiously after M. J. She never did find the culprits and Papa Joe never caught up with her.

THE BUSY SUMMER was drawing to a close but not before one last bit of drama: a bar opened up that summer on the same block where Carlos rebuilt his phony computers. It served food and the alley became cluttered with uncollected garbage. The garbage attracted rats and the rats multiplied, exacerbating an already serious problem for the neighborhood, Ma's house included. You didn't have to point this out to Ma; she commented frequently about the sudden increase in the rat population.

Three year old Little Bit was playing by herself in the back of Ma's house in late August when she spotted several rats clinging to a garbage can. She stopped suddenly, lost her balance and crashed into the cans. Stunned, she lay there for a moment and the frightened rats crawled all over her trying to escape. Little Bit panicked and screamed, flailing her arms and legs. The rats reacted and bit her on the neck, her arm and leg.

Ma, heard Little Bit scream and ran out.

"Oh, my god!" She rushed over and scooped up Little Bit as the rats scurried away. She ran the short distance to Meg's with Little Bit screaming hysterically.

Meg heard the screams as Ma was coming up the path. "RAT BITES!"

"Son-of-bitch," cursed an angry Meg and she led them into the house.

As Ma held Little Bit, Meg examined her and found the three bites.

"The one on her neck is deep, the other two are not bad."

Meg had treated rat bites before and expertly cleaned the wounds with soap and warm water. She made sure the soap was rinsed off, applied an antibiotic ointment and placed a clean dressing on the bites.

"We will have to watch her for an infection and she is going to have a scar on her neck, but I think she'll be fine. I'll change her dressing every day until I'm sure there is no problem," said Meg.

"Those stupid rats, where are they all coming from? I've never seen so many, ever!"

First Sean with his uncountable stitches, and now this. They were all outraged, especially Nettie.

"I don't like what's happening here, Meg. Do you realize that if Billy hadn't gotten there as quickly as he did when Sean was cut, Sean could have been killed!"

"I know," said Meg. "By the way, I've been meaning to ask you - how *did* Billy get there so fast?"

"Let's just say Sean had an Angel looking after him that day."

Nettie and Ma walked the alley looking for the possible source of the explosion in the rat population. It didn't take them long to discover the problem. The garbage behind the new bar was stacked up with dozens of rats crawling all over it.

Nettie took one look and burst into the bar from the back door with Ma right behind her.

"Who's in charge here?"

The surprised bartender nodded in the direction of a couple sitting at a table. The man looked vaguely familiar.

"Do you own this place?" Nettie yelled.

"No. What's your problem, lady?"

"Your garbage is her problem, pal," chimed in an angry Ma.

"It's full of rats!"

"What do I look like, a fucking garbage collector?"

"Well that just may be a question for the Health Department to decide, wise guy," calmly stated Nettie. They turned around and left.

"I knew she was going to be a problem," muttered Enrico as he reached for his cell phone.

Normally, the Health Department wouldn't get involved in garbage collection issues when it concerned the Zone but there was a child bitten by rats and three very formidable women confronting the Superintendent. They sent out an investigator.

The agent came out, took some pictures, asked a few questions and left. He ignored Nettie and Meg who had made sure that they were present. They were now totally disgusted.

"I know that weasely faced bureaucrat," said Meg. "He's one of those arrogant college types who goes by the book and has no sense at all."

"I wish I knew who owned this place," said Nettie, as they were exiting the bar. "Maybe I can help you Mrs. Ferrari."

Nettie looked over and Carlos Marcos was smiling at her.

"I own this fine establishment and I was informed about the unfortunate rat bite incident. I assume that one of your children got bitten?"

"You assume right," inserted Meg.

"You must be the famous Meg Brown? I mean that as a compliment, Ms. Brown. I know you are very respected here in the Zone.

Look, ladies, I totally agree that the garbage situation is a complete disaster. I hired a private company to clean up my share and to make pick-ups between the normal collections by the city. Also, I've hired an exterminator to kill off the rats. They can't guarantee total elimination but they can reduce the rat population considerably. I really am sorry about the child. If she needs any medical assistance, I will gladly pay the bill."

Carlos then turned to Nettie, "It seems that once more I'm apologizing to you, Mrs. Ferrari. I would have replied to your kind thank you note but Billy thought that it would be a good idea if I didn't. And he's the law around here."

"I understand how it works in the Zone, Mr. Mar... Carlos, and I do appreciate what you're doing here now. Nobody mentioned that to us. I'll thank you in person this time, good afternoon."

As they were walking back to Center Street Meg said,

"Man, that is one slick dude."

"A free computer and no rats. I'm keeping my mouth shut, Meg. Sometimes you just have to make a pact with the Devil," smiled Nettie, not so annoyed this time at feeling those same stirrings as before.

The conversation back at the bar was different.

"God damn it, Carlos! She brought a government agent in here. What's next, the fucking FBI? And for what? A chick you can't screw!"

"Tread softly, Enrico; tread real softly. You've been warned."

Chapter 15: Sandy and Roberta

WHEN SEAN WAS NINE, he was academically ahead of children his age attending public schools. Nettie thought it was time to introduce him to Dr. John and some of her other friends at the University.

"Sean can speak how many languages, Nettie?" asked an incredulous Dr. John.

"Four. And he's learning more. He has an extraordinary ability to learn language just from hearing people conversing in it." She told him about how Sean had learned Yiddish. She didn't want to go into any details about their special gift.

"If you want him to demonstrate this ability, just pick out a language spoken here and then place Sean within hearing range of people speaking it."

"You're kidding!" Dr. John paused and said... "Sean, can you speak Russian?"

"No Sir, I've never heard it spoken," Sean said politely.

Dr. John looked at Nettie and said, "Dr. Larionov and his wife are down the hall. Uh, do you mind?"

Nettie gave her okay and Dr. John set up a meeting with Sean and the Larionovs. Sean sat in their office for about ten minutes while they carried on a conversation in Russian between themselves. They were talking about their children back in Russia.

Dr. Larionov stopped and asked Sean, in Russian, if he had any questions. Sean bombarded them, in perfect Russian, with questions about children living in Russia.

Sean's performance stunned Dr. John. "Impossible, impossible," he exclaimed. "Nettie, we have to test him. We... we have to find out how he can do this!"

"No, no we don't, they won't find the answer. I just wanted you to know that he has this skill. You should see him in the sciences - especially computer science. He's way ahead of everybody else. Look, Dr. John, I'm home schooling Sean. When the time comes, I would like your help in getting him started early in his college education."

"Sure, I'd be glad to help. Look, Nettie, we should let the experts work with Sean," pleaded Dr. John.

"No," said Nettie. "But I will bring him to work with me from time to time so you can chart his progress. Okay?"

"Of course, of course. But you've got to let me at least discuss his extraordinary talents with my contemporaries!"

"Yes, you can do that. Now would you be so kind as to call Dr. Hughes in Computer Science? Tell him I'm on my way over to see him. He might want to check out Sean's computer skills." She smiled at Dr. John,

"Oh, they're sorta like his language skills!"
Nettie and Sean trekked across campus to the Computer Science building. They located Dr. Hughes's office and walked in as he was hanging up the phone. Nettie introduced him to Sean and they settled into comfortable leather chairs.
"I just talked to Dr. Telasantos. He told me about Sean, here, and his extraordinary talent. He tells me Sean may have similar abilities with the computer?"
"He does," answered Nettie. "Not only can he navigate through the most difficult programs but he can also tear any computer down and rebuild it. He can build programs and do coding too."
That got the doctor's attention. He invited Sean to sit in front of one of the computers and put him through drills that he used on his students.
After a rigorous twenty minutes, Dr. Hughes shook his head and said, "He's at an advanced level right now. Nettie, he is something special. Come on, Sean, we are going to the technical labs, I want you to show me how you can rip a computer apart!"
"Great!" Sean squealed. "That's my specialty!"
"We'll see," laughed Dr. Hughes.
And see he did.
"Nettie, that was unbelievable. Not only did he tear down and reassemble a computer, he decoded a program and created a new one. Amazing!"
Dr. Hughes hesitated and said, "Look, we do a lot of programming - and coding and repairing and rebuilding for the University. We're constantly in need of people with Sean's talent, no matter how old they are. We have worked out a special minor student exemption status with the State. You'd be surprised at how many young children we work with under this program. Their hours are strictly limited and are purely voluntary. These youngsters were born into the computer age and are really skilled. What is the cliche? Uh, we are only visitors to the information age; these children are natives - something like that."
"That's true," said Nettie. "Sean took apart his first computer when he was seven."
"Sean has more to learn but this is the place to do it. Under our program we give him credits for his time spent and when he turns fourteen he can convert his credits in for cash. What do you say?"
"Why don't you ask Sean?"
Dr. Hughes smiled and said, "What do you think Sean, would you like to do this?"
"I sure would! When can I start?"
"There's your answer," smiled Nettie. "Let's set this up the next time I'm in. Dr. Hughes, I'm going to ask you the same thing I asked Dr. Telasantos. I'm home schooling Sean. When the time comes, would you

mind helping him get an early start in his college education?"
"You can count on it, Nettie. You can count on it."

Nettie had placed Sean on the fast track to a college education. Now she had some work to do with her prize student; Skeeter would soon be thirteen. With her intelligence and desire to learn, she was ahead of students her age in most categories and was at least even in the others. Nettie knew that this was not going to be good enough. Skeeter had to be in the upper percentiles in all categories. She needed to earn a scholarship if she was going to go on to college.

SKEETER WAS MATURING into a thoughtful and attractive young woman. She had a calm, quiet demeanor and was a natural leader.

Although Skeet knew that Sandy was her mother, she never inquired about her or asked who her father was. Only once did Skeeter ask what her real name was. Meg had told her it was Abrianna Charles and all Skeeter had said was, "Oooo, thats a cool name."

Sean had just given Little Bit a computer lesson and was wrestling with her on the floor. Skeeter was on the computer surfing the local news when she suddenly stood up remaining transfixed on the screen.
Sean noticed her and said, "What's wrong, Skeet?"
"Take a look, Sean."
The headlines of the local news read: 'WOMAN FOUND DEAD IN DRUG RAID' - Below was a picture of the dead woman. It was Sandy.

Sean told Ma about the news.
"Where's Skeet?" Ma asked.
"She just went upstairs; she wanted to be alone."
"Sean, run down to Meg's and let her know what's happened. Thanks."

Ma went upstairs and found Skeet quietly sitting in a chair staring at a shoebox on the table.
"Are you all right, honey?"
"Yes, I just wish I had known her better; I'm not even sure what her name was or if she even was my mother. This box was all that I found of hers. It's just some papers and this old framed photo." She handed the picture to Ma.

"I don't know her real name, either, Skeet. But, looking at this picture, I can assure you that she *was* your mother. Just look at the young girl about your age standing next to the older lady. That young girl has to be your mother; you are a dead ringer for her! Here, look for yourself."
"Wow, I see what you mean. Well at least I know that. I'll keep this. It will be something for Little Bit and me to remember her by."

"Ma, what is Little Bit's real name?"
Ma, remembering what Meg had told her, said,
"It's Eboni. Eboni Jackson."

Meg never disclosed Little Bit's real name, Jessica Watson, to anyone. She was worried that if the authorities did come around and Little Bit was innocently identified as Jessica Watson, it might trigger an investigation and they could lose her. She couldn't take that chance. She felt It was best if only she knew Little Bit's real name, at least for now.

Meg walked in and hugged and rocked Skeeter.

"I know you didn't see her much but she was still your mother. I'm so, so sorry Skeet."

"Meg, I wasn't even sure about that until I looked at this picture." She showed Meg.

"Oh, I see what you mean. Man, you two could have been twins."

"Meg, what do you know about my father, Mr. Charles?"

Meg was in a quandary; she knew this question was going to be asked sooner or later. She wanted to tell Skeeter the truth but saw no good in that so she said, "Nothing, Skeet. Nobody knew the man and your mother never spoke of him."

"Oh, I see."

Meg now had a real concern about Roberta. No telling what Sandy's death would do to their little scam.

"Skeet, if your aunt Roberta shows up and demands that you go with her, you come looking for me and don't leave here."

"I would never go with her, Meg, and I won't let Little Bit go either!"

"Good, but just in case, I want Little Bit to stay with me for a while. Is that okay with everybody?"

"Sure, Meg," said Skeet. "Are you expecting trouble from Roberta?"

"I'd be lying if I said I didn't," exclaimed Meg.

When Nettie came home and found out the news about Sandy, she went straight upstairs to see Skeeter.

Skeeter sat in the chair staring off into the distance. Nettie went over and stroked her on the cheek.

"Don't be sad, Skeeter."

Skeet looked up at her and Nettie continued.

"Do you remember telling me the very same thing when you were a little girl? If I had a rose I would give it to you like you once gave one to me. I needed comfort then, Skeet, and you gave it to me. Now I get to do the same for you."

"I kinda remember, Nettie. Why were you sad?"

"We will talk about that sometime, Skeet, but for now, let's get you downstairs where your family is. We all love you Skeeter."

"Thanks for reminding me of that. I know you all do."

Two days later Meg's worst fears were realized. Roberta was heading up the path to Ma's door. Ma spotted her and sent M. J. out the back to fetch Meg. Roberta entered the house, went upstairs and came back down. Ma was waiting for her.

"Sandy's dead," Roberta said without much emotion.
"I've come here to get the kids; I'm their only living relative."
"You try to take those kids and they won't have ANY living relatives," came Ma's icy response.
"Don't give me any trouble, Ma, I have the law on my side."
"Any trouble that Ma gives you is nothing compared to what I'm going to give you!" It was Meg, she had her ferocious face on.
"Listen you bitch, this is none of your business and it ain't none of yours either, Ma! I'm taking those kids and that's IT! Now, where are they?" fired back Roberta.
"None of my business, huh? Well maybe it will be the District Attorney's business when I tell them about the double birth certificate scam that you and Sandy have been running all these years!"
"I don't know what you're talking about..."
"SHUT UP, Roberta, YOU BETTER GET THIS AND GET THIS STRAIGHT!" I work with the people at the Vital Statistics office. REMEMBER? They gave me access to their birth records and it was real easy to spot all the mothers who gave birth declaring that their baby's father was deceased!"
"What's that got to do with me?" asked Roberta.
"Just this: most of the babies were delivered by midwives. Two of those midwives signed most of the forms declaring the fathers were deceased and both of those midwives are in jail now for other crimes committed. Not to mention that many of those lying mothers are also in jail for numerous crimes."
"That doesn't prove shit, Meg. NOW GIVE ME THOSE KIDS!"
"Oh, it will prove something when the DA gets those jailbirds to confess to participating in your scam in return for REDUCING THEIR SENTENCES!"
"If you don't think that I won't be all over the DA's ass to investigate your little scam, you are SADLY MISTAKEN LADY!"
Knowing that she was boxed in, Roberta angrily screamed, "I'LL GET YOU FOR THIS, MEG!"
"Easy, Roberta. I think we understand each other." Roberta, furious, wheeled around and left.
"I figured you knew about the midwives, but how did you know about those other women in jail, Meg?"
"What other women, Ma?"
They both laughed uproariously.
Meg knew that she had scared her and Roberta would have to do something to cover her own butt. The first chance Meg got, she visited her friends at Vital Statistics and accessed the records. Sure enough. Roberta had her partners in crime remove from the files the birth record of one Jessica Watson. Roberta knew that Meg's name appeared on that

certificate and she could easily incriminate Roberta in fraud.

Upon further checking the files, Meg found that Eboni Jackson's name still appeared on record as well as Abrianna Charles. She bet that the transcripts of Skeet's other birth certificate had also disappeared.

It really didn't matter; neither one of the girls would ever know their fathers anyway. Meg would now forget there ever was a Jessica Watson birth certificate. Neither Little Bit nor anybody else needed to know. And besides, Eboni Jackson was a pretty cool name.

Chapter 16: The Fire

MA HAD LOST two tenants that she could not afford to lose. She wasn't keen on renting to an outsider with all the kids in the house.
"Ma, could you get by with just one paying tenant upstairs?" questioned Nettie.
"Well, I suppose I could make do. Why do you ask?"
"Because I would like to rent one of the apartments," answered Nettie. "I can afford it with my tutoring going so well and I've got an idea. If we could close off the living room in one of the apartments and install a door, we would have an extra bedroom. Then if we knock out the adjoining wall between the kitchens, we could have a pass through from the inside. What do you say? The three older kids would have their own bedrooms and Little Bit can sleep wherever she wanted to!"
"Gosh Nettie, I don't know. Are you sure you can afford it?"
"If you can, I can, and wouldn't it be great to have a bedroom all to ourselves again?"
Ma paused; then her eye's got bigger as she recognized what that would mean, "OH YEAH. OH YEAH! Now you've hooked me. All right, lets do it!" They laughed and hugged each other.
"You know," said Ma, "Billy and Meg are both real good at carpentry and I know that they would love a project!"
Billy and Meg did love a project and they got right after it. It didn't take Billy long to scrounge up an old door and some discarded lumber that had been strewn around and inside the vacant houses that the kids played in.
Soon the noisy clatter of construction was filling the house.
"I don't know who's having more fun - Meg and Billy, or the kids," Ma said to Nettie.
"I know what you mean. Meg and Billy are doing more laughing than hammering. I'm sure glad we stayed out of it and turned the supervision over to the children. They're absolutely driving our carpenters crazy with construction orders," laughed Nettie.
"Yup. You couldn't drag me up there for nothing. I'll wait for the finished product! And did you hear those kids trying to figure out who gets what room? Poor Little Bit kept saying, *But where's my room*?" added Ma.
Sean was really interested in the construction, the girls not so much. They had to move some electrical outlets and reconnect them. This fascinated Sean and he besieged Billy with questions about electricity. Sean couldn't wait to get on line to learn more.
The girls were more interested in the living arrangements. They decided to let Sean have one of the existing bedrooms. Skeet and M. J. would take the other bedroom and the converted living room for their

sleeping quarters so they could be close to each other. The remaining living room would become a computer-project room.

They pacified Little Bit by appointing her Company Clerk in charge of the computer-project room. They told her that the clerk always sleeps in her work room and that they were going to put a single bed in there for her. She was delighted and immediately figured out how to combine the two kitchens, freeing up drawers for all of M. J.'s projects.

What started out as a ploy to keep Little Bit happy turned into a stroke of genius. The little soon-to-be-four-year-old took her job seriously. Turned out she had a natural talent for organization.

First Little Bit confiscated two large project tables that Billy wasn't using and positioned them in the work room. Next she collected all of the scrap material needed for making costumes and put them into neat piles. But her most valuable contribution was keeping everybody up to date as to where and when the upcoming puppet performances were to take place. This she did by using the calendar of events application on the computer. She made sure Papa Joe briefed her on the schedule; M. J. might forget to inform her.

Sean's little computer student was fast learning organizational skills. However, they still found time for their wrestling matches and if one of the others got too close, they too were dragged into the ring. After play time, he gave Little Bit more computer lessons.

"I CAN'T WAIT for Christmas time. I just can't wait!" M. J. was twirling around with a puppet on each hand held over her head.

"Oh..." Skeeter barely looked up from her book.

"When the Christmas lights go on, that's when Papa Joe makes his rounds and it's SHOWTIME for me. Yay!"

"Yeah, I guess it's soon now," agreed Skeeter smiling up at her dancing sister. M. J. dropped to her knees in front of Skeeter, "And I really help them. I do, Skeet. Most of the kids I knew went home; they aren't there any more. I helped them get better."

"You *do* help them, M. J.," smiled Skeeter.

Papa Joe hadn't had the heart to tell M. J. that many of them had lost their battle with cancer.

Christmas season passed and spring approached. M. J. was busy figuring out how to improve her show. She wanted more personal participation, so she asked Skeet to write in a dance number for her. She sent Little Bit on a mission searching iTunes for music. Skeeter was amazed at M. J.'s ability to sense what the production needed.

The spring shows were merely a warmup for what M. J. had planned for the summer. She decided that they were going to put on a stage play: a MUSICAL.

Skeeter stared at her in disbelief, "M. J., we have no instruments, nobody to play them if we did, and no stage to perform on!"

M. J. looked surprised, the way she always looked when she was told that it was impossible for her to do something.

"You just write the script, Skeet. I'll take care of the rest."

Her plan was vintage M. J. She knew what she wanted and figured out how she was going to get whatever she needed; but she didn't have the slightest idea how the play was to be arranged. This approach forced Skeeter to become creative and independent. It provided early valuable training that would pay off for her later in life.

In M. J's mind it was simple. She would raise the puppeteering concept to new heights. Discarded and broken down musical instruments that no longer worked and nobody wanted would be perfect for what M. J. envisioned. Her band would hold the real but unusable instruments and mime to the music, just like the puppets. M. J. of course would be the star 'vocalist'. She could lip synch to anything; she's been practicing for years.

This challenge had the grownups shaking their heads,

"A band, a band, how are we going to make costumes for a band?" queried Ma.

"Oh, that's easy," said M. J. "Just find some funny hats and make the kids all wear white tee shirts with 'The Zonies' printed on them!" Yes, she even had a name picked out for her band.

"Why didn't I think of that?" said Ma.

The Kiddie Corps was put to work. As they patrolled their beats, M. J. had Corps members inform people about the play. They talked to everybody they passed on the street and to the folks sitting on their broken down porches idly passing the time of day.

Everybody knew M. J. and they were asked if they had any unplayable musical instruments that could be sacrificed for her upcoming performance. Soon she had a bent trumpet, a trombone without a slide, drums with severe puncture wounds, three harmonicas with several teeth missing, two cracked guitars with no strings or bridges, and, amazingly, a tuba that looked like an elephant had stepped on it.

They were off and running and the sad collection was topped off when Nettie brought home a keyboard, without the piano. Some Wayne State students had loaded a piano in the back of a pickup and madly chased around campus playing the school's fight song. Due to a sharp turn and too many brewskies, the piano made its escape over the side and its several splattered parts ended up on the repair table of the Music Department. That's where Nettie found the keyboard. She figured it was a good place to find unwanted musical instruments for M. J. The piano was a hopeless loss and the department contributed a scratched but intact keyboard to M. J.'s collection.

Sean was put in charge of rehabbing the motley collection back to respectability. He whistled as he inspected the battered instruments laid out on the project table by Little Bit. He started to say something to M. J. but thought better of it when he felt her hard glare behind him.
"No problem," he said, rolling his eyes and making sure that M. J. didn't see the gesture.
They all had their assignments and Little Bit kept them informed as to what each of them was doing.
They set a date for the performance; the 4th of July. Good thing. Skeeter had Independence Day for the play's theme.
Casting was interesting. M. J. wanted the performers to be between the ages of five and eleven years old, and at least one of them had to be big enough to carry the tuba. The transient nature of the Zone would make this difficult; she was going to need a lot of alternates.
Little Bit was searching for patriotic CD's to import, working closely with Skeeter. Nettie found a discount CD shop downtown and bought several recordings for twenty-five cents apiece. Evidently there wasn't much of a market for John Philip Sousa. The quicker they had the music and storyline the sooner they could rehearse.
They still had a problem. Where was this extravaganza going to be held? The Zone had no parks and they feared bad weather. They put the word out that they needed an inside venue. There were still plenty of vacant stores around.
A runner came knocking at Ma's door with a message for Nettie.

Dear Mrs. Ferrari,

I hear the children are looking for a place to hold their play. I may have just the thing for them. I recently purchased the old theater at the end of Center Street. They are welcome to use it. If you are interested please tell the runner and I will be in touch.

Carlos

Nettie stood staring at the handwritten message for several seconds, then realized that the runner was waiting for a reply.
"Um, tell Mr. Marcos that this is a very kind offer and that I will consider it and get back to him."
This could get complicated, she thought, but what an opportunity for the children. She decided not to say anything to Ma or Meg just yet; she really wanted to see the theater first. No sense getting them stirred up if the site was not acceptable. She had paid no attention to the vacant

building before, not realizing that it had been at one time the local theater.

Nettie took a walk down to the end of Center Street the next day to locate the place. A building with big swinging doors was probably the spot, she thought. While walking up to take a peek inside, the doors swung open.

"Hello Mrs. Ferrari, I thought that was you," greeted a cheerful Carlos Marcos. "I just came down here to check this place out in hopes that you would accept my offer." He was alone.

"Come on in, we can look it over together. There's no electricity so we will have to keep the doors open for light."

"Wow, this really was a theater!"

"Yeah, they shut it down about twelve years ago and left everything untouched. Ah, I knew the former owner; it was understood that no one was to tamper with the place."

The old theater was small but it had all its seats, a full stage, a foyer with a ticket booth and two aisles leading to the seats from two entrances.

"Well, it needs a complete cleaning, the lights will have to be checked and of course all the stage equipment will have to be looked at. What do you think?"

Nettie walked down to the stage to get a better look. Carlos followed her. She turned around and he was standing directly in front of her about two feet away.

Light was coming from the open doors illuminating her face. Carlos was more or less a silhouette.

"Nettie, can I call you Nettie?"

"Why, sure Carlos."

"You … standing with the light shining on you ... well, I don't think I've ever seen a more beautiful woman." He reached up and put his hand gently on her elbow.

She neither moved nor flinched and felt a tingling ripple through her body. He slowly put his other hand around her waist and pulled her towards him.

He kissed her softly on the lips then kissed her again with more force. She kissed him back. His hands dropped below her waist as he pressed her tightly against him. Their tongues met and she could feel the heat rise in her, and his fire.

Their lips separated. She took a short breath, stepped back and tried to regain control.

"Carlos, please, this, this is no good."

"You're right, Nettie, I have a beautiful place on the river, we could go there."

"That's not what I meant. You and I come from different worlds.

I shouldn't be doing this."
"Our worlds are closer than you imagine, Nettie. Give it a chance."
For some reason that angered her.
"Carlos, I teach children how to read and write and to tell the difference between right and wrong. You give people drugs that destroy their lives!"
"I'm in the process of trying to change all that," he said quietly.
"You can't change what you've already done, Carlos. I'm leaving now. I think you know I enjoyed the past few minutes. It was a nice feeling."
"I want to help the kids. Please, Nettie, let me do this."
She sensed the sincerity in his voice and said, "I'll talk it over with the family and I'll let you know. Bye."

Nettie related Carlos's offer to Meg and Ma. They were sitting at Ma's kitchen table.
"I don't get it," said Ma. "Why all this civil conscience stuff all of a sudden?"
"Simple," said Meg. "He wants to get into Nettie's pants."
"There's some truth in that," sighed Nettie. "But, after a hiccup, I assured him that it was not going to happen."
"A hiccup?" queried Ma looking at Nettie.
"Ma, the man could appear on the cover of Gentlemen's Quarterly for god's sake," stated Meg.
"Oh, I see," giggled Ma, "I wish I could get a hiccup every now and then!"
"Yeah, I could go for a series of them," chortled Meg.

"Okay, you two," laughed Nettie. "I'm glad I made your day. Look here's the reality of it, we have been constantly preaching to the kids about the evils of drugs and now we are getting in bed with ... ah, check that, bad choice of word's ... ah, and now we are working with one of the biggest dealers in the city! How do we explain that to them?"

"We don't," said Meg. All we know is that one of the residents heard our request and he made his place available to us."
"But, we do know who he is," countered Nettie.
"Nettie, all I can see is my little girl up there on that stage performing," said Ma. "She would be the happiest person on the face of the earth. And besides, she's earned it and I don't think the fact that the theater is owned by a drug dealer is going to make her do dope!"

Nettie looked at her, sighed and said, "Your argument is so much better than mine, Ma. I'll run this by Billy and then send a message to Carlos."

"Yeah, Ma's right," said Billy. "Look, the word out on the street is that there's a rift between Carlos and his people. Carlos wants to get into legitimate deals, like real estate, but his cronies like the dope business. I don't think they know anything else. Carlos does. I heard he used to be some kinda engineer or sumthin'. Who knows? Maybe this will help turn Carlos. Might be worth a shot."

Nettie sent her acceptance note to Carlos and he immediately began to clean and make ready the theater. It was late May.

M. J. had almost completed her casting. As expected, just when she found somebody willing to participate they would leave the Zone. So far she had Joey Goldstein who wanted to be the trumpet player, two little girls, Patsy and Connie, seven-year-old twins who insisted on playing the guitars and Jerry, a nine-year-old who really could play the drums. Sean was going to be on the piano, but she still needed a trombonist and a tuba player. Little Bit grabbed one of the harmonicas.

Sean and M. J. were on one of the side streets looking for a kid called Bingo; they had been told that he wanted to be the tuba player.

They were standing in front of a newspaper and variety store when M. J. spotted their ice cream cooler and bounded in. "How much for a popsicle?" she asked the clerk. He told her and she said, "Swap ya for a ticket to my play!"

"Are you M. J.?"

"Yep, the One and Only!"

"I thought the tickets were free."

"They are, but I'll still swap ya."

"Deal!" he laughed. "Here, take the popsicle and split it with your partner there. We like what you're doing, M. J."

"Gee, thanks, see you at the show!"

"M. J., where did you learn to do that stuff?" asked Sean shaking his head. M. J. shrugged and waved to an adult friend she spotted across the street.

"Hey, Jonesy! Whatcha cookin'?"

"Hey, M. J.! You and Sean come over and have some barbecue," he yelled to them. They made a beeline for the porch and in seconds they were happily munching on spicy chicken.

"Do any of you guys know a kid by the name of Bingo?" asked M. J.

"Sure. He lives next door. Do you want me to call him? If you do I'll have to put more chicken on."

"Sounds like our man, Sean."

While they were waiting for Bingo, M. J. spotted a pick- up with a large open flat bed on it, parked in the driveway.

"Who owns that truck?" she asked.

"I do, M. J.," said Jonesy. "It barely runs but I keep it in case I have to haul something for a short distance. Why do you ask?"

"Can we borrow it for our parade? We need something to put the band on."

"Sure, I don't see why not. I didn't know there was a parade."

"That makes two of us," said Sean.

"That's because I just thought of it," M. J. grinned.

"We're going to have to paint it, though. Looks like it needs it anyway."

"That it does. What did you have in mind, a nice green?"

"No, of course not! It's a 4th of July parade. We're going to paint it to look like our flag!" Jonesy paused and burst out laughing.
"Now I want to see that! I'll even furnish the paint and help paint it!"
Bingo showed up; he was a big eleven-year-old kid. He signed on and now all they needed was a trombone player.
"A parade ... a parade," said an amazed Skeeter.
"Yeah, we got a truck to put the band on and everything," replied an enthusiastic M. J.
"We'll get Billy to lead the parade in his patrol wagon with siren blaring and the works. Any kids who want to join in the fun can follow Billy... we're gonna need flags for all of them. The truck with the band will bring up the rear. Oh, yeah, we're gonna need signs advertising the show and more costumes, too. You guys figure out the details. I got to find me a trombone player."
"We will have to clear Center Street of cars," said Little Bit, taking up the challenge.
"I knew I could count on you, Little Bit," said M. J. as she grabbed her by the hands and swung her through the air.
"Let me know what you need, Skeet."

SKEET WAS GOING to have more time on her hands than what she had believed. The Kiddie Corps was about to go out of business. This is how it happened:
A Kiddie Corps member came bursting into Billy's office, "Billy, Billy, they're after me! I saw them passing dope and they started to chase me. I led them here!"
Billy jumped to his feet and ran outside just as two men came skidding around the corner. When they saw Billy they spun around and ran. One of them tripped over the foot of the other and went sprawling to the ground. Billy immediately pounced and cuffed him. Sure enough, he was carrying a package of heroin. It was starting up again, he thought - open trafficking in the Zone. There must be a new dealer here. It was far too dangerous for the kids.
Billy pulled up at Ma's; he went in looking for Skeet. "She's upstairs, Billy, what's up?"
He said nothing and walked upstairs. He told Skeet what had happened and said, "It's time, Skeet. It's gettin' too dangerous out there. You guys have done a terrific job! No telling how much trouble you've saved everybody, I can't thank you enough." He held open his arms and she came to him with tears in her eyes. "I love you, Skeeter, you truly are an Angel."
Billy left. Ma, who had followed Billy upstairs, came up to Skeet, put her arm around her and said, "I'm so proud of you."

NOW ONLY TWO WEEKS away from showtime, things were really starting to fly. The women were out scouting the thrift stores for costuming material. Billy contacted the American Legion for flags. Skeet and Little Bit were busy making signs and orchestrating the parade.

M. J. drilled her cast relentlessly as they tried to follow Skeeter's script. Papa Joe was helping with the rehearsals. The kids were having a great time. Not only were they co-participants in the musical but they became the best of buddies. M. J. loved them all. Oh, she found her trombone player; his name was Larry and he was five years old.

Skeet's script was brilliant. It told the story of a little girl who was looking for the Statue of Liberty. Little Bit was the girl. There wasn't much dialogue; the music did most of the talking. At Skeet's instruction, Sean burned the tunes Skeet required onto a fresh disc. Once the music started it wouldn't be stopped. The kids had to be on their toes. M. J. was the lead lip-syncer and directed everything.

Sean was busy helping Jonesy paint the truck and get the sets in order. The theater was about a week away from being ready. Carlos put Enrico in charge and Enrico resented it. He disliked Nettie and didn't want to be involved with anything she was involved in. Carlos insisted that everything should be in working order and he directed Enrico to bring in an electrician to check the wiring. Enrico never did; he simply turned the lights on and off to make sure they were operating.

It was the morning of the Fourth; the big day was here. The kids had been walking up and down the streets for the last couple of days with signs advertising:

PARADE and MUSICAL

Where's My Statue of Liberty?

Parade starts at noon in front of Deli

Musical starts at 2:00 P. M. at the Theater

JULY 4th

At precisely 12:00 noon, Billy cranked up the siren and with Skeet riding shotgun, the parade started down Center Street heading for the theater on the opposite end.

Billy's SUV was followed by a number of kids waving little American flags. They were followed by a blue flatbed truck with white stars painted on its top and red and white stripes down the hood. The flatbed carried the 'Zonie Band' all wearing white tee shirts with the Zonie name hand printed on them. Every member had a different hat ranging from baseball caps to military style berets. Patriotic instrumental music was blasting from speakers mounted on the back of the truck. They were broadcasting from the radio's CD player and the band mimed to the music. M. J. and Little Bit threw red, white and blue confetti into the crowd.

People lined Center Street and cheered when the little cavalcade passed. Ma, Nettie, Meg and Papa Joe cheered wildly when they rolled by Ma's house. Little Bit had just showered them with confetti. Papa Joe leaned over and said to Ma, "In your wildest imagination, did you ever think something like this could happen in the Zone?"

"Never, Papa Joe, never!"

The procession stopped in front of the theater and M. J. led her band into the building to do some last minute rehearsing. The stage lights were turned up in anticipation of their arrival. Little Bit joined Skeeter as they walked back to Ma's to change Little Bit's costume. Sean was still on the truck disassembling the mount that held the keyboard in place while it was on the flatbed. Larry stayed back to help him.

Sean was having trouble removing the bolt and was still working on it when M. J. came out to see what was taking him so long.

"What are you guys doing? We're waiting for you!"

"Almost got it, M. J. ... What's that smell?"

It took only seconds. One of the bright stage lights shorted out, sparks flew and the old cardboard ceiling went up in flames. The burning ceiling fell on the old foam rubber theater seats setting them ablaze. The brittle ceiling insulation ignited and filled the theater with dense black smoke. It happened so quickly the five band members never even moved.

The wooden building was engulfed in flames. M. J. froze for a moment then recognized what was happening and screamed, "OH NO!"

She never hesitated and dashed straight into the inferno in search of her friends. "NO!" yelled Sean. He chased after her. They disappeared into a cloud of black smoke. M. J. couldn't see a thing and was screaming, "WHERE ARE YOU? WHERE ARE YOU!"

Sean found M. J. by following the sound of her voice. He grabbed her and pulled her back up the aisle. Somehow he managed to find his way back to the door and they stumbled through it to the outside.

M. J's hair was on fire and someone threw a jacket over her, smothering the flames. It was Carlos. Sean lay on the sidewalk, exhausted. Both he and M. J. were way too close to the flames and Carlos dragged them back into the street.

Everybody at Ma's had seen the smoke and flames and came running to the theater. Meg was the first to see the kids being tended to by Carlos and rushed over to them. Sean and M. J. were coughing and each had minor burns. M. J.'s hair was completely singed on the bottom.

"WHERE ARE THE REST OF THEM?" yelled Meg.

Carlos sadly nodded towards the burning theater.

Chapter 17: Life After The Fire

SEAN AND M. J. would never forget their tenth birthdays. It would be the day that five little friends were buried. Joey, Bingo, Jerry, Patsy and Connie all perished in the fire. All but Joey would be laid to rest in the Zone cemetery. Joey was buried in a Jewish cemetery outside the city.

Papa Joe was trembling as he presided over the somber service. There had never been so many people attending a burial service in the cemetery before. The little girls' grandparents were numbed by grief. The other two had no one; they were Zonie orphans like Skeet and Little Bit.

Carlos Marcos stood at the back. Few people knew he owned the theater; he was there because he wanted to be not because he had to.

Ma and Nettie approached him after the service and thanked him for coming to the aid of the children. It was hours after the fire before they found out what he had done to save M. J. from serious burns.

"You needn't thank me. It was Sean who saved her life. She never would have made it out by herself. You have extraordinary children. I... I'm so sorry."

"We're not blaming you Carlos," Ma said. "Every single structure in the Zone could catch fire at any time. We know your people were working to make the theater as safe as possible."

"Thanks Ma, that's kind of you. I should have done more." He nodded at Nettie, turned around and slowly walked away.

"I wonder what more he could have done?" added Meg, who, with Billy, had just joined Ma and Nettie.

"What I'm worried about," said Billy, "is what is he going to do about it now? Somebody didn't do what they were supposed to do."

The children stayed close together throughout the service. They were as strong as they could possibly be for their age but nothing could have prepared them for this. Skeet was distant and in a daze. Little Bit was confused. M. J. was burned and her beautiful wavy hair had been shortened because of the fire damage. Sean had burn marks on his face and arms that glistened under Meg's healing ointment. He kept looking at M. J. feeling her anguish.

M. J. was devastated. This was her team. They were her friends. She felt completely responsible; they wouldn't have been there if not for her. She was too young to understand it any other way. The fact that she herself had been within seconds of dying didn't occur to her.

Sean sensed that M. J. was vulnerable and he was not going to let her out of his sight.

Maybe it was because none of the children understood or could comprehend death. Maybe it was because they were already hardened by life in the Zone but none of them cried during the service.

As they were leaving the cemetery Nettie lagged behind. She took a flower from one of the many that were placed on the ground around the gravesides. On her way out she stopped by Sean's grave and placed the flower on it.

Skeeter was waiting for her by the gate. Nettie realized Skeet had seen her put the flower on Sean's grave. She glanced back and said,
"That grave always looks so lonely up here all by itself. I just thought that he should be remembered too."

The fire had also destroyed a building alongside the theater and would have spread even further but it burned itself out at the intersection with the four lane boulevard. The charred remains of the buildings would remain untouched for years. All that was ever found in the debris was the melted horn of a tuba.

Meg, Nettie and Ma were having morning coffee at Ma's three days after the funeral. There was a persistent pall that hung over the Zone. The children had stopped playing. M. J. was morose and had lost her high spirited energy. The women knew it was going to take time and understood that children usually bounce back. Nevertheless, they were worried about M. J.

Nettie's grief was slowly turning to anger. Her pro-active nature had been aroused.
"Where's the closest fire station?" she asked.
"Nettie, there could have been a station right next door and it wouldn't have made a difference," stated Ma.
"I know that, but you said it yourself, this place is a tinderbox. I don't want a fire to start two blocks over and spread to our place. An efficient and available fire department could prevent that."

She had a point.

"A small station is just outside the Zone," said Meg. "But they only use it for administration; there's never a truck."
"Well, there should be," declared Nettie.
"I doubt that any of the hydrants are still working and the local shopkeepers don't give a shit about fire codes," added Meg.
"Remember where you are," Ma says. "There's some pretty powerful forces around here that like it the way it is."
"Not at the expense of children's lives," exclaimed Nettie.
"There has to be some form of compromise here!"

Meg and Ma looked at each other, each drawing a deep breath and slowly exhaling.

There would be no compromises for Carlos.

He was confronting Enrico and his brothers, Jorge and Ricardo, who had recently joined the team. Carlos had his people with him.
"Give me the name of that fucking ELECTRICIAN!" he roared. Enrico

said nothing.
"THE NAME, DAMN IT!"
"I didn't have enough time, they were all BUSY!" Enrico shouted back.
"You son-of-a-bitch," said a now outraged Carlos. He hit Enrico with a powerful backhand that sent the smaller man staggering backwards forcing him to fall to his knees. His brothers lurched forward but stopped abruptly when Carlos's men moved towards them.

"You pack up your things and get the hell OUT OF HERE! And take your GARBAGE WITH YOU," Carlos said angrily, pointing at the brothers. "If I ever see you in the Zone again I'll throw you out the FUCKING WINDOW!" This metaphor was often used by the criminal world, meaning he was going to kill him. It was a popular saying in the Zone.

"All right, I'm leaving! YOU'VE GONE SOFT ANYWAY, AND I'M TELLING YOU THAT GREEN EYED BITCH IS GOING TO DESTROY YOU!"

Carlos let him go because at that moment he would have killed him.

Carlos knew that he was deluding himself. Nettie was right; he couldn't change what was already done. There would always be Enricos out there who were his enemies - others who held grudges, and crusaders who never forgot or forgave. Even if Nettie were willing, he couldn't expose her to the dangers of the world that trapped him. That would not stop him from protecting her and her family, however, and he suspected that she was going to need it.

Nettie met with the fire chief and pleaded her case. The death by fire of five small children gave her a powerful argument. All she wanted, she told him, was for a fire truck to be posted at the nearby station and fire hydrants that worked. She subtly indicated that code enforcement was not an issue, a not so subtle acknowledgment of the special rules for the Zone that she did not like. The chief agreed to give the problem his immediate attention. Nettie didn't get what she was after and the only attention she got was from the drug dealers. They were not happy.

The Goldstein's could no longer run the deli. They had had enough. The fights, the racial slurs, the break-ins, and now the death of their only son. They put the deli up for sale and it sold immediately at the price they were asking, which was way over market value. The buyer was a real estate investment company whose stockholders remained anonymous. There was only one stockholder, Carlos Marcos. It was the third of Carlos' real estate purchases in the Zone. There would be many more in the future.

CHRISTMAS WAS COMING and Papa Joe brought his hospital schedule over for Little Bit to enter into her calendar of events.

"I'll put it in, Papa Joe, but it's not going to do any good. M. J. is just not interested. She's not interested in anything."
"Where is she, Little Bit? I'd like to talk to her."
"I think she's in Nettie's apartment. When Nettie's at work she goes there and listens to music on the radio. The door will be open."
"Thanks, Little Bit. How are *you* doing?"
"Oh, I'm okay. Sean keeps me busy on the computer and Skeet and Nettie teach me things. It's not the same, Papa Joe. We miss her."
Papa Joe found M. J. in Nettie's apartment curled up on the couch listening to classical music on the radio. She sat up when she saw him come in.
"Mozart?"
"No, wrong again, Papa Joe. It's Beethoven. What am I going to do with you? They're so easy to tell apart."
"Yeah, well you can't tell Judy Collins and Joan Baez apart either."
"True, true," agreed M. J.
"There's that beautiful smile I've missed. Hey, I just gave Little Bit a copy of the hospital schedule. You going to be ready?"
"No... not this year, Papa Joe. I...I...just can't do it, please don't ask me."
"I won't, little girl, not if you don't want to do it. It's all right."
"It's not that I don't want to, I...I...just can't."
"That's good enough for me." He held out his arms and she came to him. It was their special hug.
"Okay, we still have the Easter show; we'll see how you feel then."
"Okay, Papa Joe."

IT WAS A particularly snowy winter and the snow was sticking. Sean came running into the house during one of the storms, shouting,
"M. J., M. J., where are you?"
"I'm up here Sean, what's going on?"
"There's a bunch of new kids on the other side of Center. We've challenged them to a snowball fight. The rule is that neither side can cross over the middle of Center Street," he said excitedly.
"Come on, we need your arm!"
"Nah, I'll watch from here, you go on."
Sean was dejected. M. J. had always loved this kind of stuff; he thought for sure this would get her going again.
The snowball fight raged on and moved down in front of Ma's. M. J. watched from the upstairs window. Suddenly she threw the window open and yelled, "LOOK OUT SEAN, there's a sneaky little shit on the other side of that car!"
Upon hearing her warning, Sean's team wheeled around and looked up. "HEY, it's M. J.," they cheered and she was rewarded for her efforts

with a dozen snowballs hurled in her direction from Sean and his pals. "AHHHHHHH!" she screamed, too late... She got pounded and so did Little Bit's project table as the snowballs poured in through the open window.

"I'll kill 'em, I'll kill 'em," screeched Little Bit as she dashed downstairs and out the door to join in the fight, wearing no coat, no gloves and no boots. Risking further abuse, M. J. leaned out the window and yelled, "GO GET 'EM, LITTLE BIT, GO GET 'EM!"

The snowball fight didn't get M. J. going again but the next event did. It was Easter time and Papa Joe was planning his annual egg hunt and children's party. M. J. was lounging at Nettie's, listening to music when Sean came hopping in dressed in full Easter Bunny regalia. He hopped right on top of M. J. pinning her to the couch.

"I am The Easter Bunny and I need somebody to help color the eggs and hide them for the Kiddie's Easter hunt!"

"I'm looking for a girl named M. J. She used to do this for me and now I can't find her!"

"Get off me you lop eared rabbit," shrieked M. J. "I'm your girl! I can't believe I'm talking to a rabbit. Who put you up to this? Papa Joe?" She was now laughing at the goofy looking rabbit. Ma and Nettie, who had entered the room, were laughing with her.

"Okay, Okay, lets go see the Papa, but I'm not stepping out that door unless you take that stupid outfit off! Get the kettle out, Ma, we're going to be boiling a lot of eggs and tell Little Bit we need to get organized," she ordered as they went out the door.

"I think she's coming back to us, Ma," said Nettie with a tear in her eye.

"Thank the Lord, and thank Sean too," said a relieved Ma.

THINGS WERE PRETTY much back to normal by summertime. Sean and M. J. were visiting Jonesy when they noticed some kids playing what looked like baseball. They were using an old warehouse for a backstop. Instead of a bat they had a broomstick and they were using small rocks for baseballs.

"Hey, can we play?" yelled M. J.

"Sure, M. J., we need a couple of players," shouted one of their street buddies.

"Good, I want to pitch," she said.

Her idea of pitching was to throw the rock directly at the batter to see if he could get out of the way.

After plunking a few kids she was relegated to the outfield.

When it was Sean's turn to bat, he was drilled alongside the head in a glancing blow as retaliation. Sean's answer was to turn around and bat the other way so he could see the rock better. He actually hit one to everybody's surprise. Nobody could hit the sailing rock. M. J. got bored and started to throw rocks at everybody. She was immediately pounced on but it turned into more of a laughing match than a wrestling match. After all, this was M. J. They would have killed anybody else.

Sean was approached one day by a young mother. She wanted Sean to ask his mom if she would come by the house to 'teach her sick son'. Nettie was almost as popular as M. J.

Nettie went over to the young mother's house as soon as she could.

She had made many house calls through the years working with sick children or those who had learning disabilities. She immediately recognized that he was not sick; he was a little boy with Down syndrome. She spent many hours working with him, making progress. He was a good artist and was learning to read. Then, like so many others in the Zone, he and his mother disappeared. But Nettie's humanitarian work did not go unnoticed by the people in the Zone.

M. J. SPENT A LOT of time on line learning about classical music the winter before their twelfth birthdays. She was fascinated with the complex combination of notes it took to create music. She had Sean find out what keys you had to press in order to play a certain note on the piano. Then she had him drag out the keyboard and demonstrate it to her. He could do this easily by using his gift of recall.

Previously M. J. had Sean import her Mozart concerto #23 CD into the computer. Now she wanted him to play the music and identify each note that was being played on the keyboard.

"You want me to do what? I can't play the piano, M. J. I just know where the notes are. I don't know the sounds of them or the finger movements it takes to play them together!"

"Just ask your mom," said a confident M. J. "She will know what to do."

Nettie *did* know what to do. Actually she had always wanted to experiment with Sean's interpretive skills in music. Now would be the perfect time for it. She wanted to support M. J. in every possible way with her interest in classical music.

A while back she had translated some music written in German for the assistant to the head of the music department at the University. She did it as a favor. Roger, the young assistant, was a concert pianist.

She phoned him. "Roger how would you like to return that favor you owe me?"

"Sure Nettie, just name it." He was puzzled by the request but in the presence of Nettie and Sean he played several of Mozart's piano concertos for them.

"Thanks Roger, I wanted Sean to see those intricate finger movements up close. But I think you one upped me on the favors."

"Nah, we're even Nettie," he said pleasantly.

Nettie and Sean were alone in their apartment, the keyboard was placed on the table.

"Go ahead, Sean, it's no different than learning languages. Play Mozart's #23. Don't worry about the sound, just hear it in your head."

He closed his eyes, took a deep breath, found the music wherever it was stored and played the piece exactly as Roger had.

After he finished, he looked at Nettie and said, "Mom, this is too weird and I know that it's not normal for an eleven year old to do this - or anybody else for that matter!"

Nettie sighed and said, "Here son, watch me," and she pulled the keyboard over to her and repeated the performance.

"Wow," said an astonished Sean. "Can everybody do this?"

Nettie knew it was time. She sat Sean down and did her best to explain to him their amazing gift. She finished by sharing her theories on the energy fields.

Sean sat silent for several seconds and then said, "I'm going on line Mom, I've got to figure this out."

"I knew you would say that, Sean. Unlike me, you want to take your understanding to another level, and you should. It's a real power son; use it wisely. But for now what do you say we keep this as our little secret."

"Are you kidding? There's no way I'm telling those guys about anything this weird!"

There was a lot to be discovered about their miraculous musical abilities. Could they read any musical score and immediately play it or did they have to physically hear it? The answers to these questions were yet to come.

Nettie still wondered if Sean could play the music and not just the notes. She suspected he could; he had his father's genes.

"Okay, M. J. Here we go." She stopped the music every few seconds and transcribed on to her music sheet the numbered finger placements that Sean could now demonstrate for her. She placed them just below where the notes appeared. This was her way of learning how to play the piano without ever playing it. It was also the beginning of the classical composition that would take M. J. years to complete.

Chapter 18: Games and Names

"HEY, SOMEBODY CHANGED the password on the computer," exclaimed Sean. "I can't get into it. Do you know anything about this Little Bit?"

"No, and I'm sure Skeet doesn't either."

They were in the house alone. Everybody was off doing something.

"Look Sean, here's a note from M. J. It was taped to the refrigerator."

TO ENTER THE GATES LEADING
TO THE INFORMATION HIGHWAY
YOU MUST KNOW THE CODE.
IT HAS SIX DIGITS.
THAT IS YOUR ONLY HINT!

"OH NO! That stupid riddle game again," cried Little Bit.

"All right, it's a good hint," said Sean. "It's a digit so it has to be six numbers, one through nine, right! Okay, this should be easy, just look for things that are out of place and it should relate to a number."

It wasn't easy. It took them all afternoon to solve the riddle. They never let on to M. J. that she got 'em.

"You're going to get even, aren't you Sean?" asked Little Bit. "Just leave me out of it!"

"Oh yeah, paybacks are a necessary part of the game."

M. J. was on the alert for weeks knowing that she could be a victim at any moment. She stepped into the shower one morning and discovered that there was no water. "Hey, what's going on? There's no water!"

"You have to shower down here," hollered Sean. "I had to turn the water off upstairs because we've got a clogged line somewhere, but I'm working on it."

"Ah, crap!" She came downstairs wearing only a towel. As she approached Ma's apartment, Sean jumped out, grabbed her and pitched her through the door to the outside that he had propped open, yanking the towel off at the same time. He slammed the door shut and locked it. M. J. was standing stark naked on the porch.

Sean's plan was perfectly executed. Only Little Bit was home and all windows and doors were locked. Little Bit was hiding in the closet not wanting to be considered an accomplice.

"DAMN IT, SEAN! OPEN THE DOOR!"

From the upstairs window, Sean leaned out and said:

"TO ENTER THE GATES TO YOUR HAPPY HOME, YOU MUST SAY THE PASSWORD. IT HAS SIX LETTERS. THE HINTS ARE ATTACHED TO THE HOUSE. FIRST LETTER ONLY!"

"OH, OH... YOU, YOU... I'M GOING TO THROW YOU OUT THE FUCKING WINDOW, SEAN!"
"My, my, such language. You're going to have to confess to Papa Joe," chortled Sean.

M. J.'s ranting was beginning to attract people and a car full of teenage boys stopped and began honking their horn.
"LOOKING GOOD, M. J... LOOKING GOOD," they shouted between whistles and catcalls.

M. J. darted behind the house and hid until she thought the boys were gone; then she began her search using the rules of the game that she knew by heart. She found a slipper stuck on the downspout: okay an 'S'. It's a start, she said to herself, still hopping mad. She soon had an E, an A and an L. Realizing that the other clues were on the front of the house, she jumped onto the porch and ran to the other side searching as she raced by. The boys had come back and were waiting for her. More hoots and hollering - she was livid.

Sean leaned out the front window, "Just two more letters, M. J. You're doing good!" He ducked back in as she grabbed the biggest rock she could find.

The power of sisterhood prevailed. M. J. spotted Little Bit leaning out the back window holding up a piece of paper. There was a big letter P written on it. L, E, S, A, and now P. She got it. PLEASE!
"Okay, you jerk, I got your DAMN PASSWORD. PLEASE!"
"Very good, now say it nicely..."

M. J. gritted her teeth and drew strength from within, saying in the sweetest manner possible, "Pleeease."
"Ah, thats nice." Sean opened the door and let her in. Little Bit had a robe waiting for her. As he closed the door, he turned and ran into the hardest right cross that he would ever receive in his lifetime. He was knocked flat on his back and he saw stars. When his head started to clear, he found M. J. sitting on top of him with her hand drawn back, "What's the word, Sean, what's the word?"

Little Bit again came to the rescue. She was behind M. J., frantically waving her arms. A groggy Sean noticed her mouthing something. Then it clicked in for him and he said, "Ah, I'm sorry?"

"More feeling this time, SAY IT AGAIN!" Realizing how ridiculous this must have looked, and remembering M. J. naked on the porch with the honking cars, he started to laugh. "I'm sor...sor ..." He couldn't say it, he was laughing too hard. "You should ha..have... se...seen...yourself on the po..porch..."
M. J. was bouncing on his stomach as he laughed and that did it. She lost it and started laughing harder than Sean. Both of them were now lying side by side in convulsive laughter.

Little Bit jumped on top of them, "Does this mean the fight is over and

you love each other again?"
"Who said we stopped loving each other?" laughed M. J.
"Okay," said Little Bit, "But you've got to promise to stop playing that stupid game!"
"You bet!" they both said at once.

As they got up and walked off arm and arm, Sean said, "I don't think you should slug me any more; you're getting too strong."
"I promise," and she kissed him on his sore jaw.

NETTIE WAS PUSHING Skeet and Sean hard to ready them for the ACT and SAT exams that were coming up in the early summer. She was targeting Sean and Skeet to enter college the following fall, just after they turned thirteen and sixteen. They would now go on line studying all the preparation material available. Nettie was determined to have them ready and they were eager to take the exams.

M. J. was absorbed in music, dancing, and her puppet shows. The team was always ready for Papa Joe's hospital visits. The more innovative she and Skeet became with their skits, the more in demand they were. Everybody loved the puppets and their slapstick humor.

It didn't seem possible that Little Bit was only seven. She kept everybody in line with her disciplined organization. She also was developing a great sense of humor and loved to play jokes on her Sean.

Sean had been going to the university with his mother and working in the computer lab since he was nine years old. Nettie made sure that he wasn't putting in too much time there - he had other things to do. Although Sean was a constant source of interest to Dr. John and his friends, Nettie never consented to their requests for interviews or tests.

She opened up a bank account putting her name and 'A. J. McCleary' on it, anticipating the day that Sean could cash in his credits. She also applied for and received a social security card for A. J. He didn't know about the card or the account.

Nettie knew that when Sean applied to take the entrance exams, he would have to do so as A. J. McCleary. He was almost thirteen. Now was the time to tell him his real name and who his father was.

Nettie held nothing back and gave Sean their complete history. He was fascinated by all of it and was especially curious about his Irish citizenship status.
"Wow, that's neat," he exclaimed.

She left it up to him to decide if he now wanted to be called A. J. McCleary. Sean pondered this and said, "No. As long as I'm still in the Zone, I want to be known as Sean Ferrari. Anybody I meet outside the Zone can call me A. J. McCleary. I don't want the others to know, Mom - not even M. J. Is that okay?"

"Of course it is, son. And besides, M. J. and A. J. could get a little confusing," she laughed.

They visited Sean McCleary's grave. Sean was quiet and preoccupied with his thoughts. He never went back there.

AT FIFTEEN, SKEET was a slender brown-haired, brown-eyed African American beauty.

She and Nettie were chatting in Nettie's kitchen. Skeet enjoyed the familiar smells of lentil soup on the stove and fresh cornbread cooling on a rack. Nettie rested her chin on her hands gazing at her daughter. She never thought Skeet was anything but a member of her family.

Skeet started to say something and Nettie interrupted ... "Skeeter, do you know how beautiful you're becoming? You are so special. I just know, Skeet, that you're going on to achieve great things."

"If I do, Miss Nettie, it will be because of you. I know I had no chance living here in the Zone - a daughter of a prostitute and all that - until you came along. I owe you so much and I have no way to thank you. Yet."

"Skeet, you're not giving yourself enough credit. And don't forget your family; we all worked together, honey. For each other."

"Oh, I know, I know. I love all you guys and that's what I want to talk to you about, Nettie. I've decided to write a book."

"A book. Why, that's wonderful Skeeter! Tell me more."

"It's about all of us who live in the Zone - us kids growing up here, you, Ma, Meg, Billy, and Papa Joe. I am writing the story of the Zone."

"Wow, that's ambitious," said a surprised and proud Nettie.

"I'm going to start my research with you. Now, would you, Ms. Antoinette Ferrari, consent to an interview?"

"Why, I'd be honored Ms. Charles, fire away!"

A pad and pen immediately materialized and Skeet said, "Okay, from the beginning now: where were you born and how did you get here?"

Nettie thought for a while and then said, "Skeet, is this research information confidential?"

"Yes, I'm just learning and it's going to take me forever to gather the information and I won't begin to write anything until I get an okay from everybody."

"Boy, you're learning fast, kid," chuckled Nettie. "Now let me see, I was born in Brooklyn, New York ..."

Nettie did reveal everything about herself including her special gift, but she did not disclose Sean's real name or that the man buried in the lonely grave where she placed the flower was Sean's father. She felt that it would violate Sean's confidentiality. She merely said that Sean's father was killed just before Sean was born, giving no details. She figured that he could tell her himself at some future point.

Skeeter was gobsmacked when Nettie disclosed her gift and didn't know how to respond to the revelation.

"Wow!" she said. Then her eyes widened… "It's been passed on to Sean, hasn't it?"

"Yes. But he is more advanced. Look, Skeet, I hope you don't treat him any differently now. He would recognize it."

"Don't worry, I'm already amazed at some of the things he does. I don't think anything could surprise me about him. I, I... have to digest all of this. I had no idea! Wow! Gee, this writing is going to be fun. Can I ask you more questions later?"

"Sure, Skeet. You're going to write a great book. The Zone is a story that should be told."

"I've started to keep my own diary and so has M. J. She promised me I can read hers some day."

"Now, I would be interested in *those* stories," laughed Nettie.

"Yeah, me too. Thanks, Nettie, I'm off to see Billy. I'm going to see if he will let me look at his police log; that should give me some interesting background information!"

"No kidding! Good luck Skeet."

Chapter 19: Mr. Munoz

ON A BLEAK, overcast February morning, a tall middle-aged Hispanic man, wearing a worn jacket and no hat, walked up the path to Ma's front door.

Ma was home. All the children were upstairs and Nettie was at work. Ma answered the knock but couldn't see through the frosted storm door. When she opened the door, she was greeted by a familiar face. "Hello Libby," said Sebastian Munoz.

Sebastian was thin. His eyes were watery and his cheeks were hollow in his sallow face. Ma stared at him for several seconds and said, "You look cold, Sebastian. Come on in and get warm."

She led Sebastian into the living room. He sat heavily on the only stuffed chair.

"Can I interest you in a hot cup of coffee? I just brewed some."

"Castilian strong as always?" he asked.

"No, weaker, but just as good," offered Ma.

"You look wonderful, Libby. You've hardly changed."

Ma, never the one to mince words, replied, "I wish I could say the same for you. You look like shit. The good life finally got to ya, huh?"

"Something like that."

They chatted for about twenty minutes when M. J. appeared in the doorway. She looked at Sebastian and said, "I thought I heard you talking, Ma."

"Hi honey, come on in, I want you to meet someone." Sebastian stood up as M. J. walked into the room.

"M. J., I know we've never talked about him before, but I want you to meet your ... your father ... Sebastian Munoz. M. J. stood still, staring at him. She didn't know what to say. "I'm glad to see that you got your mother's good looks. The resemblance is remarkable." Sensing the awkward moment, he said, "You can call me Sebastian."

M. J.'s resemblance to her father was obvious, too, and she recognized it. Not wanting to engage in conversation, she merely said, after a long moment, "Sebastian will be fine. I'll be upstairs, Ma." She turned around and left the room.

"She is absolutely beautiful, Libby. You must be proud of her."

"More than you can imagine, Sebastian, more than you can imagine."

"YOUR FATHER! Are you serious, M. J?" exclaimed Sean.

"What's he look like," queried Little Bit.

"He looks like me. Go see for yourself!"

"No, not just yet," added Skeet. "Does Ma seem upset?"

"No, not at all, just as calm as usual."

They looked around at each other, with Sean, Little Bit and Skeet thinking about how they themselves would never know their own fathers.

Sebastian left the house a while later and walked back down Center Street. Little Bit spotted him and all but M. J. joined her as they peered out the upstairs window.

"How did he look, Ma?" asked Meg.

It was sometime later and Nettie and Meg had gathered in Ma's kitchen for some 'Castilian coffee'. Ma looked at them for a few seconds and replied, "He's dying, Meg - cirrhosis of the liver. He has... maybe three months."

Meg sighed and said, "Not all that surprising, Ma, the way he lived. If it wasn't his liver, it would be something else. What did he do, just stop in to say goodbye and meet his child?" she said cynically.

Meg looked at Nettie and said, "Sorry, I wasn't a big fan of Mr. Munoz. He left Ma with a child to raise by herself!"

"I'm not sure what he wanted, Meg, but he is all alone and I think he might be afraid of dying a lonely death," Ma said sadly.

"Did he ask to move in? That would be just like him," quipped Meg.

"No, no, he didn't. I don't know what I would have said if he had asked."

"You would say what you always said, Ma; *sure, sure that would be just fine Sebastian.* Oh, I'm sorry, Ma. I know how much you loved him and he's still your husband. It would be impossible for you to say no to him under these circumstances."

Sebastian returned, this time bringing a mid sized duffel bag. Ma poured him a cup of coffee.

"Have you told the children?" he asked quietly.

"No, I was waiting to see if you would show up. You weren't too sure when I talked to you."

"I was hoping that you would ask me to stay, even though I knew it wasn't fair on my part. I have no other place to go, Libby, and yes, I'm afraid."

"Well, we started this thing together, Sebastian; I guess it's only right that we end it together," she said reaching out for his hand.

Ma left Sebastian to his coffee and went upstairs to where the children were waiting. Unbeknown to Ma, Nettie had diplomatically laid the groundwork for her. They would not be surprised or upset.

She gathered everyone around the kitchen table as she sat down. "Look, I think you all know that Mr. Munoz is my husband. He is sick and he is going to stay with us for a while. I hope you understand. I know that this is your home, too, but I would like for you to make him feel welcome."

"You know we will Ma," said M. J.

"Thanks guys, I appreciate that."

The children really didn't see that much of Sebastian as the days went by, but when they did, they were polite and warm and tried to make him feel at home.

M. J. made a point to get to know him and she engaged him in lengthy discussions about her paternal family. She was delighted to discover that her grandmother was a dancer and Sebastian himself played the guitar. She knew her musical roots had had to come from somewhere. She laughed hearing about how Sebastian had met her mother at a jazz club on Woodward Avenue. M. J. enjoyed their private talks; it made her feel special to have a father. They never discussed his illness or what he had been doing since he left the Zone.

After two months, Sebastian's health declined and he become bed ridden. He died a week after that. They buried him in the Zone's cemetery. Papa Joe performed the service. The family members were all there with M. J. clutching her mother's hand throughout the service.

Sebastian's only possessions were the duffel bag and the clothes he was wearing. Ma was about to get rid of the bag and its meager contents when she noticed a leather pouch tucked away inside. There was a note sticking to its side addressed to Libby.

Libby, I hope that this in a small way
will help to make up for the grief
that I've caused you.
I've always loved you.
Please thank our beautiful daughter
for allowing me to get to know her.
Sebastian

Ma sadly shook her head and opened the pouch.

She was stunned and her hands began to tremble as she peered inside. She couldn't believe what she was looking at. There, in tidy rows, one on top of the other, were stacks of one-hundred dollar bills all neatly wrapped, fifty to a package. She gasped, sat down, and looked again. Confused and not knowing what to do, she simply reacted by putting the bag away on the top shelf of her closet. She never counted the money.

That's not all he left with her. Ma was three months pregnant.

Chapter 20: Take Me Out To The Ballgame

NETTIE HAD DECIDED long ago that Sean and Skeeter would take the ACT *and* SAT exams. Neither of them had a high school diploma and they needed to prove themselves college worthy without the benefit of a scholastic resume. They could clear this hurdle by scoring highly in both qualifying exams.

They were well prepared and patiently waiting for the tests to begin. Only Nettie was nervous. She registered them by mail using her university address for the reply.

Nettie took the children to the prescribed locations on exam day. Skeeter and Sean finished both tests in a two week period. The three of them anxiously awaited the results. Skeeter was unsure; Sean couldn't see what the fuss was all about.

In the meantime Sean was spending a few days in the computer lab working on sick computers. Dr. Hughes approached him and asked, "Hey Sean, do you like baseball? I have a couple of Tigers tickets for tomorrow's game that I can't use. Are you interested?" Sean immediately thought of Skeet and said, "Sure, I would love to go! Gee, thanks!"

When his work was finished Sean found his mom waiting for him at the language department. "Look at what Dr. Hughes gave me," he said, showing her the two tickets. "I want to take Skeet; you know how much she loves her baseball! Can we go? It's a day game and we can walk to the stadium. It's not that far!"

"Of course, Sean. You two are old enough to do that and Skeeter will be thrilled. I know she's never been to a ballgame before."

On the way home they passed a sporting goods store and Sean stopped in front of it and said, "Mom, do you think I could borrow some money from you? I can pay you back when I'm old enough to get my lab money."

"I think we can work that out," she smiled. "What do you need it for, Sean?"

"I want to buy Skeet a Tigers hat for tomorrow's game!"

"What a good idea! How thoughtful of you, Sean. She will love it. Come on, lets go in and buy it."

Sean couldn't wait to get home to find Skeet. He went bounding upstairs and found her at the computer. Nettie followed.

"Skeeter, I want to make a date with you!"

Skeeter looked up and giggled. "Do you think you can handle me, Big Boy?"

Nettie, who had followed Sean into the room, laughed, "Be nice, Skeet, he really does have a special place to take you."

"Yeah, I bet! Where're we going? To throw rocks at the rats?"

Sean pulled out the tickets and slowly waved them in front of her. Recognizing the Tigers logo, Skeeter gasped and said, "Is that what I think it is?"
"Yup, two tickets for tomorrow's game, but if you rather throw rocks at the rats I'll understand."
"AYYYY!" she screamed. "Sean, where did you get those? Let me see, let me hold them, I've never even seen a ticket before, WOW!"
"SEAN, these are BOX seats and the Tigers are playing THE YANKEES!"
"Well, I don't know what a box seat is but I've heard of the Yankees."
"Oh, I almost forgot, you can't go to the game without this," and he reached into the bag, pulled out the Tigers cap and handed it to her. "Paid for it myself," he said proudly.
Skeeter was speechless. Her eyes welled up with tears as she put on the cap.
"Don't you go crying now, you know what happens to me if you do," said Sean.
"I promise. Thank you, Sean, thank you. You will never give me a better present," she said hugging him. From that day on she never left the house without her Tigers cap.
Early the following morning, Skeeter was racing all over the house. "Hurry up, Sean, get dressed. We don't want to be late!"
"Skeet, it's 8:00, the game doesn't start 'til one," said a sleepy Sean.
"I know, but we have to get there early for batting practice!"
"Practice? I thought it was a game," said a bewildered Sean.
"It is! Don't you know anything about baseball?"
"Not much."
She got him out of the house leaving a half eaten breakfast behind. "You guys make sure you eat some hotdogs at the ballpark now," Ma said, giving Skeeter some money to stick in her pocket as they left.
At Skeeter's insistence their first stop was Billy's.
"LOOK, look what I got, Billy!" Skeet said as she excitedly burst into his office showing him the tickets.
"Hey, great hat, Skeet. Lemme see what you got here. Man, box seats for TODAY! And you got the YANKEES! Where'd ya get these?"
"Sean got them, and he bought me this hat too!"
"Man, you kids are downtown!" said a chuckling Billy. "You guys going early for batting practice?"
"Yeah," said Skeet. "It's not that far of a walk and it's right down Michigan Avenue."
"Tell you what, lets jump in the patrol car and I'll take you there. I haven't seen the old ballpark in a while, and I hear that they may be tearing it down soon and building a new one, so I better look at it while I can."

He pulled up at the corner of Trumbull and Michigan and parked in a No Parking zone. There it was, in front of them; the old but warm and beautiful Tiger Stadium. They got out of the car and Skeeter was beside herself taking it all in.

"You know," Billy says, "I used to come here as a kid when it was called 'Briggs Stadium'. We could sit in the bleacher's for FIFTY CENTS! Well, that was another day. You guys have fun now, and be careful walking home! You keep an eye on her, Sean, she's getting way too pretty!"

"Oh, Uncle Billy."

"She's in good hands, Billy," Sean said with a smile giving him a wave.

Their heads swiveled, as they checked everything out. They watched in fascination as vendors set up their stands. Tiger pennants waved in the breeze and all the wonderful baseball paraphernalia was on display.

The scalpers were already out. *"HEY, TWO TICKETS HERE, LOWER DECK, FIRST BASE SIDE, WON'T LAST LONG,"* one yelled as he nervously looked over his shoulder.

The smell of hotdogs, fried onions with sausage and popcorn filled the air. People milled about wearing Tigers caps and baseball shirts. There were plenty of Yankee caps too.

"PROGRAMS, LINE UP CARDS, GET YOUR PROGRAMS HERE!" cried the hawkers as they held them up for everyone to see.

It was bright and sunny - a perfect day for a baseball game.

"Come on, Sean. Lets walk around the outside first so we can see it all, then we'll go in and find our seats." They did just that and then toured the inside of the park. They looked at the field from every corner of the ballpark, astounded by the beauty of its huge green field and colorful scoreboard.

They made their way to their box seats behind the Tigers' dugout on the third base side of the field. Skeeter was in baseball heaven.

THE BASEBALL GAME was a nice diversion from the anxieties of waiting for exam results. Although Nettie anticipated success on their exams, she didn't want to wait for the test results before making application to the different Universities. She began to work on what the schools were going to need in order for them to rapidly process the applications for admissions. She didn't want any unnecessary delays in getting them enrolled for the fall semester.

It was a given that Sean, if he scored high on the tests, would attend Wayne State University. Because he was so young and had no high school degree, Sean was going to need excellent recommendations from qualified people in order to be accepted. Who was better to give those recommendations than two distinguished members of their own faculty, Dr. John and Dr. Hughes.

After much discussion, Skeeter decided on The University of Detroit. She, too, was going to need some inside help, and of course she had the very persuasive Papa Joe going to bat for her. He couldn't wait to meet with the admission staff to plead the case for one of his Zonie kids.

It took about three weeks but the letters from the ATC testing center for both Sean and Skeet finally arrived addressed to the language department in care of Antoinette Ferrari. She didn't open them but waited until she also received the letters from the SAT's testing center. It arrived a few days later and then she opened all of them.

She looked at Skeet's first. Then Sean's. She examined them very carefully then put her head down on her arms and sobbed quietly. Skeet had killed them both. She scored in the upper percentiles in all categories; this little Zonie urchin was going to go to college.

Sean's scores were almost anticlimactic; Nettie just looked at them and shook her head. His scores were literally off the charts. She wasn't the least bit surprised, just overwhelmed with pride.

It was late in the afternoon and Nettie hurried home with the good news. She grabbed Ma and they climbed the stairs to the kid's sanctuary. Skeet and Sean were in their quarters reading. They joined M. J., Little Bit, and the two women in the project room when Nettie called them.

Nettie never said a word but just handed Skeet and Sean their test results. Skeet was apprehensive, not being able to read Nettie's face. Sean had no reaction and merely opened the envelope and started to read its contents. He was finished long before Skeet and politely waited for her as she read hers twice. Everybody was eerily silent.

Skeet finally looked up. Nettie could no longer contain herself and with a big grin she grabbed Skeet and said, "Congratulations, honey, you flat out ACED BOTH of them." It was stunned silence, then the whole room erupted in cheers and laughter. Sean had picked Skeet up and was whirling her around. M. J. and Ma both had tears streaming down their faces. Little Bit was joyously jumping up and down. They all knew how much this meant to their big sister.

Finally M. J. ventured, "Hey, what about Sean?"

Nettie walked over to her son, kissed him and bragged to everybody, "No one has ever scored higher on either one of the tests." More hooting and hollering. Skeet gave him high-fives with both hands and said, "Way to go, bro!" M. J. hugged him. Ma was overwhelmed with emotion and pride, "I can't wait to tell the others," she declared.

They couldn't possibly have known it at the time, but this was going to be the high point of their lives in the Zone.

PAPA JOE WAITED outside the admissions office while the council reviewed Skeeter's application. Finally, he was invited in by the department head, Father Valentine.

After some routine questioning, he was asked, "Father Joseph, how long have you known this young woman?"

"Since she was two years old, Father."

"Really. How did you meet her?"

"She's a member of my parish," Papa Joe said proudly.

"You mean here at U. of D.," a puzzled board member said.

"Oh no, I mean in the Zone."

"Are you telling me she grew up in the Zone?" said an astonished Father Valentine. "No wonder she never went to school. Where did she get her training?"

"From her mother, Father Valentine, from her mother."

"Well, you tell Miss... Charles, and her mother, that we are proud to have our first student from the Zone attending our University. Also the scholarship committee will meet next week to review her nomination.

Thank you, Father Joseph, and we're kinda proud of you too. You can pick up her acceptance letter in about ten minutes if you wish, or we can mail it to her."

"No, I would be extremely happy to deliver it to her, Father."

"I bet you would," laughed the priest.

"NETTIE, THERE'S A LETTER for you at the front desk," said Dr. John with a peculiar smile on his face.

It was addressed to A. J. McCleary in care of her. She opened it and read the contents, and broke into a huge smile.

Dr. John had come to the front desk and said, "Congratulations to you and to Sean, Nettie. It was a slam dunk."

"He will have to take two years of basics, then Dr. Hughes and I will test him in Language and Computer Science. There's nothing we can teach him," said Dr. John. "He will easily pass our rigid requirements and the school will graduate him after those two years.

Tell Sean ... ah, A. J. ... that we look forward to seeing him in the fall and that he's still on the scholarship list."

They now had another reason to celebrate. The entire family gathered that evening at Ma's house. Billy used the occasion to show off the new digital camera that the department had given him. It was the first and only pictures taken of the entire gang.

Chapter 21: Carlos

THE KIDS HAD QUIETLY celebrated M. J.'s and Sean's thirteenth birthdays in July and were looking for something to do for the rest of the summer.

Nettie was exploring options in case Skeet's and Sean's scholarships didn't come through. Between Sean's bank account and her own, she had enough to get them started; but in order for them to keep going they would need the help of student loans. This was not a good option. She didn't want to saddle them with debt just as they entered the work market.

She was discussing the problem with Ma over their morning coffee. "Nettie, that's not going to be a problem. Look, I've told nobody about this, but Mr. Munoz left me with a bag full of money. There's enough for both Skeet's and Sean's education and then some," she confessed. "I kept it to myself thinking that somebody would come snooping around looking for it, but that's not going to happen. Sebastian was way too clever. I should have known."

Nettie was staring at her unbelievingly, "You... you're kidding!"

"No, it's true. Here, come take a look." Ma led Nettie to the bedroom and showed her the pouch.

"WOW, there must be, hundreds, no thousands in there! Have you counted it!"

"No, I'm afraid to. What do you say? Wanna go to Vegas?"

"Jesus, only in the Zone. Skeet's going to have a best seller. I need a drink," said a still astonished Nettie.

"You're going to need more than one, I've got more news. I had one too many hiccups," shrugged Ma, "I'm pregnant!" Nettie looked at Ma for a moment with her mouth open and then said ... "Of course you are, this is the Zone. What's next? Meg and Billy getting married?"

They looked at one another and burst out laughing.

"Hey, that's not so funny about those two; did you ever notice that they are always together?" said Nettie.

"Yeah, but they wouldn't be if they were married," and they laughed even harder.

The financial problem resolved itself. Both Skeet's and Sean's scholarships came through. They were going to receive books and tuition. Nettie preferred it this way. They now would have the incentive to study hard for fear of losing their scholarships. Not that they needed any incentive; they couldn't wait for school to begin.

Billy was as proud as could be of his Zonie college kids. It helped to take his mind off of some real police concerns. He could sense an undercurrent of trouble in the Zone. The blatant exchange of drugs uncovered by the Kiddie Corps member unnerved him. He got little information out of the man he arrested other than the fact that he worked for one of the drug dealers in the Zone. Billy shuddered as he remembered how it was before the truce. He could not let that happen again. The so called truce was tenuous at best and had the potential to become violent. To expect anything different from criminals would be naive on his part.

There were maybe five or six drug dealers active in the Zone. It was hard to keep track. Their individual internal wars made for rapid change and quick elimination. Many of the 'runners' or 'gopher's' lived in the Zone but their bosses kept them under control. They obeyed the rules of the unwritten peace or they disappeared.

The dealers needed a place to meet their contacts, store unlaundered cash, and hide their dope without the threat of police raids. The Zone provided that. More importantly, as far as the police were concerned, the dealers now had no need for establishing their logistic centers throughout the City. This had set off violent turf wars that prompted disgruntled influential citizens to demand police action. Let them have a place like the Zone.

The major dealers were still the best law enforcers. There were only a handful of them and they tolerated each other but did not trust one another. They all had a presence in the Zone. What they couldn't tolerate was one of their own people breaking Zone rules or governmental agencies like the fire or health departments making inspections.

Billy got a surprise visiter one day late in the summer. Carlos Marcos walked into his office.

"You got a minute?" asked Carlos. Billy nodded.

"Look Billy, we got a rogue dealer working in the Zone. He's an outsider and I think he's connected."

"Shit!" said Billy. "I had a bad feeling about a guy I collared a while back. That's all we need is the Mafia rearing it's ugly head."

"Billy, let us handle this one. I don't know for sure who they are or exactly where they're located here in the Zone. But I will find out and when I do, I'll pass the information along to the guys who will take care of it.

Billy, there's something else, and that's what I'm really here for. My... shall we say competitors ... have informed me that they're not too happy with my 'green eyed' friend. They get real nervous when bureaucrats start snooping around. We both know it's just a matter of time before one of Nettie's kids gets in harm's way again and she *will* react to that. She's gotta back off Billy! These guys are dangerous. I told them that they will answer to me if they get rough with her but I don't trust them. And I sure could use your help.

One more thing. I'm quite sure an ex-employee of mine is working with this unknown dealer. He hates Nettie; he thinks she was the reason I ran him off. He's one of those crazy bastards. You never know what he's going to do."

Billy looked at him intently and then said in all sincerity, "Thanks for the tip, Carlos. I worry about her too. I'll move fast to head her off if there's a problem." Billy looked at Carlos curiously as he departed from the office. Billy didn't trust *him*.

Carlos really wanted to change things in the Zone but he recognized a business opportunity, too. If he could persuade the drug dealers to set up their operation some place other than the Zone, two things would be accomplished: protection for Nettie and her family from real danger and an increase in property values. If not for its reputation, the Zone, with its seclusion created by the four-lane boulevards surrounding it, could become prime real estate property.

In either scenario, he would have to control the real estate. This was the easy part. Very few people wanted to own property in the Zone. It was too dangerous and a risky venture - not to mention the possibility that buyers might be unfairly linked to the drug business.

Other than the deli, new businesses that opened in the Zone were run by drug dealers who simply moved into the vacant buildings. They did not want to own property themselves; they preferred the cover of other people's names on the deeds of record. They were content being squatters. The real owners were long gone and had no interest in their Zone properties. They wanted to divorce themselves from any liability created by the past drug wars.

Most of the residents were leftover tenants who stopped paying rent and moved on as others moved in. As a result, most of the real estate, single family and commercial parcels, were put up for tax sales. Many of the certificates were not bought and were still for sale and those that did sell were now available at tax sale prices.

Carlos, through his real estate investment company, started on his quest to buy the Zone. He was going to have to become truly devious to accomplish his other goal: moving the drug dealers out of the Zone.

Chapter 22: Sissy

THE FALL SEMESTER had begun. Sean and Skeet started their college careers. They left the house traveling in different directions. Skeeter had the farthest to go but they both could walk to school. Neither one of them had seen the inside of a classroom before. It was a new experience and they each handled it differently.

Skeet adjusted quickly and made a lot of friends. Associating with other students who came from totally different backgrounds was a culture shock. She was thrown into a new world and was fascinated by it.

Sean was totally bored with the classroom and saw no value in it. He couldn't wait for the hourly sessions to end so he could either go to the computer lab or back to the Zone. He missed M. J. It didn't seem right that she wasn't there with him.

Ma told Meg about Sebastian's money. She would tell no one else. She asked for Meg and Nettie's advice on what to do with it. Together they made a decision. They would do nothing.

The plan was to use the money only if there was a need, and not for frivolous things. It was a comforting thought that they were not financially helpless but it would not alter their meager lifestyles. There were small luxuries that they would concede to, but only if it helped the children. For instance, a printer was purchased to link with the computer. Sean had set up individual accounts for everybody including Little Bit. They had their own passwords and relished this new privacy.

Nettie had demanded, from the beginning, that the computer would be used for educational purposes only. There would be no games or e-mail accounts because she knew, like television, this would only distract them from their studies. At no time did any of them ever ask for an e-mail address and they never complained about not having one.

Ma and Nettie bought M. J. all the CD's she wanted. Most of them would be classical music purchased for pennies at the discount store.

They came up a notch in providing clothing for the children wanting them to be respectable at school but not flashy. The kids ignored labels and picked out whatever they thought was cool. The women took nothing for themselves other than making sure Meg had enough medical supplies in case of emergencies.

Sean found plenty of time to spend with M. J. She now had him playing the concertos he had learned from Roger. She had all the finger movements written down and watched intently as Sean played the entire pieces on the soundless keyboard, keeping in perfect sync with the recorded music. She wanted him to do the same with her other composers: Liszt, Beethoven, Chopin and Brahms. He said he didn't know those pieces but would learn them. They understood that he had to hear the music performed by a live artist in order for him to play them, just like he had to do when learning languages.

He didn't have to see the finger movements or the foot movements once it was encoded. He could instantly recall them. This was puzzling and he was now more determined than ever to understand this strange ability he and his mother possessed.

Clearly, the concert hall would be M. J.'s classroom. This was her education and with Sebastian's help, Nettie took her to symphonies. Sean would go along if they were playing the music of the composers that M. J. wanted him to learn. M. J. continued to work on her composition, sharing with nobody.

Skeet was still collecting material for her book; nobody was safe from interviews. Billy would have to plead the privacy act on many of the police logs but he did let Skeet import photos of the gang taken the night of the college acceptance party. Her research file took on an important pictorial dimension.

Papa Joe found protection in the sanctity of confidentiality and Meg could only promise that one day she would organize her records and turn them all over to this persistent writer. Ma proved to be the most helpful with her historical knowledge of the Zone.

Of course the big event of the year was going to be the birth of Ma's baby. It looked like the end of November or early December for delivery time.

"I want it to be December so we can share birthdays," said an excited Little Bit. "I want to be the big sister; you guys are all too old."

"We got to have a Zonie name for her," insisted M. J. "Ma can pick the real name."

"Who said *she* won't be a *he?*" chimed in Sean.

"I did. I already have a brother. I couldn't handle another one!" exclaimed M. J., ducking a pillow being flung her way by Sean.

"Yup, I want a sister, and that's that," determined M. J.

"Yeah, well Sissy is going to be able to grow a mustache," countered Sean.

"THAT'S IT!" cried M. J. "SISSY! Sissy is going to be her Zonie name. I have spoken!"

"Are you still going to call him Sissy if he's a boy?" laughed Sean, ducking the return of the pillow.

In early December, Ma gave birth to a healthy and chubby baby girl. M. J. and Little Bit were ecstatic. Sabatha Marie Munoz (Sissy), had arrived. "I give up; all this female energy..." muttered Sean.

SEAN AND SKEET completed their first year of college and were into the summer break. It was an overcast Saturday afternoon and Skeet, M. J.,

Little Bit and Sean were walking home from downtown. They had just enjoyed a movie matinee. It was a rare and special treat for them.

They entered the Zone by one of the side streets and were strolling down the sidewalk. As they were about to cross in front of a run-down beer and wine joint, two men bolted from the door of the bar on a dead run. Two others, brandishing handguns, came tearing out behind them. The gun wielders opened fire on the fleeing men hitting both of them. They fell to the pavement and the gunmen fired several more rounds into the lifeless bodies. The two assailants turned and went back into the bar ignoring the four astonished and paralyzed children.

Wide eyed and in a state of shock, the children slowly walked past the bloody corpses.

"Lets get out of here," calmly stated Sean and they all broke into a run.

Nettie was home when they came running in, breathless and shaken. When she finally calmed them down enough to tell her what had happened, Nettie became as angry as anybody had ever seen her. "MURDERING PEOPLE RIGHT IN FRONT OF OUR CHILDREN! THIS IS OUTRAGEOUS! THIS...THIS IS UNCONSCIONABLE!" she raged. "Our KIDS could have been killed! Those CRAZY PEOPLE could just as easily turned the guns on THEM!"

Ma and Meg knew it was useless to try to reason with Nettie. She would never understand that shootings used to be a common occurrence in the Zone. Ma and Meg both realized, however, that this was different; they didn't have the children to worry about back then.

Meg spotted Billy heading down Center Street. He had heard the gunshots and was coming to investigate. She ran out and flagged him down and told him about the murders.

"GOD DAMN IT!" he bellowed. "Meg, don't let Nettie out of the house. Tell her I'll be right back!" He spun his patrol car around and headed for the bar. A half hour later Billy pulled up in front of Ma's, took a deep breath, got out of the car and went into the house. Nettie was still fuming and when she saw Billy she vented her frustrations on him.

"THAT'S IT, BILLY. THAT'S IT! This area has got to be patrolled on a twenty-four hour basis and I won't QUIT until I get you some HELP! THEY GUNNED THOSE GUYS DOWN RIGHT IN FRONT OUR CHILDREN!"

He let her rant on for a bit longer and then said, "Okay Nettie, I agree with you; I go to war with my people Monday morning. I want you to stand by until I need you and if I have to go up in front of the City Council, I'll take you with me. Fair enough?"

"Fair enough, Billy," said a calmer Nettie. "I'm sorry. I didn't mean to come down on you. I know how much you do for everybody. I, I'm just angry and upset."

"You never have to apologize for nothin' to me, Nettie. We can work this out," he said putting his arm around her.

Billy was more upset than he let on. He desperately needed to get more patrol cars in the Zone and he had to make sure that the drug dealers thought it was his idea to do so, not Nettie's. He had no idea how this would affect the fragile truce but he knew for sure that he couldn't let Nettie anywhere near that Council.

Chapter 23: Enrico

AT ONE TIME, Enrico had managed a distribution team for Carlos. He had been responsible for moving drugs and stolen goods throughout the city.

When they split, Enrico decided to go into business for himself. He had paid attention and had a line on some of the smugglers that Carlos worked with. He contacted one of them, Alphonso, a low-life who claimed to have Mafia connections. Enrico and Alphonso formed a partnership and Alphonso moved into the Zone. Enrico, heeding the warning from Carlos, did not join him.

It turned out that Alphonso lied about being connected to organized crime. In fact, the Mob was concocting a way to put Alphonso out of business permanently - they didn't like drug pushers claiming they worked for them. Alphonso and Enrico were the rogue dealers that Carlos had been worried about but still hadn't identified.

The Mob caught up to Alphonso and one of his henchmen. They cornered them in the a dirty little bar in the Zone. These were the men who were ruthlessly gunned down in front of the children.

Enrico had his foot in the door and wasn't going to be frightened off. The Mob was after Alphonso, not him. He moved his two brothers into the house formerly occupied by the recently departed Alphonso. It was going to be business as usual for Enrico.

Billy had convinced his superiors to run patrol cars through the Zone on a temporary basis. This was not a turf war, he claimed; no dealer was moving in on the other's territory. It was, however, a real threat to the carefully structured truce. A serious crime was openly committed in the Zone. If he couldn't prevent those things from happening, the dealers would take matters into their own hands to preserve the peace; and that, he contended, could ignite another drug war.

Billy's bosses had bought his reasoning and now he had to make sure the dealers understood that this was a temporary move. He was walking a tightrope. He wanted the dealers to think this was beneficial for them and he had to placate Nettie.

Enrico was feeling the heat as Billy kept the pressure on with his slow patrolling squad cars. The dealers wanted to end this surveillance in a hurry and spread the word around in their circles that they were looking for the troublemaker. Enrico stayed out of the Zone. He was growing impatient. His fledgling business was taking a hit. He couldn't understand why this incident was being treated differently. There were plenty of drug related murders in the past. Granted this one occurred in public but the hit men got out before the law came and the bodies were quickly dragged off the street and dumped into the alley. What was the big deal?

Enrico had his contacts in the Zone too and he started to ask questions. He found out that the murders took place in front of four children. Then he found out who the children were. Now he knew why it *was* a big deal and where the pressure was coming from.

"HER AGAIN! THAT MISERABLE BITCH! SHE'S NOT GOING TO PUT ME OUT OF BUSINESS!" he thundered to his brothers.

Carlos had to move quickly. His sources had told him about the men gunned down in front of children. His heart sank when he found out that it was Nettie's kids who had witnessed the shootings. He knew that any action on her part would put her in serious danger. He was somewhat relieved when Billy got in front of the situation and gave the appearance that the patrol cars were his doing and nobody else's. Carlos also knew that the drug dealers had the same information he had and they understood that Nettie could go off at any minute.

The dealers did agree that it was better to get out of the way and let Billy do his job in removing the problem. It was a short leash. They would support Billy while keeping a wary eye on Nettie. She was a danger to them.

Carlos frantically worked his contacts. It paid off. A Mob connection identified the dead men and labelled Enrico and his brothers as the outlaws. A snitch for one of the dealers reported that Enrico had been told that some children had witnessed the killings. They further reported that Enrico had flown into a rage when he discovered the identity of the child witnesses.

This put a different light on the situation. Before doing anything serious, the dealers would have first used frightening tactics to scare Nettie off, including threats to the children. But Carlos knew that Enrico would not fool around with scare tactics; his increasing hatred for her made him capable of doing just about anything.

Carlos understood that Enrico and his brothers had to go. The dealers agreed and together they made the arrangements to have all three of them eliminated.

Chapter 24: Her Light Still Shines

THINGS HAD QUIETED DOWN in the Zone and Nettie was comforted by the constant presence of patrol cars circling the streets.

Nettie took fourteen year old Sean to apply for a worker's permit. It would make him eligible to be paid at a higher rate and he would be able to convert his lab credits into cash. Also, she made him the beneficiary of her bank account, her only asset. He was old enough now to understand financial matters and she made sure that he knew where she kept the important papers: birth certificates, his Irish citizenship papers and passbook accounts. Sean was enjoying this new level of responsibility.

Returning from their appointment with the Department of Labor, they had just turned into the Zone and were walking down Center Street when they heard gunshots. Not sure of where the firing was coming from, Sean and Nettie hesitated, shrugged at each other and continued on their way.

Jorge, Ricardo and Enrico were inside the Zone. It would be a rare and chancy appearance for Enrico, but they were meeting an important contact who insisted that the meeting take place in the Zone. This was a set up.

The hit was botched right from the beginning.

Jorge was driving; Ricardo was in the back seat and Enrico was riding shotgun. They were all armed with semi automatic pistols.

The hit was to take place as soon as the the three men got out of the car but the killers' information was flawed. Enrico's car was coming from the wrong direction and the assassins' hiding places were now exposed. Jorge started to turn into the driveway when Enrico spotted the exposed gunmen. "No...! NO...! KEEP GOING... KEEP GOING!" he yelled.

Jorge swung the car around just as the gunmen opened up. The bullets took out the passenger side windows missing Enrico. It also took out the rear side window striking Ricardo and killing him instantly. Enrico had his gun out and fired off a few rounds. He looked in the back seat and saw Ricardo slumped over; he had taken a bullet in the head.

"They killed Ricardo! THE BASTARDS! THEY KILLED RICARDO!"

Jorge pulled onto Center Street with tires squealing. They approached two pedestrians walking towards them on the passenger side of the car - Nettie and Sean. Enrico recognized them.

"SLOW DOWN, SLOW DOWN! IT'S THAT BITCH! SHE CAUSED THIS!"

Jorge decelerated as they closed on the two of them. Enrico, now in a complete rage, pointed his gun out the shattered window and fired repeatedly at his helpless targets, emptying his weapon, striking both of them at point blank range. Then they sped away.

Sean and Nettie lay on the sidewalk. Sean had been hit three times in the body and had struck his head on the curb as he fell. His last conscious recollection was of his mother lying next to him covered in blood. Nettie was hit several times in the body and once in the head. It was the head shot that killed her.

HE SAW DARKNESS, then a little light, then darkness again. Then more light. Sean was regaining consciousness. It had been three days since the shooting. Sean's eyes were now completely open. He blinked rapidly and tried to focus. There were two familiar faces looking back at him and he faintly heard a voice he recognized.

"Sean, Sean, can you hear me?" Now he put the voice to the face. It was M. J.

His mind was working furiously...

"M. J. Where's Mom? I, I, had this awful dream...," he stammered with a weak voice. "Where is she? Where is she? It was so real. She was covered in BLOOD! WHERE IS SHE, M. J.?"

As M. J. held him, tears streamed down her face. Sean was confused and he looked at Meg who was also crying as she held on tightly to his hand. Seeing the two of them sobbing brought an automatic response from him as tears were now falling from his eyes too. He was frantic, "What's happening? WHERE IS SHE?"

He suddenly became quiet and said almost inaudibly, "My god, it wasn't a dream. It wasn't a dream... Mom, Mom..." He then laid his head back, choking on his tears, and slowly went inside to a place that only he and his mother could understand. He remained there for hours.

The doctors were in and out saying only that he was probably suffering from severe shock. But they were puzzled. Sean was showing no signs of shock symptoms. His eyes were wide open. Only Meg knew where he went and she kept saying, "He'll be back, he *will* be back."

And he did come back. Papa Joe joined M. J. and Meg in the room as they were standing vigil. Sean's eyes came into focus and he looked at each of them. In an unemotional voice, he said, "I want to talk to Billy."

Billy soon arrived and, at Sean's insistence, he hesitatingly told Sean everything he knew. He did not know who the gunmen were. When he finished, a tearful Sean said, "It was Carlos' friend, the man with the mustache. I saw him with the gun. I remembered him and now I'll never forget him."

ONE OF THE new patrol officers had been first on the scene. He had called Billy. Meg heard the gunshots and sirens, grabbed her medical bag and raced out the door heading toward the twirling lights of the patrol car. She was horrified at what she saw, but remained composed and took measures that stopped Sean from bleeding to death.

Billy was overwhelmed with grief as he and Meg worked to place Sean in the patrol car that would act as an ambulance. Meg went with Sean in the speeding car as it raced to the hospital. She kept pressure on his wounds as they weaved their way through traffic. Meg could not remove the image of Nettie's bullet-ridden body from her mind. She was shaken, in anguish, but fought to remain in control.

Papa Joe was there when they placed Nettie's body on the gurney en route to the coroner's. He was crushed. And no amount of praying was going to help him.

It was left to Billy to inform Ma and Little Bit. M. J. and Skeet were off somewhere. Ma, cradling her baby, could tell by the look on Billy's face as he came up the path that something awful had happened. She wasn't prepared for the tragic news and fell to her knees in anguish. Little Bit was lost and confused; she cried and clung to Ma.

"What about Sean? What about Sean?" Little Bit kept asking.

Billy waited at Ma's for Skeet and M. J. to come home. He didn't want to leave Ma alone with the two little ones. M. J. and Skeet were sitting in a coffee shop near the U. of D. campus. There was a buzz going through the place and they overheard someone say that a white woman had just been gunned down and killed in the Zone.

M. J. and Skeeter saw fear mirrored in each other's faces. They took off in a panic, running for home as fast as they could. As they raced up the path to the house and saw a grief stricken Billy, M. J. clutched Skeeter's arm and said, "Nettie." They ran past Billy into the house and found Ma curled up on the couch sobbing and in a daze. The three of them held each other and cried until they exhausted themselves.

Billy told the girls that Sean was in critical condition, but alive, and Meg was with him. He said he was going to the hospital and would report back. M. J. tore herself away and demanded to go with Billy. Skeet stayed with Ma and Little Bit as they comforted each other. M. J. never left the hospital until Sean regained consciousness.

They took turns visiting; Sean was never alone. His wounds were serious but no longer life threatening. He was augmenting the healing process with the powers of his gift, astonishing the doctors at the speed of his healing.

Everyone did their best to hide their grief in front of him, but it was impossible. They were a family and they shared in the loss and comforted each other.

Sean would drift back to his safe place whenever his grief overwhelmed him. The doctors said that it might be weeks before it would be medically possible for him to leave the hospital. He would not be able to attend the burial service. Sean wanted to be there with his family, but he knew he wasn't strong enough.

On the day of the service, Little Bit insisted on staying with her Sean. They dropped her off at the hospital and she crawled up in bed with him. They held hands and talked about other things.

There was no funeral procession, just a closed casket service at the chapel. It seemed that the entire Zone had turned out. There were hundreds of people standing outside the small cemetery all in mourning.

Dr. John and Dr. Hughes were among the mourners along with members of their staff. They were accompanied by students Nettie had tutored and the many friends she made at the University. The grandparents of Patsy and Connie, the mother of the Down syndrome child and Mr. and Mrs. Goldstein had all left the Zone but were here to honor Nettie. They were just a few of the many mourners who no longer lived in the Zone. They joined the others who wished to pay their respects to the woman whom they knew and loved.

The casket was placed between the chapel and her gravesite; it was set back several feet from the service road that encircled the small cemetery. Chairs for the family were set up in front. Mourners filled the road and the overflow stood outside the cemetery.

Papa Joe stood next to the casket as he began the solemn service. Losing Nettie was an enormous personal loss and his suffering showed as he paused and appeared to be paralyzed with grief. Skeeter, holding a red rose, shakily stood, and with a wavering voice said, "I have a poem that I would like to read to you." She gave Papa Joe a hug and began:

"Her Light Still Shines

It wasn't light
It wasn't dark
It was just gray

There was no joy
There was no sadness
It was just another day

There was no need for hope
There was no need for despair
There was no need for need

It was an existence
It was not a life
Then SHE planted the seed

The gray became brighter
Each day became more meaningful
Needs needed no explanation

NETTIE was our teacher
NETTIE was our mother
NETTIE was our inspiration

Her gifts became our treasures
Her life became our soul
Her light became our dawn

SHE has left us
But her light still shines
For in us her spirit lives on"

Skeeter set the rose on the casket and returned to her seat. This emotional tribute to Nettie from one of her children ended the service. There was nothing more to add.

At Sean's request, his mother would be buried next to the lonely man's grave. Skeeter, as she left, gathered up one of the bouquets surrounding Nettie's casket and placed it on the lonely man's grave.

Chapter 25: Changes

NETTIE'S DEATH precipitated dramatic changes. Billy was hurt and angry. He adopted a zero tolerance policy in the Zone and his superiors had no choice but to go along with him. The killing of a white woman in the Zone made headlines and the Mayor and his council were getting nervous.

Patrols were increased and Billy alerted the drug dealers; if they didn't like it, they could leave. His only concession was his agreement not to conduct any surprise searches. However, he came down real hard on any open violators, including drunks, dopers and brawlers. The dealers stayed put; they still had a sweet arrangement. They respected Billy's zero tolerance policy on open crime, and removed any of their own people who did not.

Billy no longer cared what anybody wanted; he was past retirement age and the job was no longer important to him. He felt responsible for Nettie's death.

Carlos attended the burial service but stayed in the background away from the family. His flower arrangement was twice as big as any other. There was no card. He wasn't ashamed to let people know that he loved Nettie; he just didn't want anybody to think that she had been involved with a drug dealer.

Any thought Carlos had of divorcing himself from the criminal world ended when Nettie was murdered. He, too, took responsibility for her death. If he hadn't initiated the hit on Enrico she would still be alive.

Carlos was determined to find Enrico and kill him. He would use his considerable resources and influence to accomplish this. It wasn't going to be easy. Enrico was gone.

Carlos' quest to buy the entire Zone was renewed with a passion. He sent in his legal team to file probate proceedings and quiet title suits on the few properties that had clouds on them. Then he made offers to the proper parties and purchased those properties.

Carlos was determined to evict the drug dealers no matter what the cost. His motive now was solely for profit; he didn't care about lives he might change. He had not thought this completely through and would later regret the oversight.

Meg turned seventy. The loss of Nettie drained much of the life out of her. She was tired and sad and angry. Omens of real trouble in the Zone made her feel helpless. No longer the fearless fighter, she was now concerned only for Ma and the children. She didn't care about anything else and wanted to be there for the family if, no... when, they needed her.

Ma was morose and depressed since the tragedy. She had loved her friend and thought that everything Nettie had brought to the Zone would now be lost. Her depression was affecting everyone. She was absorbed in caring for her baby, maintaining the house, and providing the funds needed for everybody's day-to-day needs. The joy was gone from her life.

Skeet was dealing with the loss better than anybody; the seventeen year old was determined to finish school as a tribute to her mentor. She got involved with the journalism club and a theater group. She studied hard and was holding a three-plus grade point average. When she wasn't at school, Skeeter spent most of her time teaching Little Bit, trying to duplicate the same excellent home schooling Nettie had provided. Skeet knew that Nettie's shoes would be hard to fill. M. J. was still her best friend, but the three year age difference started to create some separation as their lives took different paths.

Sean, recovering from his wounds, would be able to attend the fall semester. Interrupting his education was never considered. He knew how much it meant to his mother and he would not let her down.

Dr. John and Dr. Hughes visited Sean in the hospital. They encouraged him to stay in school with an arrangement that all he had to do was take the final exams in language and computer sciences; he did not have to attend those classes. If he passed the two exams and completed the required courses, the University would graduate him at the end of the year.

Sean thanked the professors and asked if they could get him permission to take accredited physics and law courses on line in addition to his last year of basics. He pointed out how unchallenging the required classes were - a waste of his time. He was carrying a four grade point average without effort. The professors assured Sean that they could get the necessary approval.

Sean began to withdraw from everybody except Little Bit. The rest of the family left him alone, hoping he would work his way through his grief.

M. J. was the most vulnerable. She was entering a stage in a young girl's life where she needed purpose and guidance. Ma, in her deep depression, wasn't there for M. J. and didn't recognize her needs.

Papa Joe was close to M. J. and he saw what was happening. He wanted to help.

"Look, we got a lot of kids your age in those hospitals," he said to her. "And they sorta get passed over at Christmas when we make our tours. How would you feel about putting on a sync performance for them and dancing to your crazy hip-hop music?"

Papa Joe had hit a home run. M. J. came alive and became the first to move on. She would help Ma with Sissy, and would work on her composition, but for now she was back in show business. This time, though, she would be entertaining her peers and she could just be herself and, as Papa Joe chortled: "Boy this is gonna be good!"

Chapter 26: Don't Mess With Him, Man

THE SCHOOL YEAR ended and Sean completed his required courses. He graduated in June with honors, earning a bachelor's degree before his fifteenth birthday. His powers of retention made academics a snap for him. Sean had accumulated enough credits in Physics to qualify for their master's program and he had scored exceptionally high on the prerequisite exams. He applied for a scholarship.

And with Dr. John and Dr. Hughes's help, he was awarded that scholarship. He wanted to learn everything he could about the mysterious energies that his Mom was so sure could explain his gift. He still had no answers, but he was meeting the right people. A. J. McCleary would be attending graduate school in the fall. The degree wasn't important to him; it was answers he was looking for and access to the people who might have them.

Sean didn't tell his family about his academic accomplishments; they assumed he was still working on his undergraduate degree. He became interested in law, particularly International law. Dr. John had asked him to work as an interpreter for one of his off campus clients, an import-exporter from northwestern Pakistan who spoke Pashto. Sean worked in the lab with students who spoke this language and he soon mastered it.

He made valuable contacts and could see the advantage of combining a law degree with his language skills. He took the law boards and passed them with ease but had no plans to attend law school; he couldn't afford it.

Sean remained distant to his family. He spent all his time in the lab or on the computer. Sean was using his academic pursuits to mask his grief and they all knew it. The family didn't want to interfere and stayed with their policy of leaving him alone. Skeet had her own schooling to worry about and M. J. was busy with her activities. For the first time in their lives, M. J. and Sean were spending more time apart than together. The family members were drifting away from each other.

M. J. was experiencing another change. She discovered boys. It would be more accurate to say that boys discovered M. J. It was inevitable. She was not yet fifteen and looked nineteen. Her flamboyance, good looks and teenage body were a lethal combination in the unprincipled Zone. Older boys, especially, were attracted to her.

Sean was walking down one of the side streets looking for M. J. on a humid July afternoon. As he approached a newspaper store, he spotted her standing in front, surrounded by a group of older boys. Sean didn't recognize any of them. M. J. was wearing tight shorts and a midriff-revealing halter. Her wavy brown hair drifted below her shoulders and one of the boys pushed it aside as he put his arm around her.

Sean was angry and wasn't sure why. M. J., apparently enjoying herself, didn't notice him until he had stopped walking and stood beside her.

"Come on, M. J. I'll walk you home; there's something I want to talk to you about," he said, not knowing why he said that either.

M. J. said nothing and suddenly felt ill-at-ease. The boy who had his arm around her noticed and said, "I don't know who you are, whitey, but this squirrel is doing just fine where she is. You better move on!"

"He's my brother," declared M. J.

"Well, this little shit doesn't look like a bro to me," he said as he took his arm away from M. J. and gave Sean a shove.

Sean was well trained in Zonie combat and knew that if you were going to engage you didn't waste time talking, you just charged ahead. He never realized how much pent up anger he was harboring over the death of his mother until that moment.

The kid never thought it could happen. With laser speed, Sean hit him flush on the jaw and the boy went down. He didn't get up. His friends stepped back with surprised looks, sensing that maybe they should stay out of it.

Sean took M. J. by the arm and said, "Lets go."

They walked up the path to their house and M. J., instead of going inside, turned and walked over to the middle of the porch. Sean followed.

"Well, at least you paid some attention to me," she declared. "Look, tough guy, those were my friends and they didn't do anything wrong. You instigated the whole thing and the only reason I came back with you was to avoid more trouble.

We've been waiting for you, Sean, but I want my brother back, not some friggin bodyguard!"

Sean was close to tears, "I, I'm sorry M. J., I don't know what I'm doing. I just miss her so much ..." He sat down on the only chair and put his head into his hands.

"Damn it, Sean, you don't have an exclusive on sadness. She was my mother, too, and I miss her as much as you do!" She glared at him: "The rest of us have managed to go on; it's been almost a year now and you gotta get back into the game!"

There. She said it. What everybody was thinking. Sean raised his head and looked at M. J. He stood taking a deep breath, straightened his shoulders and opened his arms. She came to him.

"How did you get so smart?" he asked.

"I had great teachers."

He held her for a while, then said, "Look, I'm really sorry about your friends. I'll apologize to them if you want me to."

"No, no, just stay away from them. You know how the transients are."

"Okay, but do you think you could wear a little more clothes the next time

you're with them?"
She put her hands on her hips and cocked her head.
Sean frowned, "All right, all right. It was just a thought."
Sean began to heal and the family started to do things together again. Skeeter, Sean and M. J. all considered getting jobs but Ma insisted they concentrate on their studies during the school year and enjoy the summer break. She gave them spending money.
M. J. suspected that Sebastian had left Ma some money but she never asked. They took Little Bit along as they visited ice cream shops and went to movies.
Ma and Meg still got together for their morning coffee and Sean happened to join them one day. Meg casually asked Sean about school. He replied that he would be taking some interesting courses in the fall but he really wanted to study law. However, his scholarship money didn't allow for that.
Ma looked at Meg then turned to Sean and said, "We've got the money, Sean. Your Mom, Meg and I decided quite awhile ago that we would use it for you kids. We're going to help you guys get through school and make it available for anything else that you really need. You just sign up for your law courses and tell me how much it costs. We got plenty, Sean."
Sean knew that Wayne State wouldn't allow him to enroll in two graduate programs, so he applied to The Detroit College of Law which was located right around the block. He was accepted for the fall semester. The College was flexible and he would work around conflicts by taking some night courses. *These* classes he would have to attend.
They were into the fall semester and A. J. was doing fine but Sean had his problems in the Zone. M. J.'s boyfriend - the one Sean had decked - was a local brawler. Word spread fast and Sean was tabbed with an unwanted reputation as a fighter. It wasn't long before he was challenged and Sean responded the only way he knew how... 'Don't back down and don't hold back.' His opponent was bigger and probably stronger but Sean's aggressive style allowed him to win the fight.
Sean suspected that this could be just the beginning and there was nothing that he could do about it. But then something strange and unexpected happened.
Suddenly, His potential adversaries wanted to be his friends. The word on the street was: "Hey, that white kid is pretty tough."
"I heard that he's been stabbed and shot two or three times!"
"It was now: "Hey Ferrari, how ya doin' man!" and...
"See that white kid over there with that hot chick? Don't mess with him, man, he's one tough dude!"
They stayed clear of M. J. too.
Sean and M. J. were amused by this overnight fame, "If they only knew

that I can still whip your ass, tough guy," quipped M. J.

"Well, *I* know you can and that's all that matters," laughed Sean.

"Yeah, and don't you forget it."

Sean liked this arrangement; he was no longer being challenged. He knew the potential for trouble was there and that he better be prepared. He was growing taller and filling out. For the first time he was as tall as M. J. Now he wanted to get stronger. Sean decided to experiment with his gift. He would study how muscle was developed and then go inside and direct the flow of blood and oxygen to the right spot. He was taking the next step - the one his mother had refused to take.

Chapter 27: The Frightened Turtle Syndrome

M. J. AND SEAN were turning sixteen in the summer. Sissy was two. Little Bit had turned ten and Skeet, entering her senior year of college, would soon be nineteen.

Sean had passed M. J. in height and was still growing. His successful mind-body muscle building project had chiseled him into a broad shouldered, exceptionally strong six-footer. Eventually he would grow to six foot two and weigh a sleek two hundred pounds. Sean was the spitting image of his mother with her good looks, large emerald green eyes and wavy black hair.

Sean completed the course work for his master's and was writing a thesis on the electro magnetic connection between body and mind, using himself as the case study. He was learning but still had no valid answers explaining his gift. He would continue his search.

Papa Joe and M. J. had a busy winter. Papa Joe booked her shows into hospitals all over the city. She was thrilled.

M. J. had her father's Spanish features and her mother's wonderful brown wavy hair and had reached her full height of five foot eight inches. She had a trim, curvy figure with strong but not overly muscled legs. She no longer fit into a training bra. Her hazel almost-yellow eyes complemented her light brown skin. In other words, she was stunningly beautiful!

When together, Sean and M. J. were dazzling. To Sean, M. J. was, well, just M. J. To M. J., Sean was her overly protective brother who kept her in line. Well...almost.

M. J. was just naturally sexy but honestly didn't realize her allure. Her outgoing personality was constantly being misinterpreted as flirtatious. She was no longer just catching the eyes of young boys; grown men would hit on her and be disappointed when she didn't respond.

There were a lot of seedy looking transients hanging out in the Zone this early summer and Ma and Meg were cautioning the girls to stay clear of them.

Sean and M. J. visited Nettie's gravesite and M. J. joined Papa Joe in the chapel.

"I'll be along in half an hour Sean. I know you got things to do; go ahead without me."

"Okay, see you back at the place. Talk to you later, Papa Joe."

The cemetery was four blocks from their house in one corner of the Zone. Several side streets led directly to it.

About twenty-five minutes after Sean left, M. J. started toward home taking a side street. It was in the middle of the afternoon. She passed three rough-looking characters standing on the sidewalk and said hello to

them. She had never seen them before.
She heard them coming up behind her and turned around. They took M. J. by surprise, grabbed her and attempted to drag her off between two vacant houses. They didn't know who they had gotten hold of.
An ex-Kiddie Corps agent saw the whole thing and took off running to Ma's house.
"SEAN, SEAN!" he yelled as he pounded on the door.
Sean came out and recognized the kid, "Alex, what's wrong?"
"You gotta hurry! Three guys just grabbed M. J. NUMBER 6A on the right about half way down!"
Sean was off ... Thank you, Skeet, thank you.
He was on them before they knew it. They were cut, scratched and bleeding, but they had M. J. pinned to the ground with her jeans wrapped around one of her legs. They had ripped off her panties and one guy was kneeling over her, fully erect.
He wasn't erect for long as Sean kicked his member hard enough to break it in two. He was temporarily out of the game holding on to his package screaming and rolling around in agony.
The other two thugs let go of M. J. to get at Sean. What a mistake that was! Most women under the circumstances would have pulled their jeans back up and fastened them, not M. J. She kicked her jeans completely off to free her legs and joined the battle.
Sean had drilled one of them with a punch straight to his face squashing his nose like a grape. The third attacker had Sean by the shoulders. Sean spun him around creating a target for one of M. J.'s famous right crosses. Down he went.
The guy with the shattered nose picked up a loose board and threw it at Sean hitting him in the face. Sean shrugged it off and hit him in the nose two more times sending him sprawling to the ground, gasping for breath and choking on his own blood. The thug M. J. had belted got up and Sean put him back down with a series of punches. Completely defeated, those two staggered off and disappeared.
These guys had not been trained in the Zone.
In the meantime, M. J. had jumped on the attacker still on the ground, the one who had been kneeling over her with rape in mind. She was raining punches on his now bloody face. "YOU UGLY SON OF A BITCH, WHERE YA YOU GONNA STICK IT NOW, HUH?"
M. J. was going to kill him. He was half conscious but she continued pounding him. Sean pulled her off; she was still swinging away as he was holding her in the air.
"LET ME GO! THAT BASTARD IS GOING OUT THE FUCKING WINDOW!"
"He's already out the window; come on. Fight's over."
"Bastard, asshole," she mumbled collecting her clothes. They left the

would-be rapist lying on the ground with an unrecognizable face and a penis that had become the victim of the Frightened Turtle syndrome.

Sean's face was cut and swollen where the board had hit him. M. J.'s one eye was cut and half swollen shut. Her knuckles were bruised and puffy.

As the two warriors walked home they looked at each other's bloody faces and smiled.

"We showed 'em Sean, we showed 'em."

"Yeah. We did, M. J. ..., but you're going to have to stop wearing those tight jeans. You're driving those guys crazy!"

"Oh Sean!"

They stopped at Meg's for some minor repairs.

"Geez you two, what the hell happened?"

They were going to have to save it for Billy who had just pulled up.

"I thought I'd find you two here. Give it to me, give it to me!" exclaimed Billy.

They knew better than to hold back anything on Billy, so they told him the whole story.

"GOD DAMN ATTEMPTED RAPE!" yelled Meg. "Did they penetrate you?"

"Are you kidding? Not a chance. I'll call the shots about my own body and who penetrates it."

Sean rolled his eyes.

Billy was shaking with fury. This was one of his kids.

"I don't like it, Billy. It's starting to get rough out there," cried Meg.

"Yeah, they ain't seen rough!" and he bolted out the door.

Sean was trying to evaluate his apparently superior skills in hand-to-hand combat. He thought at first that the experience of being in so many fights when growing up may have given him an advantage. He considered the possibility that the early childhood pummeling from M. J. may have had something to do with it. Whatever it was, he knew for sure that he anticipated better than his opponents and he was faster. Much faster. He suspected his gift at work here.

Another piece to the puzzle.

News travels fast in the Zone. Sean, and now M. J.'s, reputations had risen to new heights. They were no longer just the heroes of impressionable kids, but had gained the notoriety and respect of everybody in the Zone. They also made some dangerous enemies: guys who held grudges and carried weapons.

Chapter 28: Weasel Face

SEAN WAS SIXTEEN, self supporting, with no living relatives - making him eligible to file for emancipation that would give him adult status. He filed as A. J. McCleary and it was granted.

He was living a dual life. As soon as he stepped foot on campus of either colleges, he became A. J. McCleary. A. J. was the brilliant student with unimaginable academic abilities. His college peers never knew Sean Ferrari and A. J. kept to himself. Even Dr. John and Dr. Hughes addressed him as A. J. McCleary, forgetting about his other identity.

Nobody in the Zone, other than Papa Joe, Ma or Meg, had heard of A. J. McCleary. None of his family or friends ever went on campus with him and knew nothing of his accomplishments. This was precisely as he wanted it; he knew his siblings would never understand who A. J. was. And besides, he reasoned, they probably wouldn't like him.

Billy got a line on one of the attackers, a thug who worked for a dealer. Billy found him living in one of the run-down dope houses. Without a warrant, he burst into the house and collared him, confiscating an ounce of cocaine at the same time.

There was an immediate uproar in the doper's union. The cops had violated the Zonie truce. Half the dealers vowed revenge; the other half recognized that they had brought it on themselves by protecting the men who tried to rape one of Billy's kids. A schism developed within the shaky dealers' alliance and it threatened to get ugly.

SEAN'S ROUTE HOME from law school was under surveillance by members of one of the disgruntled dealers. Two of the stalkers were M. J.'s assailants. They wanted revenge.

The stalkers planned their attack methodically. Four men jumped Sean as he was returning home from one his law classes. Sean defended himself but was overpowered and had no chance. With great difficulty, they forced him to the ground and held him there spread eagled.

"OKAY LOVER BOY!" screamed the man who M. J. had beaten senseless, "LETS SEE HOW YOU LIKE IT!"

He then thrust an ice pick straight into Sean's scrotum. He cried out in pain. Then bodies began to fly in every direction.

A huge black man and two of his friends had intervened on Sean's behalf and repelled the attackers. They left the ice pick sticking between Sean's legs.

The big man stood over Sean and said, "We didn't like the odds, kid. Ya want me to pull that outta you?"

"No," he grimaced, "Somebody get Meg Brown!"

The big man nodded to one of his friends who jumped into a pickup parked along side the curb and sped off for Meg's. "Yeah, we know her," he said as Sean tried to sit up.

"I don't know nothin' about medicine, but I would lay still if I were you and wait for Meg to get here. Don't seem to be bleeding much."

"Good idea," grunted Sean as he tried to intercept the pain messages being sent to his brain.

"Thanks for the help, Mr..."

"They call me Big George and you're that Ferrari kid, right?"

"Yeah," said an out-of-breath Sean as he propped himself up on his elbow. "I owe you man. Thanks."

"Ya know, you're pretty calm for someone with an ice pick stickin' between his legs."

"It doesn't hurt that much."

"It wasn't right what they tried to do to your girlfriend and this ain't right neither," Big George exclaimed just as Meg arrived.

Meg took a quick look and said, "JESUS... Oh man... Can you tell where it is, Sean?" said a calm but anxious Meg.

"I don't think it hit any arteries, Meg, but I don't know about the damage. I know it looks worse than what it is."

"You want me to pull it out, Meg?" asked Big George.

"No, too risky. No telling what we may tear up and it's hardly bleeding so were going to leave it alone and let the experts take it out."

"Okay, lets put him in the back of the pickup, but you *can't* jostle that ice pick!" exhorted Meg.

They placed pillows on the bed of the pickup and carefully laid Sean down and headed for the hospital. Meg jumped in back with him and yelled to the driver, "Go slowly now and NO BUMPS!"

Once inside the emergency room, the doctors debated whether or not to remove the ice pick based on the x-rays alone.

"NO WAY!" yelled Meg. "Get a urologist in here NOW!"

They agreed and summoned Dr. Chesney, the chief urologist. He ordered an ultrasound and was reading the results.

"Whose idea was it to not pull out that ice pick?" he asked.

"Mine," said Meg, willing to take the blame if she had made a mistake.

"Well, it was the right thing to do," said Dr. Chesney. "An inexact extraction could have severed arteries and glands that we couldn't have repaired. As it is, the gland that carries sperm to the duct that contains the semen has been severed completely and unevenly. We can't reconnect it and we're going to have to sew up the jagged ends and double seal each one. He has undergone an involuntary vasectomy. Only this one can't be reversed because of where it was severed and how jagged the tear was. He will never have children in the natural way. He's fortunate, though; he will be able to have a healthy sex life."

They informed Sean and sent him to the surgical floor.
"It shouldn't take long. Once we extract the ice pick, it will be a relatively simple operation from there. The foreign object is not threatening any vital organs and it hasn't severed any arteries. We'll keep him overnight and release him tomorrow if there are no complications."

Dr. Chesney muttered to himself as he went over Sean's medical history. "Wow, this is the second time this kid's been stabbed. He's also had a serious knife laceration, and has been shot, taking three bullets! Don't you think it's time for him to find another place to live?" he called back to Meg as he made his way up to surgery.

The health department routinely inspects the emergency room and one of its officials was present when Sean was wheeled in. He had been carefully observing Sean's treatment and overheard Meg's conversation with Dr. Chesney.

"Excuse me, Ms. Brown, may I have a word with you?" said a man whose name tag read Stanley Berman.
Meg turned around and looked at him. She knew him by another name, 'Weasel Face'.

"What do you want?" she growled.
"The staff here seems to know you well, and I must say you have quite a reputation in the Zone. I was just wondering ... where did you get the medical training that would allow you to make important decisions like the one you just made?"

Meg knew what he was deviously trying to get from her. She felt the bile rising and at this stage of her life she had no time for jerks like Stanley Berman.

"Don't screw with me you weasel faced little prick or someone is going to make an important medical decision for you!" She stomped off to the surgical waiting room.

Billy was informed about the attack long after it took place. He immediately swung by Ma's, picked up M. J. and headed for the hospital. He had sketchy details but was told that Sean had been stabbed and been taken to the hospital for treatment. He didn't know Meg was with him.

They were directed to the surgical waiting room and found Meg. She reassured them that Sean was all right and was undergoing a relatively non-risky surgery. She gave them the details and M. J. was horrified but relieved that he was going to be fine and would be released the next day.

No one knew who Big George was. Billy later found out that he worked for Carlos and was brought into the Zone after the rape incident. Billy correctly presumed that he was sent there to keep an eye on the kids. He would make a point to thank Carlos.

Chapter 29: Virgins

LITTLE BIT AND SISSY celebrated their December birthdays together. Little Bit had become the Big Sister. She was already showing the three-year-old how to use apps on the computer.

She insisted that Sean play horsey with Sissy and the three of them were constantly cavorting around the house. Sissy fit right in and became one of the gang.

Skeet had decided to get a teaching degree. It would delay her graduation by a semester but it would be well worth it. She loved her writing and theater classes and was active in the live stage performances but was advised to get the teacher's certification as a back up. She put her book on hold while she was learning how to write it. She still had a lot more research to do.

Meg had a visit from M. J. on a cold January morning. They settled into Meg's comfy chairs and were sipping tea.

"Meg, tell me all you know about sex! I'm getting these funny feelings when I look at boys and I figure I had better know what the hell I'm doing before I start experimenting. What's it feel like? Does it hurt? And don't you go telling me to google it... and when is the best time to do it... and..."

Meg sighed, looked at M. J. and thought, why me, why me? Why not me? Ma couldn't handle it and there's nobody else. Papa Joe? I don't think so.

"I was kissing a boy the other day and he stuck his tongue in my mouth and, you know what, Meg? I liked it!"

Jesus, thought Meg, she's learned everything else in the Zone, how did she miss this one? Because we kept her away from that environment, that's why. Okay where do I begin...?

They chatted for about an hour and Meg gave M. J. straightforward answers. She didn't waste her time on the, 'put it off until you're married' routine. She knew M. J. wouldn't buy that for a second. She did, however, emphasize over and over about the need for effective contraception and protection against sexually transmitted diseases.

"Okay Meg. Thanks. I think I got it. I can't imagine using one of those condoms, though. That doesn't seem like the real thing. Maybe I can find someone like Sean who can't make babies. I sure would like to see some movies. I wonder if Billy has some? Well, gotta go. Later, Meg, and thanks. I'll let you know how I make out!"

Meg watched her leave, sat back, and slowly rapped her head with her fist.

Papa Joe had a minor glitch in his computer and asked Sean to take a look at it. M. J. volunteered to swing by the chapel to pick it up saving

Papa Joe a delivery trip. She made the stop and had the computer tucked under her arm as she headed home.

M. J. wasn't afraid of another attack. Her assailants had disappeared from the Zone and she knew a lot of eyes were looking after her. Nevertheless she always returned home from Papa Joe's taking the side street where Big George lived. She gave him and his friends a friendly wave when she saw them.

M. J. ran into Skeet at Center Street and joined up with her. Skeet was heading to Billy's to look at some old declassified police logs.

"Hey guys, come on in," greeted Billy.

"I'm going to use your washroom, Billy," said M. J., as she set Papa Joe's computer down on his desk. She walked down the hall and passed a room where two of Billy's patrol guys were on their computer. The door was closed but the office had windows all along the hallway. She did a double take as she walked by, then stopped. They were watching some confiscated porn movies. She couldn't believe what she was seeing.

Billy called for the officers and they hurriedly ejected the disc and tossed it into the drawer. They didn't see M. J. as she continued on to the bathroom.

A police call had come in and Billy sent the men out to investigate the problem. M. J. had gotten a sneak preview of raw sex being performed and now she was beyond mere curiosity.

"Hey Billy, while you guys are looking at those logs, would you mind if I take this computer back to your officer's room where I can hook up to the internet. I gotta look up something."

"Sure kid, help yourself."

She set up, found the porn disc, slipped it into the computer and started the downloading process. She had downloaded her dance videos many times and was familiar with the procedure. She would remove the video from Papa Joe's computer when she got home, then delete it from his files.

The disc was in a compatible format and it didn't take long to download. It was untitled so she labeled it 'Adam and Eve' and left it in the downloads folder. She tossed the disc back into the drawer and joined the others in the front office. Then she realized that she had never removed a file before. Uh, oh, she may need Sean's help. Oh well, she would worry about that later; the hard part was over. She wondered how the Jesuits would feel about their part in advancing her sex education.

She couldn't help giggling to herself. "What are you so chipper about, M. J.?" Skeet asked as they were walking back to Ma's.

"You look quite pleased with yourself."

"I do? Can't imagine why," she grinned. Skeet gave her a puzzled look.

Papa Joe was waiting for her at the front porch.

"There you are. I thought you were hocking my computer," laughed Papa

Joe. "Ah, ah... I went with Skeet to see Billy," she said nervously. Again Skeeter looked at her.

"Well, I'm glad I caught you. I've just been informed that I must attend a meeting at the Diocese and I'm going to need my computer. Sean can fix the minor problem later."

M. J. felt the color leave her face as she returned the computer.

"If you don't mind I will leave it with you tomorrow and maybe Sean will have time to look her over," Papa Joe said as he left.

Sean showed up just as Papa Joe was heading down the sidewalk.

"Sean, Sean, hurry. Come upstairs; I need to talk to you," said a very jittery M. J., as she rushed into the house heading for the project room.

"What's with her, Skeet? She's jumping out her skin."

"I think she screwed up Papa Joe's computer and wants you to fix it," said a fast thinking Skeet covering for M. J. I wonder what she's really up to? Skeet thought to herself.

Sean followed M. J. upstairs and asked, "What is wrong with you, M. J.? I don't think I've ever seen you like this before."

"Sean, what's the quickest way to get something off of a computer and save it?"

"Well, we can download it to a memory stick, they're pretty fast. Why do you ask?"

"Never mind. Do you have one of those?"

"Yeah, I do."

"Look, Papa Joe is going to leave his computer with you tomorrow and I need you to take something off it without telling him." appealed an excited M. J. "You can download it to that memory stick then delete the file!"

Sean was frowning as he looked at her and said, "Let's see if I got this right? You want me to invade Papa Joe's personal files in his private computer, then remove it to a memory stick, all without telling him. Is that about right?"

"Oh Sean, you make it sound like it's a crime or something!"

"It *is* a crime M. J., and I won't have any part of it! What's the matter with you? What could possibly be on his computer that you want to steal?"

"It's *not* stealing, it belongs to *me*!" She was on the verge of tears. That was the one thing that Sean couldn't handle. "Okay, okay, but you've got to tell me everything... invading a priest's computer. Geez, M. J..."

Sean stared at M. J. in disbelief; what did she do?

"WHAT? YOU DOWNLOADED PORN INTO PAPA JOE'S COMPUTER AND HE'S TAKING IT WITH HIM TO MEET WITH HIS BISHOP!"

"Sh, shhh! Sean, not so loud for god's sake. Skeet and Ma are downstairs - they can hear you!"

Sean was incredulous, then a small smile started to appear. He looked at M. J. and started to laugh.

"What's so funny?" M. J. pressed her lips together to keep from smiling herself.

Within seconds they both were bent over in laughter, "Can you, you imagine... what that... meeting is going to be like? 'Adam and Eve'. Wh... what's that... all... about Fath... Father Joseph," guffawed Sean.

M. J. finally recovered enough to say, through her laughing tears, "Sean, we might get him in trouble."

"What do you mean WE? Just pray... if you're still allowed to... that he doesn't go into his download file."

The next day Sean and M. J. watched anxiously as Papa Joe came up the path. He didn't look upset at all and was still wearing his frock, so they assumed that he wasn't discovered, or that the Diocese was treated to the best afternoon of entertainment they ever had.

He dropped off the computer and M. J. told him that she would return it to him when Sean was finished.

"Look, M. J., I'm afraid to ask you this, but why do you want me to burn 'Adam and Eve' to a memory stick? Why don't we just delete it?"

M. J. had anticipated the question and had given her answer a lot of thought. "I not going to lie to you, Sean. I have these fantasies about sex all the time now and I just want to see for myself what you're supposed to do. Don't you ever think about those things?"

"Well, yeah, yes of course I do. I have some dreams now and then that are... are sometimes embarrassing. But I never thought about looking at porn movies!"

"Well now you can. What do say we watch them together?
Come on, how else are we going to learn?" said a now enthusiastic M. J.

"I..., I don't know M. J. What do you intend to do once you see how to do it, whatever that is?" questioned Sean.

"Ah, I'll think of something."

Sean always had trouble saying no to M. J., and he had to admit that he, too, was curious and entertained his own fantasies. He had moved back downstairs and had the apartment all to himself. Little Bit moved into his vacated room and Sissy slept wherever she wanted, usually with Little Bit.

Later in the evening, when Skeeter was about to turn in, an edgy M. J. said, "Sean's going to help me with my classical music, Skeet. We'll take the computer downstairs so we won't bother you."

"Oh, you won't bother me, M. J. You know how soundly I sleep."

"We're going to have to play this piece real loud so we will just go downstairs," anxiously replied M. J.

"Okay, see you in the morning."

Sean and M. J. sat mesmerized in front of the screen.

"Oh wow," M. J. kept saying. "Wow, did you see...? Wow...
Ooh, how do they?... Is that what your...?"

"Whew," added Sean.

When it was over, M. J. uncurled from the couch and said, "I think I need a shower; I'm going upstairs."

"I know what you mean; I better not stand up," said an embarrassed Sean.

They looked at each other for a long moment. She did not want to leave and he didn't want her to go. They both knew that something was changing.

Something did change. Sean was no longer viewing M. J. as the sister he had grown up with, but was seeing the beautiful young woman that everyone else saw. He was not comfortable with that, but did not know what to do about it.

M. J. paid Meg another visit. She told her that she had watched a graphic porn video with Sean, but she didn't disclose how she had obtained it.

"Meg, maybe we shouldn't have done that. When I was watching the video, I wanted to reach out and touch Sean, and I could sense that he felt the same way towards me. I, I, don't know what to do Meg. I guess I never noticed before how appealing he was."

"Well, you may be the only female in the Zone who didn't, honey."

"Look, just because you two were raised together doesn't mean that you're blood relatives. You are completely different persons than you were just a couple of years ago. It's this new identity that's attracting you to each other, and I for one, couldn't be happier. Go for it kid."

The next few days were awkward for both of them. It was like they were seeing each other for the first time. In a way they were. It had been so natural in the past for him to put his arm around her and give her a hug. Now he was afraid to touch her.

It was only a matter of time. They were aroused and it was just too easy for them. Later that week, M. J. walked down the stairs, entered Sean's apartment, took off her clothes and climbed in bed with him. He was naked. He knew she would come.

They had kissed each other many times before but this was the first time. Meg was right. Sean and M. J. were now different people - no longer siblings. In bed they were strangers, two virgins, eager but clumsy. They groped and touched each other, never once questioning their sudden sexual attraction to one another. To them it was a natural transition. Somehow they managed but were disappointed. It had to be better than this. The second time it was.

As the days went by they treated sex as an exciting new adventure. It was torrid and pleasurable. They couldn't get enough of each other.

Having sex with M. J. provided Sean with another opportunity to experiment with his special gift. He was asking himself if it would be possible for him hold off orgasmic contractions by looking inside his body, viewing the process and delaying the release until she was peaking. With a little practice, he was able to do just that and M. J. became the direct beneficiary of his unique power.

It was perfect! Sean and M. J. were not just experimenting with sex, it went far beyond that. They adored one another, were satisfied and couldn't imagine being with anybody else. They were safe from sexually transmitted diseases and she wouldn't get pregnant. Most importantly, they knew exactly who the other person was and there would be no character surprises. Meg said it right when they were born: it really was 'love at first sight'.

Skeet and M. J. had never kept secrets from one another. M. J. told her what Skeeter already knew. Skeeter was overjoyed; the two people she loved most were together. Little Bit was still too young to understand and thought it was perfectly normal that M. J. would be sleeping at Sean's place.

All M. J. ever said to Meg was, "I went for it!" Meg had given her the thumbs up and they both had a good laugh.

Sean and M. J. really didn't know how Ma would react and so they said nothing to her. They didn't try to hide anything and would have answered honestly any questions that she may have had.

Meg was worried about Ma. She was becoming more distant and more depressed. Meg was starting to suspect that there may be more than depression going on here. She had to have a talk with her.

IN APRIL M. J. was asked to bring her sync-dance performance to a Cancer Benefit being put on by local churches and synagogues. Papa Joe had highly recommended her and the event was going to have the media coverage needed to attract donors. She was ecstatic.

It was quite an evening. The event was held in a big conference center in downtown Detroit. It was another team effort. Skeeter had choreographed M. J.'s dance routine and Sean prepared the set and handled the music.

The entire family attended and when Little Bit introduced M. J., they erupted in cheers and never sat down for the entire performance. It didn't matter, neither did anybody else. M. J. had them all rocking.

Her up tempo sync-dance was the hit of the night.

Papa Joe was bursting with pride as he introduced M. J. to some of the local media after the performance. She was approached by an elegantly dressed woman who represented a modeling agency. "Give me a call," she said, handing M. J. her business card. "We would be very interested in talking with you. Your performance was wonderful."

Back home, and gathered in Ma's living room, M. J. asked, "Do you think I should call her?"

"Sure," said Skeet, "what have you got to lose?"
"I agree," said Sean. "Call her first thing in the morning; see what happens."

M. J. did call and made an appointment with the agency.
"They want me to come down and have my picture taken in their studio to see how I photograph. Then they want to come here to take some outside pictures," she reported back to everybody.

"They want to take some pictures here in the Zone?" queried Sean. "I can't wait to see that!"

M. J. met with the photographer and her assistant at their studio. Later that same afternoon they showed up at Ma's house. She took several individual shots of M. J., directing her to strike different poses. M. J. was wearing her tight Jeans and skimpy halter. Everybody gathered around to watch. Sean had Sissy on his shoulders and Skeet and Little Bit were standing close by. Ma and Meg were on the porch.

The photographer finished and was packing up to leave when M. J. exhorted, "Hey wait a minute! I want you to take a picture of these guys; they're my family."
"Sure, why not."
"Oh no," declared Ma and Meg, and they backed off.

M. J. dragged the others into camera range; she held Sean's hand and he still had Sissy on his shoulders.
"Okay, now everybody walk toward me," the photographer ordered. M. J. was half dragging Sean toward the camera as they looked at each other, laughing. Skeet, wearing her baseball cap, and Little Bit were giggling as they tried to keep up. That's when the picture was snapped. It would be an image they would never forget.

Meg had her talk with Ma. Ma reluctantly admitted that she hadn't felt right for for some time now. She said she always felt tired and was losing weight and had pains in her upper stomach area. Meg did not like what she was hearing and, against Ma's wishes, she made a doctor's appointment for her.

After a preliminary examination, the concerned physician referred her to an oncologist. Ma was frightened now and consented to the battery of tests. Her worst fears were realized. She was diagnosed with pancreatic cancer at an advanced stage. Only those who have been told such dreadful news could really understand how she felt. She would deal with it the best she could, but she was going to need a lot of help.

Ma couldn't bring herself to tell the children. She asked Meg if she would do it for her. Meg would do anything for her friend, even this. She gathered them all together so they could hear the bad news at one time. Sissy would not be told. Meg, as was her way, didn't pull any punches and gave them Ma's odds of survival, which were not good. She would not give them false hope but did tell them that Ma would immediately enter into a treatment program. M. J. was devastated. Once again they were all in shocked disbelief but at least this time they could prepare for it. After the initial shock wore off, they tried to pull themselves together and went to see their Ma.

The model agency called. They wanted to sign M. J. to a contract and send her to New York City for training. She refused, wanting to stay close to Ma. They never called her again.

Chapter 30: Billy

SEAN AND M. J. had turned seventeen and if not for Ma's battle with cancer they would have been blissfully happy.

A. J. McCleary had entered his last year of law school at DCL and had submitted his dissertation for his master's degree to the Physics Department at Wayne State University.

More and more he was being sought out by the international business community to act not only as an interpreter but as a consultant on import-export matters. He was becoming well versed in that portion of the law. All of this was still unknown to Sean's family and friends in the Zone.

For the first time Sean was being paid real money. Combining the funds his mother had left him with his growing personal bank account, he could now pay his own way without relying on Ma.

Skeeter, now twenty, was on target to graduate in January and was finishing up her teacher's certificate requirements.

She was chatting with Sean in the project room on a brisk October day and inquired where he stood on his projected graduation date. It had never occurred to her to ask him before, although he often checked on how she was doing.

"Ah, I'll graduate from Detroit College of Law this spring," he hesitantly answered.

"Law school! I thought you were just taking some outside courses there. What happened to Wayne State?" asked a surprised Skeet.

"Um, I already graduated from there a couple of years ago," he sheepishly said.

"What! Wait a minute. I know you were taking classes there last semester!"

"Yeah, that was for my master's degree. Look Skeet, can we keep this between ourselves. I have my reasons."

She was astounded! Then, remembering her discussions with Nettie, she merely looked at him in awe and shook her head.

"Of, of course Sean... man oh man... Jesus, man!"

There was new trouble in the Zone. Guns were fired but nobody got hurt. Rumors were that *somebody* had tried to forcibly evict people and a fight had ensued. Billy was investigating but he was getting nowhere. He would soon discover that Carlos was behind the trouble.

Carlos had set up a number of investment companies, all with different names. He had had various attorneys sign on as the resident agents and only their names appeared on the public record. Carlos was the sole owner of the companies.

The investment companies were successful over the past four years in acquiring real estate through tax sales, law suits, and outright purchases.

They now owned all but a handful of the real estate parcels in the Zone. Billy, Meg and Ma were three of the few individual property owners remaining. Soon they would be the *only* property owners in the Zone other than Carlos. Carlos had intentionally not approached them. He wanted to offer them high value for their places but he had to wait until he owned the others first. He didn't want to set a precedent that would jack up the prices.

His real estate purchases had gone undetected because nobody cared. His plan was to remove the tenants and bulldoze the vacant houses, but not all at once. He had no problem removing the drifters but when it came to the criminal residents who were not dealing in drugs, he was met with resistance. They were squatters and didn't want to leave. Carlos was not using the legal eviction process, but sent in his goons to strong-arm the resisters. He didn't want his companies to appear in court for fear that his ownership identity would be exposed. He had miscalculated the squatters' resolve and now he had a real problem on his hands. Further, he had yet to confront the dealers and their people who made up the majority of the residents in the Zone.

In early November, Carlos' goons had got themselves into a hornet's nest. They thought they were evicting a couple of tenants but discovered that the appointed house was full of armed and angry people. A gunfight broke out and people were hit.

Billy and his men heard the fight and rushed to the trouble spot. They pulled up in two cars, Billy was by himself in the second car. They had no idea what they were getting into. One of his men didn't follow police procedure and jumped out of the first car with his pistol drawn. He drew fire from the house, was hit and went down.

Billy ran to his man's aid, firing into the house to give him protection. He yelled to the other officer: "Drag him behind the car, I'll cover you." They almost made it but a volley of fire broke out from the house and Billy was hit. He staggered behind his police car and fell to the ground. The officer was on the phone calling for backup and an ambulance. Carlos' goons broke for their car, jumped in and sped away. At the sound of sirens the men in the house ran into the alley and disappeared.

Billy had taken two bullets, one to the stomach and one to the chest. It was serious. The paramedics arrived, treated him, then raced madly for the hospital.

By the time Meg, Sean and Skeet arrived, Billy was in surgery. M. J. had stayed back with Ma and the kids. Hours later, when he was wheeled into the recovery room, they talked to him briefly. The surgeon was confident that he would make it, but recovery would be long.

They visited him every day and Ma came when she wasn't too sick from her treatments. Billy asked Sean to take care of a legal matter for him and not to tell Meg for fear it would upset her. He had Sean prepare a deed signing his place over to Meg. He told Sean about his small pension and bank account explaining that Meg was the beneficiary on both of them. Sean looked at him anxiously and Billy said, "It's just a precaution, son. I'll be all right." Sean took care of it for him.

A few days later when Meg and Skeet went to Billy's room, he wasn't there. The nurse at the desk said he had been taken back to surgery. They hurried to the surgical waiting room sick with concern.

About an hour later the surgeon came out and said, "I'm sorry, there were complications. He didn't make it."

The family was crushed... they loved Billy. Skeet's heart was broken; she had lost her mentor and now her 'Uncle Billy' was gone. M. J., Sean and Little Bit were overwhelmed with grief. Ma was unconsolable; she had known Billy the longest. But It was Meg who suffered most. Billy was her man and she loved him dearly. Meg was in her early seventies and she now looked eighty. The Zone was destroying her. In the back of everybody's mind was Ma's battle with her cancer. Were they going to lose her next?

Chapter 31: Please... no more

THE POLICE WERE burying one of their own. There was a funeral procession for Billy. Police cars had lined up with flags fluttering in the cold late November wind as they proceeded to Billy's burial site in the Zone. Papa Joe, grieving once again, presided over the service of one of his beloved friends.

There was a huge turnout - almost as big as Nettie's. Billy had been in his mid-sixties and had no living family that anybody knew of. Meg, Ma, Papa Joe and the children were his family. They were obviously grieving, but not as openly as they had for Nettie's service. As though they were becoming desensitized.

Meg lingered at Billy's grave long after everyone else had left. She was deeply saddened but also angry. Her anger, directed toward the Zone, had begun to consume her. She purchased a burial plot next to Billy's.

The City acted swiftly, closing Billy's police station and sporadically dispatching patrol cars throughout the Zone. They were going to let the criminals settle their own differences. They had either foolishly failed to recognize the powder keg that was set to explode or they knew something that no one else did.

Meg, with her experienced eye, did recognize the pending disaster. She had seen it before but this time it was potentially a lot worse. There were more dangerous people living in the Zone now than at any previous time. Billy, the safety net, was gone and it appeared that the City and the dealers were comfortable with that.

She couldn't stop the inevitable disaster but she could take steps to protect the children.

It became apparent that Ma was going to lose her battle with cancer; she was not responding to the treatment and was declining. Her will to live may have died when Billy did. Meg didn't have to tell the children; they could see it themselves and were staying close to Ma.

Meg's plan was to assist the children in establishing a life somewhere away from the Zone. She knew they wouldn't leave until Ma had passed on and both Skeet and Sean had finished their schooling. Those events were imminent; she prayed that the children were away from the Zone before the storm enveloped them.

Meg knew that Sean was becoming self sufficient but Skeeter and Little Bit were going to need financial help. Ma had always insisted that Skeet concentrate on her studies and after school activities so she had never worked.

Ma had almost depleted Sebastian's gift. She had no insurance and was paying for the outrageously high costs of the chemotherapy drugs out of her pocket. Meg had Billy's small inheritance and was willing to give the kids what she could. However, she didn't know how much longer she was going to live or how much money she would need if she became sick or disabled.

The problem was resolved by the man in the suit knocking at Meg's door. Meg opened the door and the 'suit' said, "Good morning. Are you Ms. Brown?"

Meg nodded.

"I'm an associate of Carlos Marcos," he said, handing her his business card. The card identified him as an attorney.

"Mr. Marcos owns a real estate investment company that's investing here in the Zone and I represent that company," he politely stated. Meg just listened. Carlos no longer cared if anybody knew that he had bought the Zone. In fact, it now served his purpose; the dealers were put on notice.

"Our research shows that you own your home here, free and clear, and that Mr. William Donovan's property was recently transferred to you." Meg nodded and again said nothing.

"Ah. Our company would like to make you an offer to purchase both parcels. Mr. Marcos has made it clear that you are to be treated differently from the others we purchased from. We are prepared to offer you top dollar for your property and furthermore we will agree to reserve to you by deed the right to live here for the rest of your life or until you abandon your home."

Meg studied him carefully and said, "How much?"

The offer was more than generous and she accepted. It took just a few days and she had all the money she needed to get Skeet started with plenty left over for herself. She deposited the check into her only account and made A. J. McCleary the named beneficiary in the event of her death. She smiled for the first time in weeks. So did Carlos. He now owned everything in the Zone save for one parcel... Ma's.

Skeet had graduated with honors and was spending a lot of time applying for employment, using the school's placement department as her mailing address. Sean had received his master's degree from Wayne State and was set to take his law finals in early May. He would graduate at the end of that month and apply to take the Michigan bar exams in August. His family was now aware of his scholastic accomplishments.

Ma had slipped badly and it was obvious that she was near death. They had brought hospice care in and someone was always at her bedside. She wanted to get her meager estate in order and asked Sean to draw her a deed conveying the house over to him and M. J. This he did, putting it in A. J. McCleary and Martha Jean Munoz's names with joint rights of survivorship. M. J. never saw the deed but knew that she and Sean owned the house together.

Ma put Meg's name on her only bank account and told the kids about

Sebastian's money. There was not much left. She died two weeks later.

Ma's death was not a surprise and it was merciful, but it didn't ease the pain. The funeral ceremony was small. Most of Ma's friends were either dead or had left the Zone. At M. J.'s request, Ma was buried two gravesites away from Nettie. There were only three sites left adjacent to the chapel. Sean knew what M. J. had in mind and it frightened him.

Papa Joe once again struggled through a burial service of a loved one. The family stood numbly by as he performed the sad rites.

"They're dying too soon," lamented Papa Joe. "Too soon." Only Meg had been in the Zone longer than he had, and he was only in his fifties.

The children were now truly desensitized to death. The people they loved were dying and so was the Zone. It no longer felt like their home. They sensed it was time to move on; there was nothing here for them.

A few days after Ma's funeral, at Skeeter's request, they gathered at Ma's.

"I've accepted a job in Chicago," announced Skeeter. "I have to be there by the fifth of May!"

Everybody just looked at one another, not sure of what to say.

"Perfect!" shouted Sean. "And when you and Little Bit get settled and I finish my exams, M. J. and I are going to join you."

Skeet had been holding her breath. What could have been another sad moment had turned into a happy one. She looked at M. J. who was smiling and nodding her head. Skeet let out a whoop and ran to the both of them. "Thank you, thank you," she said, "I wouldn't be going if you hadn't said that!" They were joined by Little Bit in a group hug.

"Hey, what about me?" It was Sissy.

"You're coming too, little one," Sean said as he swung her to his shoulders. "We would never leave you."

"And what about Meg?" she cried.

"Meg stays here, honey," said Meg. "Somebody has to look after things, but I'll visit all the time."

"I'm going to hold you to that Meg," said a serious Skeeter.

"It's a promise, Skeeter."

Meg had taken Skeeter aside before Ma's death and told her: "I know you're looking for a job away from here, and if you find one, we have the money you need to get started."

After Skeet's announcement, Meg went to the bank and withdrew ten thousand dollars in cash and gave it to her.

A tearful Skeet said, "I'll pay you back Meg."

"If you're going to pay me back then you will have to pay Ma and Nettie also! Now how are you going to do that? It's not our money, Skeet, it's yours. You have earned it."

"Thank you, Meg. I won't lose it."

And the two women embraced.

Meg had been busy for days sorting through her records looking for documents and personal notes that might be of value to Skeet and her book. She found a lot of material and had Sean scan it into the computer and burn it onto a disc.

She included the entire scenario of Skeet's mother and aunt's fraudulent scheme. She had previously destroyed the document that contained Little Bit's real name. She deleted the name of A. J. McCleary on her copy of his birth authentication form. All of the injuries, rat bites and sicknesses through the years provided a snapshot of their history in the Zone. It would turn out to be crucial to Skeet when she eventually wrote her book.

Picking up certified copies of their birth certificates was on the Skeet's to-do list. Both she and Little Bit would need them to apply for social security numbers. Skeet had had no need for one in the past.

On the very day that she was to visit the Bureau of Vital Statistics, Sean plunked the computer down in front of her and said, "Skeet, take a look at this!"

'MASSIVE FRAUD SCAM AT THE BUREAU OF VITAL STATISTICS. HUNDREDS OF BIRTH CERTIFICATES MISSING' read the headline. It continued: 'Four people were indicted for creating fraudulent birth certificates. The alleged criminal activity of those indicted presumably led to the deletion of hundreds of the incriminating certificates from the records. Three of those indicted worked at the Bureau and were arrested. The fourth, who is still at large, was an outsider named Roberta Andrews.'

Skeeter paid the bureau a visit and, sure enough, her birth certificate and Little Bit's were not on record. She would have to deal with this new complication when they arrived in Chicago.

Communication was a problem. It wouldn't be resolved until Skeet and Little Bit settled in Chicago. The kids had never set up e-mail addresses and decided to wait until they were all together before doing so. They never had a good reason to go against Nettie's wishes until now, and besides, the girls did not have a computer. They would stay in contact by phone.

Rats had invaded Ma's phone lines again. Ma just gave up and canceled the service. Meg had a phone but no message system. It was decided that Skeet would contact Meg when they were settled. They would call in the evening knowing that Meg would be there.

IT WAS time to go. Meg, Papa Joe and Sissy said their goodbyes at the house. Meg and Papa Joe were ecstatic that the two girls were escaping the Zone. Skeet made Papa Joe promise to come with Meg when she visited; he gave his best Catholic pledge.

Skeeter and Little Bit kissed Sissy goodbye. Sissy wouldn't let go of Little Bit and held on tightly until Little Bit assured her that she would see her soon. Skeet and Little Bit hugged and kissed Papa Joe and Meg, fighting back tears.

Sean and M. J. walked their sisters to the train station. Skeet had her baseball cap on. The girls didn't have much to bring with them. Besides their clothes and personal items, they had Meg's discs, Skeet's research material also on discs, Skeet's diploma, some job applications and the framed photograph of their mother.

They stood on the train platform clinging to one another and crying. Little Bit couldn't let go of Sean.

"You behave yourself now," he told her. You're getting as pretty as your sister."

"Promise me you'll come as soon as you can," cried Little Bit.

"You know I will," he said, hugging her tightly.

M. J. and Skeet held each other without speaking. Finally M. J. said, "Here," and she handed Skeet her diary. "You be nice to me in your book now, Skeeter!" Skeeter pressed her lips tightly together and said, "I will."

One last hug, one last wave, as they stepped aboard the train.

"See you in a month!"

"Goodbye. I love you!"

Sean had his arm around M. J. as they walked back. He felt her sadness. "Hey, cheer up. We'll see them in a month or so."

M. J. said nothing but looked at him in a brooding way.

A few hours after Skeet and Little Bit left for Chicago, gunshots were heard somewhere in the Zone. About twenty minutes after that, there was pounding on Meg's door. She opened it and two unfamiliar men were standing there.

"Are you that midwife they call Meg?" asked one of them.

"Yeah, I am," she answered.

"Meg, we got a guy shot. Can we bring him in? He's hit pretty bad."

"Of course. Get him in here." She cleared the table as they were carrying him in. The victim was not badly hurt and she expertly stopped the bleeding and dressed his wounds. Curiously, his lips were turning blue and he was experiencing muscle spasms.

"What did you guys give him before he got here?" she cried.

"We had some morphine so we gave him some; he was in a lot of pain."

"JESUS CHRIST! You've OD'd him! Get him to the hospital right now or he's gonna die and it ain't gonna be from gunshot wounds!"

They loaded him into the back of a pickup and one of them rushed him to the hospital as the other two walked off.

The driver tried to leave the hospital after the orderlies carried the injured man off on a stretcher but was detained by security. A health department investigator was standing by and questioned the driver. The official was complimentary and wanted to know who had so expertly treated the victim.

"That midwife in the Zone. Think her name is Meg."

"Thank you," said Stanley Berman and he spun around and left. The security paid no attention to the driver who took off leaving a phony name. Two hours later, the victim died of a morphine overdose. Stanley went directly to the head of security.

Early the following morning, two men strode up the path to Meg's house. She saw them approach and greeted them at the door. They identified themselves as police detectives and Meg invited them in.

They got right to the point, "Ms. Brown, did you treat a man here yesterday for gunshot wounds?"

"Why, yes I did. I patched him up and told the people that brung him that they better get him to the hospital right away. They put him in the back of a pick up and took off, presumably for the hospital."

"Was he in serious danger from the gunshot wounds?"

"Actually, no," Meg replied, "but somebody gave him too much morphine and it looked like he was OD-ing to me, so I hurried them out of here."

"Did you give him any morphine while he was here."

"Certainly not!" exclaimed Meg. "I'm a midwife not a doctor!"

They questioned her further about the men and left.

One hour later they returned with a search warrant, placed her in custody and took her away.

Through his connections, Big George heard about the incident and made the short walk to the cemetery's chapel to inform Papa Joe.

Papa Joe went immediately to Ma's and found M. J. and Sissy waiting for Sean to come home. Sean was taking the last of his tests that morning and M. J. expected him home shortly.

Sissy had fallen down three or four days before scraping her knee. She had felt a sting on the back of her leg at the same time, but her knee hurt her so much that she forgot to report the sting to M. J.

Sissy was admiring a bright new bandaid M. J. had just placed on her when Sean walked in.

"Look at my new band aid that M. J. gave me, Sean," Sissy said, proudly pointing at it.

Papa Joe spoke up, "Sean, we've got a problem. The cops just picked up Meg and took her downtown."

"What! What for?"

"I don't know, but I figure you and I ought to get down there and find out what's going on!"

"Let's go." He kissed M. J. and said, "Take care of our wounded soldier. We'll get back as soon as we can!"

They were not given much information at the station, only that Meg was being held for questioning while the police gathered evidence. One of the

officers must have been a Catholic because she came up to Papa Joe and informed them that Meg was cooperating but was mad as hell.
While they were talking to the officer, a man walked past and glared at them. Sean nudged Papa Joe and said, "Weasel Face."
The officer snickered, and said, "I'll try to find out how long we're going to keep her," and walked away.
She returned and reported, "Ms. Brown will definitely be here overnight. We have a short window; we either have to release her or charge her with something by the day after tomorrow. I'm not at liberty to say more; you might as well go home." That night the phone rang continuously at Meg's but she wasn't there to answer.
Sissy got sick that same night. She was vomiting and had a fever. "Boy, she's picked up a virus someplace, Sean. If she's like this tomorrow, I'm taking her into the clinic. Damn, I wish Meg was here."
They put Sissy to bed and M. J., feeling glum, went to her desk, took out her music composition book and sat down.
"She'll be all right, babe. Kids get bugs like this all the time."
"Sean, I'm beginning to hate this place, let's leave as soon as possible."
"You bet. I'm finished with my finals; we can leave as soon as we hear from Skeet."
"Sean, please don't misunderstand this, but, if for some reason I can't finish my composition, will you complete it for me?"
A chill went through Sean; he knew how intuitive M. J. was.
"M. J. you're scaring me..."
"Please Sean."
"...Well, yes but..."
"Promise me."
"Okay, okay, I promise," and he took her into his arms.
"It's everything... all that has happened. Now Sissy's sick and Meg is in jail and we haven't heard from Skeet... I guess I'm just scared, that's all," sighed M. J. curling up tightly to Sean.
Trying to cheer her up, Sean asked, "What do you think of giving everybody a present when we turn eighteen?"
"Aren't they supposed to give us presents?"
"Yeah, but I thought our birthday would be a good time to announce our engagement."
"Is this your way of proposing?"
"Yes."
"Okay, I accept. It's a good thing we love each other or I would have said no. Hey, this is going to be fun!"
The next morning Sissy was worse and M. J. was getting ready to take her to the clinic when Meg walked up the path.
"Meg, what happened?" cried M. J.
"They released me - not enough evidence." She looked down at Sissy.

"She's sick, Meg. I was about to take her to the clinic."

Sean heard Meg's voice and came bounding down the stairs,

"Meg, what were...?"

Meg cut him off...

"How long as she been like this?"

"She got sick last night, fever, vomiting, and this morning she was complaining about having a headache."

"She's got an infection and it's serious." Meg tore Sissy's band-aid off. She examined the wound and said, "This ain't it; you did a good job patching her up, M. J." Then she conducted a body examination and when she turned Sissy over she spotted several small jagged red marks on the back of her leg.

"GOD DAMN IT, SHE'S BEEN BITTEN BY A RAT. SHE'S GOT RAT FEVER!"

M. J. gasped.

"Not your fault! I was here then too, remember, and I didn't see it either. LET'S GO!"

Sean gathered up Sissy and they raced to the four-lane street and hailed a cab. They were at the hospital in no time and Sissy was quickly admitted.

They were in the waiting room when a doctor came out. He knew Meg and said to her, "She's having a reaction to the penicillin. We're trying something else. It's not good. The infection has spread!"

M. J. put her head in her hands and sobbed, "No more, please no more." Sean just held her.

It wasn't long before the doctor returned. He compassionately looked at them and somberly said, "I'm sorry. She's gone."

There was no hysteria, only numbness.

They refused an autopsy and the next day Sissy was buried next to Ma in the gravesite nearest to the chapel. Only the three of them and Papa Joe were present.

Papa Joe could offer no spiritual blessings, only sad farewells. For the first time in his life he was beginning to question his faith. Meg was silent, tired and defeated.

Sean and M. J., numb, heads hanging, clung to each other as they sadly trudged back to an empty house.

They were not going to wait for Skeeter's call and planned to leave for Chicago as quickly as they could. They would get in touch with Carlos' investment company and sell the property to him for whatever he was willing to pay. Meg would be their contact in connecting with Skeeter and Little Bit.

That was *their* plan.

The Zone had other ideas.

Chapter 32: The War

EXCEPT FOR MA'S PROPERTY, Carlos owned the Zone. Out of respect for Ma's family, he'd give them time to deal with their grief before approaching them. He would be extremely generous and was not concerned that they might not accept his offer. He did not know that M. J. was a joint owner of the property along with one A. J. McCleary.

Carlos wasn't taking any chances. Through his intermediaries, the people who made the decisions in City Hall were informed of his plans for the Zone. Carlos' plan called for the total demolition of existing structures and the building of an office-residential complex. The development would bring millions in tax dollars to the city and a fortune to Mr. Marcos. The authorities were remaining silent in the background as Carlos prepared to evict everybody, including, and especially, the dealers. They reasoned that the amount of tax dollars was worth the risk of another drug war.

Carlos called for a meeting of all drug lords who had a presence in the Zone. He straightforwardly informed the bosses that he owned the property they were squatting on and that they would have to leave. As an incentive he told them that he was out of the drug business and he would turn over his entire operation to them. They could divide it any way that they wanted to.

The drug lords listened to his offer and stated that they were interested. They wanted to discuss the matter first with their lieutenants and said that they would get back to him in a few days with a firm answer.

Carlos had his firm answer the next day. His house on the river was blown up and burnt to the ground. The War was on.

A furious Carlos Marcos brought in a troop of well-armed men and positioned them in the many vacant houses in the Zone. The drug lords had joined together and provisioned a well armed group of thugs. This fight was going to happen and happen soon.

The morning after they buried Sissy all hell broke loose. M. J. had just retuned from meeting Papa Joe at the cemetery. She was making an arrangement for a small marker for Sissy's grave.

At first they heard the familiar popping noise of gunshots. Then suddenly gunfire seemed to be coming from everywhere in the Zone. Cars raced up and down the streets with their passengers shooting at one another. Fires were breaking out and the rat-tat-tat of semi-automatic weapons was constant. In a short period of time, the Zone became a raging battlefield with hundreds of combatants participating in the deadly conflict.

Sean and M. J. could see and hear the fight being waged. They were worried about Meg and knew that sooner or later her services would be demanded. They made the short dash to her place just as a car pulled up. It was some of Big George's men.

The car was riddled with bullet holes and, seeing Meg standing on her porch, they shouted out to her over the roar of the battle, "MEG, YOU GOT TO COME QUICK. WE'VE GOT PEOPLE DOWN AND THERE'S A BIG FIGHT BY THE CEMETERY!"

She grabbed her medical bag and was about to jump into the car when Sean intercepted her. "No, Meg. Wait until the shooting stops," he implored.

"MEG, THERE'S PEOPLE DYING. I THINK YOUR PRIEST FRIEND HAS BEEN HIT!" shouted one of Big George's men. That's all Meg had to hear. She brushed by Sean and jumped in the car and they sped off. M. J. screamed, "PAPA JOE! PAPA JOE!" and she took off in a dead run before Sean could stop her.

M. J. dashed between two oncoming cars and barely escaped from being hit. Sean waited for the cars to clear before he chased after her. He didn't see the third vehicle and it hit him a glancing blow and sent him whirling in the air. He landed face down opening up a huge cut on his forehead. His head was spinning and he had trouble focusing. He staggered to his feet and stumbled after M. J. as she raced down Big George's street, oblivious to the battle swirling around her. She ran the gamut as the combatants fired across the street at each other.

M. J. spotted Meg tending to a fallen man at the edge of the cemetery. "WHERE'S PAPA JOE?" she screamed.

"He's all right," said Meg pointing across the way.

Papa Joe knelt over some wounded men trying to help them. M. J. glanced around and saw dozens of men - dead or wounded - lying in and around the cemetery.

Meg looked up at M. J. and over the roar of battle she said, "Where's Sean?"

Realizing what she had done, M. J. knew that he would be coming after her. She looked down the street towards Big George's house.

Sean was half blinded by the blood from his head wound and was fighting to stay conscious as he ran as hard as he could, trying to catch up with M. J.

The fight was heavily engaged in front of Big George's house. Big George had fallen to the ground. A man came from nowhere and was pointing a gun straight at Big George's head.

The drama played out directly in front of Sean as he ran by. It was a matter of milliseconds and Sean just reacted. He kicked the gun out of the man's hand and followed that with a forearm shiver knocking the man to the ground and sending himself to his knees. BIg George jumped up, grabbed the gun and pumped several rounds into his attacker.

"SHE'S DOWN BY THE CEMETERY," yelled Big George.

Sean struggled to his feet and started for the cemetery. He could hear Big George shouting, "HEY... WE'RE EVEN, FERRARI!"

M. J. saw Sean, covered in blood, stumbling towards her and she ran toward him.

"NO, NO, NOT THERE!" someone yelled as M. J. ran into a blistering crossfire. Sean saw her coming and knew she wasn't going to stop and he, too, ran into the same withering fire.

M. J. was hit first and was spun completely around and landed on her side. Sean was hit and slid on his back coming to rest on his side facing M. J. She looked up at Sean and smiled softly; her eyes started to flutter then gently closed. Sean stared at her beautiful face. He tried to talk but couldn't. It was the last thing he remembered as darkness came over him.

The battle became fluid and moved up the street away from the fallen Sean and M. J. Meg saw it all and screamed to Papa Joe who was now near where she was working.

"PAPA JOE! HURRY! IT'S SEAN AND M. J. They've been hit," nodding in their direction. She got up and moved as fast as her seventy three year old body could take her, catching up with Papa Joe just as he got to them.

Papa Joe was on his knees, confused, not knowing what to do. Meg got there and felt for M. J.'s pulse; there was none. Sean was breathing but unconscious. She went to work on him; it was Nettie all over again.

"She's dead, Papa Joe," Meg said calmly and coldly; there was no feeling left in her soul. Papa Joe reached down and raised M. J. up so he could get his arms around her. He held her as he sobbed. Her arms dangled from her body, hands touching the ground. "Not my baby, not my baby," he said over and over.

The paramedics were just now rolling into the Zone and several stopped by the chapel, fifty yards from where they were. Meg waved frantically to them. Two medics jumped off of their vehicle, grabbed a gurney and hurried over.

"He's alive. Give me your clipboard," she demanded. As they were placing Sean on the gurney, she jotted down, 'SEAN FERRARI Blood type O positive severe concussion two bullet wounds both exited needs blood. I, Meg Brown, certify as to his identity' and she signed.

They loaded Sean and another wounded man into the truck and headed for the hospital. Meg went to help others. She would never remember doing so.

Papa Joe lifted M. J. and carried her to the chapel and laid her across his desk. He knelt down with his hands on hers and tried to pray through his tears.

The road outside the cemetery was full of bodies, both dead and alive. The carnage was everywhere. Police were now moving in and the war ended as quickly as it started. Several houses were still on fire but the shooting had stopped.

The ambulances started to pull into the Emergency entrance. Sean's was one of the first. A triage was quickly set up; it looked like a scene out of MASH. They would soon be swamped with patients. Mass confusion. The staff had no experience in wartime casualties. They didn't know who to take next as the gurneys kept coming.

The two orderlies wheeling Sean placed him in a line and were about to leave. One of them stopped and looked at the document that Meg had filled out. It was now enclosed in a plastic cover with a string attached. He stared at the name.

"What's up, Sammy, do you know him?" asked the other orderly.

"No, but I knew his mother. Come on." He wheeled the gurney straight into the area set up for temporary operations and said,

"Take him now, the others aren't as bad!"

They treated Sean's wounds, gave him some blood and moved him out of the way as the wounded were now pouring in. He was only given a small amount but enough to bring his count up. A lot of blood would be needed and they were rationing it.

They also needed his gurney. They unhooked him from his empty drip bag, picked him up and placed him on a stretcher tying his identifying document to it. They moved him into the triage area; there was no other place to put him. Sean was slowly regaining consciousness and trying to focus as he watched the commotion surrounding him. He was almost fully conscious now and was utterly confused. He had been there for two hours. Looking around at the chaos, it suddenly all came back to him. "NO! NO!" he cried and raised himself up off the stretcher.

He struggled to his feet and headed for the door. There were stretchers scattered around occupied by wounded and dying men. People were frantically racing about, too busy to notice or care. No one stopped him.

Two orderlies came out of the operating area into triage, spotted Sean's empty stretcher and said, "Hey, there's one." They went back into the room and lifted a light skinned Hispanic corpse from one of the tables. They placed him on Sean's vacated stretcher paying no attention to Meg's identifying document, still attached. They put a blanket over the body and delivered him to a temporary morgue.

Most of the bodies were not identified and the attendants were pleased that this one was. They immediately filled out their reports, getting the required information from Sean's previous medical records. Then they sent the body to the morgue. They knew Meg and accepted her verification identifying the body. A death certificate was ordered for one Sean Ferrari.

While Sean was being treated at the hospital, the Health officials had moved in quickly once the shooting had stopped. It was their job to identify the dead at the scene.

They were systematically lining the bodies up, using the cemetery as a temporary morgue. The corpses were being treated like book entries in an accounting ledger. This procedure was being handled without dignity or compassion. The supervisor was Mr. Stanley Berman - 'Weasel Face'. The perfect man for the job.

The temporary morgue stretched in front of the open chapel. Berman was meticulously going about his impersonal business when he noticed M. J.'s body laid out on Papa Joe's desk. Papa Joe and Meg were standing outside the chapel, both of them overwhelmed with fatigue and grief. Berman walked up to them and said, "Excuse me, but that body has to be placed down here with the rest of them."

Meg glared at Weasel Face and all the fury and hatred she harbored came boiling to the surface. She lunged at him with murder in her eyes. He sidestepped her and swatted her hands away sending the frail and worn out Meg tumbling to the ground. That was Papa Joe's breaking point. "YOU BASTARD!" he screamed. He grabbed Berman by the throat and shook him furiously choking the life out of him.

Two police officers saw what was happening and rushed over. With great difficulty they separated Papa Joe's hands and Berman fell to the ground. His face had lost all color and he was gasping for breath. Papa Joe rushed over to Meg and helped her up. The two went back into the chapel and he sat her down on one of the chairs. She refused to cry. Berman had caught his breath and was ranting, "I WANT THAT MAN ARRESTED FOR ATTEMPTED MURDER! You guys saw the whole thing. Now do your jobs!"

"Yes we did," said one of the officers. "And what we saw was you knocking down an old lady and the priest coming to her aid. Now may I suggest, Mr. Berman, that you get out of here right now before we arrest YOU!"

"So that's the way it is, huh? Well you guys haven't heard the end of this!" He stormed off and left the cemetery.

They sat in the chapel in total despair. Meg and Papa Joe. Neither one spoke. Papa Joe put a blanket over M. J. and didn't know what to do next.

He heard a scuffling at the door, looked up and saw a pale and heavily bandaged Sean standing there wearing an orderly's shirt over his blood-covered jeans. Both he and Meg stood up as Sean, with great effort, walked slowly over to the desk and pulled the blanket from M. J.'s face. Sean looked at her for a long while, sagged, and Papa Joe caught him. He put Sean down in the chair that he had just vacated and both Meg and he did their best to comfort him. Sean cried silently as he retreated to his inner sanctuary.

Finally, Sean got up, put the blanket back over M. J.'s face and said,

almost inaudibly: "Come on, lets go home Meg," and they left.
A little while later a man from the health department detail came into the chapel. He addressed Papa Joe. "Father Joseph, I'm Wayne Stover. We at the department knew M. J. and Sean. We'll take her to the coroner's office and prepare the body if you wish. I will see to it that she is placed in a burial casket and I promise to have the body returned here tomorrow morning. We'll bring her identification papers with us. She will be dressed properly, Father. We hate that son-of-a-bitch, Berman, too," he added.
Papa Joe looked at him and said, "Thank, thank you, Mr Stover; we would like that." He was softly sobbing and Wayne put his arm around him, patted his hand and left.
Sean and Meg walked slowly back to Meg's place. Once inside she laboriously sank into her favorite stuffed chair. Sean pulled up a kitchen chair and sat beside her, weak, numb and unemotional. He was functioning only by sheer determination. Amazingly, he was able to suppress his grief and stay in the present.
She looked at him with her tired reddened eyes and said, "Sean, this place is evil. It must be destroyed. She reached over and grasped his hand. Sean, you must promise me that you will DESTROY the Zone... Promise me!"
Her look was so intense and penetrating that Sean had no choice. He didn't see how he could do it, but he knew that she was right.
"I promise Meg. I promise," he said softly.
"Good. Only you can do it, Sean. Only you. Don't let those evil people profit from their crime, Sean. Don't let them... win."
"I might need your help, Meg."
"I'm tired and used up, Sean. There is nothing left for me...nothing."
"Meg!"
"No Sean, let me go with the others... they're waiting."
... "Okay," he whispered, and slowly got to his feet. He kissed her on the forehead and said, "I'll look in on you later Meg. I love you."
Sean returned to his place and sat wearily down. He lay his head back and went inside his body and commenced his own internal healing process. It was early evening now and Papa Joe had entered Ma's house. Sean was still sitting in his chair lightly dozing. Papa Joe gently awakened him.
"I'm sorry, Sean, but I wanted to tell you the arrangements that I've made for M. J."
"Sure Papa Joe, please..."
Papa Joe explained everything and Sean sadly responded,
"Okay, I'll be there first thing in the morning and we will wait for them together."
"How's Meg, Sean?"

"She wants to die, Papa Joe, and I think she will find a way to do it."
"You mean..."
"We better go check on her," said Sean. He was eerily calm. "We should be prepared."
They found Meg still sitting in her chair - head tilted forward and a hypodermic needle on the floor.
"Oh Mary Mother of Mercy," cried Papa Joe. He prayed over her for some time. Sean was lost in his own thoughts. How much more could either one of them take?
They placed Meg on the bed and covered her with a blanket. That night her phone rang and rang.
Sean hadn't arrived yet when M. J.'s body was delivered to the chapel the following morning. Papa Joe directed the men to place the casket on the stand he used for burial services. He signed M. J.'s identification papers; the department would file the death certificate.
"Father Joseph, what do you want me to do with the other body?"
"What other body?" asked Papa Joe.
"We have another burial casket and Mr. Stover directed us to drop it off here. He said that you would know what to do with it."
"Oh, okay. Just lay it on the ground over there," said a puzzled Papa Joe. He walked over to the other burial casket and examined the documentation taped to the top of it.
He jerked back and exclaimed, "My god!" The name on the papers read: 'SEAN FERRARI'.
Sean showed up ten minutes later and apologized for being late.
"Sean, there's something you should see," said Papa Joe.
"Whoa!" exclaimed Sean as he read the documentation on the casket. In addition to the name, It stated that a death certificate had been issued on the day prior. Sean shook his head and went over to M. J.'s casket.
The cemetery buzzed with activity. Bodies were still lined up waiting for identification and the workers were busy with their backhoes digging graves. There were empty burial caskets stacked one on top of the other. If nobody claimed the bodies, they would be buried without preparation. There were too many of them - over one hundred had been killed and others could possibly die in the hospital. Embalming was not required by law and the burial caskets were designed to stop the spread of infections.
Papa Joe had arranged with the department to bring Meg's body over to the chapel. Sean decided not to view M. J. in her casket. He wanted to remember her as she had been in life, but after the mix up with Sean Ferrari's remains, he changed his mind. Both he and Papa Joe opened the casket and silently said their goodbye's to M. J.
Sean stood quiet for several minutes, then said,
"Papa Joe, I want to have two graves prepared up here. One for M. J.

next to Ma and the other one for Sean Ferrari, to be placed between M. J. and Mom."

Papa Joe looked at him quizzically, but said nothing.

Sean, reading Papa Joe's mind, shakily said, "Sean Ferrari died when M. J. died. That person is no longer alive and he should be buried with the rest of them."

The two men looked at each other and then Papa Joe said, "All right, how do you want to do this?"

They opened the other man's casket with Sean's name on it, lifted up the corpse and placed him in line with the others awaiting identification. "It's only right," said Papa Joe. "Now maybe his family will find him."

The workers dug the two graves and, using a fork lift, lowered both caskets, one of them empty, into their proper sites and filled in the dirt around them. Sean and Papa Joe stood at M. J.'s graveside and silently kept to their own thoughts. They would be doing the same thing with Meg later on during the day as she would be laid to rest next to Billy.

The brutal and heartbreaking day was still not over. Papa Joe had visitors from his diocese who took him aside for a private talk. Then they left.

"What was that all about?" asked Sean.

"It appears that Weasel Face is going to get the last laugh," said a somber Papa Joe. "He has told Church officials that I tried to kill him. The Bishop wants me to leave."

"WHAT? That's ridiculous!"

"No, it's true, Sean."

Papa Joe gave him the details. "If those cops hadn't pulled me off, I would've killed him. I've lost my way, Sean, and I know it. I can no longer perform my duties here or anyplace else. They are right to move me out."

"But, but where will you go? What will you do?"

"They suggested that I do missionary work, but I must remain in seclusion until, if and when, they're ready to accept me back."

"Seclusion! What does that mean?"

"It means that the Church will treat me like I'm not part of their team and I won't be. They will say that I'm no longer in the service of the Church and they will tell no one where I'm doing missionary work because they won't know themselves. I'm supposed to have chosen this voluntarily, and I guess that's true. The alternative is to leave the Church forever."

"When is all this going to happen?"

"It's already happened, Sean. The Church must move quickly. They don't want an investigation of one of their priests who's been accused of trying to kill someone! Sean, I agree with them. I need this for myself. I must get away from this awful place."

"How will we stay in touch?" asked Sean, alarmed.

"You won't be able to reach me but I will keep track of you, Mr. A. J. McCleary."

"Sean, you're not alone. Skeet and Little Bit are out there waiting for you. Thank god they left when they did. Like me, there's nothing to keep you here."

Nothing except for a promise to Meg, thought Sean, and I will keep that promise.

Chapter 33: Skeet and Little Bit

SKEET AND LITTLE BIT arrived in Chicago the day before Meg was held for questioning by the Detroit police. They were tired and upset about leaving their family and intimidated by the bustling City of Chicago. A reasonably priced hotel was found within walking distance of Skeet's new place of employment. The girls intended to call Meg's the following evening reasoning that they would have more information by then.

The next morning Skeet was at the office of her new advertising company. Little Bit waited in the lobby. This was to be an administrative morning and then the two would be free to find a temporary place to live. It would also give Skeeter time to get her social security situation cleared up.

"Good morning. I'm Abrianna Charles; I have an appointment with Brenda in Human Resources," said a perky Ms. Charles. The receptionist looked at her peculiarly and said, "Just one moment," and she called somebody to the front desk.

A young man, not much older than Skeet, came out.

"Hi, I'm Rob from Human Resources, won't you please come back, Ms. Charles," and he led her to his office.

"Look, Brenda no longer works here. I guess she didn't have time to inform you that your position has been closed due to reorganization. I still have your application and I will keep it on file. If that spot opens up, you will be the first one we will call. I'm sorry."

Skeet was speechless as he led her back to the lobby. She and Little Bit trudged back to their hotel.

"Now what do we do, Skeet?"

"I brought these back-up applications just in case something like this happened," Skeet said as she spread them out on the table.

"We've got access to a phone here and I'm going to start calling and, if we have no luck, we'll rent a cheap room and I will start pounding the pavement tomorrow. They won't beat us, Little Bit!"

"I love your spirit, big sister. And Meg's money," she said making them both laugh.

"My first call is going to be Los Angeles. That's the job I *really* wanted. They were looking for an assistant TV script writer, and I know they were interested in me. I think they wanted to hire a woman of color. They wrote back and asked me to send them a copy of all the scripts I worked on in college. I did, but told them not to mail me anything because we were moving. I gave them Meg's number for a contact."

She made the call to Hollywood and her eyes widened, "Yes, yes, I do," she said excitedly. "But I'm coming from Chicago. I have to know for sure! Thank you, thank you. Ten days. Okay I'll call the moment I get in...

no, no... I'll call before then. Thank you Ms. Collins."

She hung up and threw the papers in the air jumping up and down, pumping her arms, "YES! YES!"

"What? What? Tell me! Tell me!"

"They were just going to call me. They WANT TO HIRE ME TO BE AN ASSISTANT SCRIPT WRITER! I talked to the head person herself. We're going to L.A., Little Bit. Yes, yes, YES!"

Little Bit was happy but confused. "Skeet, what about Sean and M. J. and Sissy? L.A.'s a lot farther than Chicago."

Skeet hesitated and said, "Little Bit, we won't need all of Meg's money and we will take the bus to California because it's so much cheaper. After my first paycheck we'll send them plane tickets. We can afford that and we'll have a place for them to stay where it's warm!"

"Wow, okay," said Little Bit. "I knew you would come up with something. Hollywood here we come!"

That night they called Meg: no answer. Meg was spending the night in jail. The next morning they boarded a bus for Los Angeles. It would take almost three days to get there but that was all right. Skeet's job wouldn't start for ten days. They had no way of knowing that Sissy had died that day from her rat bite.

Skeet and Little Bit were thirty two hours into their trip and the bus had stopped for dinner. It was 7:00 p.m., eastern time zone. Skeet was looking for a pay phone to call Meg, but had no luck. She would call the following evening. Sissy had been buried that day.

The following evening at 9:00 p.m. eastern, the bus again stopped for dinner. Skeet did find a pay phone and excitedly phoned Meg's. There was no answer. Meg was dead. The War had started that day and it made the national news. The girls were too tired to read newspapers or to watch TV and completely missed the coverage.

They arrived in L.A. the day M. J. and Meg were buried. The two weary travelers found a hotel and went to bed. It wasn't until the following morning that they heard the two day old news.

Skeet had called Ms. Collins that morning and informed her that she had arrived. During the conversation Skeet was asked,

"Aren't you from Detroit?"

"Yes I am."

"Boy, I bet you were happy to get out of there before that drug war started," said Ms. Collins innocently.

"What drug war?" replied an alarmed Skeet.

"We've been traveling for days!"

"Oh Abrianna, it's been all over the news. Hundreds have been killed."

"WHERE IN DETROIT?"

"Well, wait a minute. I've got yesterday's paper right here... lets see, here we go, I'll read it to you: 'The fighting took place in a notorious drug

section of Detroit known as the Zone.' Do you know where that is, Abrianna?"
Skeeter gasped, "That's my home Ms. Collins. That's my home. I... I'll call you back."
"Of course, I'm sorry. I sure hope your family is all right, please call me, anytime."

Skeet told Little Bit what had happened and they both anxiously hit the hotel computers searching for stories on the war. They read everything possible and the only name that they recognized was Carlos Marcos. It was reported that he started everything and was being sought for questioning by the authorities.
"Good luck," muttered Skeet.

Skeet phoned Meg again, but still no answer. Later that evening they tried once more to reach her with the same result. After failing to reach Meg the following morning, Skeet became worried. She tried to contact Papa Joe and was informed that Father Joseph was no longer associated with the University.

Skeet was flabbergasted. She then called the head of the journalism department, Victoria, who was a friend of hers, and asked if she could confirm the report that Father Joseph had left the University. Victoria did confirm the report. She further stated that the school had no forwarding address on Father Joseph. Skeet was at a dead end and trembled at the thought of what she had to do next.

Skeet went on line and searched the public records for reported deaths that week in Detroit. She started with M. J. and found her name on the list. She gasped, burst into tears and was too shaken to look further. With grim trepidation, a tearful Little Bit summoned the courage to search for Sean. When his name came up she cried out in agony. "Sean is NOT dead. He is not dead! No. NO ! I refuse to believe it. Not Sean. NOT MY SEAN!"

They were powerless to console each other in their mutual suffering. It was two days before they could bring themselves to finish their gruesome task. They found Meg and Sissy's names on the list. Their entire family had been wiped out. Now Skeet and Little Bit only had each other. There was no other place for them to go and nobody to talk to.

The girls numbly set about to find a place to rent that was reasonable and close to Skeet's work. When they found one, they unpacked and discovered that the glass on their mother's picture frame had broken. Skeet was taking it apart and found two folded documents behind Sandy's photograph. She unfolded them and was astonished to find two original birth certificates. One was in the name of Monica Wilson and the other was for Jessica Watson.

The two girls just looked at each other. They examined the dates, noticed Meg's signature on Jessica's document and instantly knew that

these were their original birth certificates.
"Why did she keep these, Skeet?"
"I don't know."
"Maybe she really did love us," whispered Little Bit. "Maybe my mother *did* love me."
"Maybe," shrugged Skeet.
Skeet would file for her social security in the name of Monica Wilson and she also enrolled Jessica in the program. They would go by those names for the rest of their lives.

Chapter 34: The Zone Was Dead

THE ZONE LOOKED like a combat zone. There were burned out houses everywhere. One third of the homes were destroyed or damaged beyond repair. Many of the remaining structures were bullet ridden with blown out windows.

There were only about fifty people still living there. Sean was one of them. There was no sign of Big George or his people. Sean had no idea where they had gone. Actually, he didn't recognize a single person living in the Zone.

Sean was lonely and kept glimpsing ghosts of his family as he moved around the house. M. J. was always in his thoughts. He became reclusive; but by using the skills his mother had taught him, he successfully fought off despondency and depression. Yet, just being at Ma's was too painful so he spent most of his time away from the Zone.

Sean could afford to move elsewhere but he had two good reasons for maintaining his residency at Ma's. First, he felt that he was going to have to actually live in the Zone in order to bring the kind of legal action that he had in mind. Second, he expected Skeet to return to the Zone one day and he wanted to be there when she did.

Determined to locate his sisters, Sean even took out an expensive ad in the Chicago Newspapers. He filed lost person reports on line hoping by chance that one of them would see it. He cross-checked names and addresses, checked with Skeet's school placement office - no luck. He searched the Chicago schools for an Eboni Jackson.

Sean wished they had discussed details of Skeet's job. He only knew that she was with an advertising firm. None of the agencies he contacted had heard of her. He was going to need government help to access private information.

He realized that Skeeter would have been unable to contact Meg. She would have checked the death records after learning about the war, so believing he was dead, would not search for him. He suspected that she had been stonewalled in her efforts to contact Papa Joe. Sean, though frustrated and close to a dead end, refused to give up.

GRIEVING, BUT DETERMINED, Sean graduated from law school and passed the bar exam. He was sworn in and began doing international trade work utilizing his language skills and earning a living. He still lived in the Zone and was working on his promise to Meg.

Soon after the drug war, Sean observed an unusual amount of activity in one of the larger houses still standing in the Zone. He and M. J. used to play there; it had been vacant for years. On occasion he would now secretively spy on the house from another vacant building. He wasn't sure what he was looking for, but he had developed a real hatred for the dopers. If they returned to the Zone he would confront them.

A white man regularly accompanied the blacks and Hispanics as they constantly came in and out of the house. Sean was now certain that this was a dope operation and he assumed that the white guy was the money man.

One day the white man was roughly escorted into the house by two Hispanic men - one, bald, clean-shaven, vaguely familiar. Sean could see that the man's hands were tied behind his back and the bald Hispanic had rammed a gun into his ribs. Something set off alarms in his head and he had to get closer for a better look.

He knew this particular two story house inside and out. They had climbed all over its rafters as kids and he was aware of all the cracks and openings in the walls and ceilings. He entered the house unseen. All three men were upstairs.

One man was nervously peering out the large framed window like he was expecting somebody.

Sean could now clearly see the bald man from his rafter hiding position and he almost swung down from his perch to get at him. Sean would never forget that face no matter how much it had changed. It was *Enrico*!

The white man was tied to a chair and Enrico was pistol whipping him. "WHAT! You didn't think we knew that you were an UNDERCOVER DICK? HUH, HUH!" and he hit him again and again.

"My friends are really going to enjoy seeing your brains SPLATTERED all over this room," he shouted, raising the pistol to the helpless man's head.

A large amount of cash was piled on a desk and a stack of what looked like cocaine bundles was heaped in a corner: the mother lode. This guy was in big trouble.

Sean had to act quickly if he wanted to nail Enrico and save the man's life. He knew how to get into the adjoining room undetected. He had done it many times before when hiding there, waiting to scare the bejesus out of M. J. In seconds he had lowered himself into the other room and immediately made his move. Sean only knew one way: go in, go fast, don't hesitate.

He burst into the room where the three men were located, surprising his prey. He hit Enrico with a crushing blow knocking him flat on his back. Without breaking stride he grabbed the other Hispanic - it was Jorge - as he was reaching for his gun. Sean lifted him off his feet and threw him through the large window taking out everything but the frame. Jorge landed face first two stories below.

Then he turned his attention to Enrico. He had staggered to his feet and lost his gun. Sean pummeled him with hard purposely aimed blows to the face, turning it into pulverized flesh. Enrico was being driven

straight back but Sean would not let him fall.
"REMEMBER ME?" Sean screamed. "REMEMBER ME? HOW ABOUT MY MOTHER? SHE HAD GREEN EYES!"

He could see the recognition in Enrico's eyes as the last blow sent him tumbling out the same window that his brother had exited. Sean had literally thrown both men out the fucking window. M. J. would have been proud.

Sean peered out. The brothers lay motionless below. A car had pulled up. The occupants must have witnessed Enrico's flight. They turned around and sped away, squealing their tires in the process.

Enraged and breathless, he tried to calm himself turning his attention to the badly beaten, but conscious, man.

Sean untied him and said, "Who do you want me to call besides an ambulance?"

"Can you get my cell phone; it's in the drawer." Sean found it and handed it over. With shaking hands, the injured man managed to make the call he wanted to.

"All right, you can call the paramedics now - for them, not for me," he said, nodding in the direction of the shattered window. Sean made the call, retrieved a wet towel from the bathroom and tried to clean the man's battered face.

"Who are you?" he asked Sean through puffy lips.

"I could ask you the same question. I hope you're a cop or those guys are going to come back."

"I am. I'm not-so-undercover Agent Steve Lowenstein, FBI," he said extending his hand.

"A. J. McCleary. I live in the neighborhood."

"You're kidding! I take it you know those guys?"

A. J. didn't answer. They heard sirens and soon there were men running up the stairs.

"Jesus, Steve, nice fight but you shouldn't have been so rough. We wanted to question those guys. Who's your friend?" asked a burly man as he entered the room. The next fifteen minutes were used for explanations and introductions. The paramedics arrived, patched up Steve and took the brothers away. Miraculously, they were still alive.

"A. J., here's my cell phone number. How can I reach you?" inquired a grateful Steve Lowenstein.

"There might be a substantial reward. There's maybe six million in cash here and millions more in street value cocaine. I will make sure you're considered for the reward if it's available. There's always a turf fight for these kinds of things."

"Okay," said A. J. "Look, I may call you on another matter that you might be able to help me with. If nothing else we can have lunch."

"It's a deal," said Steve. "Call me anytime."

The two men did have a meeting. A. J. needed to talk to Lowenstein. "Well, you're looking better than the last time I saw you, Steve," grinned A. J. "Yeah, well, thanks to you, people can still see me."

The two had an instant liking for one another and chatted amiably as they were enjoying their coffee.

"Look, we like to know everything. My people did a surface check on you and it turns out that you're an attorney. I never would have pegged you as a lawyer. Those guys usually run from fights. Our records show that you recently purchased a home in the Zone, and that's as far as they took it."

"Some investigators!" replied A. J. "Tell them to dig deeper. Steve, I need some favors. If you can't do it, that's okay."

"I owe you big time, A. J. Trust me; I'll make the effort."

A. J. leaned forward and said, "Several investment companies own all the property in the Zone. I'm convinced that the same man is the owner of all the stock in those companies. I think you know him; his name is Carlos Marcos. He cleverly keeps his name off of the public records but he spreads the word that *he* is the companies. I need proof of that. Any suggestions?"

"Okay. That's an easy one. Marcos *is* the sole stockholder to those companies. I'll give you the name of the attorney who drew up the papers for Marcos. He turned pigeon and is working for us. I'll make sure he cooperates with you."

"Thanks. Now here's the tough one. My two sisters are missing. There is no foul play; we have just lost contact. Long story. Their names are, Abrianna Charles, age twenty one, and Eboni Jackson, age thirteen. Both are very attractive with dark hair. The last I knew, they were in Chicago."

"That's it?" asked Steve. "Let's see, two young Caucasian girls last seen in Chicago. Right?" he said facetiously.

"Ah, not quite," said A. J. "They're black."

"Oh, I see, you mean soul sisters."

"No, I mean sisters."

Steve looked him and said, "Just who the hell are you, McCleary?"

"I'm an attorney, remember?" laughed A. J. "Oh, one other thing, they won't come looking for me. They think I'm dead."

"Do I want to know about that?"

"No."

A. J. HAD THE last bit of evidence he needed for a law suit he had been working on for months. He had to tie all the investment companies together as a single entity, and that entity was Carlos Marcos. A. J.'s recorded deed showed that he was the surviving owner of the only property the investment companies didn't own. It would give him standing to sue on the many counts contained in his complaint. He filed the suit. It rocked the city. The news services reported in front page headlines that:

'CIVIL SUIT FILED AGAINST CITY TODAY IN CIRCUIT COURT BY A RESIDENT OF THE ZONE'

'The City, Individual council members, Health Department, Police Department, Fire Department, and other governmental agencies, several private investment companies, Carlos Marcos and six other known drug dealers were some of the named defendants.

More serious counts alleged in the complaint are set forth below, they are:

1. City officials conspiring with the named known drug dealers to grant them a safe haven from proper searches and police investigations

2. Denial of the residents' rights to basic services

3. Inadequate and insufficient police protection directly resulting in the deaths of dozens of residents

4. Unsafe and hazardous sanitation conditions leading to sicknesses and rat bites resulting in death and disabilities to the residents

5. Investment companies conspiring with city officials for favorable treatment for a takeover of properties within Zone number 87

6. Negligence by the City in not taking measures to prevent the recent drug war when they had sufficient notice. Such negligent action resulted in death and injuries to residents.'

The suit named many city officials, not as co-conspirators, but charging them with a breach of duty to the public, abuse of power, and malfeasance of office. The Health Department was particularly targeted, with one agent, Mr. Stanley Berman, cited on specific counts.
It further stated that the investment companies and known drug dealers should not profit by their illegal actions.

The suit went on described how the above actions and government conduct adversely affected the plaintiff's real property rights, denying him the use and enjoyment of his home and making his residence untenable and a dangerous place in which to live. In addition to actual damages, the plaintiff also asked for punitive damages.'

A. J. knew that the defendants might get some of the counts summarily dismissed, but he filed them anyway. He also recognized that he couldn't prove punitive damages on many of the allegations. His real goal was to get the public in an uproar and force the defendants, who feared exposure, to negotiate.

And what an uproar it caused! News of the allegations was splashed all over TV stations and the internet. City officials were being bombarded with questions that they feebly tried not to answer.

The immediate response was to send patrol car after patrol car into the Zone where no more than a dozen people now resided. The Zone was no longer a convenient place for criminals to live.

The streets were barricaded as the health department declared that it was a threat to the health of the public to go into the Zone.

Protests groups stormed City Hall demanding that something be done about the rats.

Politicians seized the moment and demanded the scalps of their political enemies who were now in power. There was a clamor for sub-committees to investigate administrative abuse of power.

The drug dealers were moving out and Carlos Marcos was reported to have fled to South America.

The most dramatic consequences to the civil action filed by A. J., were the *criminal* indictments of Carlos Marcos and his drug friends on numerous charges. The prosecutor's office had cleaned house and a new and aggressive set of young guns were trying to make a name for themselves. While the long-tailed rats of the zone were causing concern for the public, other rats were suddenly coming out of the woodwork supplying incriminating testimony against the drug dealers.

Enrico and Jorge had survived and turned informers, now willing to testify against their former friends in exchange for reduced sentences. They had been convicted on drug charges. They never were charged in the murder of Nettie; there were no corroborative eye-witnesses alive to testify against them.

STEVE AND A. J. were enjoying one of their regular lunch meetings and talking about police work when Steve said, "Oh by the way, there won't be any reward for the bust. The City has demanded we turn the money over to them. We're in a real turf fight over the cash. Sorry. If anything changes I'll let you know."

Steve and A. J. were becoming the best of friends. Steve had started a nation wide search for Skeet and Little Bit. He reported that the girls had no birth certificates or social security numbers, no phone numbers and no credit cards. "And we don't even have a picture of them. It's like they fell off the face of the earth," said an exasperated Steve.

A. J. thought about it and said, "Steve they've somehow discovered their real names and are using them." He then had to explain Sandy and Roberta's scam to him. That gave Steve his first lead and he was hot after Roberta.

A week later Steve met A. J. for lunch. He brought his girlfriend, Amy, and her stunning blond cousin, Helena, along, hoping that she and A. J. would hit it off.

"I found Roberta, A. J. She's in Cleveland, but she won't be able to help. She's dead - a drug hit."

"Great, back to square one," said a disappointed A. J.

"Do you remember a fire in the Zone about eight or nine years ago?" asked Steve.

A. J. nodded.

"We were doing satellite surveillance of the dopers then and videoed the whole thing. Any chance your sisters might have been caught on our cameras? Pictures would help."

"Yes, there's a good chance... Steve, I just thought of something. A photographer shot some pictures of a, ah, a friend of mine for a modeling role. All of us were in one of the pictures and it's not that old. The agency is located down by the river. The model's name was M. J. Munoz."

"Great, I'll check it out."

"Look, I gotta run," said a suddenly glum A. J. "Nice to meet you Amy, Helena. Call me if you get anything, Steve. Thanks for all the work," and he left.

"Was it something I said?" sighed Helena.

CARLOS' CRIMINAL CASE took a sudden turn. He had cut a deal with the District Attorney's office regarding the charges brought against him. Carlos agreed to supply the evidence needed to convict local public officials who for years had been on the take. A plea bargain was entered. In return for Carlos' incriminating testimony, some of his felony charges would be reduced to misdemeanors and others reduced to third degree felonies. He would serve no jail time and could safely return to the U.S. However, he would be required to transfer all of his real estate holdings in the Zone to the City. The prosecutors agreed that no drug dealer should profit from his crimes.

This new development in the criminal case gave A. J. an opportunity to settle his civil suit and he pounced. He offered a settlement wherein he would agree to dismiss his suit against all of the defendants releasing them from any liability.

In return, he demanded that the City completely raze all buildings in the Zone, exterminate the rats and change the zoning so the land could be used only for a public benefit and not for profit. Further, the cemetery was to be permanently maintained by the city.

For himself personally, as compensation for his damages, and his attorney's fees, he wanted one million dollars. He would, however, in lieu of cash, accept a lien for that amount to be placed on the property formerly described as the Zone. If his lien was not extinguished within a one year period, the property would then be deeded by operation of law outright to him.

It was a fair deal and the government officials accepted it. They could not chance a jury trial. All parties agreed to the settlement offer.

SKEET AND LITTLE BIT were slowly adapting to their new environment and trying to put the Zone behind them. They were dealing with their immense loss and courageously moving on.

Little Bit attended public school for the first time and excelled. She never gave up hope that her Sean was still alive. She couldn't sense that he was dead. However, she did not pursue a search, nor did she check to see if someone was searching for her.

Skeet was doing well in her new job and had begun to write her book. She googled Detroit and discovered that the Zone was about to be demolished as a result of a court settlement. She backtracked the news and was able to follow highlights of the suit.

She paid little attention to the parties and had no need to go into the court files. The captioned reporting provided all the information that she needed to complete her book. Skeet was delighted that the Zone was going to be used for a public purpose. At least now she could have a positive ending to her family's story.

A few days after Monica read about the Zone's demise, Nancy Collins came into her office and said, "Hey, we're sending a writer to Detroit to help on a project. I know you're from Detroit. You interested?"

Skeeter caught her breath. She wasn't sure she was ready for that but she knew that she had to bring some closure to her life in the Zone. A trip to the cemetery would do it.

"Yes Nancy, I would like to go," sighed Skeet.

"Good. A week from tomorrow. I'll have Flo make the arrangements."

A. J. STOOD in the cemetery, facing away from the graves of his family, watching bulldozers topple over building after building like they were made of matchsticks. Thousands of rats scurried for their lives; a sanitation crew hosed them down with poison as they tried to escape. Everything was being demolished and removed, including the roads, utilities, and sewers. At A. J.'s request, Ma's house would be the last building to be demolished. He thought it appropriate that his family home should outlast all the others. It stood for everything that the Zone did not.

When the demolition process was complete, other than the cemetery, the land was entirely barren. Traffic on all four-lane boulevards was visible. Nothing was left standing, not even the chapel. There were no rats. The Zone was dead.

In his mind, A. J. relived his life in the Zone as he gazed out at the emptiness. Shaking his head, he softly uttered under his breath, "A promise kept, Meg."

A. J. HAD DECIDED to practice law in Washington D.C. where all his international clients were. No longer was there any reason for him to stay. Clearly Skeet would not be returning to the Zone; it was now two years since she and Little Bit had left for Chicago.

He rented a small storage locker in downtown Detroit. It held the piano keyboard, the obsolete computer, his penny whistle and M. J.'s uncompleted music composition. On the locker's shelf, he placed the envelope Steve had given him containing the satellite video of the parade on the day of the fire and M. J.'s modeling photograph collection. There was nothing left to do but leave.

Steve drove A. J. to the airport. It was A. J.'s twentieth birthday.

Skeet, aboard a plane flying into Detroit, was musing over the fact that it was July 7th, M. J.'s and Sean's birthdays. She smiled remembering all the fun parties. She was still smiling as she deplaned.

A. J. was early and watched as his plane arrived, coming out of Los Angeles. He had a strong feeling about Skeet and was thinking about her as he stared out the window. He didn't notice the young African-American journalist walk by, skinny jeans clinging and boots clicking as she slung her leather computer bag over her shoulder and headed for the baggage claim area.

. . . .

A. J.

PART TWO

Chapter 35: Moving On

MONICA PEERED ACROSS the four lane boulevard into the Zone. She could not believe her eyes. Nothing. There was nothing.

She could see the Zone's perimeter clearly outlined by the other three boulevards. Some of the cemetery markers were visible and a few tall trees were left standing; it gave her a reference point.

Monica crossed the boulevard, gaged where Center Street once was located and entered the Zone. She was recording everything for Jessica with her camera.

The smell of poison hung heavy in the air. Small signs warned of pesticide use.

Walking to where she thought her home once stood, she stopped, looked in every direction and was astonished to see how small the area really was. Monica had dealt with her grief and was not saddened by what she observed. It was now part of her history and she welcomed the opportunity to relive it - determined to remember the happy times and the joy of her family life.

She hesitated, then walked toward the cemetery calculating that she was on the street where Big George once lived. She stopped about fifty yards from where the gravesites began. Monica had no idea that she was standing in almost the exact spot where M. J. and Sean were caught in the crossfire and had fallen under its withering fire.

The little service road encircling the cemetery was untouched by the demolition. She slowly followed its path in the opposite direction from Papa Joe's office-chapel, knowing that her trail would bring her back to where the chapel once stood.

Monica knew where her Uncle Billy's grave was and when she came upon it she smiled warmly thinking of his big chair that she sat in as a child. She chuckled to herself remembering the 'kiddie corps' that she saddled him with, allowing him no say in the matter. She talked to him silently and prepared herself to move on.

Monica glanced at the grave next to Billy's and as she started to walk away, abruptly stopped and became transfixed on the grave's marker. It read:

MARGARET BROWN 'MEG'

She let out a small gasp and for the first time since entering the Zone felt a catch in her throat and tears welling up. She fought hard to stay in control. A thin smile crossed her face as she remembered with tenderness this remarkable woman and all that Meg had done for her. Monica lingered there for a long time talking silently to Meg. She was grateful to whomever thought to place her next to Billy. It was the perfect thing to do.

Monica was glad she happened upon Meg's resting place first; it gave her the emotional strength to face what was ahead. She came to the turn in the road where, away from the other graves, the lonely man was buried. The grave was still marked by its temporary peg with no name on it.

She was now standing at the foot of Nettie's grave beside the lonely man's. Monica had been there many times before and she spoke quietly to her.

Sean was laid to rest next to his mother and M. J. next to him.
"I love you guys," murmured Monica as she stood between them. "Little Bit and I miss you every day. We think about you..." She didn't dwell on their deaths but on the lives they had shared, the adventures, the laughter. When she knew it was time to leave, she knelt with one hand on each marker, "I will never forget you. Little Bit will always remember..." She could no longer hold back the tears ...
"G...goodbye... Bye"

She moved on to Ma's grave next to M. J.'s and to Sissy's who was laid to rest next to Ma. She talked to them for a while then stepped back and viewed all of her family's resting places. Each one had an unassuming but respectful marker placed on their graves. They were the same as Meg's and she wondered who had ordered them. She took photos of each grave to show Jessica.

The exit from the cemetery was next to where the chapel once stood. She exited and headed for the four lane boulevard, stopping to look at the gravesites and reaffirming her vow to complete the book about the Zone and her family who once lived there.

Monica felt that in order to write her story she needed more information on how Sean and M. J. died - the circumstances surrounding their deaths.

Papa Joe would know the details but she had had no luck in connecting with him. This time she went straight to the Department of Human Resources at The University of Detroit.

Arriving unannounced at the department, she introduced herself as Monica Wilson, a personal friend of Father Joseph, and asked for his forwarding address. She was politely informed that the department had no idea of his whereabouts and that it was church business.

In anticipation of this response, Monica had written a letter to Father Joseph. Now she handed it to the assistant and asked that it be delivered to him when he returned to the University. The assistant took the letter and filed it in Father Joseph's personal file. Monica left the Human Resource office with little hope that her letter would find Papa Joe, but it was worth the chance.

A representative of the Federal Bureau of Investigation had also visited the university's Department of Human Resource some months earlier. He wanted to know if the school had an updated student employment placing file on Abrianna Charles. The school did not and the agent also left a letter; he had requested that it be placed in her file. It was marked 'Confidential' with instructions for the department to give it to Abrianna if she ever contacted them for any reason. It was signed by Steve Lowenstein. Steve had missed finding A. J.'s sisters by a whisker.

Monica's next stop was to the Health Department; they handled all the verification of deaths and prepared the death certificates.

Once again she introduced herself as Monica Wilson, but this time she stated that she was a writer working on a book about the drug war and wanted to talk to whoever was in charge at that time. She believed this might give her the entree she needed. It worked. She was told to wait and a Mr. Wayne Stover would be out to talk to her.

Mr. Stover invited her into his office. Monica explained that she was writing a book about the Zone and had friends who were killed in the drug war.

"I'm trying to find out just how they died and you are my last hope," sighed Monica.

"A lot of people died that day, Ms. Wilson, and we did not conduct an investigation on each individual's death. Neither did the police. It was classified as a drug war with random shootings. What were the names of your friends? I'll pull up their files and see if we have anything extra on them."

"That would be greatly appreciated, Mr. Stover. Their names were Sean Ferrari, M. J. Munoz, and Meg Brown."

"Why, I knew all three of them, Ms. Wilson! I was personally involved with all of their death verifications."

Monica's heart skipped a beat and she said, "Oh, please tell me what you know!"

"Well, I'll try to recall what I can. Of course, I wasn't there at the time of their deaths, but here is what I remember: the major fighting took place by the cemetery and Sean and M. J. were caught in a crossfire on a side street real close to there. Meg and Father Joseph were helping with the wounded and I'm quite sure M. J. and Sean came to assist. That's when they were hit. The paramedics reported that they were lying side by side and Meg and Father Joseph were attending to them. M. J. died on the spot and Sean later died in the hospital. That's pretty much it, Ms. Wilson. And Meg - she literally worked herself to death. Given her exhausted condition and the stress of losing her friends, she collapsed and died of natural causes. They were all buried the same day."

Monica sat frozen to her chair. It was one thing to know of their death and quite another to hear how they had died. Finally she sighed, "Thank you Mr. Stover. I had to know."

"I'm sorry, Ms. Wilson. I wish there was more I could tell you."

"You've helped me more than you know, Mr. Stover. Thank you."

Monica had accomplished what she came for and, when she finished her work assignment, she hopped a plane and returned to Los Angeles. She had her closure and felt certain that she probably would never return to the city of her birth. She and Jessica were moving on.

A. J. TOO was moving on. There was no reason for him to stay in Detroit. He had lost his entire family and had no home. His only solace was that Skeet, Little Bit and Papa Joe were out there somewhere and he would never stop looking for them.

The nation's capital was A. J.'s destination. Because of his language abilities and scholastic brilliance, he had developed a substantial international law practice two short years after passing the bar. Many of his clients were from the D.C. area and the agencies and embassies he worked with were there. It was the logical move.

He had never been outside the city limits of Detroit.

A. J. had another reason for moving to Washington. He would have access to the Library of Congress, The National Academy of Sciences and other Institutions that could provide valuable information in his scientific quest. The law suit was over; the Zone was history. Now he had time to devote to what he had always known would be his calling in life. He was determined to uncover the mystery of his powers and use the information for the benefit of others. This was his mother's legacy and he was going to honor it.

A. J. knew he had the unlimited potential to make all the money he needed by practicing international law. He would make as much money as possible, not for acquiring personal possessions, but to provide the assets needed to pursue his scientific and humanitarian goals.

Washington D.C. would serve him well.

Graduate degrees were of no particular interest to A. J. in and of themselves. The scholastic requirements were not a challenge for him and therefore somewhat boring. However, he did discover early in his law career that others were impressed with how many letters followed a name.

Academic achievement won the attention of important people and opened doors for him. He understood that he had to be taken seriously as a scientist and an international lawyer if he were to attain his goals.

Once A. J. determined that Washington D.C. was the place for him to start, he applied and was accepted to the Georgetown University's Graduate Law School. He would pursue a Master of Law degree in their Global Health program, feeling certain that his scientific research would eventually lead him to work in the health related fields on an international level.

A. J. was reflecting on his new life's adventure as his plane was about to land at Dulles International Airport. He would practice law in the Federal Courts which he was licensed to do, establish an international consulting business near the International Trade Center of the Capital, offer himself as a linguist fluent in many languages, do extensive research in the study of electromagnetic fields utilizing all of the Capital's available resources and pursue a Master of Law degree in Global Health.

Wow, where did all this energy come from? he asked himself. How was he going to keep it all together? "Oh, Little Bit, where are you when I need you?" he chuckled. Yes, he was going to continue his search for his sisters.

A. J. was taking in Washington's beautiful vista from the air. This was his first air flight. He felt he had just been born into a new world. He had never lived anywhere except in the Zone. He had never stayed in a hotel, never had a date, never driven a car. He also had more experience in life than any other twenty year old on the planet. A. J. was not intimidated.

Chapter 36: Beautiful Becky

THE YEAR WAS flying by for A. J. The University recognized his unparalleled scholastic abilities and allowed him to take as many course hours as he wished. He was poised to receive his master's degree in Global Health at the end of the spring semester.

Many of A. J.'s international business clients from Detroit were stationed in D.C. so it was easy for him to establish his consulting business. Soon he was negotiating import-export contracts for multinational companies. He frequently moderated meetings attended by speakers of different languages. His language abilities and knowledge of international law immediately become well known in the Capital's international business circles. As the demand for his services grew, he began to recognize his value and charged his clients accordingly.

Through networking, international government agents stationed in Washington were quick to discover this young attorney from Detroit who demonstrated unique language talent. They began to openly court A. J. to assist them in complicated international commerce dealings with the United States. He could rapidly learn their languages and his powers of retention and recall of international rules and laws were exactly what they needed. A. J. became a familiar face in the halls of the U.S. Department of Commerce.

A. J.'s growing list of high placed government contacts were beginning to pay dividends as he sought their help in introducing him to the scientific community. He was relentless in his research of electromagnetic energies. Through his contacts, he was corresponding with some of the finest scientific minds in the field. He studied everything they recommended that related to the subject. He began to expand his goals beyond merely understanding his gift.

The research was telling him two things: first - living human cells could definitely receive outside energy contained in the frequencies of electromagnetic fields. Second - an unwritten alliance between research scientists, politicians, and religious groups in the United States were resisting any serious development in this area as it related to health issues. They classified it as occult science.

A. J. shuddered to think that this coalition was interfering with science in order to protect their own special interests. It was different in Europe, particularly in France, Italy and Germany. Those countries encouraged this science.

A. J. ran into the same problems his mother did when she had attempted to understand electromagnetic energies in relationship to their unexplainable gift. The research and technology was not there; he had to develop his own theories. He was in the process of doing just that. It didn't take long for him to realize that he needed help. Difficult and complex math issues kept popping up. He didn't have time to learn how to solve them so he started a search for a trained advanced mathematician.

He visited the math department at the University and was greeted by a student assistant. A. J. introduced himself and described the kind of expert he was looking for. The student assistant stated that there was only one person he should consider: Dr. Rebecca Waxman. She wasn't affiliated with the University but rented space in the building. Dr. Waxman, he claimed, was an expert in calculus, logarithm, algorithm and just about everything else.

"Becky's office is down the hall, last door on the left past the restrooms," he volunteered. "Oh, and, um, good luck!"

Not quite sure what he meant by that, A. J. headed down the hall. He was in for a surprise because he was about to meet a woman like no other he had met before. 'Becky' was brilliant, fascinating, complex, and had a mouth on her that would make a Zonie cringe. He would come to absolutely adore her.

A. J. found her small office; there was no name on the open door. He walked in and found Dr. Waxman sitting in front of a row of computers with her back to him. She was fully engaged with whatever she was working on and operating all the computers at one time. She appeared to be extremely agitated and was muttering to herself.

"Pardon me. I don't mean to disturb you, but I'm looking for Dr. Waxman. Would that be you?" A. J. politely asked.

"Of course it's me, who the fuck did you think it was, Dr. Seuss?" She still hadn't turned around, "Look, geek, you better get it right this time or I'm coming down to the Computer Science department and RIP THE DIRECTORS BALLS OFF! GOT IT?"

A. J. had been watching her struggle with the obvious computer glitch and said, "I'm not from Computer Science and I sure wouldn't want to be in the director's shoes but I think I can fix your computer."

Becky turned around for the first time, looked A. J. up and down and said, "Who the fuck are you?" She was a large woman, not fat, just big. She had long sandy blond hair toppling over her cat's eye glasses. She wasn't conventionally beautiful but curiously attractive nevertheless. He guessed her to being in her late twenties.

"My name is A. J. McCleary. You installed new software on your number one computer and it's not compatible with the others. Right?"

"Brilliant, Sherlock. Did your millionaire mommy and daddy put you through Harvard just to tell me that? Tell me something I don't know!"

Ignoring her insults, A. J. said, "Okay, I will. There's nothing wrong with your computers; the software on the main computer is faulty and it needs reprogramming. I can do it in five minutes. You interested?"

"Why the hell should I trust you?"
"Mommy sent me to Harvard and I know everything," laughed A. J.
Again she looked him over, this time in greater detail. She figured he couldn't be worse than the other technicians and besides, he had immediately recognized the problem. "Okay, give it a go, Preppy. No one else has been able to fix it and if you screw it up remember what was going to happen to the director's balls!"
"How could I forget? Slide over to number two computer and keep it open to this program." She did as he suggested and A. J. pulled up a chair and went to work. He tore into the program's diagnostics, made a few corrections and said, "Okay, here we go."
He got up, gave Becky the first chair and watched as she furiously worked the computer. She had a full size monitor hanging on the wall above the main computer and was tracking the other five devices on that. All six computer screens were filled with mathematical formulas and equations, each operating differently from the other.
A. J. had never seen anybody operate a computer with such speed before, and she was running *six* of them!
"Okay, hotshot, I'm impressed. They're all in sync," she said.
"Not quite. Number six isn't tracking like it should. You missed it."
"WHAT? You arrogant little Ivy League shit! I never miss anything!" she screeched.
"Did anybody ever tell you that you look beautiful when you're mad?" chuckled A. J. "Here let me show you. That little icon in the corner shouldn't be there; it should be clear like the others."
"Did anybody ever tell you that you were a smart ass?" replied Becky.
"All right, I didn't miss it in the equation," she said, "just in the computer language."
"You are absolutely right, Becky, but it has to go or it will give the wrong signal." A. J. went over to computer number six and reconfigured the program. "There, now you are perfect."
"Thank you, and who said you could call me Becky?"
"You did." He smiled at her.
It wasn't much but there was a little smirk on her face as she said, "All right, you can call me Becky. Now what the fuck was your name and what the hell did you come in here for?"
He liked Dr. Rebecca Waxman. He could see through her bluster and recognized a superior intellect. She clearly had no patience with less intelligent people and wanted to be left to herself. A. J. had to gain her respect; she was exactly the person he needed. He instinctively knew there could be no professional secrets between them and she would demand full disclosure. He was prepared to give it to her.
Becky sat quietly as A. J. briefed her on who he was and what he wanted from her. Her eyes lit up when he talked about electromagnetic

frequencies and what he was trying to understand about them. He told her about his gift leaving nothing out.

Becky was impressed with his obvious intelligence, a quality she admired most in a person. She knew few people who were as smart as she was. However, she had her doubts about his alleged powers and needed substantiating evidence. “Okay, hotshot, you know computers and you know science, but I think your so called ‘gift’ is flat out bullshit! How old are you, anyway?”

“Twenty.” A. J. walked over to the number four computer and briefly studied the puzzle of figures that filled its screen.

“Give me a blank screen on your main computer, Becky, and let me work from it.” She hesitated, then created the blank screen. A. J. sat down and commenced to fill the window with an exact duplicate of what had appeared on computer number four.

Becky compared the two windows, not quite believing what she had just witnessed. She stood silent for a while and quietly asked,

“Do you understand what those equations mean?”

“I haven’t the slightest idea; that’s going to be your job.”

She paused, stared intently at A. J. and asked, “These electromagnetic frequencies - what are you going to do with them once you’ve figured out how they biologically affect the human body.”

“Cure cancer,” he quietly said.

“Holy shit!”

They both recognized the beginning of a lifelong friendship. From that day forward, A. J. always referred to her as his ‘Beautiful Becky’.

Chapter 37: Captain Kirk

BECKY AND A. J. sat in a trendy Georgetown bistro enjoying lunch and going over some data.

Drinking a tall beer out of a frosty mug, she raised her glass, "Well, a belated happy birthday and congrats on the Master of Law degree. Now that you've turned twenty-one, Boy Genius, are you going to have a drink with me?"

"Sure, why not? Order me something that won't make me throw up!"

"Jesus, he's going to have a beer. What's next? Chasing women?"

"Hey, one thing at a time! I still haven't figured out why I should pull the chair out for them?"

"Yeah, I noticed," laughed Becky.

"See, that's why I love you, Beautiful Becky, you don't care!"

"Got that right, lover boy. Now what's this news you've got for me?"

"The Pakistanis have asked me to act as assistant council in their border disputes with Afghanistan and China. It affects many of their country's northern tribes. Some of them speak different languages or dialects; that's where I come in. The case goes before the World Court in The Hague. I'll be leaving in two weeks, probably be gone for the rest of the summer."

"Wow, you're moving up fast kid. Can you speak Chinese?"

"Yeah, I've been going to a lot of Chinese restaurants lately."

"Look, that's the other thing I want to talk to you about. As you know, my quest in trying to understand my language gift has introduced me to the science of electromagnetic energies as it relates to curing disease. That's what is really important and now I want to direct all of our energies to that. Hopefully we'll get some answers to help explain this gift as we continue to explore the health related issues.

Becky, I know that we've just started but we're going to shift gears. We've been concentrating on applying some of our own theories to any research material concerning electromagnetic fields that are available. For instance, scientists create wave frequencies in their labs; then by the use of oscillators and other devices, they introduce the wave into diseased or malfunctioning human cells in an attempt to treat them."

Becky took a sip of beer and looked up, "And your point is...?"

"Just this. The powers here in this country find that method flawed, scientifically incomplete, dangerous, and objectionable for their own questionable reasons. I have no need to challenge the establishment, so we are now going to concentrate our research on working with the existing frequencies running through the electrical circuits of the human body."

"Whoa, slow down there, young Einstein. Are you telling me we are going to attempt to cure diseases by reprograming the existing electrical frequencies of the human body?"

"See how smart you are? Yes, that's exactly what I mean. I want to use the body's own frequency patterns to treat malfunctioning human cells. This approach will be safer than using random waves created by mechanical electrical devices and therefore more acceptable to the establishment. It also should be more effective.

"Here comes your beer, A. J. You better finish your thought before you start drinking?"

"Yeah, good idea," he grinned.

"Look, by utilizing published research and much of my own, I will attempt to prove that human body organs emit recognizable frequencies that pass out of the body. Those wave patterns are unique to each individual and can be identified as those that belong to him or her. That's the first step.

The bands are short but they're there. We need to identify the particular organ's frequency, then capture, catalogue, and store its electronic footprints. A computer receptor capable of doing that will have to be created. It will probably be contained in a microchip. That's the second part."

"Yes, go on...," Becky said, nervously twisting a cocktail napkin in her fingers.

"The third part is to diagnose the collected waves and if it's discovered that they're corrupting the circuitry causing diseases, we fix it. Ah, that's the hard part."

"We fix it. I see, and just what's my part in all this?" Becky took a gulp and looked at him questioningly.

"You, Lady Einstein, will do the math to help me build the program that restores the corrupted frequency pattern back to health and then returns it to the ailing persons circuitry to resonate with the diseased cells. Easy enough, huh?"

Becky looked at him for a long moment and said, "So let me get this straight, Captain Kirk. You are going to discover new science on human frequencies, invent a microchip that will receive, identify and store those waves, then send reconstructed frequencies back to the human body to cure their diseases. And you want me to figure out the math that will help create a program that will integrate all this. Have I got that right!"

"Boy, you mathematicians sure get right to the point."

"A. J., you're giving me a headache. Ah, just from a mathematical perspective, how many integrations am I going to be working with?"

"Oh, let me see, we have billions of people living on this planet, each one has billions of cells. Well, you do the math," he said. "It's got to be a mathematician's dream come true! Right? ... Becky, what's wrong? You look funny. Are you okay?"

"Don't bother me, I'm having a mathematician's orgasm. Ohhhhh..."
"Becky, stop moaning; people are looking at us!"
"Ohhh, Ahhhhh, Ohhhh...," crooned Becky, laughing at her embarrassed lunch companion.

A. J. WOULD SPEND the rest of the summer in Europe. He enjoyed The Hague and his experience with the World Court, making valuable contacts that would prove important to him in the future. He was only an hour away by air from Geneva - a scheduled stop for him.

Most of A. J.'s international clients were based in Geneva. It was home to the World Health Organization, the International Union Against Cancer, the European seat for The U.N., the International Trade Center for Europe, the World Trade Organization, the International Red Cross, just to name a few.

A. J. had never seen mountains before and fell in love with the alpine peaks and hilly terrain on the bay of beautiful Lake Geneva. He sensed immediately that he had to live and work there in order to accomplish what he was trying to do. Europe would be receptive to his cutting edge radio-biology and he was taking the next step up as an international attorney. Geneva would be his home for the next three years.

On his return to Washington, he found a stack of mail to sort through. One of the letters was from the City Commissioner's Office of the City of Detroit. A. J. had anticipated an attempt by the city to negotiate his lien to a smaller amount. What he had not anticipated was the hard financial times Detroit was going through. The city was near bankruptcy.

The commissioners had always intended to retire the lien; it would have been a cheap purchase for such a now desirable piece of vacant land. They had many inquiries from investors about the availability of the property. But the fact that the zoning restrictions insisted upon by A. J. when negotiating his settlement only allowed for the construction of something for the benefit of the public and not for profit always ended the negotiations.

The city still wanted the land to use for the expansion of their government offices which would satisfy the zoning requirements. It didn't matter; they were broke and couldn't afford to retire A. J.'s lien at any price.

The letter stated that they were not going to retire the lien and acknowledged that A. J. had become the outright owner of the Zone under the operation of law provision of the Court's order.

They did add that they had been approached by prospective investors including the owners of the Detroit Tigers professional baseball organization. The Tigers were considering it as a possible site for their new ballpark. The city indicated that they would not oppose a zoning change for this type of use if A. J. was interested. He was not.

He sat in almost stunned amazement as the reality set in. It was dreamlike - a Zonie kid owning the Zone. From time to time A. J. had considered what he would do with the land if indeed he became the owner. It was too preposterous to give it much thought. The truth was he knew exactly what he would do with it, but had dismissed the thought as pure fantasy. He was excited and in disbelief that his fanciful vision was actually within his reach.

There was an e-mail from Steve; they had stayed in contact over the months. Still no word on Skeet and Little Bit. He also wrote that because it was not official FBI business, he had to designate the file inactive. However, it would remain in the cross reference files and if their names appeared anywhere he would have notice of it.

A. J. hit him back thanking him for all he had done and advising him of his plans to move to Geneva. He felt that the girls were slipping away but vowed to himself that he would renew his search with great vigor when he returned from Europe.

He quickly made his plans, completed some unfinished business and, after a strategy session with Becky, headed for Geneva. He would stay in constant contact with her throughout his stay in 'The City of Peace'.

Chapter 38: Geneva

GENEVA TURNED OUT to be everything A. J. thought it would be: picturesque, colorful, bustling and home to some of the most beautiful women in the world. He was beginning to take notice of such things, suspecting that there just might be a life beyond work and academics.

A. J. discovered Geneva's lively open air cafes that catered to artists and musicians; he enjoyed their bohemian spirit and avant-garde styles. He frequented the symphony halls, the opera and ballet theaters and even the rollicking pubs. A new world was opening up to him.

Winter in Geneva was a surprise. He had always grumbled about the cold, gray, damp and miserable Detroit winters. The air here was fresh and clean and there were many bright and sunny days. He took up skiing and discovered athletic abilities that he didn't know he had. He loved the thrill of racing down a mountainside and then sipping hot coffee drinks by a warm fireside at the end of the day.

A. J. had enough money to live a decadent, expensive, luxurious lifestyle, but he chose not to do so. He dined in good restaurants but rarely had more than one drink. He rented a beautiful flat overlooking the harbor; it was upscale and home to him. This was his only concession to excessively enjoying the fruits of his substantial income.

This new lifestyle was a bonus for A. J., but not a distraction. He came to Geneva to work on what he knew was important and he filled his days meeting with clients and contacting the different world health and humanitarian agencies based in Geneva.

A. J. knew that in order to move forward with his theories, a new and revolutionary microchip had to be invented. He set up his own research lab in his flat, complete with equipment, parts and software needed to build a microchip. He found all the essential information on the net and put his powerful mind to work to accomplish the task. He could handle much of the mathematics but would call on Becky when he needed her magic.

His master's graduate degree in Global Health, together with his enormous skills, gave him the credentials necessary in the practice of international law. He was becoming a well known and respected international law attorney.

A. J. was invited to assist the French at the World Court in their country's dispute with Iran over nuclear power issues. He made some of the argument on the floor speaking French, one of the Court's official languages, and answered challenges in Arabic when the Iranians claimed they were being misinterpreted. This language ability impressed the Court and the international attorneys who were present. A. J. was a rising star in the European international community.

She spotted him as he walked into the harbor-side cafe and sat himself at a table on the outside deck. It was a beautiful late spring morning and A. J. had just ordered a coffee when she walked up and introduced herself.

"Hello, I'm Sheila Belair. May I join you?" she said with a French accent, flashing a beautiful smile that displayed perfect white teeth. Her dark hair was pulled into a neat chignon; she was tall and elegant. Her pencil skirt and silk shirt were cinched with a large turquoise studded belt. She was perched on stilettos as she comfortably stood in a vintage fashion model's pose. He guessed her to being in her mid thirties.

A. J. did not rise but merely gestured to the unoccupied chair and said, "It was waiting for you."

"Thank you." She gracefully slid into the chair handing A. J. her business card.

He looked at it. Sheila was spelled 'She-lagh' and the title, President, followed her name. The name of her company was embossed in raised letters:

Bella Lagh
International Modeling Agency
Geneva, Switzerland

"My personal attorney has highly recommended you, Mr. A. J. McCleary. He pointed you out to me the other day as we were dining in the same restaurant. I recognized you immediately when you walked in here. I hope you don't mind me interrupting your morning coffee?"

"No, not at all. Do I know your attorney?"

"No, he said he never met you. He doesn't practice international law but he knew you by reputation. Nobody with talent can hide in this city, Mr. McCleary."

"Please call me A. J. Your card says you're an international company. Are you having problems with the new set of rules some of these emerging states are troubling us with?"

"Exactly. That and several other problems that have been dogging us. My models come from all over the world and as you know there is no one contract that fits everybody. There are tax issues, jurisdictional problems, visas... It just goes on and on. We're a big company, A. J. and we have attorneys everywhere. What we need is someone who is able to coordinate things - the language barriers are extremely troublesome. I'm told that you speak many languages. Would you like to help? We pay top dollar and you would be working with young beautiful chicks and one old hen - that would be me."

"Now, did you really think that I could turn *that* kind of an offer down," smiled A. J. "And if you're an old hen, then I'm ten years old!"

They both laughed and She-lagh said, "My number's on the card. I'll be here all week; the office is just a few blocks away."

"I'll check my schedule and give you a call," said A. J.

"Great," and she got up to leave. She-lagh extended her left hand to A. J., expecting European chivalry. She didn't get it. He still hadn't figured out why they expected the chair to be pulled out for them, let alone this. She smiled and gave him a little wave.

He watched her walk away; she had spectacular legs.

She-lagh and A. J. had a late afternoon appointment two days later, meeting in She-lagh's plush and expansive office complex. A. J. was waiting in the reception area but wasn't the least bit bored as he casually observed the constant flow of beautiful women coming and going. He became a little self conscious when he noticed that they were checking him out, too.

"Sorry to keep you waiting," She-lagh said as she came out to greet him. A few of the models stopped when She-lagh herself appeared in the reception area. She took notice and said, "These are some of our models, A. J."

"Ladies, I'd like you to meet A. J. McCleary. And, no, he's not a model; he's an attorney and more than likely you will be working with him."

"Oh?" a slender blond said, as they each politely introduced themselves to him.

As they were walking away, She-lagh said, "You know, you *could* be one ..."

"One what?"

"A model of course. We work with a lot of men. You're tall, in great shape, handsome, and with those wonderful green eyes we could place you easily. And your youth helps, too." She looked at him differently when she said the last part. It didn't go unnoticed.

He met with She-lagh and her executives in an elegant conference room. The meeting lasted for a couple of hours and She-lagh's people were impressed with how swiftly A. J. grasped their problems. A. J. was impressed with their preparation and willingness to accept advice. They agreed to work together.

After the meeting broke up, She-lagh escorted A. J. back to the reception area. "Look, I'm going to grab an early dinner at one of the private restaurants we have around here. Why don't you join me?"

"You know, I would enjoy that. I've been real curious to see inside one of those places. I'd be glad to join you. Thanks."

A. J. did enjoy himself. The ambiance was quiet and relaxing and he enjoyed She-lagh's company. It was a typical European style dinner; nobody rushed anything. She ordered a bottle of wine with dinner and drank most of it. "Well, it's time that I get out of here; I have a busy day tomorrow. You wouldn't mind walking me home, would you, A. J.?

It's dark and I don't live far from here."
"Sure. Of course I will," he replied. She slipped her arm through his and they strolled towards her place. He knew what this meant; she had been giving him signals all evening.
A. J. hadn't been with anybody since M. J. He couldn't imagine being with someone else, but it was now four years since M. J.'s death and as his memory of her receded, his need for a woman was becoming too powerful to resist. He had a lot of money, especially for a twenty two year old. He knew he was a sexually appealing man in a city teeming with alluring single women. There was about to be another turn in his life.
She-lagh didn't even invite him in; she just opened the door and assumed he would follow. He did.
"If you want, pour yourself a drink," she said, nodding towards an ornate bar, "I'll just be a moment."
She returned wearing a short creamy silk nightgown.
She padded barefoot back into the room, walked over to the bar and poured herself a glass of wine. She took a sip, then placed the delicate long stemmed glass on the bar.
"Aren't you going to join me? I hate drinking alone," she murmured as A. J. sidled up to her at the bar.
"No, I'm not much of a drinker."
She reached up, put her arm around his neck and gently pulled him towards her. They kissed. He could taste the wine and it excited him. They kissed again, this time it was ardent and hot.
"Come, lets get comfortable," she purred and led him to her bedroom. He was being seduced by an older woman and was loving it. She was in charge, the quintessential cougar. He offered no resistance.
She-lagh slipped out of the silky nightgown and sat on the bed watching as A. J. undressed. She was sitting on the edge of the bed as he approached. He began kissing her on the neck then slowly moved down to her stomach. He gently laid her back as he dropped to his knees. Her legs were dangling off the bed and around him as he tasted her.
He stayed there for several minutes bringing her to a point of uncontrollable arousal. Being in control was no longer important as she urgently felt the need for him. Through her body language she demanded that he enter her. She frantically slid back into the bed pulling him on top of her. Then her hand guided him inside.
She-lagh was used to her young men prematurely climaxing. A. J.'s mind took over and he didn't release until she was fully satisfied.
They lay side by side and she gently ran her hand over his stomach.
"How in the world did you get all those scars, A. J.?"
"Oh, I kept running into things when I was a kid growing up."
"Look A. J., I'll be leaving for Paris at the end of the week. I share an

apartment there with my boyfriend."

"Oh, geez, She-lagh, if I had known that..."

"No, no... it's all right. He's twenty years older than I and he understands that I go out with men younger than I am and he goes out with other women. It's just the life we choose to live; we love each other madly.

Because of that, I never sleep with any other man more than once. You are really tempting; it's been a long time since I've had such ... but I don't want to screw things up between him and me. I hope you understand."

A. J. understood and was relieved. He did not need to get involved with an older woman - a client at that.

They would go on to develop a close friendship and he always felt grateful to She-lagh for helping him break free from the memory of M. J. He would never forget M. J. and would always honor her, but now he felt that he could move forward and maybe love again.

His social life took off. He got to know many of the models and was often seen around town with them. It was the perfect situation. The models were in Geneva for training and when they completed their courses, She-lagh sent them all over the world. Rarely did they return to Geneva.

It was not as if he spent every day with them. He still devoted most of his time to work and research. But when he felt like having female companionship, the models were always there. He took them to fine restaurants, ski outings and occasionally to one of the countless social events he was invited to. They loved it, knowing that their stay in Geneva was temporary and there would be no career ending involvements. It helped that She-lagh would just roll her eyes when the girls inquired about him. They understood.

It was really unfair on A. J.'s part, but he couldn't help comparing the models to M. J. These girls' priorities were hair and manicure appointments, something that M. J. would have had no need for. M. J. understood life for what it was; the women that A. J. was dating were sophisticated and educated but never really challenged by life.

Chapter 39: The McCleary Chip

IT HAD BEEN a year and a half since A. J. had arrived in Geneva and he was frustrated in his attempt to build the essential microchip. Becky kept after him to send her more work, but for the most part he could handle the math problems himself and that's what was frustrating him. He hadn't yet been able to create the chip that would lead to the integration of human frequencies. That's where the complex math problems would come from and Becky's talents would be needed. And he still hadn't developed the science necessary to complete the first step.

Then A. J. caught a break. Three French scientists with whom he had shared electromagnetic research information had made a significant breakthrough. They were able to conclusively demonstrate that each human being's individual organs had a unique and identifiable transmitting wave pattern.

Further, It was demonstrated that each individual organ wave contained at least one of the same identifying unique frequency markers that was present in the others. Taken together, the wave patterns were as conclusive as DNA testing in identifying people. The French scientists put the study on line to share with the world. A. J. was ecstatic; the first step in his quest had just been taken for him.

The researchers had provided the science. A. J. made it operational. Utilizing the information in the study with his now massive research, A. J. was able to build his microchip. The chip acted as a receiver but only recognized natural occurring human electronic waves. It could be integrated with existing operating programs when placed in a computer, cell phone or any other electronic device. It could even be placed in a credit card. The chip was activated when the new owner turned the device on.

The keyboard of a computer, the face of a cell phone and other electronic devices would all have a sensor that transmitted an electronic message to the chip. The message was the unique electronic wave of a purchaser's skin organ created by the touch of the individual. The wave was then stored to memory.

From that point on, the operating systems could be programmed to recognize only the owner's touch and no other person could use the device. Then it would function like any computer or electronic instrument.

The computer's programming was far more extensive than the other devices. It could be programed to receive *all* the transmittable organ frequencies of the individual and identify each organ. Because of the stored characteristic marker found in the skin frequency, the program could sort through any competing waves and filter out ones that didn't contain the identifying marker. What was left was the individual's electronic organ footprints recorded to memory. It was brilliant.

The method used to activate the processors was revolutionary. It was the perfect security protection; you could lose your credit card, phone, or even your computer and nobody else could access it. This went far beyond finger printing technology.

The business possibilities were endless but that would be for someone else to develop. Nevertheless, the second step in his long journey had been accomplished.

She was the first one he contacted. "Becky, I did it! We have an operational chip! We can receive, identify, store and transmit the frequency data of a human organ. We can now take the next step! You're about to go to work. Vacation's over!"

"What? You're shitting me!" answered an excited Becky. "Jesus, you're really going to do it, aren't you?"

"No, Beautiful Becky, *we* are going to do it! I'm sending you the equations. Start thinking BIG. We've got to build the program that will recognize corrupted frequency patterns, reconstruct the waves and then figure out how to transmit them back to the human body. It may take a while, but it can and will be done! Oh, the chip's got tremendous commercial value. I'm going for it; we need the money."

"Ohhhh, Ohhhh, ummmm, I think I'm having another mathematician's orgasm, Ohhhh..." she moaned.

"Becky, take two Xanax and go to bed!"

A. J. ANNOUNCED his electronic invention in scientific journals. The firestorm it created was totally unexpected. Apparently a major international electronics company had been privately working on the same thing. This was a surprise; they were not out in the open like A. J. was. He had beaten them to the punch.

"It is a blatant patent infringement and a theft of corporate secrets," exclaimed one of the executives. "We'll sue him in every jurisdiction in the world!"

"My, my, you sure do know how to piss people off, A. J.," She-lagh said, as she read the newspaper accounts to him over a morning coffee at the cafe.

"Boy, I guess. Good thing I'm an attorney."

"I don't believe this trash for a second," she said, "but I think they mean business. What are you going to do about it, anyway?"

"I'm going to irritate them even more. I'm going to do nothing. Through the journals, I'll declare that the microchip is a trade secret and off limits to all concerned."

"Yup, that should really piss them off. Now I know how you got all those scars, A. J."

Not everybody was angry with him. Many companies applauded his work and wanted to do business. News of his invention was widely reported in the business pages of European newspapers; they referred to it as the 'McCleary Chip'. It was barely noted in the U.S.

Any business with security issues would be interested in the McCleary Chip and that would be just about everybody. No wonder the complaining executive was furious; it was money out of their pockets.

Governments at all levels took notice. With proper programming, the chip would have an enormous impact on the identification process relating to police work, customs, drivers licenses and other situations. The Intelligence agencies and military people were particularly interested.

A. J. wanted to reap the commercial benefits from the McCleary chip but he didn't want to be involved in the business end. He would either sell the chip or license its use. Somebody else could commercialize it. He expected to be financially rewarded but he was only interested in actively taking the next scientific step.

There would be other problems. He had yet to hear the concerns from the religious right or the anti Big Brother theorists. This was not going to be easy.

It didn't take long. The outraged company filed suit in the United States Federal Court. They alleged patent infringement, civil theft of trade secrets and other business complaints. The rest of the business world was watching.

A. J. didn't hesitate. He electronically filed a motion to dismiss on jurisdictional grounds. He cited that he was also a citizen of Ireland, that the invention was created in Switzerland where he was a resident and that the United States had entered into many treaties recognizing foreign jurisdictions in these types of personal intellectual properties actions. The Court agreed and dismissed the suit, infuriating the plaintiff. The fight would move to A. J.'s back yard in Geneva.

Chapter 40: Monica and Jessica

MONICA FIDGETED on a leather couch on the set of a Hollywood TV studio. The moderator, Patrice Harden, chatted, trying to put her at ease. This was Monica's first televised interview since her book came out; it would be broadcast by tape to a national audience.

"Okay Monica, here we go."

"Good morning viewers. Welcome to *The Literature Hour*. I'm your hostess, Patrice Harden. This week, we have taken our show to Hollywood, California. We'll be reviewing three great books this morning and interviewing some very special people, who just happen to be, you guessed it... *The writers!"*

"Let's open our show by introducing one of those very special people, someone who's done all sorts of writing. Let's see, she's written and directed TV scripts and plays. She's currently a screen writer and now she's had her first book published. And she's only twenty-six years old! Meet this talented young author sitting next to me, America: Monica Wilson.

Monica, you're from Los Angeles by way of Detroit, are you not?"

"Yes, that's right, Patrice. I was born and raised there. I came to Los Angeles with my sister just before I turned twenty-one."

"Well, you've certainly accomplished a lot in your short time here but what is interesting to me... no, what is fascinating to me, is your life growing up in Detroit!

And that is what your book is all about. Look, I grew up in suburbia; I can't even relate to what you struggled through. My gosh, that entire area where you used to live isn't even there anymore!"

"No, it's not. The only thing left is the cemetery."

"Folks. This is must reading - a true and compelling story. Monica, I don't want you to give away anything to your prospective readers, but could you tell us a little about the book? Here let me hold it up, you've titled it 'The Zone'. Where did that name come from?"

"The police used to identify their areas of patrol by designating them as zones, followed by a number. I grew up in an area that was so notorious for its crime that they didn't even use the number; it was simply referred to as the Zone and everybody knew exactly where it was."

"Wow! Speaking of names, you didn't even find out that your name was Monica Wilson until you left the Zone. Right?"

"That's right. We never knew anybody's real name; we all had Zonie names. Mine was Skeeter."

"And you were never referred to by any other name in the Zone?"

"No, just Skeet."

"You wrote your first play in the Zone. Tell us about that."

"It was a puppet show," chuckled Monica. "My sister, M. J., was a real performer. She was always putting on little skits and I'd write the scripts for her. I was eleven when we did the first one; she was eight.

Patrice, I don't want people to think that I was a lost child growing up as an orphan without love. I had a wonderful life and protective family. True, only my sister, Jessica - we called her Little Bit - was related to me by blood, but the people who cared for us were the most loving family imaginable. That's what the book is really about, how we grew up protected by love in a very dangerous place."

"Monica, that love really comes through in the book. Tell me, where did you get all your background information?"

"I actually began gathering the material when I was fifteen. I interviewed my adult family members for much of it and had M. J.'s and my diaries. There were medical records and police reports that my family gave me. And of course I had my own memories."

"Read it, people. You won't be able to put it down. Thanks for being on the show, Monica. The best of luck on the book and your promising career."

"Thank you for the invitation, Patrice."

Little Bit was excitedly waiting for her in a small Beverly Hills cafe.

"Skeet, Skeet, over here," she called out as Monica entered the cafe. The girls still called each other by their Zonie names when they were alone. Jessica could hardly contain herself, "How did it go? When is it going to be broadcast?"

"I was scared to death. The lights were blinding and I didn't know what I was going to say. Nothing was rehearsed; they wanted it to be natural and spontaneous. It's going to be aired Monday morning, two days from now!"

"What was she like, Patrice Harden? Was she as cool as she appears to be?" eagerly questioned Jessica.

"We talked for quite awhile before the cameras started to roll, and I really liked her. She was genuinely interested in me and the book and gave me her business card. She wants me to call her if I ever get to New York."

"Wow, let's go," laughed Jessica.

Little Bit had turned eighteen. She wasn't much taller than when she left the Zone. Topping out at five foot two and weighing one hundred and five pounds fully dressed. She was as pretty as her sister with large brown eyes and a curvy delicate body. That was deceptive; LIttle Bit was Zonie tough!

Jessica had completed her studies at a magnet high school with honors. She had exceptional computer skills and was enrolled in a junior college business school. Her natural organizational skills made a future career in business a given. She was already keeping track of her sister's bank accounts and schedule. She had plenty of time to devote to her active social life and she moved easily among Monica's stylish friends.

The sisters lived together in an upscale L.A. neighborhood, not too far from Hollywood.

They were walking into their two bedroom apartment and Jessica was still firing questions.

"Did you see the book displayed in the bookstore window? Wow! There it was! *THE ZONE*. I couldn't believe it. I ran into the bookstore, grabbed the book and started shouting - MY SISTER WROTE THIS BOOK. MY SISTER WROTE THIS!"

"Little Bit, you didn't!" laughed Monica.

"I did, I did!" Jessica said with a big smile.

"I... I still have trouble reading it," she sighed.

"I know, Little Bit."

"Skeet, he's still alive. I just know it," she whispered.

"Honey, I stood at the foot of his grave. I talked to the health official... He would have found us by now if he were alive, Little Bit."

"I realize that but I just don't sense that he's... he's... gone," she murmured. "If only we could find Papa Joe..."

"Okay, okay," sighed Monica, clutching her sisters hands.

They were up early Monday morning, anxiously waiting for the program to begin.

"Good morning viewers, welcome to *The Literature Hour*..."

"Skeet, I am so proud of you," said a teary Jessica. She had reason to be proud: the book would be in the one hundred best sellers list at its peak and would be widely acclaimed in the Los Angeles area. Monica would soon receive inquiries from her motion picture friends. She retained the movie rights.

Chapter 41: It Was Time To Go Home

THE CASE WAS filed in an international court in Geneva. The Court was going to hear *all* expert witness testimony. This would take months.

As the proceedings dragged on, it was clear that the plaintiff's arguments were fallacious and without merit. A. J. paraded one member of the European science community after another to testify in his behalf. He was able to establish, through their testimony, that he had been working on the project for two years and nobody knew that the plaintiff was working on the same thing.

If it were a prize fight, it would have been stopped weeks ago. It soon became obvious why the plaintiff filed a law suit that they knew they couldn't win. First, they were hoping to force A. J. into disclosing his trade secret. He was far too smart to let that happen. Second, they wanted to delay A. J.'s commercialization of the microchip as long as possible. This would allow their technicians time to build their own chip. They would then rush to have it patented and take it to the market. The Court was becoming impatient with their tactics. The plaintiff was running out of options.

THE WORLD SCIENCE Symposium was held in Paris that year. A. J. introduced the microchip to a world-wide audience. He demonstrated how it worked on a live person. He asked She-lagh to be his subject. She was thrilled to help out. They had the perfect friendship. They were not romantically involved and they liked and respected one another.

She showed up with navy blue leggings, a matching loose silk sheer shirt and her signature stilettos. She had everybody's attention as A. J. diagramed the whole process on large overhead screens. His invention even out-dazzled She-lagh's appearance. It made headlines in Europe but was only footnoted in the U.S. science publications.

The presentation just may have been the knockout punch regarding the law suit. The invention was now receiving universal attention and businesses would soon be clamoring for it. The plaintiff couldn't afford to be shut out from the market. They started to send their feelers out for a settlement.

After the symposium, while A. J. was greeting the guests, he was approached by a Russian diplomat who introduced himself as Dr. Ivan Larionov. This tall, distinguished looking man seemed familiar to A. J.

"I apologize for staring at you, but have we ever met before?" A. J. inquired.

"I don't recall, Mr. McCleary, but I did spend considerable time in the U.S. I worked for Wayne State University in Detroit for a while. Could we have met there?"

A. J. remembered. He smiled at the man and said, "Yes, that was it. Well, I never thought that I would get the chance, but thank you."

"Thank me, for what?"

A. J. laughed and said, "I want to thank your wife too. You both taught me how to speak Russian when I was nine years old."

"Nine years... oh my, you were the little boy Dr. John Telasantos introduced to us. You had that amazing ability to... oh, wait till I tell my wife!"

The Russians were interested in the chip and A. J. promised to contact Larionov when he was in a position to market his electronic invention.

A. J. was getting all kinds of offers. Dr. Frederick Howe, the Dean of the Department of Physics at The University of Virginia was one of the few American scientist who had attended A. J.'s presentation. Dr. Howe was very interested in the electromagnetic science A. J. was pioneering and he invited A. J. to the Virginia campus to discuss furthering the research. "Yes," said Dr. Howe, "We would make our labs available for your research and support you in any way. We know you're a language specialist and we can certainly make room for you on our faculty. In fact, I'd even design a Ph.D. program for you if you're interested. Your reputation is widely known in the educational circles, Mr. McCleary."

This offer got A. J.'s attention. The more he thought about it, the more it appealed to him. He wanted to return to his homeland for a number of reasons - finding Skeet and Little Bit was one of them. He would also be within two hours of Becky. Further, he had received an e-mail from Steve. Steve had switched teams; he was now working for the CIA and was stationed in Langley near Washington. A. J. also needed to visit Detroit.

"A. J., SLOW DOWN FOR CHRIST SAKE. WHAT ARE YOU TRYING TO DO, KILL US?" screeched She-lagh. They were on a French winding country road and A. J. was driving her Alfa Romeo. It was the first time he had ever driven a car.

"WOW, SHE-LAGH! THIS IS GREAT!" shouted A. J. over the road noise.

"TERRIFIC. I'M GLAD YOU'RE HAVING FUN. NOW STOP AT THE NEXT HUT HOUSE CAFE. I'VE GOT TO BREATHE AGAIN!"

She-lagh regained her color and was still a little shaky as she sipped her red wine. A. J. waved his beer mug around while telling anybody who would listen how exciting it was to drive a race car.

"It's only a race car if it's on a track, A. J. Remember that," scolded She-lagh. "Okay, okay, I'll try to remember. Let's get back on the road!"

"Oh no, not until you promise to drive at a safe speed. Beside's I'm hungry; let's have lunch."

They were enjoying steak frites in a casual but romantic setting.
"You'll add to your scars driving like that, A. J. Those things tip over you know!
Hey, you never did tell me how you got those scars."

"Well, let me see, I was stabbed once, slashed a few times, and shot five times. Not to mention a zillion cuts, bruises and black eyes."
"A. J., I'm serious. What happened?"
"Oh, did I mention an ice pick being rammed up my scrotum?"

"A. J. ...! Oh forget it. So, you want me to take you around to symphony halls and museums while you're in Paris?"
"Yes I do. I'm interested in seeing their architectural designs and floor plans."
"What are you going to do, build one of your own?" chided She-lagh.

"Something like that," replied A. J. "Come on, let's get going. I promise to obey the speed laws but you have to drive when we get back to Paris."
"Of that you can be certain!"

THE PLAINTIFF RECEIVED a crushing report from their research team. It would take them an estimated minimum of two years to accomplish what A. J. had done. The plaintiff had backed itself into a corner. They were not going to produce the chip and they had alienated the one person who could do it for them. Further, the case was winding down and it was certain that A. J. was going to prevail and move forward with the commercialization of his invention.

Sensing his advantage, he informed the plaintiff that he was taking the case to its completion. He added that he would issue licensing rights of the chip to anyone who wanted it, but never to the plaintiff. He was bluffing. He wanted to end the matter quickly and didn't care if the plaintiff had commercial use of it. But they were going to pay dearly for the rights.

The plaintiff had another problem. They had carefully planned a public sale of their common stock and were trying to time the sale to occur just after they announced the patenting of their frequency chip. All was now in jeopardy.

They had arrogantly underestimated A. J.'s resolve and now would have to deal with him under his terms. The plaintiff requested a conference; A. J. consented and an agreement was hammered out.

The company was prepared to offer for sale billions of dollars worth of common stock to the public. They were holding back a large percentage of the stock for future distribution to insiders. A. J. wanted that insiders stock. In return, A. J. would give them the exclusive commercial rights to the microchip. He also agreed to give them the indispensable equations.

He further insisted that rights to the use of the chip would be granted to anyone conducting scientific research for health purposes. A. J. would retain the exclusive right to the equations for any scientific purpose and agreed not to reveal them to anyone else.

The company balked at this at first but soon realized that it would involve only a small part of the market. They consented to all his demands.

The deal was finalized and A. J. became incredibly wealthy overnight. He would sell the stock as a secondary offering one year after receiving it to gain the most favorable tax advantage.

He decided to return to his homeland.

A. J. received his stock but it would be weeks before he was in a position to leave Europe. He contacted Dr. Larionov and told him of the deal struck with the plaintiff. He offered to share scientific information with the Russian government. The doctor thanked him for being up front and said they would be interested in working with him on the scientific level.

He paid his tax obligation to Switzerland and notified his research friends and other organizations that he was leaving Geneva. He assured them that he would continue to share information and thanked them for all of their help. They welcomed his scientific collaborations but were sorry to see him leave.

He called Dr. Howe to set up a tentative appointment in Charlottesville, Virginia. He had decided to continue his research in the U.S. He had no idea that this decision would put him in direct conflict with powerful forces opposed to his work.

She-lagh was his best friend in Europe and it was going to be difficult to say goodbye. Their farewell was more emotional than what either of them had expected. They would miss each other and promised to always stay in touch.

A. J. would turn twenty-five in a few months. Monica's book had been out now for two years and had disappeared from the shelves of bookstores. A. J.'s reading was centered around scientific journals, history and classic literature. He never knew her book was out there; it was not circulated in Europe. He had not seen his sisters for seven years. It was time to go home. He boarded a plane and headed for Washington. Becky was picking him up at the airport.

Chapter 42: Rinni

ROSHINI AMEEN, 'Rinni', was born in the worst possible place on the planet to be born a woman - a small tribal village in the far northern corner of Pakistan near the border of Afghanistan and China.

Rinni was brought into a world of secular tribal law and religious fanaticism in a place where females had no rights. They existed for the sole purpose of serving the male. If a woman disobeyed or objected to her treatment, she was killed.

After the age of twelve, girls were sexually abused by the men of their tribe or any visiting male from one of the neighboring tribes. It was common practice for male members of their own family to sexually assault them. Many of them were forced to endure genital mutilation. They were never allowed to enter the outside world without wearing a burka.

The treatment of women in this small tribal section of the world offended the doctrines of even the most fanatical religions found anywhere on earth. The tribes practicing this brutality towards women were ignored by the rest of the world - as though they didn't exist. Their numbers were in the thousands and they lived in such a remote area that nobody cared. The men were so lawless and violent that no one uninvited came in and nobody left without consent.

Numerous tribes surrounded this isolated society and they all disapproved of such abusive treatment being practiced by their neighbors. But did nothing about it.

"AYYYEEE," she shrieked, and a hand quickly covered her mouth. "Dal, it's me, Rinni! Quiet! You will wake the others!"

Daleela Khaleel, like Rinni, was in her early twenties and was a member of a secret underground movement of young women under Rinni's leadership. After centuries of abuse, these brave women had banded together to make war on the barbarous men of their isolated region.

"I'm sorry, Rinni, I was having another nightmare. I'll be all right in a moment."

"It's okay. I had them, too, after my mother was butchered by those animals! Hurry. Zay is waiting for us."

Zaynab Shaheen was the third leader in this growing army of determined and vengeful young women. Most of these warriors were unclaimed females or widows. Rarely did a man live with them but these savages would simply enter the women's homes for pleasures whenever they desired.

It was the middle of the night. The invisible warriors, shrouded with black burkas, silently slipped out of their homes to rendezvous with other black clad young women. The purpose of the gatherings was to organize. They met in three different locations; Rinni, Dal, and Zay were leaders of the individual groups. The groups operated in coordinated secrecy. If any of the women were caught outside at night, they would be executed on site. These girl guerrillas were both brave and lucky; they had yet to be discovered and were getting close to commencing their surreptitious attacks.

There was a confusing and brutal civil war raging in neighboring Afghanistan. The men from Rinni's isolated region formed combat teams and crossed the border to fight for whichever side hired them.

Unbelievably, many times they would be engaging their own tribal members. They were paid killers without conscience.

Most of the area's men stayed in camps surrounding their villages waiting to be hired for combat. Mercenaries - terrorists from tribes outside the region - were also engaged in the conflict and it wasn't uncommon for them to be at war with men from Rinni's villages. They spoke dialects sometimes recognized only by their individual tribes. Rivalries and hatreds developed quickly confusing the issue even more. This played into the hands of Rinni and her followers.

Rinni's plan was simple. It was designed to create war between the tribal groups with the hope that the outside tribes would annihilate the men from her villages. The women would assist the outside tribes any way they could - gathering information, acting as spies, and engaging in the physical combat themselves. They were determined and full of hatred for their abusers. Actually, they hated all men. They had known no other except these sub-humans. They had never been loved by a kind father or brother; nor had they experienced sex with gentleness.

The women, too, had a dark side. After being beaten and raped so often, they had developed an insensitivity to life. They would find it easy to commit atrocities themselves.

It was time. The out camps away from the main body of men were easy targets; there were three of them. Each was inhabited by only a handful of men and they had no sentries. There was no reason to expect trouble; nobody ever came near their region. The women had thoroughly scouted them and knew exactly how many men were in which tent.

Invisible in black clothing, they silently crept into the quarters of their sleeping and unsuspecting prey. They pulled out sharp kitchen knives and efficiently slit the men's throats. Then they cooly cut the testicles off each corpse and tacked them to trees. The women were back in their hovels before daylight.

Experienced professional special forces couldn't have done it any better. No one was left alive and they had moved without being detected. In fact, the bodies were not even discovered until long after daybreak.

The hanging of the testicles was brilliant. Nothing would infuriate these fanatic macho men more then to have their manhood literally and symbolically attacked. Nobody would even dream that the assailants were female; they were considered inferior, weak and incapable of functioning in a man's world.

These unprincipled and miserable excuses for human beings went into a blind rage. They promptly gathered into disorganized fighting units and headed straight for the camps of the nearest hostile tribe.

Rinni's plan was being carried out to a degree of success that even she couldn't believe. The warring sides tore into each other in fierce combat that lasted for days. The outside tribes recognized an opportunity and united to strike down these hated people. They devastated the men of Rinni's villages and drove them back to their isolated region.

Many of the retreating men forced their way into the homes of the females who now outnumbered them three to one. Most of them fell asleep from pure exhaustion; the women made sure they never woke up.

Dozens of bodies were dragged into the streets. When the battered combatants saw what was happening, they fled to the other side of the mountain range and regrouped. Their forces were down to less than one thousand men but they were still dangerously armed. The women numbered over three thousand and were joined by young male sympathizers who had not signed on with the paid killers.

A most interested party was observing the conflict. The American CIA was looking for a base of operation in this remote part of the world. It was handed to them on a silver platter. They immediately detached a small but well armed unit that got in between the black clad fighters and the dangerous men with guns.

Chapter 43: Robo-Cop

"WELL WOULD YOU look at the boy wonder, all grown up and famous! Check out those carry-ons, bulging on all sides, chock full of money!" greeted a smiling Becky.

"Hey, Beautiful Becky!" A. J. called out. He dropped his bags and threw his arms around her. "I missed you and your insults. I've started to get soft!"

"Don't worry, I'll get you lined out, Playboy. Come on, let's have a beer. I want to hear about your adventures!"

Becky insisted that he stay with her and her partner, Genevieve, until he got settled. A. J. really liked Genevieve Gross; they had mutual interests. She was a lawyer, a feminist, and almost as outspoken as Becky. She had grown up poor in a tough Jewish neighborhood in Queens and would have made a great Zonie.

They planned to celebrate his twenty-fifth birthday at a local Georgetown pub. A. J. invited Steve, who was still at Langley. A. J. couldn't wait for Steve and Becky to meet. She hated cops.

A. J. and Steve arrived at the pub before Becky and Genevieve who were meeting them there. They were catching up on each other's interesting lives as they waited.

"What made you leave the FBI for the Company?" inquired A. J.

"Oh, all the usual reasons, but I also wanted to work on an international scale. The opportunity presented itself and I jumped. As a matter a fact, I landed my first foreign assignment this morning. There's a small tribal war developing in northern Pakistan. We're going in to protect some innocent women from the wrath of terrorists. At least that's what the world is supposed to think. I have my doubts… Leaving in two days."

A. J. thought it would be a good idea to prep Steve before Becky arrived.

"Steve, you will love Becky once you get past the initiation process."

"What the hell does that mean?"

"You'll see. Just remember, if you pass muster you will have a loyal friend for life. Stay cool. She really won't mean what she says; it's a test. There they are!" A. J. says waving to the two women. "Oh, she hates cops."

"WHAT? Terrific, A. J., just terrific!"

"Becky, Genevieve, I'd like you to meet a good friend of mine, Steve Lowenstein. What's everybody drinking?"

"Lowenstein. You Jewish?" airily asked Becky.

"Yes I am," replied Steve.

"You a banker, lawyer, comedian... or what?"

"Ah, I work for the government."

"No, really... in this town?" snickered Becky.

Here we go, thought A. J.
"Please tell me you're not a fucking accountant."
"Ah, no, actually I'm in ah...ah security," sheepishly answered Steve.
"Security. Are you one of those guys who scopes out women's bodies through the security check machines at the airport?"
"No. I work in the government's intelligence division."
A. J. held his breath.
"A fucking spook. Government Intelligence. That's an oxymoron! Who are you spying on in here? It must be Genevieve, she subscribes to Mother Jones."
Steve was saved by his cell phone, "Excuse me, I have to take this," he said and answered his call.
"No problem, Robo-Cop. What would you do if you were taking a leak?" said a smiling Becky, obviously enjoying herself.
Steve folded his phone and said, "Sorry, duty calls and I've got to leave you folks. A. J., my schedule has been moved up and I'm leaving tomorrow. I'll call you when I get back.
Well, did I pass, Becky?" he laughingly asked as he grabbed her hand and patted it. "Nice to meet you Genevieve," and he turned around and left.
"Nice guy for a cop," said an approving Becky.
Steve passed an official looking man as he was leaving. The man glanced at Steve and walked directly towards A. J.'s table.
"Oh, not this jerk," exclaimed Genevieve.
"What do you want, McGee? This is a private party!"
"Nice to see you too, Gen. Actually, I'm here to deliver something to Mr. McCleary," and he handed A. J. two documents.
"I don't suppose you would sign for these, Mr. McCleary?"
"Hit the road, asshole," declared Genevieve. He left.
"He's a private Dick, A. J. And I think you've been sued."
"Man, I just got here," he said as he read the documents in lightening speed. He handed them to Genevieve.
"Wow, you're walking in high clover. You're a co-defendant with the largest electronics company in the world. What kind of collusion and fraud are these birds talking about? Do you even know Messrs. Barry Zimmerman, Martin Kleinman, and Robert Galen?"
"Nope, never heard of them, but I assume they're disgruntled stockholders of the electronics company. We settled a law suit a while back. I guess these guys didn't sign on to the agreement.
I suspect they're also behind this other matter. It appears that the IRS is also questioning the deal," said A. J. "And I'm sure the SEC can't be far behind."
A. J. was learning a valuable lesson. The problem with making a lot of money is that everybody's always trying to take it away from you.

"Do you know the attorneys involved, Genevieve?"
"Yes, I do. They're like sharks in the water!"
"Do you want to take them on? I'm leaving for Charlottesville and I haven't got time for this."
"Sure, I would love it."

"Okay you're hired, for both cases. Just keep me informed. We'll spend a day together once you get familiar with the complaints and plan our strategy."
"The quicker the better; this ought to be fun!"
"Glad I made your day, Genevieve. Now let's have lunch," smiled A. J., adding, "Becky, you were kinda easy on Steve. You're slipping."

A. J. signed on to the university's doctoral program. Dr. Howe made it simple for him. He breezed through the language requirements and would take the necessary physics courses on line. The school was interested in him conducting his cutting edge research at their institution and they wanted his thesis to be written under their program. They also made him a member of the faculty. He would be teaching language.

In late November Genevieve called A. J. "I just concluded meetings with both the IRS and the SEC. They reviewed the supporting documents you voluntarily gave them and determined that you have complied with all their silly rules and regulations. They are both discontinuing their investigations."

"Good job, councilor; that should get the plaintiff's attention."
"Yeah, they wanted me to tell you that they're really after the company for bargaining away their insider stock and you were a necessary party to the suit. They hoped you understood that it was 'just business'.

I told them that I hope *they* would understand that it is 'just business' when we file our suit against them for knowingly and purposely misrepresenting your personal information to government agencies."
"Boy, you *are* having fun, Genevieve, I love it!"

WHEN STEVE ARRIVED in Pakistan in July, he realized his suspicions about the assignment were well founded. The CIA, indeed, was not intervening to protect innocent women from terrorists and murderers, but working with guerrilla fighters who were militarily engaging their oppressors. The fighters just happened to be female.

He recalled a briefing given to him by Special Agent Bob Browne who was the on-site operational manager for the assignment.

"Steve, these ladies are no ladies!" he had declared. "I mean, these gals go on patrols looking for the killers from their villages. Christ, if an unidentified man wanders into their territory, they surround him and stick butcher knives against his throat."

"Jesus!" exclaimed Steve.

"Yeah! These women are clever and resourceful - somehow they've managed to get some arms and ammunition. Fearless they are and their leader is merciless. She's young - mid-twenties maybe; they call her Rinni. We've let them know that we are on their side but they don't trust us for a second."

"Why should they?"

"They shouldn't. So far we've managed to stay between those paid killers and Rinni's people. We had a shootout with a handful of them last week and killed them all. The ladies in black merely nodded their approval. As I stated in my report, It appears that their numbers are growing as word of their liberation gets out. Women from nearby tribes are joining them. They're bringing children - some of the kids are young boys who want to fight!" added Browne.

"Thanks for the update. Look, I've been sent here to try to set up a political alliance with these, ah ... women. This is a real movement and we're going to try to help them get recognition from Pakistan. Of course we want to be their friends; we like their location and will stay as long as possible."

AS THE MONTHS went by, Steve was able to establish a shaky relationship with Rinni and her people. They used neighboring tribesmen as interpreters and, even then, communicating was difficult. It slowly became clear that Rinni would settle for no less than an outright assault on the men camped on the other side of the mountain. They were going to need modern weapons, and a lot of them.

Steve knew that even if Rinni's forces were successful, they would need help in structuring some form of local government to control the villages in her region. Receiving recognition from Pakistan would be essential and they would need guidance in how to deal with Islamabad to achieve this. Getting Rinni and her followers to understand would be difficult.

In early winter, Steve gave his operational manager a briefing on the latest orders from Washington.

"Look, Bob, they want you to stay here and militarily train these fighters. If we don't, they will attack those guys and probably get slaughtered. They're outgunned and have no combat training. There are lots of men from the surrounding tribes who want to join with Rinni in her fight but are totally undisciplined. All of them must be trained and the men have to recognize the women as their leaders. We're going to supply the arms."

"Man, that's a tall order!"

"Agreed. Furthermore, it appears that certain feminist powers on the Hill have been informed about these amazing women and want to put them on public display. This will help Rinni and her people get recognition and also promote the politicians' own agendas. They are rallying behind Rinni and are pushing hard for her cause.

Rinni and her warriors haven't the slightest idea of the magnitude of their fight and who their friends are. My job is to explain what she is up against and convince her that she needs our help. She has to know this is more than a mere tribal conflict. I'm going to try to talk Rinni and some of her fighters into coming back to Washington with me to meet their supporters. That's essential if the politicians are going to make their case for Rinni's fight. They need to see and talk to the leaders of the women combatants. And parade them around Washington."

"Steve, even if you can get them to go to Washington, how are they going to communicate? Nobody, and I mean NOBODY, speaks their language! Their dialects are sometimes not even understood by their own people and we are never sure what they are saying!"

"Oh, I think I know someone who can converse with them in their own language and dialects," stated Steve. "First I have to get Rinni there!"

STEVE, RINNI AND DAL boarded a plane for Washington on a cold February morning. The women were not wearing burkas, only simple head scarves. Zay would stay behind to command the guerrilla force.

A. J. had a busy week scheduled. His research lab was in full swing but was producing little results. He had volunteers for the experimental research but was having unexpected problems finding their bodies' compatible resonating frequencies. The process was much more complex than what he had imagined. Becky agreed.

A. J. considered having Genevieve search for a top-notch investigating firm to find Skeeter and Little Bit but dismissed the idea. Through Steve, he had access to better resources than they did. So he would conduct the search himself and began the process of retracing all of his previous investigative work, looking for new information and new resources. This was a mistake. A. J. never thought about googling the Zone. It simply was no longer a source and would be considered useless. However, this just might be one the first things a less informed investigator would do. They would have found Monica's book.

A. J. was in the process of sending an e-mail congratulating and thanking his three French scientist friends who had recently been jointly awarded the Nobel Peace Prize for Science. They had publicly acknowledged A. J. and others for their contributions.

Another e-mail was coming in.

A. J., I'm back in D. C. I need your help, please call, Thanks, Steve

Chapter 44: Twins

"STEVE, WELCOME BACK. Let me guess - they want you to go undercover and I have to teach you how to speak Pashto!" A. J. laughingly said over the phone.

"Close, real close, but what I need is for you to teach some Pashto speaking friends of mine how to speak their own language!" replied Steve.

"Ah! Dialect problems, huh?"

"You got it! But that's just the beginning..."

Steve gave A. J. a short briefing and said, "I'm going to send you what we have on these tough women. We want you to work with them before we take them public."

Pausing to digest what Steve had just told him, A. J. asked, "Steve, I heard Becky threaten to do it, but these young women ACTUALLY cut off the testicles of their enemies?"

"Yup, and tacked them on to trees for effect!"

"Whoa. I'd better be nice to them!"

"Does that mean you will help us? I don't want to put the pressure on, but you're the only game in town. Besides, I already told them you'd do it. They wouldn't have agreed to let me bring them here if we didn't have *A. J. McCleary*."

"How did I know that? Yeah, of course I'll help. I admire that kind of courage."

"Good, we'd like you to meet with them in a location half way between D.C. and your campus. We've got a spot in mind; it's a security issue.

Steve had selected an upscale hotel for the meeting place. He rented a large suite where the two women would stay during the indoctrination process. It was complete with two bedrooms, kitchen, living room and a small den.

Both appalled and angered, A. J. let out a slow whistle as he reviewed Steve's file. Someone in the agency had done an exceptional job gathering information on how the women of Rinni's villages had been abused for centuries. He welcomed the opportunity to talk to Rinni and Dal about what they had endured. A. J. knew this would be a sensitive issue with them and he would have go slowly.

A. J. was nervous approaching the hotel suite on the top floor. He dressed casually, assuming that men in suits might intimidate the women. He did not know exactly what to expect but wasn't prepared for what he was about to get involved in.

Steve opened the door at A. J.'s soft knock. "Right on time, A. J. Come in and meet our guests." The two stood side by side wearing embroidered tunics with long trousers, heads and faces uncovered.

Steve made the introductions but A. J. never heard him. He stood transfixed staring directly at who, he somehow knew, was Rinni.

His heart began to skip beats. Stunned and shaken, he let out a slow breath. If M. J. had had a twin sister, he was looking at her. Everything: the dark color and length of her hair, the light brown skin, height and body type, her expressive face, and the eyes - oh the eyes. They were M. J.'s, but in color only. Rinni's glare was threatening, dark and suspicious. Put off by A. J.'s stare she coldly stared back at him.

Sensing the awkward moment, Steve suggested, "Ah, you might want to say hello to our guests in your best Pashto."

A. J. recovered somewhat, smiled at Rinni and apologized for his rudeness, trying to explain why he was so taken aback. She seemed to understand but he wasn't sure. The look did not soften. He knew he had made a mistake. He instinctively sensed that, from here on, he would need to be gentle and calm. He suspected that this was going to be like befriending cautious and untrusting wild animals. They had good reason, he conceded. Try as he may A. J. could not take his eyes away from Rinni.

Steve motioned for them to sit in the living area and after the two women hesitantly settled into comfortable chairs, A. J. began talking to them.

Understanding his pure Pashto was difficult but between some recognizable words and hand gestures they realized that he wanted them to talk to each other. They complied and whenever there was a pause, he gestured to them to keep talking. They looked at one another and continued their dialogue. A. J. listened intently as he stared off into the distance. After another pause A. J., speaking Pashto in the women's peculiar dialect, said, "Please go on."

They were shocked. Rinni and Dal glanced at each another and A. J. repeated in a soft voice, "Please."

They talked non stop for another ten minutes and were amazed when A. J. joined the conversation.

"How did you do that?" exclaimed Rinni. "Nobody but the people in our village understands our dialect!" A. J. smiled and said, "It is really a pleasure to talk to you two. Welcome to America."

Steve was speechless - blown away by A. J.'s language abilities.

"I know. I can't explain it either," A. J. said. "Understanding foreign languages and dialects is something I could always do. I know that all of this must be confusing to you but that's what I'm here for. Don't be afraid to ask me anything; if I don't know the answers I'll sure find them out for you."

For the first time, A. J. could see the two starting to relax. "Rinni, I'm not sure if you understood me earlier or not, but let me apologize again for staring at you. A while back I lost someone very dear to me and you remind me so much of her. I'm sorry."

She ignored the apology and said, "What do we call you?"

"A. J., two letters," he said. "And your friend here is called Steve."

"Is *that* what he was trying to get us to say?" said Dal.

Rinni wasted no time; she was straightforward and business like. "We came here to get guns and ammunition. Steve insisted that we meet the people who are going to give them to us. Take us to those people so we can leave. A. J. repeated the demand to Steve. "Tell them we are going to do that, but we have to work around the politician's schedules. They don't understand the politics. I'm afraid I'm going to have to lean on you; nobody else can talk to them. Break it to them slowly - that they're going to be here for weeks! I can see that you're delighted with that prospect but they aren't going to be happy. And, A. J., forget it. They hate men!"

This was not going to be easy. A. J. had no idea how to proceed. The women were intense and had the most penetrating eyes he had ever seen. "You'll have your guns, Rinni, but some powerful people want to get to know you first. Let's make sure they don't get the wrong impression. You're very important to us; give me time to explain that to you. I promise, I will always be honest."

They said nothing. He smiled at Rinni. She showed no emotion whatsoever.

Chapter 45: The Americans Love Them

RINNI AND DAL had seen airplanes but had never been on one. They had only a vague idea of where they were going when boarding the plane in Islamabad and couldn't comprehend the distance. The drive from Dulles to the hotel had been unnerving and they were exhausted.

Steve had arranged for a female agent to be with Rinni and Dal whenever he wasn't there. She was with them the morning after their arrival while Steve was attending a conference held by Congresswoman Nan Keller, head of a sub-committee on women's rights.

"I'm sorry, Congresswoman, we are not going to allow anybody from a political congressional staff to interview our two guests or take part in their training," stated Steve's boss, Robert Haynes.

"All right. I know we are on the same team. I'll leave it in the hands of you experts; just give me plenty of notice when they're ready."

A. J. returned to the hotel the day after their initial meeting, bringing his computer and a small globe. He had had a session with the CIA's psychological team and they were in agreement on how to proceed. They would stay in the background and only Steve, the female agents and A. J. would be in physical contact with the Rinni and Dal.

A. J. decided to slow his research so he could spend time with their two guests. He could see how important it was to prepare them before they were turned over to Congresswoman Keller. Also, he couldn't get Rinni out of his mind.

He began with basic geography, reasoning that once Rinni and Dal saw how big the world was and how many people lived in it, they might understand the global impact of their cause.

He would not make the mistake of believing they were unintelligent simply because they were uneducated. Already, they had demonstrated intelligence dealing with the evil men of their villages

A. J. started slowly by showing them a map of the world on his computer. He pinpointed where they lived and zoomed down to the precise location then pulled it back and repeated the process. They immediately identified with the mountains. He had Rinni drag her hand across the map from her home to Washington D.C. and reminded her of their long flight. She took her finger to the edge of the map and said, "What's beyond that?" They were getting it.

Setting the globe in front of them saying "There are no edges, Rinni," he slowly spun the globe from D.C. to Pakistan. They were silent as he pointed to D.C. on the globe and then on Google map, focusing on the Capital building. Then he showed them videos of the people and traffic with the Capital in the background. Their eyes widened as they began to understand. He did the same thing with Islamabad. They got it!

Their curiosity and natural intellect took over and the questions started. It was a beginning and a good one. The next several days were spent introducing them to American civilization. The questions kept coming. He answered some of them in English and had them repeat the question also in English. They understood that he was teaching them the language and, slowly, they came to appreciate it.

Over the next few weeks, A. J. and Steve took them exploring public places to demonstrate that men and women could exist in harmony. The men were also trying to make them more comfortable around people. It was hard to gage what effect this was having; Rinni and Dal didn't say much and were beginning to show signs of restlessness.

Wherever they happened to be, A. J. made sure he was never alone with Rinni. It was a natural thing for him to hug someone. However, under these circumstances, he determined never to physically touch either one of them.

Rinni and Dal always turned in after dinner. It was their time to discuss the day and have their quiet talks.

"Rinni, the men in this country appear to be different. Take A. J. and Steve for example: they're polite, considerate and are really concerned about us. They're not just acting. I think they would fight anybody who tried to harm us. A. J. is so protective and I've never seen any man look at a woman the way he looks at you. I know you don't want to hear this, but it's a kind and gentle look. Loving."

"He's not looking at me, Dal. He's looking at someone he's lost and I happen to look like her. It makes no difference, anyway. We will be leaving shortly and neither one of us have time to see if these men really are different. We have a war to fight, remember?"

"Yes, I remember. I think it's time for us to start pushing them. I'm beginning to get the impression they aren't giving us the complete picture yet. We've learned a lot and maybe we're not ready, but I'm getting anxious."

"Me too," said Rinni, "I know we need to learn more but we have to get back to Pakistan... Okay, let's push them."

They were conducting their normal early morning educational session in the suite when Rinni interjected, "A. J., It's time for us to prepare for our fight back home. We want to know how Steve and his team are going to help us!"

A. J. interpreted and Steve glanced at him and said, "Not just yet." Dal interrupted A. J.'s reply, "No, it's time, Steve. It's time!" Both women had that hard piercing glare. They were not going to be put off. No interpretation was needed.

Steve gave A. J. a surrendering nod, "Okay, A. J., I guess it's time. I'm not going to argue with them."

A. J. cabled his computer to a large flat-screen TV and googled in a map of northern Pakistan and a broad area of the Islamic countries that surrounded it. He pinpointed their tiny villages and said without emotion, "Your small fighting force is surrounded on all sides by thousands of armed men who are determined to annihilate you."

He showed them a graphic satellite video of the armed camps and their locations. "If you were to win your fight and establish a cohesive form of government run by women, it would be a religious and cultural defeat for them and you will become a perpetual target for their jihad."

They sat like rocks staring at the evidence, not even blinking. Rinni unemotionally and in a flat tone said, "We would rather die than to go back to that life."

A. J. pulled his chair around and faced them. Taking a chance, he gently grasped their hands and softly uttered, "You are not alone in this fight; you don't have to die."

Steve explained that people all over the world identified with their cause and added, "Rinni, Dal, with the help of Nan Keller and her powerful forces, a significant amount of pressure could be put on Pakistan forcing them to give you some protection. Nan is a member of our government and is a crusader for world wide women's rights. Your cause is important to her."

Rinni and Dal listened attentively as Steve continued:

"We want you to meet with her, not only as fearless warriors, but as true leaders in the fight for women's rights. They want to proudly introduce you to the world. *Then* we are going to introduce you to the leaders of Pakistan."

Neither of them spoke as A. J. continued his translation. They were focused, tense. "It's important that you be able to play both roles," Steve said. "That's why we have been so deliberate with your preparation. We agree that your enemies on the other side of mountain must be defeated and that you must lead the fight. They are not outsiders but men from your villages and you would be fighting to establish your freedom from their barbarous yoke. Then your new political friends here could make their case, on your behalf, that you are a true viable entity. Pakistan would have to acknowledge you."

Steve was prepared for the next step but had wanted it to come later. He showed Rinni and Dal videos from all over the world that documented women's advocate groups demonstrating for their individual causes. He would use the globe to show where these groups were located in relationship to where they both lived. He had extensive coverage of Nan, featuring many of her battles. Rinni and Dal really took notice when she was shown leading rallies to stop female genital mutilation.

Dal looked at Steve and said in passable English, "You make me understand. You can fight with us!"

"Yes, we wait. We learn more," offered Rinni.

A. J. was beaming with pride at his prize English speaking students; they smiled back. It was the first time he had seen them smile. Rinni's smile took his breath away. She looked directly at him. Her eyes had softened.

Weeks later, Rinni and Dal played their roles superbly as Nan escorted them around Washington. They wore embroidered tunics and appeared comfortable and confident but both women retained the bearing of warriors. The Pakistani ambassador was impressed. He reported back to Islamabad... "These women are formidable and cannot be dismissed. The Americans love them."

Rinni and Dal were being trained to fire automatic weapons. Steve had kept his promise much to the delight of the two leaders.

A. J. was curious; he had never fired a gun of any kind. Steve obliged and allowed him to participate in this part of the training.

"It's nice to be on the other end of one of these things for a change," he commented. Steve looked at him curiously.

A. J. accompanied them on their final day of training. They had been drilled in mountain combat and briefed in the up to the minute satellite intelligence as to the position of their enemies. That information would be kept current.

Their training was over. They were returning to Pakistan.
Steve was going with them. The warriors said goodbye to A. J. at the hotel. Dal and Steve discreetly left Rinni and A. J. alone.

"Thank you, A. J. for... a lot of things."

"Rinni..."

"No," she interrupted. "It's better this way. I have visions in my dreams, A. J. and I've come to believe them. I am returning to my country to fight a battle. I will survive the battle, but not the war. My enemies will not go away, I know that now."

"Rinni..." again she interrupted, "Shh," and she put her hand to A. J.'s face. "I have never touched a man like this before," she said softly. "I'll miss you."

Rinni turned and left. A. J. couldn't bear to follow.

Chapter 46: Loose Ends

A. J. HAD BEEN distributed his stock more than a year ago. It was time to sell. The company made the right choice in settling the suit. Teams were poised to bring new products to the market, and with the McCleary chip, they were able to do that on an international scale.

The stock took off and, in less than a year, its value increased by two and a half times. The executives had been telling the insiders this would happen. They pointed out that the increase in the value of their personally owned stock would more than make up for the loss of their insider stock that was given to A. J. All but the three disgruntled stockholders had bought into that reasoning.

A. J. had an investment plan in place when he sold his stock on a secondary offering. He set aside money for taxes and traded heavily in the foreign markets with which he was very familiar. Like everything else A. J. attempted, he was successful. Money came easily to him. He was wealthy and he wanted to share it.

"They've had it!" exalted Genevieve. "The three bozos want to settle with the company and they want to release you if you release them from our suit. The court won't accept the settlement unless you sign off!"

"Tell them no. I won't sign off to any settlement until those three bandits agree to pay me one hundred thousand dollars each. The McCleary chip has already returned millions to them on their personal stock."

"Wow, you're tough!"

"No, Genevieve. I merely refuse to play that game of suing somebody to force them into a settlement they don't want. I would rather fight them all the way and lose than to give in to their high handed tactics."

Genevieve got back to him. "Galen wants to agree to your terms. He said he didn't want to sue in the first place but was placating the others. He's happy with his stock increase and doesn't mind paying your demand. The others are furious with him, but I don't think he cares."

Two days later the other two grudgingly capitulated. They took it personally.

The school year ended and A. J. planned to concentrate on writing his thesis. He would not be teaching. He also had been sporadically working on an architectural project begun in Europe. He enjoyed designing things and had a particular project in mind. Once again at a dead end with finding Skeet and Little Bit, he was frustrated to the point of inaction.

His research lab was put on hold. A. J. was having trouble concentrating. He missed Rinni and was beset with worry.

A. J. had planned to go to Detroit and decided now was the time; he needed the distraction. He knew what he wanted to do with the Zone and that's what his architectural project was all about. A. J. had promised himself that he wouldn't use his money merely to make more money. He wanted to contribute to worthy projects.

When he arrived in Detroit, he met with the city's planning department to see if his idea was feasible. It was. Then his search began for architects, engineers and builders.

The city was abuzz about the likely loss of their beloved baseball team, the Detroit Tigers. The owners had been unable to find a satisfactory location to build their new ballpark and were looking at sites outside the city.

Word got out from the planning department that the owner of the Zone was in town. The operational manager of the Tigers, Ed Bradley, contacted A. J. in a last ditch effort to try to convince him to sell them the Zone. He agreed to talk to him.

A. J. declined their offer. He had plans and did not need the money. When A. J. asked him why they couldn't renovate the old park, Bradley replied that they had wanted to do that but the cost of renovation had exceeded their budget. It made better financial sense to build a new one.

A. J. remembered his and Skeet's day at the old stadium. He recalled how she and Billy loved that place. He was saddened and knew that Skeeter would think keeping the Tigers in Detroit and playing in their old stadium was a worthy project.

"If you were to receive a donation to cover the excess cost of renovation, would you consider keeping the Tigers in Detroit?" he asked Bradley.

"Yes, of course. That would change our thinking completely."

"Good, because I would like to be that donor."

Bradley was speechless. A. J. continued, "I do have one stipulation, though. I want you to set aside a section of one hundred seats in the bleacher area to be designated as the 'Billy' section. Tickets to those seats are to be distributed free to people who can not afford them. Also, I want a plaque to be placed in the designated section honoring Billy. And I wish my gift to be anonymous."

Regaining his composure, Bradley, elated, stated that he would schedule an immediate meeting with his management team and get back to A. J.

Bradley called the next day. "We're all in agreement and couldn't be happier. We accept your generous donation, Mr. McCleary. But we have one question: who's Billy?"

"Billy was a police officer here in Detroit. He served for more than thirty years and was killed in the line of duty. His name was Lt. William Donovan and he was a rabid Tigers fan."

The necessary papers were drawn and A. J. made arrangements for the transfer of funds. The Tigers would be staying in Detroit; and to the delight of many, they would be playing ball in their grand old newly renovated ballpark.

A. J. hired an architect to put finishing touches on his plan for the Zone. He would work with the architect's suggested engineers and builders. He had tied up his loose ends and left Detroit feeling pleased with what he had accomplished.

He phoned Becky and informed her of his plans. Then he bought a one way ticket to Islamabad.

Chapter 47: Pakistan

"GOOD MORNING A. J. Nice to see you again. What brings you to Islamabad?" asked the government agent A. J. had worked with at The Hague.

"Hello, Omar. It's nice to see you too. I'd like to say that I'm here on business or pleasure but I've come to ask a favor of you. If you can't accommodate me, I will certainly understand."

"You did us a great service at The Hague, A. J., and my government would welcome the chance to assist you if it is at all possible."

A. J. got right to the point. "I'm traveling to a remote area in the northern part of your country and I need a guide and safe passage to my destination."

Omar hesitated for a moment and said, "Would this happen to have something to do with those women training for combat near the Afghanistan border?"

"Yes, it would. I don't want to deceive you or your government, Omar. I'm here on my own behalf. My government doesn't know the reason for my visit. I helped train two of those women and they have become friends of mine. I'm here to help them if I can."

Omar twisted in his chair and said, "Your honesty is appreciated, A. J., but I have to tell you, those courageous women are not as popular here as they are in the U.S. Many would like to see them, ah, shall we say, eliminated."

"I know, Omar. I'm going to try to help prevent that from happening."

"All right, but this is not something my department gets involved in. However, I work closely with those who handle that sort of business. They will remember you and you're not asking for much. Let me see what I can do. You've done the right thing by informing us of your intentions. And for the record, I'm one of the many who want the female warriors to succeed. In the meantime, enjoy our interesting city and I will contact you as soon as possible. Try the Talkingfish restaurant; it should suit your western tastes!"

A. J. had not informed Steve that he was coming to Pakistan. He didn't want to compromise Steve's delicate assignment and felt it would better if he operated without the assistance or knowledge of the CIA.

Two days later Omar sent instructions to board a bus in Islamabad, take it northwest to a city called Mingora and to wait at the Mingora bus station for his contact. A. J. did as instructed and shortly after arriving there, two heavily bearded men dressed in mountain tribal clothing approached him. "You speak Pashto?" A. J. nodded yes.

"Come with me, I'll give you information as we travel."

They climbed into a battered jeep and headed northwest toward the wild and lawless tribal areas. A. J. rode in the front seat. The men were armed.

"We're taking you to a frontier province region north of the tribal area on the Afghanistan border. You will spend the night in one of our camps and then you will be taken by horseback to a trail that will lead to your destination."

They were soon bouncing across impassable mountain roads for what seemed like hundreds of miles. They finally reached their crude campsite and after a quick meal cooked over an open fire, A. J. crawled into a cot and fell asleep.

The following morning A. J. was on top of a horse with a guide leading the way. He had never been on a horse before and prayed that the horse knew what he was doing. He was enticed by his new friends to swap his western clothes for something more suitable for the rugged terrain that he was entering. He could only imagine what Steve's reaction would be.

They rode for hours in the mountainous country. At one point the trail narrowed to three feet with vertical drops of five hundred feet on both sides. A. J. forgot about the reins and anxiously held on to the saddle horn with both hands. Much to his relief, the guide finally stopped at the crest of a hill and pointed to a valley below.

"You'll have to walk from here. Make sure you have no weapons of any kind and stay on the trail. At the other end of this valley someone will greet you. Just hope they are not the women!" With that he turned and left, taking A. J.'s horse with him.

Once in the valley A. J. was completely in the open. He knew that he would surely have been spotted by now and was more than a little jumpy. The trail started to ascend back into the mountains and his breathing became heavier. The trail narrowed as it passed through a break in the rocks.

"If you weren't American-looking I would have killed you!" a high pitched voice called out to him from somewhere in the rocks. He or she was speaking the dialect of Rinni's people.

"I *am* American and I'm looking for my American friends who are the guests of Rinni and Dal!"

"Walk past the big rock in front of you and stay on the trail. If you have any guns I will shoot you. Just keep on walking; I'll be right behind you."

A. J. obeyed and as he walked past the big rock he could see his captor, a young boy twelve or thirteen years old.

They walked straight up for about a half of a mile and then the trail started down again. Below them he could see a sprawling camp and beyond that, at a lower altitude, he could see a village.

"I will leave you now. If you come back up this trail alone, I will shoot you!" A. J. turned and smiled at the young boy with the big gun,

"Thank you for the escort. I'll tell Rinni what a great job you did." The boy grinned and headed back up the trail.

A. J. paused and reviewed the landscape. The camp was set up in military fashion and was active but not overrun by men or women. The village was nestled below the hill where the camp was situated. A semicircular bowl of high mountainous terrain enveloped the village on all sides except for the far end. There was a small open valley on that end that lay directly in front of a high and steep jagged range of mountains. A. J. was certain that Rinni and Dal's enemies were camped on the other side of that mountain range. There were plenty of trees offering cover for small military forces.

The village disappeared from sight as he descended the trail towards the camp. As he came closer he could see that the area served as a supply depot for guns and ammunition. There were small barracks lined up in military fashion. He paused and walked directly into the camp heading straight for the largest barrack. He was not noticed. Just as he was approaching the barrack, two men came out the door studying a large map. A. J. smiled and said, "Hey, where can a guy get a beer around here!"

Startled, Steve looked up … "HOLY SHIT, A. J.! WHAT THE... HOW THE… WHERE THE HELL DID YOU COME FROM?"

"Well, I had the bus drop me off at the trailhead a few yards back and was escorted the rest of the way by your well armed and mighty sentry. Boy, you have tight security around here!" Both men laughed as they embraced one another.

"Good thing you didn't fool with him - the way you're dressed he would have shot you as an enemy - I'm not kidding. Besides, that was one of Dal's nephews; you better treat him with respect."

"Really, I should have known; he was all business just like Dal."

"This is Bob Browne. He runs things around here. Bob, here's the guy Rinni and Dal think so highly of, A. J. McCleary."

"Pleased to meet you, A. J. I would appreciate it if you didn't tell anybody how you got in here undetected. I'd get fired."

"I came in the back door. Obviously you're not concerned with intruders coming from that direction. Your troubles appear to be on the other side of that range behind the village."

"Nice assessment, A. J.," said Steve. "You came through friendly territory; those guys have our backs. But what ARE you doing here, as if I didn't know?"

"Sorry Steve, I couldn't let her go into danger without being there. Look, I won't get in the way and I can really help in the intelligence end by interrogating any prisoners captured. I'll understand their dialects."

"What prisoners? A. J., they will literally shoot the wounded! They won't stop until every one of the bastards are dead!" exclaimed Steve.

"Jesus, how many are they up against?"

"We figure less than a thousand; it's hard to tell. We've had some defectors come over the mountain but Zay captures them, asks a few questions and executes them on the spot! They've stopped defecting."

"Wow. Zay - is that Rinni and Dal's... the one they left in charge of the fighting force?"

"Yeah, she's absolutely ruthless," added Bob. "A cold blooded killer and perfect for the job. Hell, we had guys join up from the other tribes but when they refused to serve under her command she shot them! She's not like Rinni or Dal. There's no reasoning with her, but, boy, do the troops follow her orders! They are a remarkable fighting force, A. J., fearless and disciplined beyond belief. They're gonna win this fight. Those idiots on the other side of the mountain underestimate them."

"We also have about one thousand fighters under arms who are now sufficiently trained for combat, almost all of them women. This will be a short fight," said Steve. "You ought to see Rinni's battle plan - challenging but simple and efficient. She will take a third of the troops around the right flank of the mountain, Dal will take the same number around the left and Zay will charge straight up the mountain with the remaining forces. It should all be over in a day. No one from the outside is interfering. They know that we're here and they won't take sides for political and religious reasons."

"Steve, we both know that the real fight comes after the battle. Have they given that much thought?" asked A. J.

"Yes, that's Dal's department and she has some novel ideas. I'll share them with you later."

"Okay, I can't imagine you guys staying out of the fight."

"Why, A. J., we're here as advisors! That's after we send hundreds of missiles to their designated targets of course," chuckled Steve.

"I will be in the rear of Dal's forces with my intelligence team. Bob will do the same for Zay's. And I won't even try to stop you from joining the team following Rinni. A. J., Rinni's got the last call on that; it's her ballgame."

"Yeah, I know, Steve. One last question: where is she?"

Chapter 48: Take No Prisoners

STEVE WAS GIVING A. J. the grand tour from a military jeep. "This is the main village where Rinni and Dal live. There are four other smaller villages tucked away in the mountains but they're pretty much deserted. The inhabitants have moved into the main village for security. The village is continuing to grow as word spreads about the women's fight. There are a lot of children here as you can see; most are boys. If they survive in their struggle, the next generation should balance out the genders. It's really exciting to watch this transition evolve. I'm glad to be a part of it.

Rinni is with her fighting group encamped at the upper end of the valley. Dal is at the other end and Zay is in the middle. They're waiting for me to inform them of the attack date. I'm waiting for confirmation of the time set for the rocket attack. It could come at any moment; that's why the leaders are with their people. You got here just in time."

A. J. nodded and asked, "What happens after the rocket attack?"

"They'll move into position during the confusion of the exploding missiles and will launch their attack after the bombardment stops. They can be ready in a moment's notice to move out but that won't take place until the early morning hours under the cover of a moonless night. Before the rocket explosions.

Come on. We'll drive out to Dal's encampment; I need to confer with her on some matters. Then we will swing by Zay's so you can meet her. I'll drop you off at Rinni's on the way out."

Dal looked up as Steve drove into her headquarter area, "A. J., what a surprise! Does Rinni know you're here?"

"Hey Dal, you look great in your combat clothes. How do you like mine?"

"You look funny," laughed Dal. "I'll try to keep my fighters from shooting you."

"No. She doesn't know I'm here. Don't tip her off, I want to surprise her, too."

"Oh yes, you'll surprise her, all right. Are you going to stay for the action?"

"I hope to be part of the action, Dal." Dal shot a glance at Steve who shrugged and said, "Rinni's call."

After meeting Zay, A. J. whistled, "Steve, that tiny, pretty girl is the most fierce looking woman I have ever seen! She actually sent shivers down my spine and she never spoke a word!"

"Yeah, that's Zay. She hates everybody. I'm glad she's on our side."

Rinni saw them as they drove in. She showed little emotion.

"Special delivery, Rinni!" Steve exclaimed as A. J. jumped out of the jeep. "I should have an update for you shortly. I'll be back," and he drove off.

Rinni looked at A. J. without smiling, "You shouldn't have come. This is

not your fight."
"I couldn't stay away."
"Don't make me out to be her, A. J. You don't want to lose her again."
"You're not her, Rinni, and you're not mine to lose. I'll stay out of the way but I will be close by."

Rinni stared at him and saw his determination. She knew it was useless to try to dissuade him. They were standing by a shed she was using as a command post.

"Come with me." She took him down a narrow path that led to a small bivouac area protected under the cover of large trees. Her small army was encamped there, clad in black and heavily armed with automatic weapons that they were busily cleaning. Almost all of them were women. They were separated into six distinct groups of about fifty fighters each. She stopped at each group and identified A. J. to them. "If you see this man on the battlefield, don't shoot him. He is one of us. A red scarf will be tied around his arm!"

She turned and A. J. walked next to her as they headed back towards the shed. "Each small unit has their assignments. Steve's pictures have identified where our enemies are located and we intend to kill them all. There will be no prisoners taken. They know we're here but they will never see or hear us coming. Their superior male belief systems makes it impossible for them to believe that we are a fighting force.

You will stay in the rear with Steve's men and the medical teams. I must lead those women and I can't do it if I'm worrying about you. I need your word on that, A. J.! Refuse and I'll place you under arrest." He knew she meant it.

"You have my word, but if you're in trouble, I'm coming!"
She smiled for the first time and said, "Of course you will."

They looked up as Steve skidded in bringing his jeep to a bouncing stop.

"It's a go, Rinni! You're moving out at 0300! Zay will be one hour ahead of you; she's got to climb."
He nodded in A. J.'s direction.
"He will be with your guys, Steve, and will move with them," declared Rinni in remarkably good English.
"Good. Grab that pack in the back, A. J. You'll need it for tonight."

He then tossed A. J. a holster and a sidearm.
"It's supposed to be for self defense, but shoot every one of those sons-a-bitches you see!

Rinni, I'm supposed to have a camera guy with me, but I want your okay on that!"
"Yes. But no pictures of my casualties!"
"Done. See you two on the other side. Put them down early tonight, Rinni. Sleep is important. One of my guys will wake you. Do what she

tells you, A. J.," he said as he wheeled the jeep around and left.

Rinni filled A. J. in. "We're going to move within one hundred yards of our battle positions and wait for the rocket attack. Then we will occupy those positions during the confusion. When the shelling stops, we all attack at once. Dawn will just be breaking. We will have outflanked them and Zay will force them directly into our fire.

You guys won't move until the shelling stops. Wait until you hear our automatic weapons firing and come up as fast as you can. You'll be in jeeps so you should get there in a hurry. We need the medical teams and the updated intelligence. I'll be in the first group; we will keep moving. The second group will hit them and then the next, and so on. You can follow me, A. J., but don't catch up... There you've got the whole plan. It should be all over by noon."

Night fell. Steve's men arrived and rolled out their bags behind Rinni's warriors. Rinni returned from visiting her teams and set her blankets down near the men's.

A. J. walked over and plunked his pack next to her. "Is there room at the inn, Commander?"

"Yeah, but behave yourself. My girls are trained killers and they will be watching."

"Don't worry," he smiled. "Do you think your troops will get any sleep? They must be frightened no matter how well-trained they are."

"They're not afraid, A. J. Unlike your people, they've lived with death every day of their lives. Dying is of little consequence to them. They lust for revenge."

"What about you, Rinni? Do you feel the same?"

"I told you that I will survive this fight. I know my fate, A. J. I'm not certain about yours so don't take any chances. You're not supposed to die."

"Rinni ..."

"We need sleep," she interrupted. "We will talk more after the fight."

"Okay," he said quietly.

He could not sleep. Rinni was sleeping restlessly. Suddenly she started to utter little cries. A. J. sat up and looked at her. She was trembling and frantically pulling the blankets around her. He reached over and touched her hand; It was ice cold. He grabbed his blanket and threw it over her. He got under both blankets and pulled her close. She was facing away from him. Suddenly she was awake and stiffened when she felt A. J.'s body next to hers.

"Rinni, it's me. You're cold; I'm trying to warm you!"

She understood, "A. J., It was just a nightmare. Happens to me all the time and I get real cold," she uttered between chattering teeth.

"All right, but I'm not going to leave until you warm up."

He realized that he had both arms tightly wrapped around her and was grasping her hands pulling her closer to him. He caught himself and reacted by releasing her hands.

"I'm sorry, Rinni. I wasn't trying to …"

"Shh." She took his hands into hers placing them on her breast... She was no longer trembling.

Chapter 49: The Fight

"RINNI, A, J., it's time."

The agent moved on when he saw they were awake. Rinni was up in a flash and headed for her fighting groups. A. J. laced his boots, checked his sidearm and put on a light jacket. It was a chilly fall morning. He was standing next to his pack when Rinni returned.

She walked up to him pulling out a red scarf from her black tunic as she approached. She tied it around A. J.'s arm just above his bicep. "There," she said. "It belonged to my mother. I'll remove it when the fighting stops. Join the others, A. J."

The men sat in their jeeps as the women came within ten feet of them, heading into the valley. They were so quiet and darkly dressed that they would have passed unnoticed to an unsuspecting eye. More women moved in behind the jeeps. They were from the village and would follow on foot to the battlefield to help with the wounded.

Rockets slamming into the other side of the mountain lit up the sky as their deadly warheads exploded. The sound was frightening.

"Where are they coming from?" questioned A. J.

"Don't ask," came a reply.

Then came silence and the men tensed. A clamoring of automatic weapon fire broke the silence.

"Lets go," shouted one of them. "NO!" came the squad leaders reply. "That's coming from Zay's area; she would be first!"

Another wait, then distinctly and from much closer came the sounds of fire from Rinni's fighters. "MOVE OUT," came the order and the jeeps raced full throttle across the valley. There was no need for silence; the battle was raging.

Daylight was breaking as the jeeps rounded the far edge of the range. They were now on the other side of the mountain, racing through the foothills where the camps of the enemy were located. The magnitude of the assault had caught their unsuspecting enemies completely by surprise and the rocket attack was devastating. Rinni's trailing groups were finishing off what the others before them had started. The jeeps pulled up behind the last team; it immediately became apparent what their orders were. They were shooting the wounded. There was only one casualty dressed in black and a medic had jumped out to treat her wound. The small convoy of men moved on.

As they moved further, they could see what was happening. Rinni's forces had completely encircled their assigned enemy camps and were driving the fleeing men towards Dal who in turn was driving her foes towards Rinni. Zay's forces had come pouring over the top of the mountain and hit them from behind, sending the confused men in both directions. Caught in a huge vice, they were being slaughtered. Many had thrown up their arms in surrender but were mercilessly gunned down.

Fighting was now concentrated in the center and, after dropping medics off at earlier battlefield sites, the jeeps pulled to within one hundred yards of the battle. The area was in the middle of a collection of boulders and deadly skirmishes were taking place between large rocks at close quarters.

A. J. was frantically searching for Rinni. He couldn't find her. One of the men handed him binoculars. As he panned the field he suddenly stopped, lowered the glasses and refocused. He spotted Steve kneeling over a fallen woman in black on the far edge of the battlefield. A. J. could see their enemies moving and threatening to get behind them. Most of Dal's fighters had advanced past Steve's position.

From out of nowhere came another woman in black firing furiously and driving the attackers back into the rocks. It was Rinni. She had seen Steve and the fallen fighter and had rushed to their aid, but in doing so she separated herself from her forces. They were outnumbered and in trouble.

A. J. took off in a panic, scooping up an automatic weapon that lay on the ground. He was almost there when several wide eyed frightened men came rushing out of the rocks trying to make a break for it by running through Rinni, Steve and the fallen fighter. A. J. opened fire and stopped them cold, chasing them back into the rocks. Rinni hadn't seen the danger; things were happening too fast.

Steve leapt to his feet and fired off several rounds with his .45 to targets just behind A. J. who felt the wind of the bullets as they whizzed past his ear. Two gunmen toppled over as they were taking dead aim at A. J.

Rinni was now treating the fallen woman. It was Dal. Her leg was badly shot up and Rinni had a tourniquet in place. Steve was dragging her to her feet.

"TAKE HER OTHER SIDE, A. J. AND LET'S GET THE HELL OUT OF HERE!" shouted Steve. The four of them raced side by side to the waiting jeeps and medics. Dal's arms were around both their necks and they gripped her by the waist with her one good leg barely touching the ground. Rinni was right next to them firing away as the killers still tried to get behind them.

Steve's men circled back and got between the four of them and their attackers. Rinni's forces broke through, shooting at anything that moved. The camera, mounted on the jeep's hood, was on automatic and its powerful lens had recorded the whole escape. Then it was over. There were scattered gunshots as the women, true to their word, were killing any enemy who survived. With the consent of Pakistan, helicopters were ordered in to evacuate Rinni's most seriously wounded. Dal was one of them. It would take a huge medical effort to save her leg.

The women's casualties were incredibly light due to their thorough training and discipline. They counted thirty-five dead and fifty-two wounded. Most of the dead belonged to Zay's fighters; they had borne the brunt of the attack as they fearlessly charged into the entrenched defenders. Zay was one of the dead.

"She was unbelievable," said an amazed Bob Browne.

"They met resistance all the way down and she never took cover, not once. She just went from spot to spot on a tear, killing everyone in front of her. She almost made it to the bottom but got too far out front and was gunned down. The women in black have themselves a true hero."

Chapter 50: The Supreme Irony

MEDICS PLACED DAL in a transport helicopter alongside several other wounded warriors. Dal asked for A. J. go with her on the trip to the Islamabad hospital. She wanted to make sure her wounded fighters understood the seriousness of their injuries and that the doctors understood them.

Steve leaned over Dal and said, "I'll bring Rinni and some of your troops to visit you in a few days; she's going to be a little busy for now. Hey, I get the first dance when you're ready!"

"The fight's over, Dal. They're all dead," coolly stated Rinni. "Hurry and heal fast! We've got a government to set up and you're badly needed. See you in a couple of days."

"I'll be waiting Rinni," Dal whispered through her pain.

Rinni turned and said to A. J., "Stay with her; she's not afraid of killers but I think she's terrified of doctors." She took the red scarf from A. J.'s arm, "You keep this. It brought you luck and I want something for you to remember me by." She tucked it in the pocket of his jacket.

"I don't need a scarf for that, Rinni." A chill ran through his body. He didn't know how to reply.

He boarded the helicopter and shouted to Steve, "Nice shooting, partner, thanks. I don't think those guys liked me!"

"Yeah, you're right. They liked you about as much as those guys back in Detroit liked me. I hope we're not taking turns saving each other's bacon because if we are, YOU'RE UP!

Take care of the ladies, A. J. See you in Islamabad."

With the aid of the American's small earth-moving equipment and trucks, Rinni and her victorious fighters dug a mass burial pit away from the foothills of the mountain. All the despised dead men were buried with no markers. Their guns, ammunition and useful belongings were collected and stored in the village. Little evidence remained that a great battle had taken place on that side of the mountain.

A special cemetery in the heart of the village was designated as the final resting place of the heroic women warriors. Rinni kept her little army intact and stationed them on both sides of the mountain. Steve's people were invited to stay as long as they wished.

Two days later, Rinni, with a handful of her fighters, joined Steve and members of his team as they loaded themselves into a helicopter and headed for Islamabad.

Within days, word of the women's historic victory made world news headlines. Most people had no idea what was unfolding in that remote region. They were about to be educated. Now that the war had turned out successfully, releases to the wire services were orchestrated to offer maximum impact as it related to human and women's rights.

The news was supported by 'credible' on-site reporting backed up by indisputable pictorial evidence. The casualty counts were hard to believe. So few of Rinni's fighters had died and the entire enemy force was annihilated. The actual accounting of the battle would astound the world.

Countries from around the globe acknowledged the event and toasted the women for their achievement. Islamabad broke into a spontaneous celebration with thousands of people demonstrating in the streets. The demonstrators were mostly women and college students who sensed the enormous shift in the cultural and political attitude of the region.

The Pakistani government sent a detachment to the hospital to protect Dal and her wounded comrades. Word had spread that one of the leaders and many of the fighters were being treated there. The public was crying for names and pictures of the warriors. The CIA, at the urging of Nan Keller and interested women's rights groups from around the world, obliged them. This was pre-planned; they wanted the truth to be told and did not want the women's accomplishment to be negatively spun and diminished by the lies of their enemies.

Training photographs of Dal and Zay, identifying them as two of the leaders, were released to the news media. Part of Bob Browne's account of Zay's incredible death charge down the mountain was released making her an instant national hero. Thousands of Dal's admirers gathered outside the hospital cheering and waving placards with her image on them.

But it was Rinni who fascinated and captivated. She was credited as the architect of the movement and its unquestionable leader.

The photo of Rinni blasting her way through their enemies who outnumbered them became the iconic image of the war. A. J., Dal and Steve had been carefully cropped out; what remained was a closeup view of Rinni running toward the camera looking to her left at the men who were trying to kill her. Flames were spitting from her automatic weapon. She was bareheaded, wearing black combat clothes, jet black hair flying in the wind. Her remarkable beauty and unmistakable courage made her absolutely irresistible to the media and to Islamic women around the world.

Pakistani military personnel met Rinni's helicopter. Leaks, intentional or not, were rampant in the government and notice of Rinni's arrival was made public. Rinni and her fighters were escorted to the hospital in bulletproof vehicles. Steve discretely did not accompany them. He was frantically working the phones but he was helpless to provide the necessary security. He did not have the manpower. Steve's team had to rely on the Pakistanis who, so far, were doing an excellent job.

Rinni was overwhelmed. Her picture was everywhere and she was astonished by their raucous reception.

They were rushed up the hospital steps but Rinni stopped at the top and looked over the crowd that had flocked to the area - thousands of them wildly chanting ... "RINNI ... RINNI ... RINNI!" She was still wearing all black. Embarrassed, she waved and ducked into the hospital. The spontaneous roar of the crowd was deafening.

Dal sat in a wheelchair with her bandaged leg extended. The doctors had saved her leg but it was certain that she would always have a limp and would need a cane to walk. She was thankful for their wonderful effort. She, A. J. and two of her fighters were watching Rinni's arrival and turbulent welcome.

Rinni and her companions burst into the room, "DAL, LOOK AT YOU! We heard." She rushed to her friend grabbing both of her hands. "You ARE going to be dancing!"

"Well, maybe a slow one," Dal sighed. "Rinni, can you believe what's going on out there?"

"No, but if you think you're off the hook, you're wrong!" she smiled. "We passed a door in the hallway that leads out to a balcony; what do you think, A. J.?"

A. J. caught on quickly, "You got it! Lets go!" He wheeled Dal out of the room and made a beeline for the balcony door. Dal laughed as he opened the door and Rinni wheeled her out to the balcony railing with the other women following.

The crowd saw them and instantly recognized Dal from her posters. It was her turn. "DAL...DAL...DAL," they yelled out! She waved back. "RINNI...DAL...RINNI...DAL"... It was bedlam. The media was having a field day. Soon the rest of the world would get their first glimpse of these two remarkable women. A. J. stood behind. Rinni turned to look for him. They made eye contact and smiled. A. J. couldn't have been prouder. Or sadder.

Later that day a few key Pakistani ministers entered the hospital from the rear entrance. They were greeted by Steve and his boss, Robert Haynes, who had just arrived.

"Thanks for acting so efficiently," Haynes said to the ministers.

"There's a lot of fire power within fifty miles of their village!"

"We know that and we have made our decision. Can we visit Ms. Ameen and Ms. Khaleel?"

"Yes, they're waiting for you."

After the formal introductions, with A. J. interpreting, the Defense Minister said, "We offer our congratulations on your magnificent victory. Please understand that for political reasons we could not publicly support you. You have won over the hearts of millions of our citizens and the minds of many of us in our government. We are now prepared to give our support and help protect you from certain reprisals by your enemies." Rinni and Dal listened intently.

"To do that, by special resolution, we are going to designate your region as a protectorate and create a district status for you. You will have absolute autonomy to run your district as you wish but you will be under our military protection."

Rinni tilted her head and mouthed the word, 'protectorate'.

Dal continued a stony faced silence.

"Protectorate?" Rinni asked aloud.

"Yes. We intend to establish a garrison in the mountain range where the battle took place and have constant patrols in the immediate areas surrounding you. Mr. Haynes' country has offered their satellite and electronic help which we have accepted. This will go into effect immediately."

"And, what about our fighters?" asked Rinni.

"We will refer to your forces as police and they will be under your control with no interference from us. You can call yourselves mayors, presidents or anything you want. Just tell us how you wish to be addressed. I know you haven't had time to think about it but at some point we're are going to need a name for your district.

We will introduce the resolution to the parliament tomorrow and give you a copy when it is passed, which it definitely will. Special ministers will be assigned to you and you can work through them on any problems that need our attention. I know you're tired so we will go now. Once again, congratulations on a battle well fought and we look forward to working with you."

After they left, Rinni and Dal embraced and came as close to tears as they ever would. They looked at Steve and A. J. "Thank you," Rinni said.

Steve had arranged accommodations for everybody at the same hotel. They bid Dal goodnight and headed for the elevator.

Rinni stopped at the balcony and walked outside into the early night air. A. J. followed. They were left alone as the others waited in the lobby. The crowds were gone and Rinni gazed at the sky.

"She's going to need a lot of help, A. J. I know you won't forget her when you go back to your country." He started to say something but Rinni cut him off. "No, this is not your home and you have important things to do elsewhere. I would never have left here."

"Rinni, it frightens me when you talk like something has already happened."

"It has, A. J. It has. I told you, I know my fate and I'm at peace with it. My journey isn't over; it's just beginning. Dal and the others understand that. Take comfort in what they say. You've given me a gift I never thought I would have. Unlike the others, I know now what it is to love and be loved by a man. I can't ask for more out of this life, A. J. I can go to my new journey with a feeling of fulfillment. Thank you for the gift and be happy for me."

They traveled in separate cars to the hotel; it was important that the CIA remain in the background. Rinni and her small group entered the hotel at a secured entrance at the same time Steve and A. J. were coming in the front door. A. J. suddenly stopped and shouted,
"CAN YOU HEAR IT?"

The concussion from the explosion blew Steve and A. J. back out the door. They lay on their backs stunned and disoriented and could faintly hear sounds of screaming and then sirens. Thick smoke filled their nostrils and clouded their vision.

"STEVE, STEVE, are you all right?" coughed A. J.

"Yeah, I think so," Steve replied.

They managed to stagger to their feet and stumble away from the smoke. They stood at the side of the hotel and looked at what used to be the back of the building.

"Oh no, that's where Rinni went in," calmly stated Steve.

They raced around the corner of the building and saw that the entire back portion of the poorly constructed ten story hotel had collapsed on top of itself.

A. J. spotted Rinni's car lying on its side and he and Steve ran over to it. The dazed security driver was crawling out the window. He recognized Steve and A. J. and said, "They had just walked into the building when it went off. I'm sorry."

They both knew that nobody could have survived that kind of total destruction.

It took weeks to clear the rubble. None of the bodies were found. Security cameras away from the building recorded the suicide bomber entering the building seconds behind Rinni. It was the supreme irony. The bomber was female.

Chapter 51: Rinnistan

THEY SAT IN DAL'S hospital room two days after the bombing, waiting for a visit from A. J.'s friend Omar Karim.

"She knew she was going to die, Dal. She told me you would understand how she knew and I was to take comfort in what you would tell me."

Dal tried to explain, "We, as women, have always been told that our lives are meaningless. We've come to believe that our salvation occurs when we die; then we move on to a new and better life. We look forward to death and are not afraid. We are religious in our own way and look for signs that tell us when we are to begin our new journey. Rinni's signs came to her in her dreams, like a vision. Her visions came while we were in America, A. J."

"I know. She told me," he said somberly.

"Rinni saw in her visions that her martyrdom would be the face, the symbol, of our new life. She was too humble to make such a statement so she spoke to me about it in vague terms. Rinni would have been pleased to know that she would still be helpful to us after she moved on. The women are happy for her and Zay and the others who were killed. That's why we are not in mourning."

"I'm not sure I understand all that but ... go on," said A. J.

"What we were learning in America confused and frightened us. We worried that If our lives became to easy we would no longer be able to accept death as the next step in our journey."

"We *do* think of death as a tragedy; your beliefs are foreign to us. But, you are happy now?" asked A. J.

"Our goal from the beginning was to rid ourselves of the brutal men who were killing us, not to establish a wonderful new life. We welcomed your support, but we had no idea that it would lead to this. We only wanted to be left alone so we could die with dignity when the time came.

I don't want our people to have any illusions about their existence here in this lifetime. I just want them to be safe and to live without fear. All this world-wide attention - how is it going to affect us? We are determined to keep our lives simple but not so difficult."

"That might be impossible, Dal. You will be overwhelmed by well intentioned people who will want to change your lives. Steve talked to me briefly about how you want to run your District. It sounds modest but I liked your idea about opening up those old trade routes to outsiders."

"Yes, our little village is ideally situated for trade and always has been. Those old northern roads that were once joined together in our valley connected many different cultures by land routes. The Pakistan defense minister indicated to me that they might be building an airstrip on the other side of the mountain to supply their garrison. If we rebuilt those old roads, it would certainly open things up for trade here in this region. Our lives would be enriched in many ways."

"Yes, I heard about that possibility; that's why I invited one of Pakistan's trade agents to meet with you. Omar Karim is a friend of mine and he's the one who saw to it that I got to your region safely. You can trust him; he supported your fight. He's a good man, Dal."

Omar arrived a few minutes later and greeted Dal, "It is a pleasure and an honor to meet you, Ms. Khaleel. You and the women of your region have earned our respect. I'm so sorry about Ms. Ameen; the people of our country came to love her and then lost her the same day. You can rest assured that her new friends here in Islamabad won't let the world forget her."

"Thank you, Mr. Karim. Rinni will never be forgotten."

"A. J. spoke to me about your idea for the old trade routes. I had no knowledge of their history until he told me about them. I did my own research and I see why they were so important. I would like to help; in fact I've informed the trade minister that I wish to be appointed as trade agent for your district if you decide you want one."

"You know, Mr. Karim..."

He interrupted, "Please call me Omar."

"All right, Omar. Trade and Defense are the ministries I'm interested in. Your help would be welcome. You know, I've never called a Muslim man by his first name before. It's only fair that you call me Dal."

"Another honor, Dal. I will make the necessary arrangements."

They would become good friends and Omar would turn out to be the most important man in Dal's life.

"You are a natural diplomat, Governor," smiled A. J. after Omar left. "You're going to do just fine."

"Governor. Is that what I'm supposed to be called?"

"Sounds good to me. Look, I don't know how you'll to react to this, but you're going to need money if you are to remain autonomous and not financially dependent on Islamabad. I'm in a position to see to it that you get whatever you need. How about making me your unofficial finance minister?"

"I don't know anything about such matters, A. J., but if you think I need one, I can't imagine anybody I could trust more than you."

"Great, I'll set it up and no one will get their hands on your treasury except you and me," he smiled.

"A. J., I have no real concept of money. How much are we going to need?"

"Oh, about as much as it would take to renovate a Major League baseball park."

"Well, okay, whatever that means," sighed Dal.

A. J. had found another worthy cause for the dispensation of his wealth.

"Hey, have you thought of the name for your district yet? I'm going to need it."

"Yes, I have. It will be called Rinnistan!"

Congresswoman Nan Keller had been working feverishly behind the scenes once the women's victory was assured. Her diplomatic efforts helped convince Islamabad to set up the protectorate. She was sickened and appalled at the murder of Rinni and was joined by sympathetic forces around the world demanding that Islamabad do more. They responded positively and agreed to build the airstrip and add additional garrisons in the area. It was made clear that Rinnistan would be defended against anybody who would want to do it harm.

By winter, Dal had recovered enough to return to Rinnistan. The garrison was up and running and work had commenced on the airfield. Dal concentrated her large and disciplined police force within the growing village. She had daily contact with the military who maintained a small headquarters in the village. The main garrison was on the other side of the mountain but others were on the way and they would patrol the entire area.

A. J. remained in Islamabad and coordinated with Omar in handling Rinnistan's growing needs. They would stay in contact after A. J. left. A private account was set up for Dal, and A. J. would fund whatever she needed to administer her district. Pakistan's assistance would be mainly in supplying manpower. Omar loved the challenge and he became a treasured and trusted friend.

STEVE HAD BEEN reassigned and had left the area and A. J. returned to Virginia. Try as he may, he couldn't view Rinni's death as Dal and the others did. He agreed that they never could have established a real romantic relationship but, unlike Dal, he mourned her passing.

When they were in the U.S., Rinni and Dal talked at length to A. J. about their lives in Pakistan and the history of their people. It had both fascinated and revolted him. He had been with them practically since beginning of their struggle for liberation and was there at the end when they achieved victory.

A. J. wasn't ready to completely let Rinni go. Hers was a story that needed to be told and he was the perfect person to tell it. He knew the history and had personally joined the fight. He decided to write a memoir about the struggles of the women of Rinnistan.

The next few months were spent completing his doctoral thesis and writing the memoir. He was getting frequent updated reports from Omar and channeled whatever funds were needed to Dal's account. His Detroit project was almost to the permitting stage and he was excited about it.

A. J. enjoyed D.C. and spending time with Becky. Genevieve would join them on occasion. One beautiful spring day, Becky and A. J. were strolling through the Capital area.

"I intend to try some new approaches, Beck, but I'm just not ready to commit full time to our project and you and I both know that's exactly what it's going to take. Life keeps throwing little curves at me and I get distracted."

"Ah..., I wouldn't call fighting terrorists in Pakistan a little curve! Look, I know you're going to figure this out and I haven't been sitting idly by either, but I must admit this is really complicated. Good idea! Let's take a break and we'll hit it again. In the meantime lets go have a beer!"

Chapter 52: Old Friends

IT WAS NOW late summer and Dr. A. J. McCleary was in Detroit meeting with his builders. The last permit hurdle was cleared and construction of his fanciful dream was about to begin. He was the sole officer and director of the corporation that he called, 'The New Zone Development Company'. All contracts and construction related matters would be run through this company.

When A. J. took a final site walk-though with his architect, Arthur Hoskins, he noticed a man standing near the cemetery.

"That guy shouldn't be here; he must have ducked under the construction tapes. I'll have him removed," stated Art, as he reached for his cell phone.

"No, uh, just a minute. I think I know that man," said A. J. "Wait here. I'll be right back."

The man turned when he heard A. J. approaching. A. J. stopped about ten feet from him and they stood staring at one another. A. J. spoke first...

"Hello Big George."

"JESUS...! SEAN... MAN, YOU'RE SUPPOSED TO BE DEAD!"

They shook hands and Big George said, "Oh, what the hell. I've never hugged a dead guy before." They both laughed and embraced each other.

Big George had just been released from his prison term for charges relating to the Drug War.

"Look what they did to the old place, Sean! Just as well. There was nothin' but trouble here. Suppose they're going to build tall office buildings or somethin'; those executives won't have any idea what they're sittin' on," he grinned. "You're lookin' good, kid! I guess you're here for the cemetery, huh?"

"Yeah, just visiting. How about you?"

"Me, I'm here 'cause I have no place else to go. I'm broke, 'cept for the spending money the warden gave me. Now I'm an ex-con and nobody wants me. I thought some of my old cronies would still be around, but shit, they're either dead or still in jail. I can't find nobody."

A. J. paused and said, "Are you looking for a job? I mean a real job, not your old kind of work."

"Yeah man, I gotta eat and I ain't never going back to the joint! Shit, I'll wash dishes, clean sewers, anything. You know of somethin'?"

"Yeah, I think I do, how would you like to be a cop?"

"A WHAT! Sean, you must still be half dead. A COP! Oh, that's funny."

"I'm talking about a security cop, one without a gun. You interested?"

"Hell, yes. I was kinda in the security business when I worked for Carlos.

You can tell my new bosses that I've got experience," he chuckled. "Seriously Sean, I can do that kind of work. Can you put me on to somethin'? Will they hire an ex-con?"
A. J. pointed and waved at the survey markers, "I'm involved with the construction that's about to begin here and we're going to need a security guy to watch over things. I do the hiring - and the job is yours if you want it."
Big George was in disbelief. "You..., you're shittin' me! A Zonie rat in charge of all this? Sean, I love it, man. When do I start?"
"Right now. Come on, I want you to meet somebody. Oh, Big George, I'm known by a different name. It's A. J. McCleary now."
Big George glanced at the cemetery and said, "No problem. I've never heard of that guy in there, A. J."
He introduced Big George to Art. "This is our new security guard. If anybody has a security issue, have them contact Big George here."
They spent the rest of the day together, visiting a uniform supply store, a bank, and a cell phone retailer.
"I don't know what to say Sea...A. J. I, I, won't let you down, man. You've got my word."
"I remember that to be pretty good," grinned A. J. "I'm not worried.
We'll stay in touch by phone. Keep your own hours. You don't have to be there all day but make sure the construction guys have your number. The night shift could be troublesome. I'll get you help if you need it; don't be afraid to ask."
They shook hands. A. J. looked at the dark and scarred man and said, "I just love seeing old friends." It brought a smile to Big George's face.

HE HAD JUST left Dulles Airport and was checking his inbox on the taxi ride home. There was a message from Omar:

A. J. Next month will be the first anniversary of the Great Battle. Dal is planning a big celebration. The dedication of Rinni's memorial is the main event. Dal would be disappointed if you couldn't make it. We finally got in touch with Steve. He said wild horses couldn't keep him away! Please let me tell her that you're coming. Omar

A. J. replied immediately:

I'll be there, Omar. Those horses can't stop me either.
My best to Dal! A. J.

Another e-mail was from a Japanese scientific research group in Tokyo. A. J. had put his thesis on line to be reviewed by anyone who had similar scientific interests. His paper focused on how electromagnetic fields affect the human body and how the human body affects electromagnetic fields. The Japanese group was conducting research on the same subject matter. They were interested in exchanging ideas with him.

He was meeting Becky in Georgetown and gave her a call.

"Hey Beautiful Becky, we still on for lunch?"

"Yes, did you bring me a present?"

"Well, kind of. I got some people from Japan interested in what we are doing; it could be helpful."

"Great. I want expensive jewelry and you give me fucking scientists!"

"You never wear jewelry!"

"I'll start."

"Is Genevieve available? I need to talk to her."

"Yeah, she's right here but she's in a pissy mood. I think she's unhappy with the idiots she encounters in her job."

"Perfect, that's what I want to talk to her about."

"What? Her idiots?"

"Becky, just bring her along."

A. J. knew he would never be able to devote the personal time necessary to adequately watch over all of his pursuits. He was going to need some help and had exactly the right person in mind for the job.

They were enjoying lunch at Becky's favorite sushi bar. Between bites of his sashimi and sips of Japanese beer, A. J. queried Genevieve: "The practice of law starting to get to you?"

"No," she replied. "It's the jerks who practice it that are getting to me! I don't care if I ever see the inside of a courtroom again."

"Would you be interested in having an office practice that served only one client who paid you very well?" asked A. J.

"As long as I don't have to go to court, I'm interested," she said enthusiastically.

"I've got a similar problem, Genevieve. I enjoy being involved with many projects but I hate the business end of it. I like to initiate, design and create things, but I don't want to manage the ultimate product. Becky will confirm that I have a lot of irons in the fire. For instance I have just commenced a multi-million dollar building project in Detroit. I'm funding the development of a small community in Pakistan. I'm involved in important research which will eventually have to be channeled into a foundation, not to mention a personal investment portfolio whose assets are larger than many third world countries."

"You're kidding."

"No, I'm not. Look, I have to deal with accountants, brokers, and bankers on an international scale. That's my court room and I don't like it either. I need a business manager to get between me and all of that so Becky and I can get to work."

Genevieve put down her chopsticks. "Yeah, yeah... go on."
"You can set up your own staff, hire assistants and consultants, create an umbrella type business organization, or do whatever will work for you. Just keep careful records and put *everything* in computer accounts that only you and I can access."

"Well, Gen, you wanted a new challenge," Becky chortled. "He will be demanding. But he's cute."

"A. J. ..., I can't do what you do. Nobody can. I'd be in over my head!" exclaimed Genevieve.
"You don't have to. I'll make the decisions and point you in the right direction. You just have to do the leg work, gather information and watch all of our associates like a hawk. For instance, your first assignment, after you set up the operational organization, will be to go to Detroit and meet the construction gang. You've got to make sure they aren't over budget and are not stealing us blind. Bring in construction consultants; learn from them and then dismiss them."

"I've never been to Detroit; do I need a passport to go there?"
"No," laughed A. J. "But where I once lived and where the project is located - it was like a foreign country. You'll love it! Wait 'til you meet Big George!

But do get your passport up to date. You'll be traveling to Islamabad shortly to meet with a wonderful guy who will fill you in on our Pakistan project. I'll be there next month myself. Someone has to be watching things back here while I'm away. See why I need you and any team that you assemble?"

"I... I... Let me think about this."
"Genevieve, I wouldn't ask you to take this job if I didn't think you could handle it. Your biggest assets are that you're smart and hard working. And besides, you've got the brilliant Beautiful Becky to fall back on. What do you say?"

THEY WERE FLYING out on the same day. A. J. was heading for Islamabad and Genevieve was going to Detroit. The two of them sat with Becky in the airport lounge.

"I like your idea of setting up separate foundations for our individual projects, Gen. We will dissolve the development company in Detroit as soon as construction is finished and replace it with a foundation. The one you're designing for Rinnistan is the perfect vehicle to use there also. Becky, we will need the same thing for our work. We're going to set up our own research lab sooner or later and it won't be for profit. Like the other projects, I want my financial role to be kept confidential.

Creating an investment corporation whose sole purpose is to make money to fund the foundations is exactly what I had in mind, Genevieve.

But it's precisely that kind of set up work that I dislike. Thank you for doing it for me."

"Are you kidding, A. J.? She loves it," said Becky. "I've never seen her so cheerful!"

"Yeah, I love spending other people's money," laughed Genevieve. "While we're on the subject, if our investment company gets any bigger, we are going to have to find our own building somewhere. You don't have any more projects in mind do you, A. J.?"

"I don't choose them, Gen; they just seem to find me."

A. J.'s flight was called first and he got up to leave for the gate. "Genevieve, you don't have to do it now because you're so busy, but I would like you to find me a top notch private investigating firm. We'll talk more about this later. I'll be in touch you two!"

"I wonder why he needs that? You know, it's going to take about four persons to do what A. J.'s been doing," sighed Genevieve.

"Tell me about it, Gen. Tell me about it."

Chapter 53: The Memorial

A. J. WAS IN A small fifty passenger prop jet preparing to land on the airstrip built by the Pakistani military. It was in the valley on the other side of the mountain from Rinnistan. He was with Omar and forty-two other passengers, most of whom were tourists.

"Did you see that huge satellite dish on top of the mountain?" asked Omar. "With the help of your money, it is Rinnistan's first joint project with Pakistan. It'll serve as the communication station for both the military and Rinnistan. It is in the exact spot where Zay went over the mountain! And," he added, "It provides an excellent reference point for the tourists.

You know, I think tourism is going to be bigger than trade. People from all over want to see what these women have accomplished. This small airline is only a beginning," proudly stated Omar. "Work on the roads will begin in the spring and the government has agreed to build the power relay station to serve the entire region. Again - thanks to your help - Rinnistan will bring power into the village once the main lines are close enough. You can't believe the number of volunteers who are helping. Many are engineering students from Islamabad. They set up camp in the mountains and are loving it."

The landing was surprisingly smooth and after deplaning they hopped into a waiting jeep. They drove around the mountain and headed for Rinnistan along the same route Rinni's small force had taken several months ago. The trail was now a real road. They drove through the pass, across the valley and into the village.

"Wow, you guys have been busy," cited A. J. as they entered. "I'm impressed!"

"Well, the basis for the land plan was already here. With all the trees, we were able to cut out a perfect grid and construction started along those tree lines. It's like a canopy covering the village and is quite appealing. Merchants are coming in from Islamabad to serve the tourists and the eventual traders; they have even started to build a small hotel. But the real attraction is Dal's police force.

The outsiders are fascinated by them. They've kept their black combat clothes and added some insignias and sharp looking red berets. They are really impressive and are deadly serious about their duties. If a man tries to come into Rinnistan armed with weapons, the police politely ask him to leave and if he fails to do so within a reasonable time, they shoot him. It's very effective. They did that only one time; the message got out."

"They shouldn't have asked so politely," quipped A. J.

Omar smiled and added, "Most of the women in the police force fought in the Great Battle and they're as disciplined now as they were then. They absolutely adore Dal and so do the villagers, especially the children.

They follow the police around as they make their rounds and get all excited when the women acknowledge them. The children flock to Dal when she comes by every day. The interesting part is that most of them are boys. Their respect for her will never go away and it's wonderful to see."

"What an amazing turnaround! Rinni would have been proud," sighed A. J.

"Dal took over an abandoned food storage building and turned it into her government quarters; it's made of rock. Once the students got hold of it, they created a respectable and attractive home for the District of Rinnistan.

There's the governor's mansion!" grinned Omar. "And there's the Governor." Dal was coming out of the building. She leaned on her cane and had a noticeable limp, but other than that she looked the same - as trim and pretty as ever. She looked up when she heard the sound of the jeep.

"A. J., I was hoping that was you!"

"Hello Governor," A. J. responded and grabbed her hand in both of his as she extended it to him. That's about as far as she could go with any public display of affection.

"You look great and Rinnistan is such a wonderful surprise. All of you are to be congratulated," said a beaming A. J.

"Thanks, A. J., but we have a long way to go. Come inside, I want to show you something."

She led him into her small office and pointed to a large color photograph hanging on the wall behind her desk. "Look, Steve sent this to me. One of these days I'm going to display it in public."

A. J. went over to it and smiled. It was the un-cropped photograph of the four of them making their escape, beautifully framed and behind glass.

"Wow! We actually did that?" asked A. J.

"Yes. My leg and I thank you," smiled Dal. "That combat picture of Rinni is what the sculptor used for her statue. It came out perfect. Come on, let's walk over there."

She led A. J. to what she called a Memorial Garden. Situated under a stand of trees and flower beds was a life size bronze statue of Rinni. She was struck in the image of her combat photo that had circulated throughout the world's journals. The dedication ceremony would take place the next afternoon.

A. J. stared up at the statue for a few moments and lowered his head. Dal gently squeezed his arm and she and Omar walked away leaving A. J. to his thoughts.

Behind the statue were graves of the fallen heroes with Zay's larger tombstone in the front, complete with a detailed account of her death charge down the mountain. The Garden would be the final resting place of all the women warriors and another section was set aside for those of the police force and future police who did not fight on that day.

The three of them strolled through the village and Dal gave A. J. an update, “We are going to build a school and we have decided that along with the normal studies, we are going to teach Pashto as it’s supposed to be spoken, and English. Missionaries have contacted me offering to administer the school. I told them they could do that but could not advance their own religion. All but one declined. An independent religious missionary organization from the U.S. accepted our terms and their representative will be here in a couple of days. I think we can do it, A. J. Our people will not become soft and yet they will be protected and educated.”

“I’m speechless, Dal. You and your women are wonders. Look, in that regards, I am almost finished writing a memoir about you and Rinni and the whole movement. I was hoping you would approve.”

“Of course I do. She needs to be remembered, A. J., and I know you will be truthful. It’s important that the story be told accurately. I thank you for doing it.” A. J. nodded his head in gratitude.

Steve arrived the following morning and stood with A. J. at the dedication ceremony. They were delighted to see so many foreign dignitaries there, including a staff member from Nan Keller’s office.

“They’re going to make it, Steve. You guys can be proud of this one.”

“Yeah, we get to win one every now and then. It makes up for some of our mistakes. You were an important part of the team, A. J.; the guys in Washington won’t forget.”

The next day they said their goodbyes to Dal and once again Steve and A. J. parted company, promising to stay in touch.

Omar accompanied A. J. back to Islamabad. “Omar, I know that Genevieve has been in contact with you and she will be here in a few weeks. You will be dealing mainly with her. She has set up a special foundation for Rinnistan and I want her to personally meet you and Dal. You’ll enjoy working with her but I will remain in contact. And thanks for keeping my financial help confidential.”

“Thank you, A. J., for everything. Dal and I are looking forward to meeting Genevieve.”

“Good. Can I buy you a cab ride back to town?”

“No thanks. I have to meet Dal’s missionary teacher here at the airport in a few hours and get him on a hop to Rinnistan. You take care, A. J.”

They shook hands and A. J. left for his hotel and - first thing in the morning - for Japan.

Omar searched through his bags and found the sign he needed. This airport is way too crowded, he thought to himself. He will never be able to find me without this FATHER JOSEPH sign.

Chapter 54: Los Angeles

THE MEETING WITH the Japanese scientists went well. They were doing research on the same subject matter as A. J. and, like him, were not making much progress in curing diseases through electromagnetic energies.

A. J. had planned to go home after the meeting but his new friends encouraged him to attend an important symposium in Honolulu on the first of the following month. He would meet others from all over the Pacific Rim who were also studying the subject.

After a call to Genevieve, A. J. felt comfortable enough to stay in the Pacific. He took a side trip to China to visit some Geneva friends then flew to Hawaii, welcoming the three weeks before the symposium to relax and complete the memoir. A. J. spent the first week putting final touches on the memoir. When satisfied, he put the document on line. He notified Nan Keller about the piece and knew that she would alert her friends to the link. He was not concerned about making money but just wanted the story of the women's struggle to be circulated in the educational and political circles. He would spend the next week cruising the islands and studying the latest research on electromagnetic energy.

He had just returned to Honolulu and was checking his latest messages.

There was an interesting one from a Dr. Ian Griggsby:

Dear Dr. McCleary, I am a scientist who has devoted his entire career to working with people who have the unusual ability to control certain body functions by the use of their minds. I read your doctoral thesis on line and I think we can be helpful to one another. I KNOW that outside electromagnetic energies can deliver messages to the human brain. You might be interested in my evidence.

I am currently on sabbatical in Los Angeles, please e-mail me if you're interested in my work.

A. J. was more than interested. He re-routed his return to the U.S. through Los Angeles and set up an appointment to meet Dr. Griggsby during his layover.

Another e-mail caught his attention; it was from a Los Angeles film agent named Rachel Holloway. She had read his memoir on Rinnistan and believed the women's war story had potential movie value. She was impressed that his accounting was from personal knowledge and invited him to contact her. The thought had never occurred to A. J. that Rinnistan's story could best be circulated by way of the big screen.

He was interested but knew that he would probably not have the necessary time to devote to such an endeavor. However, the more he thought about it, the more he could see benefits to Rinnistan and to women's causes. He thought that he should at least talk to Ms. Holloway while he was in Los Angeles.

A. J. replied to Rachel's message and told her when he would be in her neighborhood, adding that he would call but was on a tight schedule and probably wouldn't be in Los Angeles for more than a day. She said that it would work for her and to make sure he called.

IN ANOTHER PART of Los Angeles, Monica had just come home from work.

"Uh, oh, Skeet, you're not happy," observed Little Bit as Skeeter walked into their apartment and plopped down on the couch.

"No, no. I'm not. I'm ANGRY! I saw the first cut of the movie and If I hadn't written the story I never would have known that it was about the Zone! Those guys lied to me! They said that they would stay close to the book's storyline and THEY'VE TOTALLY GONE HOLLYWOOD ON ME! Happy I'm NOT!

M. J. comes off as a sappy slut and Sean a wimpy white boy! Everybody else appears to be non-existent. And I only saw a small part of it! Wylie tells me that what I saw is pretty much the way the entire film is going to be cut! I'm just sick," she said bending over and holding her head in her hands.

"Oh no," cried Little Bit. "There must be something you can do about it."

"No, I gave them complete control when I contracted with them. I thought that I was being smart going with a fledgling film company. I was certain that I could trust them; they hadn't become big, powerful and arrogant yet. Boy was I wrong."

"Can't Wylie Morris do something? I mean she's a big star and actively campaigned to play the part of M. J."

"Yeah, she's not happy either. She's going to contact her attorney and have her raise hell! But, I'm not sure that's going to do any good. Oh, how could I have been so stupid? Stupid!"

Chapter 55: Ten Years

A. J. GOT INTO Los Angeles on the late flight and would meet with Dr. Griggsby in the morning. If he had time after that, he would call Rachel Holloway.

Dr. Griggsby and A. J. met at a downtown restaurant for an early morning breakfast. Dr. Griggsby was about twenty years older than A. J. and was from the mid-west.

"I teach kinesiology at Northwestern University in Evanston, Illinois, A. J., and have been on staff there for twenty-one years. We work with athletes, dancers and other physically active people, focusing on the brain's ability to send electrical energies to distressed areas of the body, usually the muscles. We try to expedite the healing process by having them mentally direct stimulation to the injured area. I also work on body building. That, of course, is a brief, incomplete oversimplification of what I do."

"I've taken the time to read your work, Ian, and I'm familiar with what you do. Our work is similar, but I deal with controlled *outside* electromagnetic energies that are re-introduced into the body. But, as my paper reflected, I'm also intrigued with foreign energies that somehow get into the body's circuitry on their own."

"That's why I contacted you, A. J. I'm on leave here in L.A. working with an American Indian who lived in the valley just outside of Los Angeles. He was one hundred years old but he looked and behaved like he was fifty. He claimed he used his mind to stay young; that's why I was interested in working with him.

Now, here is what is going to interest you: he could speak ancient old world languages that haven't been spoken in centuries. He was totally illiterate and it was impossible for him to learn those languages from anybody here on this planet. Nobody can speak them."

"You've really got my attention, Ian, but you keep referring to him in the past tense. Is he still with us?"

"No, he died two days ago. He told me the day before he died that it was time for him to move on. He was perfectly healthy! A. J., he claimed he learned ancient languages from hearing people speaking to him... in his dreams! I recorded him carrying on a conversation with himself in those languages and I forwarded it to language experts. They confirmed the authenticity of the old tongues.

Now, here's the kicker: this Indian man said he learned to stay young by listening to his dreams. Voices told him to go inside his body and look for little men running to and fro from his brain. He claims he was instructed to direct these guys to his organs with orders to rejuvenate them. He swore he could see that happening! I never taught him mental exercises, I just observed. A. J., I believe him on a personal level but find it preposterous scientifically."

A. J. was stunned. He remembered his mother telling him to do something similar when he broke his arm as a child. He looked at Dr. Griggsby for several seconds and said, "Ian, I'm going to tell you something that I've never made public, mainly because it's scientifically preposterous and I didn't want to be perceived by the scientific community as some sort of wacko!

I, too, have seen the little men. It first occurred when I was a child. I called them trains because they ran along little tracks. My mother also had the ability to look inside her body." Then A. J. shared his and his mother's experiences with the phenomena. "I've learned to direct those trains to help keep me fit. I've been doing it all my life."

Now it was Ian's turn to be stunned. "A. J., do you know what this means! Look, many sports doctors have not bought into the theory that the mind can initiate the healing process or produce superior athletes. With your conscious ability to direct those energies..."

"Whoa, slow down, Doctor. I'm not an athlete and I don't intend to become one!"

"It might help your research, too."

"How so?"

"Well, if we can dramatically show that the brain is the *transmitter* of electrical energies to the cells of the body but is being directed to its destination by the mind of the persons themselves - in this case you - then is it not reasonable to think that the controlled outside energies that you're working with should be sent to the brain first?

"You're saying: have the outside programmed frequencies resonate with the brain organ first then let the brain do the routing?" asked A. J.

"It's just a thought but you're going to have to *first* show that the mind can affect the body's cellular behavior. You know how science operates - one step at a time. You sure you don't want to be superman?"

"Yes, I'm sure; but I like the idea of programing the brain with controlled outside frequencies. My research partner, Becky, and I discussed this possibility at some length but we put it on the back burner. You know, that just might help explain how your Indian spoke those languages." Not to mention how he and his mother learned, he thought to himself.

A. J. had heard enough. He canceled his flight back to D.C. and decided to stay in L.A. for a while so he and Dr. Griggsby could work together. He had gotten more out of that breakfast appointment with Ian than he had with any of the symposiums he had attended. He called Becky and told her to start rethinking their research approaches.

Then he phoned Rachel Holloway.

"Yes Mr. McCleary, she is expecting your call but is busy with some clients now. Are you staying in the downtown area?"

"Yes, I am. I'm at the Sheraton."
"Good, that's right here in the financial district; we're only a block from you. Rachel wanted you to come right over if you were nearby. There are some people here she'd like you to meet."
She gave A. J. the address and he walked to her office building. The agency was on the top floor. He got off the elevator and strolled down the spacious halls to the end unit. Before he opened the huge double mahogany doors, he gazed out the window at the end of the hall. He could see the city and the mountain and the Hollywood sign.
He opened the doors and entered a paneled foyer furnished with sleek modern couches and tables. There was another set of doors - etched glass - directly in front of him. The plushness of the office made him laugh to himself at the way he was dressed. He wore jeans and a pullover sweater. He long ago stopped wearing the uncomfortable suit and tie.
A. J. paused, then opened the glass doors. The receptionist greeted him, "Rachel's office is at the end of the hallway. She's expecting you, Mr. McCleary." He thanked her and headed down the hall. He found the office door open and walked in. Rachel stood behind a large desk. An attractive dark haired woman was a few yards away talking on a cell phone and a third woman, with her back to A. J., was leaning over the desk reading something laid out in front of her.
Rachel was tall, trim, and had long wavy sandy blond hair that flowed over her shoulders, partially covering one eye. She looked up and greeted A. J. who had stopped about ten feet from her.
"You must be Mr. McCleary. Come in; you're not interrupting anything," she cordially said.
The woman on the cell phone waved and moved away as Rachel began to walk around the desk to shake his hand. The person with her back to him straightened but remained focused on what she was reading; A. J. glanced in her direction as he started toward Rachel.
Suddenly he stopped and whirled around. The woman reading was familiar even from behind. His mind started to race. Where? Where ...? She turned and looked directly at A. J.
She became rock still, gasped and put her hands to her mouth. A. J. turned ashen, dropping his computer to the floor.
They stared at each other, both in shock, both trembling, both disbelieving...
He whispered more than spoke... "Skeet...Skeet..." then, "Skeeter ..., SKEETER!"
She started towards him, stopped, her eyes glazed over, tears gushed out: "SEAN...SEAN...SEAN!" she screamed, took another step, stopped again, and then ran to A. J. jumping into his outstretched arms.
"Wha...," exclaimed Rachel, OH MY GOD!"

Wylie Morris just stood there, not believing what she was seeing.

Tears streamed down A. J.'s face as he clutched Skeeter. He looked at her, still in disbelief. "I..., I couldn't find you Skeet. I tried so hard but I COULDN'T FIND YOU!" he sobbed.

"We thought you were dead, Sean! NO. I ... I thought you were dead. Little Bit never gave up hope, NEVER! Oh, Sean, Sean, she was so right!" cried Skeet.

They stood there for many seconds holding each other, both too emotional and choked with tears to speak.

Finally, A. J. managed to say, "Little Bit, Little Bit, my baby, is she here? Is she all right?"

"She's fine Sean; she's right here in L.A. Oh, I won't know how to tell her, she'll fall apart!"

"Can we call her? Can we go where she is?"

"Of course, of course," she answered, as they continued to hold on to each other.

"Oh Skeet, it's you, it's really you!" And he stroked her face.

"Sean, I thought, I thought you were... dead." More tears.

"I'm so sorry, Skeet. I figured I could find you and explain."

Rachel and Wylie stood there with gaping mouths.

A. J. sensed their presence, looked over and said,

"I'm sorry, this is my sister; we've been separated for ten years," and he hugged Skeet even tighter.

"You don't have to apologize to us, Mr. McCleary. WOW!" exclaimed Rachel.

"I guess we will have to change the ending, Monica!" stated Wylie.

"Monica? Is that your name, Skeet?"

"Yes, and who... who is Mr. McCleary?" she asked. Her head was spinning.

"What's Little Bit's name?"

"Jessica," Skeet replied.

"Jessica! Oh boy, do we have a lot to catch up on. Can we call Little Bit now?"

"Yes, yes." Skeeter separated herself from A. J. and reached for her cell phone. "Oh, gosh, she won't answer; she's in class. I'll call the landline at home and leave a message for her to call me. I'll, I'll try to be calm." She reached her recording ... "LITTLE BIT, LITTLE BIT, call me right away! It's important. Don't do anything else. JUST CALL ME!"

"That's calm?" quipped Wylie.

Skeeter, recovering from her shock, asked, "Sean, what are you doing here? Who's Mr. McCleary?"

"Skeet, McCleary is my real name. You know the lonely man buried next to mom?"

She nodded yes...

"Well, that's my father. His name was Sean McCleary. Mom gave me her initials, A. J., for my first name."

"I knew there was some kind of connection between the two of them," said Skeet. "But I never would have guessed *that*!"

"Skeet, they're all dead," he sadly said. "M. J., Meg, Sissy..."

"I know, Sean, I know. Papa Joe?"

"He was forced to leave the church; I don't know where he is...Skeet. So much happened that day. It got so confusing.

The Zone's been demolished, nothing remains but the cemetery."

"I know. I was there."

"What? When?"

"About two years after Little Bit and I left the Zone. The smell of the rat poison was still strong. I saw your grave, Sean!"

"Oh, Skeet. We must have just missed each other. I left the Zone right after it was demolished."

"Where did you go?" Skeet asked.

"I went to Washington D.C. I was there for little over a year; then I was in Europe for almost four years. You were supposed to be in Chicago, Skeet!"

"Look, why don't you two go into the conference room. You've got so much to talk about," offered Rachel.

They accepted her offer and sat side by side on a stuffed couch leaving the door open. They would talk then hold each other then talk some more. Skeet couldn't stop crying and then A. J. would cry too.

Finally, Skeet got up and walked on shaking legs back into Rachel's office where the other two were waiting.

"Rachel, do you have a copy of *The Zone*? Sean wants to read it - the book, not the screenplay."

"Sure, there's one in the other room. I'll bring it to you."

"Here, keep it, Sean, I've got others," Rachel said as she delivered the book to them.

"It's A. J.," he chuckled. "Sean's reserved for my sisters. Thanks, but I'll be finished in a few minutes and you can have it back."

Rachel looked on as A. J. flipped through page after page ... "Is he…?"

"Yes, he is Rachel, every word."

He would smile, then look solemn and after about ten minutes he closed the book and looked at Skeet.

"It's wonderful, Skeet. You captured it. You told it as it should have been told. I have only one criticism - you left yourself out! He looked at Rachel and said, "She played a much larger role in all our lives than she portrayed in the book."

He held Skeet's hand and said to Rachel, "In all the excitement we didn't discuss what I came here for. Can we reschedule? I plan to be here longer now."

Wylie walked in and A. J. said to her, "I'm sorry, I don't know your name. You must be a friend of Skeet's?"
Rachel and Skeet both snickered. A. J. had no idea that she was one of the most recognizable actors in Hollywood.
"You know, I needed that, A. J.," she laughed, realizing that he really didn't know who she was. "I'm Wylie Morris and, yes, I am a friend of Monica's."
He still didn't know who she was.
"Sean, what did you come here for?" asked Skeet.
"I've written something too, Skeet. Rachel found it on line and thought the movie industry might be interested. She invited me here."
"It's that story on the Pakistani women I told you about, Monica; it's really compelling," stated Rachel.
"Sean, what do you ...?" Skeet's cell phone rang, "IT'S LITTLE BIT, I don't know how to tell her, Sean!"
"I don't know either; I just want to hear her voice. Hurry, hurry and answer!"
"Little Bit," she started ...
"SKEET, WHAT'S WRONG, WHAT'S WRONG? I've never heard you like that before! WHAT?"
Skeet couldn't help herself, she started to sob.
Little Bit cried out, "OH NO, it's bad news!"
"OH NO, NO. Little Bit, it's the best news possible."
She was crying now, and just blurted out: "HE'S ALIVE, LITTLE BIT, HE'S ALIVE!"
There was dead silence on the other end, finally, calmly, Little Bit said, "Please tell me you're talking about Sean... please."
"YES, YES, HE'S STANDING RIGHT NEXT TO ME!"
Her screams were deafening even through the phone. Skeet had to yank the device away from her ear. Rachel and Wylie smiled and shook their heads as A. J. reached for the phone. Skeet, still crying, handed it to him. Rachel wrapped her arms around Skeet as A. J. waited patiently for Little Bit to stop sobbing.
Little Bit gasped for breath, "SKEET, I WANT TO TALK TO HIM, PLEASE, PLEASE!"
"It's me, baby, it's me," Sean said as calmly as he could.
"OH SEAN, SEAN," she wailed. "IT'S YOU, IT'S YOU, I KNEW YOU WERE ALIVE! I JUST KNEW IT! I JUST...just... Talk some more, talk some more, please!"
"I'm coming to see you, Little Bit, as soon as we hang up. Oh, god, how I missed you guys."
"Sean, SEAN, I, I want to LOOK at you, I want to TOUCH you!" Hurry Sean, hurry. I'll hang up now. HURRY!"
"We're on our way, Little Bit. We're coming."

Little Bit was waiting for them in the parking lot. A. J. spotted her and bolted out of Skeet's car as it came to a stop.
"SEAN!" Little Bit screamed running towards him. She jumped into his arms and wrapped her arms and legs around him, crying, hugging and kissing him all at the same time.

He held her, kissed her and rocked her in his arms. What was said was only heard by them. Little Bit would not let go as Skeeter led them into the apartment.

Chapter 56: Skeet Studios

THEY STAYED UP most of the night, talking, laughing, crying. Early on, Skeeter appeared wearing her Tigers baseball hat.
"Is that the same hat?" asked Sean.
"Yup," said Little Bit. "She guards it with her life!"
Sean started to tell them about the 'Billy section' in Tiger stadium but thought better of it; he wanted that to be a surprise. He told them nothing of his Detroit project. That would be the bigger surprise.
Sean wanted detailed accounts of their lives from the day they left the Zone, but he only spoke in general terms about his. They never suspected that he was incredibly wealthy. He spoke mainly of his academics, scientific research, and international law career. The girls were careful not to talk about that awful day in the Zone. They would let Sean tell them what happened when he wanted to. They were not sure themselves if they wanted to hear the details.
"Sean, how did you get involved with the women from Pakistan?" asked Skeet. "Rachel is really interested and it takes a lot to get her attention."
"I'll tell you what; hand me your laptop, Little Bit. Thanks ... I'll pull up the link for you, Skeet. It will answer all your questions."
"Oh, just a second, Sean, I have to touch the computer first. It only responds to me - security. I don't know how they do those things!"
Sean and Little Bit were sitting on the floor chatting while Skeet was perusing the memoir. "You've got to be kidding me," said Skeet. "No wonder Rachel is so excited."
She put the computer down. "Little Bit, you've got to read this. This is all true?"
"Every bit of it, Skeet. They are the most courageous women imaginable. No, they are more than courageous...
So Rachel is your agent, and it was pure happenstance that you were there when I arrived?"
"Yes, she's also Wylie's agent and is the promoter for both of us. We are working together on a ... film."
"Oh, is Wylie a writer too?"
"Sean, you've been out of the country too long. Wylie is one of the top movie stars in Hollywood," laughed Little Bit.
"I thought I would die when you asked her what her name was today," Skeet grinned. "You really have never heard of her?"
"No, I had no idea who she was. I never go to movies or read the entertainment page. She's quite pretty though."
"Yeah, you might say that," said Little Bit.
"You make movies too, Skeet?"

"Sean, I guess you'll find this out soon enough. We're making a movie on the Zone. It's already in production. Wylie plays M. J."
He sat there blankly looking at her... "Skeet, she's not a SISTER!"
That made both girls break out in laughter, "Did you ever hear of makeup?" chortled Skeet. Besides, her mother's a sister, that makes her a half sister. Anyway, M. J. was mixed. Remember?
She's a good actor, Sean, but they won't let her play the part like we want it to be played. That's why we were at Rachel's; both Wylie and I are mad as hell at the producers for what they're doing. We wanted advice from Rachel. I was reviewing the screen version when you came in. It sucks! They're killing my book, Sean, you won't recognize the Zone in the movie."
"What did Rachel advise?"
"She wasn't hopeful. I signed a contract giving them complete control. They even made both Little Bit and me sign waivers giving them the right to tell our story!"
Sean paused and said, "They didn't get my waiver."
Sean was up early and was on the phone to Genevieve who had just returned from Islamabad, "That's all I know about them, Gen - the names of the principals and the name of their film company. Find out what you can. I'm in a kinda hurry on this one. Oh, forget the private investigators; I found them."
"Found who?"
"My sisters. They're here in California."
"I didn't know you had sisters!"
"In that regard, both you and Becky should read this book. It's called *The Zone."*
"I read that book a couple of years ago; it was great! I was going to tell you about it. I think *The Zone* is a story about your property in Detroit. Oh my god! That's where I heard the name Big George before; I never put that together!"
"The book talks about two girls: Skeet and Little Bit. They're my sisters, Skeet wrote the book."
"WHAT? A. J., they're black!"
"Really?" chuckled A. J.
"How was your trip to Pakistan?"
"That Dal is some lady, A. J. You do know that Omar is crazy in love with her. I read your memoir on the flight back; don't you do anything easy?"
"That wouldn't be any fun! Put Becky on. Get back to me as soon as you can on the other matter."
Little Bit came in yawning. She went over to Sean putting her arms around him. "It's you, it's really you. Like, I can't believe you're standing right here in my kitchen." The tears welled up again.
"I've dreamed of this day too, Little Bit. I knew you guys were out there

somewhere... somewhere."

He looked around, smiled and said, "Cool place you have here, kind of a step up from Ma's, huh?"

"Yeah, we really like it. Skeet makes enough money to move closer to Beverly Hills, but we're comfortable here and that's not really us, anyways. Besides, Skeet is not home that much. She usually stays with Jeff."

"Who's Jeff?"

"Oh, guess we forgot that part. Jeff is Skeet's white boyfriend. They've been together for two years. You would like him, Sean. He's an accountant for one of the big film companies. He's quiet, unpretentious and he absolutely adores Skeet."

Skeet came out wrapped in a soft terrycloth robe.

"There she is! My famous celebrity sister," grinned Sean as he gave Skeet a big hug.

"I was up earlier and I poked my head in here to see if that was really you sleeping on the couch. I still can't believe it!" and she hugged him back.

"Skeet, do you have an office downtown?"

"No, I'm a writer. I just need my computer and a place to sit. I usually hang here or at Jeff's and I use Rachel's office if I have to meet somebody. Oh, I didn't tell you about Jeff..."

"Little Bit filled me in; I can't wait to meet him. I'll be gentle," he smiled.

"No, I was wondering if you're going into the city. I'm meeting someone there; I just have to give him a call about the time."

"Sure, I have to get back with Rachel and Wylie on what to do with those jerks. I'll drop you off wherever you want to go."

"Skeet, later this afternoon I might have some ideas about those jerks. Can you tentatively schedule a time for me to meet with the three of you tomorrow? Don't do anything until I've had the opportunity to check a few things out. Remember, I'm an attorney and I now have a stake in your movie too. I won't let them do it, Skeet."

"Uh, oh! You know what that means. Done deal," exclaimed Little Bit.

"Yeah, I feel better already," smiled Skeeter.

Sean and Skeet were leaving the apartment. "Dinner on me," said Sean. "Take me to your favorite place. Bring Jeff, Skeet! What are you doing today, Little Bit?"

"I'm going to read about the women from Pakistan. Have fun, kids. Hey, can I invite one of my boyfriends to dinner?"

"How many boyfriends are there?" Sean said, looking at Little Bit like a concerned father of a teenager. Little Bit would turn twenty-two in a couple of weeks.

"Don't ask," said Skeet. "Yeah, bring the rapper, the one with the gold teeth!"

"WHAT? WAIT A MINUTE..."
"Let's go, Sean." Both girls were laughing.

Ian and A. J. sat in a downtown L.A. coffee house.
"Ian, Becky agrees. She feels it's important we first establish that the mind can direct brain frequencies to parts of the body before we reveal that we are programming the brain with outside electronic messages. We are a long way off."

"Yes, you can't jump steps even if the results are positive. The powers to be won't let you use it. Then what good is it?" mused Ian.
"Okay, now what is it that you want me to do?" asked A. J.

Ian answered: "First I want to run a series of base tests to determine the physical level of your body's abilities. It'll be conducted by researchers at UCLA with the help of the athletic staff. We want and need credibility."
"What kind of tests?"
"We want to know how much weight you can bench press, how fast you can run, how far you can throw a ball, those kind of things. Once we've established a maximum performance, we will retest you - say every six months or so. During that period you will send your little electronic trains carrying brain frequencies to the nerve centers of designated muscle fibers, creating impulses. That will cause the muscles to contract demanding an increase in the blood flow that carries all the nutrients needed for growth and strength.

You will do nothing in the way of exercise that would contract your muscles. Your training schedule will be monitored; growth and strength will come from your mental abilities, not from weight lifting. We'll tell the scientific community that you mentally sent those messages, which will be true. It won't convince a lot of skeptics, but it will help validate my work. We won't tell them that you visibly observed and directed the trains.

It's not a great leap from there for you to claim that you're using the same electronic routes and procedures to send your outside restructured frequencies to the distressed areas."

"Okay, but how will the scientist know if I'm dogging it or not, just to establish a low baseline?"
"You will be constantly monitored for blood pressure and oxygen flow; they'll know. Plus your own credibility is at stake here."
"All right, but I see one flaw. Because of my fitness, my baseline is already high. Substantial improvement may be insignificant or I *may* become a superman!"
"Good point. Lets hope you're wearing a cape."

THEY DISCUSSED the movie in Rachel's office. A. J. was appalled by the completed cuts. He looked at Skeet and said, "To release this trash would be an insult to you and to our family. I'm going to stop it, Skeet. No reflection on you, Wylie; you're only following the director's instructions. It's not your fault either, Rachel. You did your job and got the best deal for Skeet. You can't control what the producers and directors are doing.

Here's what I've found out," said A. J. "Your filmmakers are in financial trouble - hanging by a thread. They're past due on their payments. Evidently your contract put them close to the edge financially, Wylie. Don't be surprised if they want to renegotiate it."

"Boy, you're well informed. They've already hinted at that; my claws came out and they backed off. Rachel told them to forget it."

"Okay, here's what I'm going to do: my attorney will threaten them with a law suit if they go forward with the movie story line as is. They're going to be surprised that I'm still alive and will see their potential liability. It's possible that this may force them to stop the film altogether. If that happens, Wylie, we are going to need you to threaten suit for a breach of contract.

All right, with all that said, don't worry about the movie or your contracts. If those jerks don't agree to change the script and do it right, I've got somebody interested in buying them out. Then the movie will be made the way Skeet wrote it.

I'm going to sit down with Skeet and tell her exactly what happened on that terrible day. It will be up to her to rewrite the ending any way she wants to. I'm going to ask you to keep the information about the investor confidential; it could affect the negotiations." What he didn't tell them was that he was the investor.

Rachel and Wylie looked at each other and Rachel said to Skeet, "Has he always been like this?"

"Always," laughed Skeet. "Little Bit said, it's a done deal, and it is. This problem is over!"

A. J. turned to Wylie and said, "I can see that you're perfect for the part. Nobody knew M. J. like I did. I'll work with you to help you understand what she was really like if you want."

"A. J., I would absolutely love to have your help. I know I haven't captured her yet and I really want to do it right. Thank you."

"Skeeter, I have M. J.'s model photos taken that day by Ma's house, you remember?"

"You're kidding! I sure do remember. Boy, Wylie, this will really help. You will be able to see what we all looked like back then. Where did you get them, Sean?"

"Long story, Skeet. I also have videos of the theater fire; that should help with the settings."

"Oh my god, Sean, I don't know what to say… I've got a lot of writing to do. Man!"

Genevieve made the demand to the movie company pursuant to A. J.'s instructions and was stonewalled. Anticipating that probability, there was a backup plan in place. Genevieve contacted the investor group that had financed the film company. She told them that for a reasonable discount she had a client who wanted to redeem the debt owed by the film company to the investors. In return her client wanted to be assigned the notes of obligation executed by the borrower, and also the contract between the parties. The financiers fell all over themselves accepting the offer.

Then Genevieve notified the film company that she represented a client who had purchased the promissory notes formerly held by the film company's investor group. She went on, stating that the loan would not be extended and demanding complete immediate payment, pursuant to the terms of the agreement.

The film company knew they couldn't come up with the money and wanted to renegotiate the note. Genevieve declined and offered a settlement wherein all of the company's stock would be transferred to her client in lieu of the debt. The stockholders had very little of their own money invested. Seeing that they had no alternative, they agreed to the exchange but wanted to be released from the personal notes they had signed and to be held harmless from any suit brought by Wylie Morris.

The film company was surprised and relieved when the counter-offer was accepted. They never knew they were dealing with A. J. who had now become the owner of a movie studio - sets, cameras, the whole works. You can do this kind of thing when you have unlimited resources.

A. J. disclosed to everyone that he was the investor. The girls now had a glimpse of their brother's wealth. They were astonished but not surprised.

A rewritten version of 'The Zone' would soon be in full production.

A. J. made Skeet president of the company and set up a plan in which she and Little Bit would be issued all of the stock over a period of years. Skeet was free to run the company as she wished; she had the full service of A. J.'s investing firm for consulting purposes.

A. J. FINISHED HIS testing with Ian and his associates. Ian returned to Evanston and A. J. prepared to head back to D.C.

"Can't you work out of here?" pleaded Little Bit.

"No, I really can't. Look, would you consider leaving California to come work for me?"

"You bet. Just tell me where and when and I'll be there," she brightened.

"Wait for my call on that, Little Bit. It will be coming."

Skeet had taken to her new business status with a flourish; she was born for this type of work. The business end of the film company, renamed 'Skeet Studios', would be handled in D.C. Skeet would be in constant contact with Sean.

A. J. said his goodbyes to everyone and left for D.C. In flight, he opened a note from Wylie:

Thank you, A. J. Now I feel like I know her - and you. Call me when you're back in town. W.

....

DANELLA

PART THREE

Chapter 57: Getting Close

BECKY WAS HOT. "GOD DAMN IT! Every time I think I have a resonating match, it comes crashing down on me! This THING is going to KILL ME!"

They had made enormous progress. She was working with a wave frequency taken from a volunteer's cancerous pancreas. For the first time, they had a subject who had been using a device that contained the McCleary chip. They had a recorded frequency of her healthy pancreas and didn't have to reconstruct the diseased one.

The frequencies of the healthy pancreas were downloaded and Becky was trying to computer resonate them with the subject's recorded brain frequencies. They were using a program she and A. J. had written that would register the compatibility of the waves but crash if it wouldn't resonate mathematically. They would not attempt a computer transmission of the healthy frequency to a human brain for delivery to the organ unless it first worked in the program.

Rapidly the McCleary chip was changing the way electronic companies did business but it had done little to advance the study of electromagnetic energies - until now. Researchers all over the world were exchanging information on their subjects' abnormal frequency patterns that indicated a cancer, but they had nothing to compare it to. Previously normal patterns in the subjects were never identified and stored to memory. With the practice of storing a person's organ frequencies in computers using the McCleary chip, a virtual library of information was being collected. Now it would be feasible to electronically recreate a healthy pattern if they didn't already have one. That, too, had to be introduced into the human body.

It was becoming clear that the dominating frequencies of cells within the organ had to be mathematically integrated also.
This was a daunting task and was the reason they had so far been unsuccessful. With the body's billions of cells and neurons interacting, it

was easy to understand how cancers could spread and how difficult it was to treat.

They were getting close and they knew it. That's why Becky was frustrated. Every impulse was different and had to be re-calculated separately for *each* subject and then integrated with the brain's frequencies. There were millions of combinations.

"It ran for five minutes before coming down. I thought I had it."

"You almost did, Beck. Let's just recalculate the last few integrations; I think I'm beginning to see a pattern here."

"No shit. How come I didn't see it?"

"Because you're a mathematician and I'm a scientist."

"What the fuck does that mean?"

"I don't know. I was just trying to make you feel better," laughed A. J.

They stayed with it and were finally successful. After countless hours they had a computer-generated resonation.

"Why am I not happy? We did it," said an exhausted Becky.

"Because if we have to do this with every individual cancer patient, they would be dead before we could help them. Okay, it's a breakthrough, and there is a pattern here that might reduce the processing time if we can develop it. Baby steps, Beautiful Becky, and we still have to transmit that frequency out of the computer into the human."

This opened up a whole set of new problems. The transmission from the computer to their human subject did not work. The individual died before they could cure this latest problem.

They were not going to be able to do this alone; it was going to take international networking and cooperation. A. J. was being contacted regularly from cancer research organizations around the globe as they shared information. The researchers were going off in all directions and losing valuable time with duplicate studies. A. J. was about to launch his own research lab and saw the necessity of organizing the flow of information coming from hundreds of sources. He knew just the person who could do that for him: Little Bit was about to get her call.

"HI, BABY, IT'S ME. What are you and Skeet doing for dinner tonight?"

"SEAN! Are you here in L.A.?"

"I will be later on today. I've got to meet the boys at UCLA so they can see how strong I am. I also have something I want to talk to you about and I want to see how the movie is coming along."

It had been six months since he left L.A. and A. J. was looking forward to being with his sisters again. He was about to hail a cab at the L.A. airport when a familiar face greeted him from under a floppy straw hat and sunglasses. Wylie Morris smiled from behind the wheel of a silvery Porsche. "Hey handsome, need a ride?

You'll have to excuse the get-up; it acts as a disguise. Monica told me you were coming to visit us and I volunteered the limo service but you will have to settle for my little car instead."

"Wylie! What a nice surprise. Impatient cabbies make me nervous," grinned A. J.

"Well, hop in before security runs us off. The cab fare is lunch at my favorite hideaway."

"Great. You can fill me in on the production. I can't wait to hear the latest updates. Skeet keeps me informed but I don't think she tells me everything."

They enjoyed a lobster bisque at a quiet seafood bistro, "Boy, this is every bit as good as we get on the Chesapeake. Thanks for bringing me here."

"Yeah, Rachel and I come here often. Monica joins us when she can. She is one busy lady, A. J.; she tries to do everything. As you know, Jeff has joined her and is a big help in dealing with the numbers. And Jessica is a wonder, she keeps everybody in line."

"Oh yeah," laughed A. J. "She's always been good at that."

"We're right on schedule and it looks like we could wrap this up by next spring," said Wylie.

"There was a lot of re-writing to do and thanks for putting your foot down, making certain that Skeeter was more involved. Monica fought us all the way but what a difference it made in the storyline. You were so right."

"Yes, I kept sending her e-mails reminding her about some of our adventures. She was always a big part of all our lives and I think she honestly forgot about that."

"Look, A. J., we're getting into the more intimate scenes between you and M. J. I don't think Monica has a complete understanding of that part of your relationship. She's relying a lot on M. J.'s diary but I'm starting to drift a bit. I think I need your help."

"Sure. What do you want me to do?"

"Well, before you leave, would you spend some private time with me away from the cameras? It would make a difference. I sometimes get a little uptight in those moments and can't relax with all those eyes peering at me."

"Yeah, I can understand that. Just tell me where and when."

"Great. I'll review the parts I'm having trouble with and we can get together at my place when you have the time."

They drove straight to the studio where Skeet and Little Bit were waiting for them in Monica's office.

"Sean!" cried Little Bit rushing over to him. He grabbed her and swung her in the air, just like he did when they were kids growing up. "You want me to put you on my shoulders and take you for a ride?" he grinned.

"No, no, Sean. She'll do it," chimed in Skeet as she ran up for her hug.

The four of them toured the sets and A. J. looked on as the actors recreated the day of the parade.

"Wow, that's incredible, Skeet! If I didn't know any better I would have thought I was standing in front of Ma's house."

"Yeah, those videos you gave me solved a huge problem. We now have a lot of footage, not all in sequence yet, but I think you will begin to get the feel for what we're doing."

They made their way back to Monica's office and Wylie said,

"I gotta run, guys. I have a walk-through to do. Where did you get that maniacal director anyway, Monica? Marine boot camp in San Diego?"

"Something like that," teased Monica as she shuffled through scripts. "You know how I like to give unknowns a chance."

"Well, glad to help. I hope I survive. I'm not as tough as the real M. J. Call me, A. J. I'll have the scripts ready and we can go to work. See ya."

"Uh, oh. Look out, Sean, I think I know what that's all about," grinned Little Bit.

"What? Come on, she just needs help with some of the personal stuff, thats all."

"Right, Sean, right," smirked Skeeter.

After dinner the three of them were relaxing in the girls' apartment and A. J. commented on how his cancer research project was coming along.

"Skeeter, I think we're getting close to a major breakthrough but our efforts have hit an operational snag. There is so much information being reported to us every day that it's becoming impossible to keep track of it all. Also, we are not being explicit enough in our requests for data from our friends and too much time is being wasted... We're not organized."

Skeeter looked at Little Bit and said, "I think what our brother is trying to say is that he needs you."

"Skeet..."

"It's all right, Sean. Little Bit and I have talked about this. Look, we are in the business of making movies, and you're in the business of saving lives. She's my right arm and I'll miss her terribly but if you need her, her place is with you and your team. And besides, she's been waiting for your call."

"Thanks, big sister," Little Bit said clutching Skeeter's hand.

"Yeah, thanks, big sister," Sean said, clutching her other hand.

The following morning A. J. had his long overdue meeting with Rachel to discuss the Rinnistan memoir.

"This would make a sensational documentary or historical movie," cited Rachel. "In either event it goes unsaid that Skeet Studios would handle the production. If we decide on a movie, Wylie is the logical choice to play Rinni. We wouldn't even have to change her makeup."

"Okay to both propositions. We'll let Skeet decide what format to use. I'm leaning towards the movie."

"Yes, and so is Wylie," said Rachel.
"My only request is I want The Zone to be released before filming begins on Rinnistan. Of course I'll discuss all this with Skeet."

"Good. I'll talk with Monica too and see how she wants to handle the promos. I'll start lining up some screenwriters for her. God, life is strange, A. J. I mean, look how all this has come together. Amazing."
A. J. smiled, "I know. I can't wait to see the next act."

SHE WAS A MOST polished seductress. The girls were right. Wylie Morris didn't need any help with the script. She was so smooth and clever he actually thought they were rehearsing a love scene. Wylie was reading the lines perfectly but when she unexpectedly initiated a passionate kiss he knew that she had other things in mind. At first he was put off by the deception and said so.

"Wylie, why didn't you just invite me up for a drink? I would have gotten the message."
"Okay, why don't you join me for a drink?"

A. J. stepped back, looked at her and thought to himself: Here is one of the most beautiful woman in the world offering herself to me and I'm playing games with her. Idiot.

"You have any cold beer?" he chuckled. Wylie laughed but before she could retrieve the beer he took her into his arms and returned the kiss. She wasn't going to be solely in charge. Clothes started to fly and in seconds they were in bed. With his ability to control his orgasms she was overmatched and loved it.

They saw each other many times over the weeks to come; they both were in the relationship for the sex. Wylie Morris was a woman who knew the power of being beautiful and would not saddle that power with single relationships. A. J.'s past tragic experiences would not allow him to get close to a woman again. It actually worked for them as they became both friends and lovers.

"DAMN IT, A. J. You were right."
They had almost completed the exercises and the results were disappointing to Ian.
"Your scores are higher, even comparable to the strength of professional athletes, but not significantly better due to your high baseline. Okay, lets complete this. We're going to see how much farther you can now throw a baseball." They were standing at home plate at the college stadium. He had scored high on the previous testing, throwing the ball three hundred and twenty five feet - not bad but not major league either. He took aim at the centerfield fence some four hundred and fifty feet away.

A. J. took a couple of hops and promptly threw the ball clear over the fence. It was eye popping. The scientists were astounded.

"That will do it, A. J. That will DO IT!" said an excited Dr. Ian Griggsby. "Incredible! Nobody can do that. Nobody! What an improvement. Did you do anything different in your mental exercises?"

"You know, I did. Whenever I sent the trains to my arms, I visualized myself throwing the ball farther and faster than before. I didn't do that with the other exercises."

"A. J., we really have something to work from now; this is exciting!"

An assistant baseball coach at the college observed the testing and sauntered over to the scientists. He was carrying a hand held radar gun used to measure the speed of a ball pitched. He looked at A. J. and said, "With that arm, I would like to test how hard you can throw the ball from the pitcher's mound to the plate. What do you say?"

"He says yes," replied Ian, anxious to see the test himself.

The gun consistently measured one hundred and fifteen miles per hour. "I know some professional scouts who would be interested in talking to you," said the blown away coach. "Thanks, but I have a job," joked A. J.

They discussed the next step in their joint experiment while enjoying coffees at a cafe on the UCLA campus.

"A. J., I know you're headquartered out of Washington, but would you consider setting up your research lab at Northwestern? Our interests are mutual and I have scientists in our field visiting practically every week. We have just made a giant leap and joint participation in our type of experimenting would be beneficial to both of us. I would openly support your research and together we should be able to make a persuasive argument to the doubters."

"You know, there would be an advantage to that and I'm sure my business manager would prefer that I stayed away," he grinned.

"The University is liquidating some of its real estate assets and I happen to know that a Victorian office building near the campus is about to go on the market. It would be the perfect size for your lab; there's even a small auditorium. You would also have access to student assistants."

"You're making a great pitch, Ian. I'll talk it over with Becky. I won't go anywhere without her."

"Good. One other thing. There's an oncologist right in Evanston who works solely with children cancer patients. She has set up a clinic and she's not happy with the progress being made in the search for a cure. She's constantly looking for alternative methods and a while back she contacted me to learn about the mind-body techniques that I work with. She would be really interested in your studies and I bet she already knows about you."

"It's getting better, Ian. It's getting better."

Chapter 58: They're Just Babies

BACK IN WASHINGTON, A. J. discussed the move with Becky and Genevieve. "We're going to set the lab up where?" cried out Becky.
"Northwestern University, just outside of Chicago."
"I know where it is. I was born and raised on the North side and did my undergraduate work at The University of Chicago!"
"That means you're happy?"
"Of course I'm happy. I get to go home - what's left of it."
A. J. let that pass. Becky had always been secretive about her past.
Becky was becoming uncomfortable anyway with the rapidly growing investment firm Genevieve was building and wanted a more academic surrounding. The move would be perfectly timed for her.
Genevieve wasn't all that thrilled. She didn't like the idea of being separated from her partner, knowing that their career paths would travel in different directions.
"Great. You're going to leave me in D.C. to run this business in an office complex that is way too small to operate efficiently and you're taking Becky with you? Tell me why I shouldn't be pissed off?"
"Ah... your expense account would allow for as many visits to Evanston as you wish to take?"
"That's a start. What else?"
"Ah... you can move this office to any place that you want - no limitations on the size."
"Bingo! Becky, make him provide a home for you that has plenty of room for some of my stuff! I'm beginning to like this move a lot better!"
"You got it, Gen. I have a great place in mind. I know the neighborhood," said Becky, delighted.
"You two are tough," sighed A. J.
The building in Evanston was perfect for their research lab and A. J. purchased the large three story turreted nineteenth century structure. It was just off campus, close to Ian's office. The auditorium would be kept as is but everything else needed extensive remodeling. A. J. would use the third floor for his living quarters.

"WELL, WHAT DO you know, Sean? I finally get to live in Chicago," said Little Bit in the cab ride from the airport.
"Yeah, I was thinking the same thing. It only took you eleven years to get here.
You've got a job waiting for you this time and it's going to be a challenge, starting with the lab and office design. I can't wait for you to meet Beautiful Becky. You're going to think you're back in the Zone when

you hear what comes out of her mouth," laughed A. J.
"Is she going to put me through the test?"
"Not a chance. She read the book and is genuinely excited about meeting you. You already passed the test."

They bonded instantly. Becky towered over Jessica and naturally wanted to protect her like a little sister. But she found out that this little girl didn't need any help as Jessica took charge and things were immediately placed in order. Jessica loved being around Beautiful Becky and it *did* remind her of her life in the Zone.

Nobody was happier with the move than Ian. He was already blogging about what he considered a successful experiment with A. J. that validated his mind to body theories. A. J. wasn't so sure, but he met with the visiting scientists when they came on campus and discussed the value of the tests as it related to their field of study.

A. J. and Becky explained to Jessica in great detail what they had in mind for their lab setup. Jessica grasped it right away and made substantial improvements on the efficiency of the floor plan. She designed the layout so they could easily expand when the time came.

The 'operations room' would have individual work stations in it. Their computers would be hooked up to a large screen where A. J. could view all incoming information. This room was connected to the auditorium by a double swinging door.

Several rows of auditorium seats would be removed and replaced with long work benches. The seats would then be placed side by side behind the benches. The room would resemble a NASA command center with the stage acting as a director's perch. The student assistants would do their work from here.

"Shit, Jess! I never would have thought of that," said an impressed Becky.

They temporarily took over the existing offices, setting up their computers as the remodeling was about to get underway.

"The first thing we're going to do is get a technical guy in here so we can wire this building properly," exclaimed Jessica.
"I need to immediately download all your sources so I can sort this mess out! How the hell have you two been operating? This is a disaster!"

"I told you she would be upset, Beck. It's best we just get out of her way," sheepishly added A. J.
"No shit. I'll be in my soon-to-be-demolished office, Jess, if you need me," said Becky as she quickly made her escape.
"Coward," A. J. called after her.

DR. DIANE WHITIKER ran the Children's Cancer Medical Center located near the hospital. A. J. and Ian met with her in her office.

"It's a real pleasure meeting you, Dr. McCleary. I'm familiar with your work. I try to read every study on alternative treatments for cancer. I was surprised when I figured out you were the A. J. McCleary who invented The McCleary Chip."

"What? I didn't know that, A. J. You are full of surprises," said a truly surprised Ian.

"Well, it all kind of just evolved. What's important is the use of the chip in researching treatments for disease. I focus on that."

"I know you must have hundreds or thousands of researchers and medical people on your web site contact list and I'm proud to say I'm one of them," stated Diane.

"What? You are? When did you sign on?"

"A couple of weeks ago. I've been reading Ian's blogs and searched out your site."

"Little Bit's going to kill me," he mumbled.

"Who's going to kill you?"

"Oh, my new chief of staff. She's not happy with my organizational skills," chuckled A. J.

"Dr. McCleary..."

"Please call me A. J." he interrupted.

"Okay, A. J. I've actually been following for some time now all your on line studies and the studies of others who are storing organ frequencies by using the McCleary chip. I've been praying for a breakthrough in your work. I've got a lot of sick kids here."

"I know you do and that's why I asked Ian to introduce us. I was hoping you would allow me to do some experimental research on your patients."

"And I was hoping you would ask me to do that. I believe the answer to curing cancer is to treat the electrical energies of the human body, exactly what you're working on. A. J., I have a roomful of terminally ill children. Their parents and I are willing to try anything at this stage. Just tell me what you want me to do. And I don't have to tell you that every second counts."

"I think we're getting close, Diane. As a matter of fact, we accomplished a computer resonating match just recently but the patient died before we could take the next step. Becky - my partner in all this - and I know the urgency and we get frustrated when people die before we can help them. I don't know how you can do it, facing all that anguish everyday."

"It's hard, really hard, but none of us give up," sighed Diane.

"Okay, here's what I would like you to do. Immediately get your kids to start using devices that have the McCleary Chip..."

"A. J.," she interrupted. "I started doing that months ago. I told you I'm a believer in your research and I want to make every option available to them."

"Wow. You're way ahead of the others. I'll have Jessica contact you as soon as we leave here. We're going to have to download all your stored information."

"A. J., I did something else. I not only stored their frequencies but I repeated the process every single day. You will have a day-to-day history of their cellular and organ frequency changes."

A. J. was gobsmacked. "Diane, Diane! This is precisely what we are attempting to set up now. We're looking for a predictable pattern to the evolution of frequencies indicating diseases. This could save us months, maybe years! Okay, like you said, not a second to waste. I'm going back to the lab. Becky will want your most terminal patients' information first."

"I'll have that ready for her, A. J. Suddenly I don't feel so helpless! I don't want to sound too metaphysical, but this can't just be luck: you meeting Ian, then moving your research lab here and getting together with me..."

"Yeah, I know what you mean, but we have work to do."

THREE OF DIANE'S patients were the most urgent. 5 year old Silvia, Kyle, 7, and Brandon,10. They all had leukemia. Silvia was in the final stages.

Becky and A. J. had several sessions with the three children re-testing them on a device they built that only contained body frequency information.

"Okay, lets review this," said an anxious A. J. in a meeting with Becky and Jessica.

"Scenario number one: We had a healthy frequency and didn't have to reconstruct it. It computer resonated but we couldn't get the brain to integrate with it when we transmitted.

Scenario number two: We had an unhealthy frequency and with Diane's recorded information we were able to work backwards and reconstruct a probable healthy one and that also computer resonated. We couldn't get the brain to accept that one either. At least we were able to identify a real pattern in the signals with Diane's kids. It saved us a lot of time but we're taking days instead of hours to accomplish a computer resonation. We must do better!

Little Bit is in contact with many of our research partners around the world and will send them unhealthy frequency patterns we have collected from individual cases so they can attempt to reconstruct them. They will forward the combinations they have tried back to Becky who will constantly post them so there will be no duplicate efforts. That will give us hundreds of researchers working on the same frequency instead of only Becky. We are way understaffed but we'll solve that problem by using student assistants when the information comes pouring in."

Jessica excused herself as her phone rang.

"Okay, next we are..." Jessica returned looking like she was on the verge of tears.

"Little Bit, what's wrong?" asked a concerned A. J.

"That was Diane. Silvia died five minutes ago," she sobbed.

"Oh no," gasped Becky. She put her hands to her face.

Nobody said a word for several seconds. Finally A. J. spoke: "We cannot allow ourselves to do this. We can't get close to these children; they're terminally ill and we are not yet in a position to help them. Others will die and it is not our fault."

"They're just babies, A. J.," sobbed Becky.

"I know, I know. Little Bit, when it's appropriate, ask Diane to assign the children numbers. That's how we will identify them from now on. We have to stay detached if we are to be effective or we will rush something and make it worse."

Kyle died a month later. Ten year old Brandon was the last identified patient.

INFORMATION AND DATA were steadily coming in. It was collected by the students who forwarded it to Jessica who in turn sent it in orderly fashion to researchers on her network. Becky coordinated the return information and A. J. oversaw everything. They were in operation and it was efficient. Now this powerful team was ready.

Chapter 59: The Brandon Foundation

"IT'S NEVER GOING to work, Becky. The brain simply won't recognize computer reproduced signals, healthy or reconstructed ones!" declared A. J., discouraged.

"Okay, what will it recognize?"

"The organ's own frequency.

Look, we now know Brandon's healthy frequency patterns and we can send them up to the ionosphere together with their magnetic powers. If we make the signal strong enough, maybe it will attract his own wandering healthy frequencies with its similar like impulses and bounce them back to our receptors. We will put the computer next to Brandon; the bands will be large enough to invade his body receptors too. It could resonate with his brain waves."

She looked at him intensely for a long moment and said, "There is absolutely no science on that; you are really reaching."

"Of course I am. There's no science on that because nobody has tried it. The hard part was reconstructing an unhealthy resonating frequency and we're the only ones who have accomplished that and the only ones who developed a computer resonation of a healthy frequency."

"You're going to be accused of playing with powers that only belong to God!" exclaimed Becky.

"Do you think that Brandon and his parents really care about that?"

"No, I don't, A. J. I don't... Lets go see Diane."

They met with Diane and were joined by Brandon's parents.

"It's close, real close Mr. and Mrs. Harris - maybe two days at the most. I'm not going to give you any false hope. Dr. McCleary here is pioneering a new technique in the treatment of cancers. He is asking your permission to use this process on Brandon. It is painless and has never been done before. He's working with magnetic impulses."

"Dr. Diane, we have all the confidence in the world in you. You have fought so hard. I know you won't make our decision for us, but what do you advise?" asked Mr. Harris.

"There is no other option. You have nothing to lose."

"I knew you would say that. Okay Dr. McCleary, do what you can. We are not expecting you to succeed; we won't be disappointed."

A. J. nodded, set up his computer and sent the computer resonated frequency up into the ionosphere.

"Look, Mr. and Mrs. Harris, we have no scientific evidence that this will work. We're trying to retrieve Brandon's healthy body frequencies that are floating somewhere out there in the upper atmosphere. The program we're using is designed to attract our return signal. If it is received by the computer's receptors, the band should be large enough to also interact with Brandon's very weak body frequencies. Hopefully, the healthy waves will resonate with his brain frequencies and will then be directed to Brandon's blood cells. That's all there is to it, Mr. and Mrs. Harris. Now we just wait."

"Oh, I wish Brandon could hear this. He would love it; he's a Trekkie!"

Brandon was lying, sedated, in a bed next to A. J.'s computer. The waves had merely a few feet to travel.

For the next few hours they took turns coming and going out of the room. The computer screen remained blank.

Diane saw it first. "A. J., get in here. SOMETHING'S HAPPENING!"

A. J. and Becky rushed into the room. "It's our signal coming from somewhere," declared A. J. "The bands are interacting with Brandon's body frequencies. We will have no idea what it contains until his body absorbs it. Our program will show if it resonates with the brain."

"Jesus!" screeched Becky. "It's oscillating... IT TOOK! IT TOOK!"

"What does that mean?" cried Mrs. Harris, clutching A. J.'s arm.

"That means we're in a place where no one has ever been. Now we need the brain to do its job and route the good guys to Brandon's blood. Diane, lets keep a running count on the white blood cells!"

"I've already started, A. J. I've got it on the monitor. My god, there are so few red cells! We won't get an accurate reading for another ten minutes."

Not a word was spoken until the reading came through. "The RED COUNT'S UP! It's low but it has risen. We're... REVERSING IT. IT'S WORKING, IT'S WORKING!" shouted Diane.

Two weeks later Brandon was sitting up in his bed asking how his beloved Cubs were doing. His red cell count was almost back to normal.

A. J. and Becky were paying him a visit. They brought a brand new Cubs hat with them. "Here you go, slugger. You'll be needing this in a few months; your friends are waiting for you," grinned A. J.

"Gee, thanks, A. J. Mom and Dad told me what you and Becky did. Thanks for that, too."

"Hey, don't forget Dr. Diane. Next to you, she's the real hero."

"Yeah, I know. She's my buddy."

A. J. was reviewing with Diane what had just transpired. "I don't know what happened out there in that dark world Diane; I can only speculate. We do know that the returning signal had qualities that the transmitting signal did not but were nevertheless very similar. The waves kept coming and the brain recognized it. How the brain functioned after that is a mystery that may never be understood. This is not science but we intend to repeat this procedure with patients all over the world until our positive results are overwhelming and we will have to be listened to."

"You know they will come after you, A. J.," said Diane. "Powerful people will be threatened."

"I suppose, but it won't stop me. There are a lot of Brandons out there and I now know I can help them. How can anybody stand in the way of saving peoples' lives?" It was a rhetorical question.

Genevieve formed a cancer foundation for them named the 'Brandon Foundation'. They already had to expand their facility and it was just beginning.

SENATOR HARRY C. DAVIS was a United States Senator from Alabama. He had a reputation for being honest and hardworking. He also was ambitious and was being considered as a candidate for the Presidency of the United States. The senator was fifty-four years old, five foot ten, slightly overweight and balding. He was conservative and the preferred candidate of the evangelical right of his party.

He met with his advisors in his Birmingham office. After the normal political briefing, one of his advisors said: "There's a report that just came over some of the medical web sites about a scientist in Illinois who successfully cured a child's leukemia by using frequencies coming from somewhere in space. He claims it was the patient's own body frequencies floating around out there."

"Man! Won't those non-believers ever quit!" exclaimed a disgruntled Senator Davis.

"This guy might be different, Harry. He seems to have the support of some pretty influential people in the academic world."

"Okay, you stay on top of it, Bud. He might need watching; lets see what we have on him. The man probably has never been in a church in his life."

BARRY ZIMMERMAN and Martin Kleinman were chatting over a cup of coffee and reading the financial section of the Washington Post.

"Would you look at this!" exclaimed Zimmerman, "the McCleary Chip is back in the news. That fucking McCleary has used it to cure a kid's cancer."

"Let it go, Barry. Sounds like he's doing some good for Christ sakes."

"Never. That son-of-a-bitch stole a hundred grand from me. Maybe the public should be informed on what a thief and fraud he is. I'll knock him off his white horse!"

"Oh man, the Masked Blogger is about to strike again," sighed Kleinman.

There was more trouble on the horizon. A. J. got a call from Steve.

"Hey, A. J. ... Sean, or whatever the hell your name is, I just finished reading The Zone. I don't think your lost sister got the ending right."

"No, she didn't but the movie is going to set it straight. Wait 'til you see the guy playing you. He can't take a punch either," chortled A. J.

"You could have told me, you know. I might have liked you better," quipped Steve.

"Okay, some serious news. Your two friends, Enrico and Jorge, have just been released from prison. Lets hope they've been rehabilitated and behave themselves. If they read a revised Zone or see the movie, they will know who A. J. McCleary is. I don't trust them."

A. J. hesitated, thought about his mother, and said, "Thanks for the heads up, Steve, but I can't worry about them. I've moved on. And besides, I didn't put them in jail; I just threw them out the window!

Hey, when are you coming to Chicago? Becky was asking about you. She said she wasn't finished with you yet."

"I think I'd rather face terrorists," replied Steve, which made both of them laugh.

Chapter 60: The Masked Blogger

THE BRANDON FOUNDATION team was buzzing with excitement and unbridled energy. They doubled the number of student assistants and had a waiting list of eager young men and women willing to participate in the struggle. Word had spread fast that a new and successful approach in the treatment of cancer was being developed in a research center right on their campus.

Jessica sent the news by way of their group contact lists all over the world. They were soon inundated with requests to work on thousands of cancer patients. That, of course, was impossible so they shifted gears again.

Another work station was set up in the operations room and would be occupied by Jessica's new assistant, Marcia Bryson. Marcia was in her mid thirties, married, had two children, and taught yoga. She was a no nonsense efficient type whose talents were immediately recognized by Jessica who shared the same qualities. She would be in charge of six of the most advanced and brightest students who would be part of the operational team but located in the auditorium.

Marcia and her team's chief function was to create a network comprised of doctors and cancer clinics from all over the world and train them by way of videos on how to gather the frequency information from patients using the McCleary chip. The doctors and clinics would transmit the patient Information back to the foundation. This data would be collected by the battery of student assistants in the auditorium. Then it would be sent in orderly fashion to Jessica who would forward it to the research labs.

Becky had her own team of mathematical whiz kids stationed in the auditorium helping her detect patterns that would save an enormous amount of computer resonating processing time. Everybody knew that shortening the process by mere seconds could save hundreds of lives. Their goal was to immediately identify a resonating pattern for specific cancers. Once cancers were identified in the patients, the process of sending their computer generated healthy organ frequencies out into the atmosphere could begin. The technique of frequency resonating was constantly being upgraded by the foundation as they recognized more and more similar patterns in their human studies.

The foundation's role was now being clearly defined: it had become the central headquarters in a coordinated effort to defeat cancer and other diseases through the use of electromagnetic frequencies. All information from the electromagnetic treatment of patients from around the globe was being funneled to the foundation through a networking program set up by Jessica. They were rapidly building a pool of cancer frequency patterns to be used in their advanced research.

Their work was becoming a true international effort and was drawing a lot of attention from the scientific world. The information was still considered experimental and, so far, the public was mostly kept unaware. Not all the attention was positive.

IAN HAD NO patience with skeptics and obstructionists and he published the results of the mind-to-body techniques he had used on A. J., describing in detail his one hundred and fifteen mile fast ball.

A. J. consented to the publication and validated Ian's work citing the successful treatment of Brandon's cancer as an example of the brain sending a controlled introduction of outside energies along the same body circuit routes that Ian was working with. Dr. Diane added her substantial medical credibility by confirming the reports set out in the publication.

Ian's publication predictably brought out many skeptics and they used their own web sites for negative attacks on the study. They labeled A. J.'s research as non-scientific occult science and many called it the work of the devil:

'Why, the notion that a person's electrical body frequencies are floating around in the heavens is preposterous! Are they telling us that they are even out there after a person dies? This is an all out attack on the precepts of good science and Christianity! These people must be stopped! Where are our leaders on this issue?'

The foundation refused to get involved in that rhetoric but merely reported cases of successful treatments, identifying their human subjects from around the world. They provided links to clinics that were reporting the personal accounts of their patients who were cured. This was not convincing governments, the science community, and certainly not the established medical professionals. Their critics were giving Ian's publication no credibility and, when questioned, were steadfast in demanding a twenty to thirty year successful track record before commenting. So far, the skeptics were effective in keeping the public uninformed.

RACHEL PHONED A. J., excited: "Congratulations, A. J.! And thanks. You just saved me a lot of work!"

"You're welcome, Rachel, but what are you talking about?"

"Don't you ever watch the news? You have been nominated for a Pulitzer prize for your work on Rinnistan!"

"No kidding! I thought only politicians and educators were interested in the story."

"Hardly. Evidently it was widely read in Asia and here in the U.S. by a lot of interested people. You're becoming famous, A. J. The timing is perfect; we were about to announce that Skeet Studios had just committed to do a production on the women warriors from Pakistan. We can now add that the movie will be based on a true story written by A. J. McCleary who was recently nominated for a Pulitzer Prize for this work. It's a promoter's dream!"

"Well, I'm glad I'm making your job easier, Rachel, but how is this going to affect the press releases on The Zone coming out next week?"

"Yeah, we've been discussing that at length. We've pretty much decided to go with a statement that parts of The Zone had to be re-written because of astounding new disclosures about the death of one of the main characters, Sean Ferrari, also known as A. J. McCleary. We will say nothing else. With your growing notoriety we figured this was the perfect tease. Shamelessly pure Hollywood. We are also constantly reminding people that this is a true story and our revisions are not fiction."

"And how am I supposed to answer when I'm asked if I'm the same person as the character in the movie?"

"Tell them to wait for the movie to come out."

"No, I couldn't do that. If asked I'll answer honestly, but I'll tell them to see the movie for the specifics."

"Fair enough and probably a better way to handle it, A. J."

His notoriety was also the subject of a phone conversation he had with Ian. "A. J., I just had lunch with the Director of Player Personnel of the Chicago Cubs. He's a good friend of mine. I've done a lot of work with his ballplayers over the years; I told him about you. Now before you say no.."

"No!"

"Ah, like I said, before you say no, he's invited you out to Wrigley to pitch to some Major League hitters."

"You know I'm not interested, Ian. It's not necessary in our work and I'm way too busy to be playing games. No and No."

"I told him you would say that and he was wasting his time, but baseball guys have a hard time taking no for an answer. They can't imagine anybody not wanting to be a professional ballplayer. All I have to do is call him. A. J., don't discount the publicity. The more exposure we get the more pressure is put on the medical profession.

Look, you don't have to sign any contracts. Just show up and strike everybody out. I'll call a press conference and explain who you are and describe your success with Diane's kids. I'll claim the Cubs are very interested in you."

"Ian, what makes you think I can strike them out?" laughed A. J. "Don't I have to throw it over the plate?"

"You and I both know that you can send that ball anyplace that you want to."

"Maybe. But I've never done it; and besides, what makes you think they will want to sign me?"
"Are you kidding? You throw a one hundred and fifteen mile fastball past their hitters and they will mortgage the franchise!"
Ian might have a point, A. J. reflected. He was frustrated with the medical establishment. If he could just get a significant number of doctors to experiment with his procedures ... no telling how many lives could be saved in the process. Publicity may get the attention of those who have discounted their work because it is not standard practice.
"Okay, set it up, Ian, but on one condition. You tell them that I'm doing this for the scientific exposure and they have no chance of getting me to sign a contract."
"Fine. They will agree because they won't believe you. Who in their right mind would turn down a Major League contract?"
It was early April and the Cubs were between games. Plenty of reporters were on hand as word got out about the tryout. A. J. arrived wearing sweats and running shoes; he had to borrow a glove. Most of the Cub players had the day off. The few who did show up for extra batting practice agreed to bat against this unknown pitcher. A. J. only threw to a few batters. It was enough. They couldn't hit him and the catcher couldn't hold him. They called it off before somebody got hurt.
Ian held his press conference explaining that A. J. was actually a scientist working on a cure for cancer. Ian further stated that Dr. McCleary was getting great results by using mind to body techniques in his treatment of children stricken with cancer and that he used the same techniques to develop his un-hittable fast ball.
It was reported in the sports bylines that: '*The Cubs are about to sign a fireballing phenom'.* The article described accurately how A. J. had developed his fastball and that he was a scientist. The special interest story was bigger than the sports story. The Brandon Foundation was making headlines.

"WHAT HAVE YOU GOT on him, Bud? I'm starting to get a lot of heat from my base. They want me to discredit him. They honestly see him as a threat not to just their political philosophies but to their religious beliefs," said a concerned Senator Davis.
"Okay, we've got a lot on him but we are double checking everything. This guy has to be getting credit for things that he couldn't have possibly done. I mean he is apparently disgustingly wealthy, but most of his money is held offshore so we are having trouble getting accurate financial reports. We suspect that he might have CIA connections. He is a renowned scientist who has been acknowledged by Nobel Peace Prize winners and, incredibly, he has been nominated for a Pulitzer Prize for a

story he wrote about terrorism. And get this - now we hear that he is a central character in a movie called The Zone and he is identified in this so called true story by a different name!"

"Oh, this has got to be a scam," exclaimed the Senator. "If this weren't so important it would be funny."

"You want a real laugh? The Chicago Cubs are trying to sign him as a pitcher. Evidently he has a one hundred and fifteen mile fast ball, apparently developed by some mind-to-body technique."

"What? Oh, I've got to meet this guy's marketing man. This is hilarious," laughed Senator Davis. "This should be easy. Lets just expose him as a fraud he must be."

"We may not have to do that. Evidently the 'Masked Blogger' has unloaded on him. We're getting the information now."

"Good. Let our friend know that we are behind him, but keep us out of it."

"I already did," cited Bud."

BARRY ZIMMERMAN had been a power broker for years, accumulating contacts with Washington insiders and working behind the scenes for many lobbyists. He wasn't used to losing and never forgave the electronics company for forcing him into a settlement with A. J. It was either giving in to A. J.'s demands or losing a lucrative account.

A. J. never knew of Zimmerman's political connections or his business relationship with the company. He did suspect that this man was the kind to hold a grudge and was about to find out how true that suspicion was.

It first started out as a game for him. He loved to tweak his enemies, and they were plentiful. The internet provided the perfect venue. He began to blog, utilizing all the dirt he had collected over the years. His blog was widely read because it was so personal and targeted powerful people. It contained just enough truth to give him credibility. Zimmerman had a real talent for straddling the fine line between slander and gossip. He recognized early on that if he disclosed his identity he would never be able to work in Washington again, so he adopted a pseudonym: 'The Masked Blogger'.

Living in Washington, Genevieve was the first to see it. She actually was a fan of The Masked Blogger and searched for his blog every Monday morning. She loved to see the untouchables... touched.

She sat straight up spilling her coffee as she read his latest diatribe. "Holy shit! He's talking about A. J.," she gasped.

Hello, readers! Boy, have I got a dandy for you today. It appears that a certain so called scientist working out of a college in the Chicago area has declared that he can cure cancer by summoning spirits from the Universe and infusing them in a person's body forcing them to exorcise the cancer! It would be funny, but he actually is trying it on children! Can you imagine the false hope he is giving the parents of those children?

Well, I've done my homework and here is what I found out about this quack. The guy is well known in Europe but not for his science. He has passed himself off as a linguist and a international attorney. (nobody has ever seen his license) But his real achievement is his proclivity for chasing women. He somehow charmed the president of a big modeling agency in Geneva and after his fling with her he went to work on her models. They were seen in all the Geneva hotspots.

He was finally run out of Europe when he was sued for stealing patents of a major electronics firm. He made his way back to America and was sued again for civil conspiracy. He is also in trouble with the IRS and the SEC. How's that for one who claims he can cure cancer!

Oh, there's more. A lot more. Our hero has an investment firm somewhere in D.C. Without question, he is funding groups that have known terrorist ties in Pakistan!

And here's the real kicker! Our boy has somehow landed in Hollywood! That's right. He is the subject of a movie about to be released called The Zone; it's supposed to be a true story about a white kid growing up in a Detroit ghetto. He's the white kid and it does give the movie some credibility. He's a classic example of the adage... 'you can take the kid out of the ghetto but you can't take the ghetto out of the kid.'

Oh yeah - the movie is about our boy all right, because that same Casanova who charmed the models has worked his magic on the lead female star of the feature. Just ask all the beat writers in Hollywood.

Okay, I'm going to close with a tease. Chicago Cubs, you ought to be ashamed.

Chapter 61: The Un-Masked Blogger

GENEVIEVE PHONED BECKY. A. J. and Jessica joined them in a conference call. They had the blog on the main computer.

"Does anybody know who this Masked Blogger is?" asked A. J.

"No," said Genevieve. "But he's widely read and a lot of people want to believe everything he writes."

"My question is, what are we going to do about it?" asked Becky. "I mean, this could have a serious affect on the foundation."

"I suspect that's exactly what he's trying to do - discredit our work," offered Jessica. "But why? We haven't made any claims. We're just accurately reporting the results of the experiments."

"I've been following this blogger for some time now and this is really unusual for him. He attacks politicians or New York business men all the time but never scientists! I detect something else going on here. Any ideas A. J.?" questioned Genevieve.

"I've been warned that this kind of thing would happen. There are a lot of powerful people who don't like what we're doing and it doesn't do any good to try to understand their reasoning. It won't change their behavior. I'm afraid that this may be only the beginning."

"Are you suggesting that we do nothing?" asked an increasingly angry Becky.

"The last thing we should do is get into a pissing contest with this guy, Beck; that's just what he wants," stated Genevieve.

"Yeah, I agree with that. We have to take the high road," sighed Jessica.

"Okay, lets keep operating the same way and not even acknowledge the blog. But this might be impossible with all the attention it's sure to get. Little Bit, it might be a good idea to start looking for a public relations person to insulate us from the media. We need somebody to report our research anyway. You're way too busy to do that."

"I agree, Sean, but we're not the only ones affected by this idiot. How about Skeet Studios? Wylie? That model friend of yours? Rinnistan, Diane, Ian, the University and the Cubs?" queried Jessica.

"Yeah, and don't forget the Investment company," cited Genevieve.

"Good point, guys. They might have something to say publicly and it's their right to do so. I don't want them to fight our battles but we are just going to stand back for now. If it becomes necessary, I'll make an appropriate statement. Lets just wait and see."

Rachel, Skeet and Wylie were the first to call. "Sean - we're just now reviewing this outrageous blog. I'm personally offended, Wylie is mad as hell and Rachel is loving the publicity. What do you want us to do?"

"I think Rachel has the right idea. Ride the publicity and keep promoting the movie as a true story, which it is. Just flash your beautiful smile at them, Wylie, when they start with their personal questions. It will drive the hacks nuts."

"Okay, but I don't like it. Sean, you don't deserve that," exclaimed Skeet. "At some point this guy has to be challenged."

"Yeah, and I want the name of your model friend. We should compare notes," added a sarcastic Wylie.

A. J. got an e-mail from She-lagh:

Hey, my girls in New York tell me that you and I made the news. Were you fooling around with my models? I get this kind of crap all the time, A. J., so it doesn't bother me, but I know that such absurd publicity could be harmful to you and your foundation. Just tell me what you want me to do. I can attest to what you were really doing over here. You know you can contact me anytime - better yet, come visit me. Love ya, She

Steve, who was stationed back at Langley, called. "We don't know who this guy is, A. J., but he's taken shots at us before and he's indirectly implicated us with this funding of terrorist bullshit. I know you're not asking but we'll support you and give you anything we turn up on this jerk."

"Thanks, Steve. We're keeping our heads low but he has implicated a lot of people who are my friends and I may be forced to issue a statement."

"Okay. And don't worry about Dal. It's not likely she will hear about this and the Pakistanis know the truth. I'll be in touch and you do the same if anything else comes up."

"Yeah, I will, Steve. I don't think we've heard the last of him."

Something else did come up. A. J. got a call from Bob Galen.

"Dr. McCleary, this is Bob Galen. Remember me? I was one of the guys who sued you awhile back but dropped the suit when you agreed to what I thought was a reasonable settlement."

"Yes... yes I do. At the time I understood your position on the matter. You were being pressured by your co-plaintiffs. What can I do for you now, Mr. Galen?"

"Thanks. I want you to know that I support what you're doing with your research. I, of course, have personal knowledge of the potential of your chip as it relates to health issues. And that's what I'm calling you about. I'm outraged at what the Masked Blogger is doing. He has gone too far this time and I know why he has attacked you. If you're interested, I'll share some information that should be helpful to you."

"Oh? Yes...yes. I'm very interested in finding out all I can about this man. He could do us a lot of harm with those absurd charges. We are saving lives and all we are asking is for an honest chance to explain what we are trying to do."

"I believe you, Dr. McCleary. Look, I know this man's real identity. You know him too and when I tell you his name you'll understand why he's targeting you. He used to be a friend of mine but I no longer have any respect for him. He doesn't care if you save millions of lives, he just wants to personally hurt you."

"You say I know him?"

"Yes. He was one of my co-plaintiffs in our suit against you. His name is Barry Zimmerman. I can't give you any more than that; you will have to take it from there. He is connected to a lot of powerful people, Dr. McCleary. Be careful. He can be ruthless. The only thing I ask is that you don't identify me. I'm relying on your confidentiality."

"Okay. You've got my word on that - and thanks."

"Yeah, good luck."

A. J. phoned Steve as soon as he hung up with Galen. "I know the blogger's name, Steve; it's Barry Zimmerman. A few years ago I received some money from him settling a law suit. Evidently he took it personally. I can't swear to the reliability of my source or give you his name but I wanted you to have the information."

"That name sounds familiar, maybe from my Bureau days. I'll run a check and get back to you. If your informer is correct and we expose this guy, it will make a lot of people happy."

"Right. The sooner the better. My e-mails are starting to back up."

It was the reference to the Chicago Cubs that did the trick for the Masked Blogger. He wanted A. J. identified but cleverly never referred to him by name. The Chicago sports writers first put two and two together and figured out who the blogger was talking about. They identified the subject of the blog as A. J. McCleary and made their findings public. It was forcing A. J. to make a statement he didn't want to make.

The foundation was being inundated with calls and e-mails. Reporters were walking right into the lab unannounced and making it impossible for them to work. In response, carpenters were brought in and quickly constructed a small reception area sealing off the rest of the building from unwanted guests. There was plenty of room for the construction; in front of the auditorium was a substantial lobby.

Another office was built behind the reception area for Jessica. She was freed up to a great degree by Marcia and her students and could now concentrate more on the business end of the foundation's endeavors.

The first order of business was to decide how to answer all the questions being directed at A. J. regarding his scientific pursuits and his personal life.

Dr. Diane was extremely upset when they met at the foundation to discuss the problem.

"How dare that nameless coward accuse me of compromising my patients and lying to their families! A. J., Ian and I are going to call a press conference to defend ourselves. We want you to join us. Our phones have been ringing off the hook."

"Okay, I agree. Diane, why don't you and Ian give a detailed account of our joint efforts through your individual websites. The foundation will alert the news media as to your statements and announce that I will address the blogger's allegations at an open press conference the day after tomorrow. That way you two won't have to answer stupid questions and I can be brief and to the point. Then we will jointly state that we have nothing else to say."

Everyone was in agreement and Jessica put the word out about the press conference. They were going to hold it at their research center but there was so much interest they had to move the conference to a large banquet room in a major hotel in downtown Chicago.

An hour before the scheduled time, Steve called A. J.

"We got him. It's Zimmerman all right. We easily traced him on the web. If you want to expose him, feel free to allude to the tracking but don't mention us. Invite him to challenge you; his political supporters will be unhappy if he obliges and would silence him in a hurry. We know who *they* are too and, believe me, they won't want any part of this."

The banquet hall was filled to capacity and the people were noisily settling into their seats when A. J. walked up to the podium. No large cameras were allowed into the room, only laptops and smart phones. The address would be videoed and uploaded to YouTube. There were maybe two hundred people present and many of them were sports reporters... A. J.'s fastball.

Diane, Ian, Becky and Jessica sat in the front row. Brandon and his parents were seated next to Diane with Brandon sitting in the end seat next to the center aisle. He wore his Cubs baseball hat.

A. J. addressed the crowd: "Good afternoon. I'm Dr. A. J. McCleary and I'm associated with The Brandon Foundation. I believe you are familiar with my work and the work of Dr. Diane Whitiker and Dr. Ian Griggsby. They are sitting in the front row next to Dr. Rebecca Waxman, my partner, and Ms. Jessica Watson, director of the foundation."

"I'm sure you are aware that Dr. Whitiker and Dr. Griggsby have already responded through their web sites to certain allegations contained in a widely circulated blog that inaccurately described our joint efforts. As scientists and doctors we did not want to respond to such irresponsible reporting but in order to protect the foundation and our personal credibility we have chosen to reply.

I will not take up your time defending the science in which we are involved. Dr. Whitiker and Dr. Griggsby have already done that and I concur completely with their statements. We have never claimed to have a cure for cancer; actually we've had more failures than successes. But we have had many cases where the cancer has been completely eliminated. If we had saved only one life by the use our techniques, it would have been worth it.

However, as I said, I'm not here to argue the science, I'm here to address the personal attacks on me. It reflects on the foundation and is therefore unacceptable.

Let me first state that NO, I am not going to sign a baseball contract with the Chicago Cubs. And YES, I can pitch a baseball at speeds that are virtually un-hittable. I agreed to the tryout to showcase our research and I was upfront about that. Check Dr. Griggsby's documented report for verification by other credible scientists depicting this successful experiment.

A few years ago I had the occasion to work with two Pakistani women who were leading a guerrilla war against male oppressors from their village. I authored a memoir on that experience which will be made into a movie called 'Rinnistan'. Yes, I am that same A. J. McCleary and yes, I financially support their great cause.

When I was growing up in Detroit, I was known by another name - Sean Ferrari. The reason for the two names is explained in another movie about to be released based on a true story called 'The Zone' written by Monica Wilson. Monica and Jessica Watson are my sisters, also explained in the movie. Every bit of the story is true. It will premiere in Detroit this fall.

I have been attacked in that same blog written under the pseudonym, The Masked Blogger. I did not know why he targeted me until I discovered the identity of this man. Several years ago I invented a microchip popularly referred to as The McCleary Chip, the same chip we are effectively using to fight cancer.

The blogger held stock in an electronics corporation that was working on the same thing. I won the race to perfect the chip and they sued me in Europe. The plaintiffs had second thoughts about the suit and pressed for a settlement which resulted in the blogger and others not being transferred insider stock. It was distributed to me as part of the settlement. Check my web site for the court case number and you can follow the suit.

The Masked Blogger was irate, and when I came back to America, he and two others personally sued me and the electronics company. They also filed fallacious complaints with the IRS and the SEC. The blogger and his co-complainants were not successful in these actions either.

The un-masked blogger's name is Barry Zimmerman. And, Mr. Zimmerman, if you wish to continue with your deceitful and cowardly behavior, I'll be glad to share your web tracking records with the public. All those people you have offended in the past just might be interested in these."

That statement set off a buzz throughout the room as reporters quickly attacked their computers and grabbed for their phones.

A. J., annoyed by the distractions, waited for it to quiet down and proceeded. "Enough about him. I want to close by introducing somebody else to you. Sitting in the front row is a young boy with a Cubs baseball cap on. His name is Brandon Harris and our foundation is named after him. Brandon is the ten year old whose life was saved through the joint efforts of Dr. Whitiker, Dr. Waxman and myself. He had terminal leukemia and was literarily within hours of death. By effectively using our electromagnetic procedures, he is back playing baseball with his friends. His mother and father are sitting next to him."

Brandon then unexpectedly stood up, took off his cap and waved to the assembled crowd, most of whom were reporters. His parents stood with him and his mother could not hold back the tears.

A hushed silence came over the room. It started slowly but a spontaneous and loud applause broke out and Brandon burst into tears. It was as if he really hadn't understood what had happened to him until this moment.

He suddenly ran to the podium and threw his arms around A. J. It was a poignant scene and when A. J. walked Brandon back to his parents, he made brief eye contact with a woman in a red dress holding a smart phone that she forgot to use.

STEVE WAS THE first to reach A. J.

"That was GREAT! You got a standing 'O' in this room. That son-of-a-bitch is finished, hoisted on his own petard! YES!" He pumped his arms.

Then it was Skeet. "Way to go, bro! We are dancing in the streets here in Hollywood!"

"Yeah," chimed in Wylie. "Remind me never to get you mad at me!"

"Once again you did my work for me, A. J. Priceless publicity!" added Rachel.

"Ah, Sean, did you forget to tell me something? I mean it's just a minor thing, like the premiere of The Zone being held in *Detroit*?"

"Sorry Skeet, I wanted to surprise you, it just blurted out."

"Yeah, I'm surprised all right. Detroit isn't exactly Hollywood. Have you given any thought where we are going to hold this gala?"

"Yes, and that's a surprise too. You won't be disappointed."

"Okay, but when are you going to tell me about it? We only have a couple of months to prepare and Rachel is now showing definite signs of apoplexy."

"I'm glad you asked," laughed A. J., "because this Saturday you're joining Little Bit and me in the Motor City. I won't close the deal unless you approve."

"You're kidding. I can't, I've got to… that's only three days away, Sean!"

“Sorry; you’re already booked. The three of us back home; isn’t it exciting?”
“WHAT HOME?”
“See you at Metro, Skeet, we’ll talk later.”

THE SCENE AT Senator Harry C. Davis’s office in Birmingham was a different story.

“Well now, we totally underestimated this fella, haven’t we?” calmly claimed the Senator. His staff said nothing.
“I mean he took down poor Zimmerman in just a couple of sentences.

He’s for real, gentleman, and he’s obviously got connections in places we can’t touch. He couldn’t have acted alone in exposing Zimmerman and he did it in such a manner that the great Masked Blogger can’t be allowed to reply. Am I making myself clear?”

“Yeah, you are,” stated Bud. “Okay, he’s smart, tough, has resources and now he is attaining credibility which will certainly create a following for him. He’s formidable, all right, Harry. How should we handle him?”
“How? With great respect, that’s HOW!” thundered the Senator. “He’s no chicken shit politician. As a matter of fact, he’s not political at all and that makes him really dangerous! He’s vulnerable, though. He is dealing in unacceptable and to many people frightening science and he has no religious qualities that I can see. That turns off a lot of folks but, unfortunately, it also makes him susceptible to the lunatic fringe we know is out there. So we do nothing to incite those maniacs. IS THAT UNDERSTOOD?” His staff nodded in agreement.

“We treat him publicly with the highest respect. We compliment him on his accomplishments and in the same breath we suggest that we would like to see more substantiating scientific evidence in his work. You know something? I think he will agree with that. And I’ll tell you something else: there isn’t a person in this room who wouldn’t kiss his feet if he did find the cure for cancer. No sir, we support him when he’s scientifically proven and we fight him like hell if he leaves God out of it!”
“If that happens, how are we going to fight him, Harry?”
“Let’s win the nomination first. Then if we go all the way we will have the power to do a lot of things.”

The Masked Blogger never did reply. Barry Zimmerman left Washington and could not be reached.

TWO BASEBALL FANS found the video on YouTube.
“It’s that FUCKING FERRARI KID! I told you I thought it was him beating the shit out of me! He’s not dead after all, Jorge, but he’s going to damn well wish he WAS!” yelled Enrico.

Chapter 62: Welcome Home

SEAN AND LITTLE BIT were waiting for Skeet at the end of the walkway. They waved to her and she hurried over to them. "Boy, I miss you guys," grinned Skeeter.

"You're right on time, Skeet; we just got here ourselves." Sean returned Skeet's fist bump and playfully bounced her springy curls.

"You look great, big sister. I like the new 'do," added Little Bit.

"Yeah, I decided to go Hollywood for you."

They hailed a cab, handed their carry-ons to the cabbie and headed into the city.

"We're staying at the new Pontchartrain. We'll check in and leave our stuff, then we're going to Tiger Stadium! The game starts in about an hour," said an excited Sean.

"What? Oh, what a wonderful surprise!" exclaimed an even more excited Skeeter.

"Oh, no. I don't have my cap!"

"I'll buy you another one," laughed Sean.

Skeet's eyes widened as they strolled up to the renovated building. "Wow, what a great makeover. And yet it still looks the same. I'm impressed. Where's our seats?"

"Sorry, Skeet. It's a sellout and we're going to have to sit in the bleachers."

"Ah, that doesn't matter. I'd sit anywhere."

They bought their tickets and entered the gate marked 'Bleachers'. It was noisy and had the unmistakable smells of a baseball park, much to the delight of Skeeter. They followed the signs and Little Bit spotted it: "Look, Skeet! That sign over the ramp in front of us. It says THE BILLY SECTION."

"I believe our seats are this way, ladies." And A. J. led them up the ramp.

"I wonder why it's called the Billy section?" quizzed Skeet.

Bolted to the wall where you entered the bleachers was a prominent plaque. Sean stopped in front of it and the two women gasped as the likeness of their beloved Uncle Billy jumped out at them.

"Oh my god," they both cried in unison. They read the memorial with glassy eyes. Skeet reached out and gently stroked the plaque. She turned to Sean and said,

"You did this, didn't you?"

They worked their way through the crowd and found their seats on the bleacher benches. Pointing to the area behind them, already filled with raucous bleacher bums, he said, "Those one-hundred seats are freebies, courtesy of Uncle Billy."

They were still excitedly chatting about their ballpark experience as they walked down Woodward Avenue the following morning. They were across the street from the Zone and traffic was heavy. Little Bit was nervous about visiting the cemetery.

They crossed familiar streets and Skeet asked, "We didn't pass where Center Street was, did we?" They peered in between the passing cars and Little Bit said, "I don't remember that brick wall being there."

"I don't either. Oh my god, what is that? Look, it's beautiful with all those flowers banked up against it. It stretches for blocks! Sean...?"

"Skeet, there's an ornamental gate with bars in it, right where Center Street should be."

"You're right, Little Bit. Lets cross over and see... Sean?"

He just smiled and led them across the street. The gate was set back with the wall angling on both sides towards the gate and connecting to it. It was attached to two pillars; one of them had a stone carving on it:

THE ZONE

They were speechless and stood staring at the gate when slowly it started to slide open and disappeared behind the brick wall. Skeet and Little Bit hesitantly stepped back as a security guard approached them. He spoke to them in a deep voice: "Nice to see you again, Skeeter, Little Bit. Welcome home."

They were stunned. They looked at one another, then back at the guard. He was huge, his name tag read GEORGE.

Skeet suddenly recognized him. Little Bit had never seen much of him as a child and couldn't place him.

"Oh my gosh, it's Big George! Big George, what are you doing here? What is this place?" cried Skeeter.

Big George looked at Sean and said, "What? You didn't tell them, Boss?"

"Boss! Sean tell me, what's going on here?"

"Yeah Boss," chimed in Little Bit, "that would be a good idea."

"Okay. I'll fill you in while Big George takes us for a ride." He pointed to a four seat security golf cart.

"Yeah, jump in ladies. I'll give you the grand tour." The gate closed behind them as they entered the Zone.

The little cart traveled on a double lane concrete road for about fifty yards and Big George stopped as the road divided into a boulevard. There was a street sign at the intersection: CENTER STREET.

"I can't believe we're in the Zone!" screeched Little Bit. They both looked at Sean and he nodded his head.

"Oh, gosh, oh my gosh." They sat there for several minutes and took it all in.

Scattered flower gardens were surrounded by manicured lawns. Small ponds lay between high berms. There were trees - most of them pine and newly planted. The boulevard median exploded with color - blue and purple flowers in blossom, small evergreen bushes and patches of red-orange geraniums. The brick wall completely enclosed the Zone with another entrance gate located at the opposite end of the boulevard.

"Your movie ends with us missing each other at the airport, Skeet. If there were to be a sequel it would reveal that I ended up owning the Zone. I'll give you the details later, but for now let's continue our tour."

Big George turned onto the boulevard, drove for a bit then crossed over the median and angled away from Center Street on a double lane ancillary road surrounded on both sides by more landscaped beauty.

They pulled up to a single structure next to a small parking lot. Skeet and Little Bit couldn't believe their eyes. There, standing in front of them, was an exact replica of Ma's house.

"I don't believe it, I don't believe it," they kept saying as they exited the cart and walked up the familiar path to Ma's. In front of the small stairs leading to the porch was an engraved plaque, identifying the house as belonging to Libby Munoz ('Ma') and giving a synopsis of its history and naming all of the people who once called this place home. They read all their names and anxiously entered the house.

It was all there. With Sean's remarkable powers of retention, he had been able to replicate everything down to the smallest detail, including the furnishings. The girls walked around in disbelief. They wandered through Ma's kitchen remembering the smells and happy times and then ascended the stairs. It was as if they had never left - the bedrooms, the small kitchen, and the project room were perfectly reproduced.

The project room was complete with Little Bit's single bed and her work table. Puppets and socks were arrayed in an orderly fashion. School books were tucked away on shelves and a computer was set up. It was the same Mac that Carlos had given them.

They weakly sat down at the kitchen table. It was surreal - a moment back in time they never thought they would relive.

Sean joined them as they searched for words. Nothing came out. Once outside, they stood looking at the house, lost in thought and memories. They gazed down the road and could see another building partially hidden by trees.

"Come on," Sean said softly. "There's more."

As the cart moved slowly towards the building, they glimpsed the cemetery on the other side of Center Street. They could see the top of what appeared to be a large structure just in front of the cemetery.

They recognized it immediately, the small apartment above a garage - Billy's police station. An eighteen year old patrol car was parked in the driveway. Everything was the same when they entered the station. Even Billy's big chair was reproduced; Skeet couldn't resist and crawled into it. His hat was somehow retrieved by the curator and it was displayed proudly on his desk. Skeet put it on.

"Your movie is going to make these places famous, Skeet. People are going to want to see it. I didn't build it for that reason, though; I did it as a memorial to our family. I was determined that they wouldn't be forgotten."

"You always amaze me, Sean."

"Yup, big brother. Always," added Little Bit.

"Okay, now for the rest. Lets go, Big George."

They cut back to Center Street, and headed in the direction they came from but on the other side of the boulevard.

Big George crossed the median once more and stopped before entering a wide one way winding lane.

"This is not the real Center Street," he said, "the road we're on turned away from Center a little ways back. Center Street is just up ahead at the end of this lane but it ain't no longer a street."

They slowly continued passing by more berms on both sides with scattered pine trees behind. Maples and oak trees had been planted, too, and when they matured it would be a colorful wonder in the fall. At the foot of the berms, gardeners attended rows of flowers that appeared to be directing them to a destination. The lane straightened out and Big George stopped.

The girls gasped. In front of them was a huge structure that filled the landscape. To the right they could see the cemetery lying just on the other side of a large pond. A shining new chapel was prominent as it nestled among the tall trees that had not been bulldozed. To the left was a large but well landscaped parking lot. Directly in front of the building was a roundabout with a number of statues filling up the middle area.

"Sean, what is that?" asked an incredulous Skeet.

"That, Ms. movie producer, is where your premiere will be held. We call it The Center Of New Beginnings. But it's more than that. I think you'll both understand once we go inside."

The building resembled a European museum with it's brick facade but had contemporary architectural lines emphasized by tall narrow windows. It was not square but designed with cuts and angles that rambled and were set back from the columned portico that served as the main entrance. Beautiful gardens filled in the cuts and trees were planted everywhere, surrounded by lush lawns. A spectacular stained glass dome topped the high brick walls.

They were overwhelmed. "Wow," was their only responses as they tried to take in everything at once.

Big George stopped in the middle of the roundabout and Sean said, "I think you may want to get out and take a look at the statues."

They climbed out and walked up the pebble path leading to the statues. The bronze figures up on pedestals sat amidst waving grasses. They recognized the scene and stood with open mouths, staring.

Beautifully cast in Bronze were the life size figures of Sean, M. J., Skeet, Little Bit and Sissy. The figures were positioned exactly as they were in the photograph taken in front of Ma's house the day of M. J.'s modeling interview. Sean had Sissy on his shoulders and was holding M. J.'s hand as they smiled at each other half running towards the camera. Skeet and Little Bit were next to them; Skeet had her baseball cap on. Spelled out on the bottom of the pedestal in large engraved letters was:

CHILDREN OF THE ZONE

The girls walked completely around the display, "Awesome... unbelievable. Sean, when did you do all this?" asked Little Bit.
"It's been a couple of years in the making. I had lots of help."
Back in the cart they drove into the drop-off area behind the roundabout. "I'll leave you guys here. I have to open the gates to the cemetery," smiled Big George giving a salute.
He continued down the one-way lane that circled back to the main road.
"How did you find him, Sean?" quizzed Skeet.
"He just showed up on the property and I hired him right away."
"What a neat thing to do."
They walked up marble stairs and were standing in front of several eight foot cathedral glass doors. Sean opened one and they walked into a large breath-taking lobby. It was designed in a semi-circle with portraits of famous stage performers on its paneled walls. The floor was marble, completely outlined with four slats of hardwood joined together. Hanging from the high ceiling were rows of modern crystal chandeliers. In the middle was a directional marquee encircled by a handcrafted bench.
Skeet and Little Bit looked at the marquee. They had thought there was nothing left that could shock or surprise them; they were wrong.
In fancy large script, enclosed in beveled glass, it read:

Enter The M. J. Munoz Symphony Hall from either side.

The Nettie Ferrari Children's School is located in the East Wing

The Libby Munoz Museum and the Meg Brown exhibit are in theWest Wing.

Cafe and Lounge located in both Wings

Skeet and Little Bit were now numb and close to being overcome by emotion. Sean held both their hands, "Oh Sean, Sean, this is so wonderful," sobbed Skeet. Little Bit just looked at him nodding her head in agreement.
First he took them to Nettie's school. It had large Mahogany doors with windows instead of walls at its entrance. Once inside they stood in a

small foyer decorated with children's bright paintings. A warmly lit and wide hallway led to the classrooms. A substantial library and a visual arts room loaded with computers were located across from them.

At the end of the hallway under lights from tract lighting was a beautiful large scale portrait of Nettie. Sean had commissioned a well known contemporary portrait artist to do the work. The image he used was the photograph taken of her and others by Billy the night of the college acceptance party at Ma's.

"The school won't be in operation until the fall. We are still looking for a director and qualified instructors. The idea is to invite under-privileged kids from the inner-city to attend. We want to turn it over each week to allow as many children as possible to participate in this enriched program. The classes will all be introductory in an attempt to interest them in academics. There will be classes designed for children from kindergarten up to and including high school age. Anyway, that's the plan. We'll know more in the fall."

"What a perfect tribute for our mom, Sean," said Little Bit, gazing up at Nettie's portrait.

"Yes," added Skeet. "She would be so proud."

They moved on to the museum. Sean introduced the girls to Helen Donaldson, the curator.

"We are still collecting artifacts and are a long way from our grand opening. You would be surprised at the number of ex-Zone residents who are contributing. It's astounding. A. J. has some stuff for us too. We are going to have a large portrait of Ma hanging near the entrance here," she said.

"The museum is not only dedicated to the history of the Zone but A. J. wants us to focus on displaying how a social environment can decay and be reborn. All of you are are shining examples of that. You lived in that dangerous place and not only survived but thrived! That's the real lesson we're trying to communicate and that's the one A. J. wants the public to see. Everybody's story will be told, including those who didn't survive.

The Center will fund studies and bring in sociologists to conduct symposiums on the subject. The Zone will be a centerpiece. We are counting on you, Ms. Wilson, for a major contribution from your studio. We plan to feature your movie and the book as the prime exhibit."

"Ah, I sort of volunteered your services, Skeet."

"Well, I sure hope you did! Anything you want, Helen, is yours. I'll turn everything we have over to you and the actors would love to contribute. You can even have my baseball cap."

"Terrific. We sure would like Meg's medical records; we need it for her exhibit. We're going to have a large portrait of her, too... and Billy, and Papa Joe."

"It's all yours, Helen."

They entered the Symphony Hall from one of the side entrances walking through its tall door. It was massive, seating five thousand, with a large tiered balcony section. Every plush seat had an unobstructed view. The paneled walls were etched with likenesses of musical instruments, dancers and performers. The performance stage was huge with a generous back stage area. Wall sconces lit the room with a subtle glow.

There was an orchestra pit and four side stages but the most amazing feature was the magnificent stained glass ceiling that dominated the center of the Hall. The contractors guaranteed its acoustic qualities.

Skeet and Little Bit had been in shock all morning, but now they were in awe.

"What do you think, Skeet? Will it do for your premiere?"

"You've got to be kidding, Sean. I have never seen anything like this anywhere. Hollywood, New York, no place!"

"Man! Wait 'til Rachel and Wylie see this, Skeet. They're going to be in tinsel heaven!" laughed Little Bit.

"Should I be taking pictures, Sean?"

"Not necessary. We have brochures and a virtual DVD for you. We will let you decide when we should go on line with the videos."

"Come on. I want to show you the intermission area; the balcony, orchestra and mezzanine share the room."

The intermission room had a bar on each end with comfortable couches and stuffed chairs scattered about. But its most dominating feature was a large portrait of M. J. copied from one of her modeling photos. There was a short history of what she did for the people of the Zone and elsewhere.

Her two sisters stood in front of the painting, smiling.

"God, she was beautiful, Sean."

"Yeah, she was, Skeet. She sure was," he said softly.

After a complete tour of the hall they exited through a back door. Decks on both sides of the building served the cafes. Their bright yellow table umbrellas created a warm and lively contrast with the surroundings. Behind the building was a large pond, residence to many ducks and geese. Beyond that was the cemetery. Paved paths converged at the pond and the quaint walking bridge that took pedestrians across.

They walked across the bridge and entered the cemetery at the opposite end from the chapel. They were no longer surprised at anything they saw.

"Boy, who would have thought..." sighed Skeet.

The lawn between the graves was healthy and green. The service road was paved with narrow curbing and drains that fed into the pond. All of the markers and tombstones were straight and the rows were properly identified by tiny respectable signs. There was a small parking lot specifically set aside for the cemetery; it had its own gated entrance.

There were three or four cars parked and a few people were placing flowers on graves that until now had been forgotten.

The three of them followed the road and came upon Billy's and Meg's graves. Both sites now had monuments on them. This was Little Bit's first time back since she left the Zone almost twelve years ago. They paused for awhile, each deep into their own thoughts. Little Bit was sniffling as they moved on.

The turn in the road brought them to their family plots. They all had monuments like Billy and Meg's. This time, however, the lonely man's resting place had an identifying monument like the others.
It was etched with his name, Sean McCleary, and the dates of his birth and death. The chiseled inscription stated that he was survived by his wife, Antoinette J. Ferrari (Nettie) and his son, A. J. McCleary.

Sean looked at his sisters and said, "She always considered herself married to him - a certificate wasn't necessary."

They took their time and stopped in remembrance over each of their family member's individual gravesites. Neither of the girls questioned the monument on Sean Ferrari's grave; they knew the story.

The chapel was replicated but made larger and constructed in marble and stone. It was open like before but the portals were now prayer stations. Through the portals they could see Papa Joe's desk and religious artifacts made to survive the winter weather. Over the entrance, engraved in the stone, were the words:

FATHER JOSEPH CHAPEL OF THE ZONE

Inside was a plaque titled 'Papa Joe' with his likeness and a brief history of his service to the Zone.

They were about to enter, but noticed a man with his head down praying at one of the stations. They politely waited outside chatting for a few minutes. Sean turned around when he heard the man shuffle toward the door. It had been a day of surprises and wonder for Skeet and Little Bit and a day of happiness and satisfaction for Sean. But now it was Sean's turn to be surprised.

His hair had turned gray and he was heavier but there, standing in the doorway of the chapel, was Papa Joe. The girls turned when they saw Sean looking at the man. They, too, looked at him and now for the first time since they entered the Zone, both of them lost their composure.
"PAPA JOE, PAPA JOE," they screamed and ran to him. The three of them clung to each other in a scene of indescribable joy.

Sean waited for them to separate. Papa Joe walked to him and the two men embraced and held on to each other for several seconds, both of them sobbing.
"God bless you, son. God bless you."

PAPA JOE, after years of stellar missionary work, was welcomed back into the Church. He had just finished a meeting with his superiors and decided to visit the cemetery in the Zone.

Papa Joe was shocked by the transformation of the Zone and he unashamedly knelt in prayer by the gate. He was astonished and delighted when he was greeted by Big George who invited him in. It was Big George who informed Papa Joe of Sean's, Skeet's and Little Bit's upcoming visit. He solicited a promise from the big man not to disclose to the three that he had been there. Papa Joe wasn't sure he was ready for a reconnection just yet. But he made note of their scheduled arrival and told Big George that he would contact him when he decided what he was going to do. He didn't regret his decision.

After their emotional reunion, Sean and the girls delayed their return to Chicago and L.A. so they could spend some time with Papa Joe. The four met for breakfast. "I'm not sure where I'm going to be assigned, but count me in as a guest for the premiere. I wouldn't miss it for the world," said a happy Papa Joe.

"We wouldn't hold it without you," smiled Skeet.

"Yeah, you're my date, Papa Joe, and you can't get out of it," grinned Little Bit.

"Okay, it's a date!"

"Sean, I forgot to tell you that I worked with a friend of yours, the Governor of Rinnistan."

"You know Dal!"

"Yes, I helped set up their school just after you left. Your name came up often and I decided it best not to let Dal and the others know that I knew you. I was still on probation and no one was supposed to know where I was. They couldn't say enough good things about you, Mr. McCleary."

"Man! I just missed you. Hey, Skeet's next movie is about Rinnistan. You'll have to make an appearance."

"I don't think so," he grinned.

They all agreed to stay in constant communication when they parted company the following morning.

BACK IN L.A., Monica couldn't stop talking about The Center For New Beginnings. "Rachel, Wylie, you should see the Hall. It's enormous! And can you imagine holding the premiere in the exact location where the entire movie takes place!"

"No, no, I can't. This is too good to be true," said a delighted Rachel. "We're short on time, you guys," she continued, "I've got a lot of work to do. We have to fill that place."

"Oh, that shouldn't be difficult," offered Wylie. "After A. J.'s press conference I'm getting calls from people I haven't heard from in years."

"Yeah, me too," said Rachel, "and businesses by the dozens are after me for tickets. They're asking for hundreds of them and this is after the Detroit location was announced."

"Okay, I'll leave everything in your capable hands, Rachel. Wiley and I are meeting with your Rinnistan screenwriters in the morning. We want to hit the ground running after the premiere. I still can't believe it - the biggest day of my life and it's going to take place right where I used to live. Look at me, I'm so excited!"

"And we are excited for you, Monica," smiled Wylie.

MARCIA WAS AT wit's end when A. J. and Jessica walked into the operations room. "About time you guys got here. Those people are driving me crazy!" She was referring to the persistent presence of reporters.

"Becky's been no help; she keeps telling them to get the fuck out of here."

"Not a bad approach," laughed Jessica, "guess I better start reviewing those applications for a PR person."

"Yeah, good luck. There are hundreds of them.

I did put my most outspoken student at the reception desk and she's handling all non-research related calls and e-mails. She's holding them at bay but we need somebody to talk to these people. Not Becky!"

When things quieted down, Jessica began to review the applications. It would still be weeks before they hired someone; they were too busy with other matters at the moment.

One of those concerns was how to keep pace with the constant flow of information coming in.

"A. J., we are making real progress. I'm almost ready to declare a specific pattern on some of the cancers. But as you know, they change so quickly that we sometimes get overwhelmed. Our kids are great, but we need those faster computers," explained Becky.

"Yeah, I know and I'm meeting with the experts tomorrow. Like we discussed, we'll buy the fastest supercomputer we can get our hands on and if we have to build one to our specifications we'll do it, regardless of how long it will take."

Chapter 63: Danella

SHE WAS BORN in Westport, Ireland, a coastal town on the west side of the country north of Galway. Her mother, Colleen Flannery, was an Irish lass from Northern Ireland. Colleen married a French diplomat, Henri Jean Fochett. They had one child they named Danella Marie. They pronounced her name Duh-NELL-ah.

Danella spent her early happy childhood years in Ireland. She was a cheerful carrot top with big bright sea-green eyes. When Danella was five, the family moved to her father's homeland, Paris, France. Just after Danella turned ten her beloved mother succumbed to cancer. The little girl's heart was broken.

Everything about her Paris surroundings reminded the ten year old of her mother and she withdrew and became melancholy. Henri was offered a transfer to Quebec City, Canada and, feeling a change of scenery was just what Danella needed to get her over her grief, he accepted.
It *was* exactly what she needed and she flourished in this French speaking Canadian city.

Henri flourished too, and although not wealthy, the two of them lived comfortably on his six-figure income. Henri never re-married.

Another career opportunity presented itself and Henri accepted a job as a diplomat serving France in the United Nations. Henri and Danella moved to New York and set up home in a swanky section on the East Side close to the U.N. building.

Danella celebrated her eighteenth birthday that year. Her red hair had turned a beautiful dark auburn shade that made her large sea-green eyes appear even paler. She was fully grown now, five-foot seven, with a perfectly proportioned body. Her figure was more athletic than model like. She had a tiny waist that made her ample breasts look larger than what they were and her legs were those of a dancer, which she was. She knew she was blessed with a great body and would always take special care that it stayed that way.

By all standards Danella was beautiful. But she went out of her way to hide that beauty. She pulled her hair back, wore big round glasses, used very little makeup and dressed in frumpy clothes. This puzzled her father but he never tried to change her. What could never be changed was her sparkling personality, her wit and her natural Irish good humor. She also had an Irish temper; it rarely surfaced but when it did...

Danella chose to go away to college. She selected Cornell in Ithaca, N.Y. Her reasoning being that it was close enough to her friends in Canada and not far from New York and her father.

Danella blossomed at Cornell, majoring in Journalism and Modern Languages with a minor in Art and Design. She added Italian and

Spanish to her already fluent French and English. Her highest grades were scored in journalism and she won a national award for her writing. But it was her activities in the Drama Club that she enjoyed the most and made her well known on campus. Her talents as actor, dancer and singer led to starring roles in musicals. She often joined jam sessions at local coffee houses playing guitar and piano.

Danella graduated with honors in the required four years. She married her college sweetheart, which qualified her for permanent resident status, and they both landed jobs in the Big Apple - she with a high powered public relations firm, and he as an advertising agent. It was the All-American story. Then her world came crashing down.

The couple had moved in with her father on a temporary basis which delighted him and saved them a lot of money. On a warm sunny Saturday, Danella's husband and her father decided to spend the day at the race track. Danella opted to stay home. The two men she loved would never return. The cab they were riding in was broadsided by a drunken truck driver killing both of them.

She struggled through her grief and slowly recovered. With her father's savings, life insurance and pension death benefits, Danella was financially set for life. However, emotionally she needed to work and stayed with the public relations firm, but became bored and restless. What she really wanted to do was get into journalism. She loved to write and through her public relation connections, she landed a job as a beat writer for a small newspaper in Chicago. It didn't pay much but she wasn't unhappy about leaving New York.

Danella was twenty-four when she landed in Chicago. She worked for the paper for two years, learned the ropes, and made a lot of connections. With her pleasant personality and sometimes outrageous sense of humor she also made many friends. Looking for the freedom of being independent, she struck out on her own and became a freelance reporter.

The University of Illinois is one of the major research Universities in the country. They had recently installed a supercomputer to handle their research requirements. One of Danella's first freelance reports featured the new supercomputer. She became fascinated with the system and the technicians became fascinated with her. They allowed her to sit in on the training courses. A quick learner and a whiz at computers, she became well versed in the monster machine. This was the type of reporting she loved to do; it challenged her and she learned in the process.

Danella had found a home in Chicago. She liked her new professional freedom, became a Cubs fan, and enjoyed the museums, theaters, and social events. But like most curious and talented young people, she felt an urge to do more, to be involved with something really important. She had no idea what that might be.

Being a Cubs fan and in the reporting business, the story about the scientist who had a one hundred and fifteen mile fast ball caught her attention.

She had had a call from one of her sport reporting friends,

"Hey Danny, this is Pete. Did you see the Masked Blogger's latest blast?"

"No, I didn't, and for the one hundredth time, it's Danella!" she scolded in her normal good natured way. "You know I hate being called Danny. Do you enjoy annoying me?" she teased.

"Oh, no, no, noooo…, I know better than to get you riled up," he had snickered. "I just forgot. Anyway the blogger is zeroing in on the Cub's scientist with the un-hittable fastball. You should check it out."

She *did* check it out and then mumbled to herself, "Either that jerk is on to something or this guy is from another planet."

Pete called again. "Danella... see I remembered. The fireballing scientist has called a press conference, presumably to announce his signing with the Cubs and to denounce the blogger. I've got an extra pass. It's scheduled for tomorrow. You interested?"

"Yes, I am. Where is it going to be held?"

"Downtown. I'll e-mail you the all the particulars and meet you there. It's supposed to be a packed house."

They arrived at the press conference a little late but found two seats near the front row. She was wearing a red dress and carrying a quilted shoulder bag; it was unusually formal for her.

From the second A. J. took the podium, Danella couldn't take her eyes off him. She not only was mesmerized by his appearance but by the relaxed way he handled himself and the essence of his address. She recognized that this was a man of substance and that he was being truthful. His short bio captivated her and aroused her reporting instincts. She had to learn more about him.

Danella gasped with the rest of them when he revealed the Masked Blogger and she yanked her phone out of her bag.

She had become choked with emotion when A. J. walked Brandon back to his seat. Sitting a couple feet away, she could see on A. J.'s face the deep feelings he had for Brandon and she sensed his sincerity and commitment to his work. The emotions she experienced surprised Danella. She was usually in total control. Something had moved her and she wasn't quite sure what it was.

She felt a stirring inside but dismissed the notion that it was an attraction to A. J. He dated movie stars, she told herself. What chance would I have with him? No, it was more than that: he and the others were attempting something that she had to be a part of. Danella had never forgotten the pain of her mother's death from cancer.

She practically ran to the cabstand after the press conference and went straight home. Ten seconds after entering her apartment she was on the internet searching for links to the Rinnistan memoir and The Zone. She dove into the stories. Later she googled The Brandon Foundation. It caught her eye right away; a request from the foundation for resumes from anyone having experience in public relations. She printed out the application form and hurriedly filled it out.

Chapter 64: It's A Masterpiece

EVERYBODY WAS BUSY in the weeks leading up to the premiere. The foundation was building on its successes but the amount of work was overwhelming. They desperately needed a supercomputer and one was being built for them. It couldn't arrive soon enough.

Jessica was wearing many hats and needed help. She was the main coordinator of all the incoming and outgoing research data. She ran the administrative end and handled the constant requests for information by a curious media and educational organizations.

A. J. was becoming a source of interest as more and more stories of his achievements and adventures circulated.

"You need your own press secretary, Sean. This is getting ridiculous," cried an annoyed LIttle Bit.

"Yeah, I know. It's distracting and irritating. Also, we need to disassociate ourselves from those anti-Christ scientists who are claiming that our research proves we never die but live on in an electromagnetic world and can be contacted."

"No kidding! We're getting calls from religious freaks blaming us for doing the work of the Devil. They're scary people, Sean!"

"Oh man, how close are you to hiring that PR person?"

"Well, with all the scrutiny we are suddenly under, it's a real slow process. I mean we can't even ask for their gender for god's sake let alone their race or religion... not that we care. They can only identify their first name by using an *initial*. And we have to consider *all* the applications and can't even have them send photographs! What makes it really tough is that there are so many qualified people applying. Their narrative on why they want the job will be the decider."

"Okay, I'm glad you stopped taking applications. Pare it down to five finalists, then the four of us will get together and make a selection. Hey, I'm also getting us some technical help; we'll need it when the new supercomputer is up and running."

"Great. Things are moving faster and faster, Sean. We are barely keeping up with it."

PREVIEWS OF THE ZONE had hit theaters, TV, and the internet. Prior publicity had generated an enormous interest and Skeet's team was trying not to become overly confident. The book had seen a rebirth and it was flying off the shelves.

"That's it! The Hall is sold out," cheered Rachel. "Wow, and we still have three weeks to go! All the hotels are booked and the City of Detroit is in a festive mood. I just got a request from their Chamber asking for

more promo material."
"Yeah, we're getting the same requests at the studio, Rach, for both the Zone and Rinnistan," exclaimed a delighted Skeet.

"Landing The Detroit Symphony Orchestra was perfect, Rachel."

"Yes, thanks. They're already rehearsing on stage and are happy not to be in the pit. Setting up the VIP tables in that area is going to work out great; we'll have to keep that list short, though. Boy, this is the fun part. I'm getting fitted for my gown tomorrow, can't wait," she giggled.

SOMEBODY ELSE couldn't wait for the event either.

"Are you sure you know what you're doing with that stuff, Enrico?" asked Jorge. "Plastic explosives can be tricky."

"Oh yeah. Remember, that ex-government guy was pretty specific. He showed us where to place the shit and how to detonate it by using just a cell phone. He even had blueprints of that music building!"

"I don't know, I don't like it. Why did he approach us? He must have other guys who could do the job."

"I fucking told you. His contacts told him how much we hate that guy and we would work cheap! I don't know why they want his ass, or how they found us, but I don't care. We get to take him OUT!"

"Yeah, him and hundreds of other people too."

"Right. That party is going to be a BLAST!" Enrico laughed loudly at his own joke.

THEY WERE GATHERED in Jessica's office.

"Great job, Little Bit. All five of these finalists are really qualified."

"Yeah. Marcia and I were just commenting on that, A. J. This is going to be tough," cited Becky.

"Okay. Does anybody want to make an argument for any of the finalists?" asked Jessica.

"Yes. I do. I was really moved by that D. Fochett's narrative. Her story about her mother's death from lung cancer was very compelling. She really wants this job."

"Becky, how do you know the applicant's a female? It was so perfectly written. It followed our request not to indicate gender," stated Jessica.

"Don't ask me how I know, I just do."

"Yes, and it helps that she or he knows what networking is all about," added Marcia.

"Well I don't care if she's a he or a she. D. Fochett was also my first choice. Want to make it unanimous, Sean?"

"You're making it easy for me, guys. That candidate is such a beautiful writer, I was really captivated. The sincerity just poured through. Okay, it's unanimous. Bring D. Fochett in for the interview, Little Bit. Unless he or she has two heads hire her... ah, him, so we can get on with our jobs.

WHEN A. J. was in Detroit with Skeet and Little Bit, he took the time to empty out the small storage locker he had kept for years. There wasn't much inside: the keyboard, the computer, his penny whistle and M. J.'s sealed music composition. He turned the whistle, computer, and keyboard over to Helen for the museum and took M. J.'s composition back with him to Evanston.

A. J. placed the composition on the small office desk in his upstairs living quarters. Only Little Bit visited him there; it was his unofficial private sanctuary. For weeks he ignored the sealed package, sensing its heavy emotional content. But he knew that he needed to open it and he did.

Inside the composition book was a neatly folded note:

Sean, I know it may be a long time before you open this. If I have not completed the last movement, please do it for me. You'll know what to name my work after you finish the score. The composition is full of hints and so is this note. I love you, M. J.

He just sat there shaking his head. "Even now the riddle game," he said smiling. "Only M. J. ..." He reluctantly read the piece in his normal speed, playing the notes in his mind. He then slowed down and replayed it, again and again.

"My god, I can't complete this. It's a masterpiece!"

It was now less than a week before the premiere. They planned to go to Detroit together the day before the event. Skeet, Rachel and Wylie were already there. A. J., Jessica and Becky had not seen the final cut of the movie.

Taking Little Bit aside, Sean explained, "I'm leaving for Detroit today. Something important has come up and I have to be there."

"Sean, is anything wrong?"

"No, no it's just something I have to take care of. I'll call you." He left immediately.

BECKY AND JESSICA chatted in the reception area while waiting for D. Fochett to show up for the interview.

"What was all that carrying on in the auditorium the other day, Jess?"

"Oh, that was Sean playing computer word games with the students. He sits up on stage and sends phrases to them and they complete the sentence guessing his endings which are usually hilarious. He's divided the room up into two teams and keeps score. Each kid has a team code name like Super Geek, Baby Girl, Awesome Blossom...well, you get the picture. The teams accumulate points and at the end of the school year the winning team who has correctly completed the most sentences wins a new laptop for everybody on their squad. They have so much fun."

"Is that what he does in there when I'm not with my students? I thought he was training them. Word games for god's sake. Man, new laptops for the winner, and what do the poor losers get?"

"Don't tell anybody but he's going to buy them *all* laptops," grinned Jessica. "Of course, I lost my head. Just like him, Jess," laughed Becky. "Just like him."

"Too bad A. J. is going to miss meeting our new PR. Uh, oh, I think this must be her coming up the front steps. Told you she was a she."

"Whoa, talented and good looking to boot. You be nice, Beck. We need her."

"Hey! I was the first to speak out for her remember?"

WHEN A. J. GOT to Detroit, he went straight to the Hall. The orchestra was wrapping up a rehearsal when A. J. approached the conductor and handed him a copy of M. J.'s composition. "Maestro, as a favor to me, would you look at this piece and tell me what you think. It's important and pertains to the premiere."

"Well, of course, Mr. McCleary, I'll read it tonight. Come by tomorrow about this same time and I'll have a review for you."

"Thanks, I really do appreciate that."

He found Big George at his office. "What have you got, Big George?"

"Maybe just the jitters. One of the guards spotted a couple of seedy looking guys hanging by the Hall. There's a lot of traffic here now and it wouldn't have gotten my attention but the gates were closed, 'cept for the cemetery. When my guy approached they took off. No description. Like I said, jitters on my part, maybe just some curious onlookers. Thought I should tell you, though."

"Well, I'm glad you did. Nobody has reported any threats so you're probably right."

"Yeah, maybe, and thanks for all the added security. The Detroit cops were here yesterday to coordinate things. Seems funny bein' on the same team."

"We need all the help we can get," smiled A. J. "There will be a lot of famous people here and we have to look out for them."

"And for you too, Boss."

He caught up with Skeet and the ladies and they all went out to dinner that evening. "A. J., the Center is absolutely beautiful and M. J.'s Hall is spectacular," Rachel bubbled. "We are busier than hell and Wylie has been all over the media broadcasts."

"Yeah, this is fun. I had no idea Detroit was making a comeback and I'm glad we can help," added Wylie.

"I'm still working on the VIP list, Sean. We know that the two front tables will be occupied by the four of us plus Jeff, little Bit, Papa Joe, Becky, Marcia, Ian, Diane, Genevieve, and Steve, and any dates they bring along. The other tables will seat the Hollywood crowd, but I'm really struggling with the dignitaries we don't know. The space in the pit is not very big," sighed Skeet.

"You're on your own there, Skeeter, but it would be nice if Dr. Telasantos, Dr. Hughes, and Wayne Stover had good seats."

"I didn't forget, Sean. They've all replied and will be sitting in the front row with the cast and crew."

"Ah, that's great, Skeet. They were awfully good to us and Mom.

After tomorrow I will be out of contact for a few days on some personal matters so I probably won't see you guys until Saturday. It's a good thing. I'd just be in the way."

The following afternoon he kept his date with the conductor.

"A. J., where did you get this? Who's the composer? The timing, the rhythm, the mingling of the light and dark, all those movements, so emotional, that is incredibly hard to do! Who wrote this?"

"You're standing in the Hall dedicated to her memory. It's the only piece she ever wrote."

"M. J. Munoz composed this? But she was only a young girl. I'm, I'm... astonished!"

"Yes, me too, but I watched her write it. It's hers.

Look maestro, I know you're on short notice, but her composition *must* be in the program. It's written mainly for piano, with harp, flute and percussion filling in. It shouldn't be that difficult for your orchestra to prepare for."

"Maybe not the orchestra," exclaimed the conductor, "but how about the pianist? Nobody could be ready in just a few days to play that complicated piece! And it's not complete. The last movement is hanging."

"You're right, of course. Here's what I would like to do..."

A. J. went back to his hotel room and did not emerge until the day of the premiere.

"What is she trying to do? I can't finish the last movement unless I understand all the others and I'm not getting it," he mumbled to himself.

A. J. spent the next two days and sleepless nights trying to understand, reliving the days when M. J. was writing the piece. He was frustrated knowing that this was her legacy and he was letting her down; he couldn't allow that to happen.

I'm concentrating too much on the movements, he thought to himself. Maybe I should try to discover the title of the composition first and see where that takes me. She said I will know how to name it. Look for the hints.

"Okay, M. J., lets play the game first if that's what you want."

Now he was looking at the composition differently, searching for hints, using the same techniques he did when he and M. J. had their riddle wars. Look for anything out of place he told himself. Anything.

He searched every page, every note... Finally, "THERE...there it is," he shouted out loud. "Oh, you've outdone yourself this time. Clever, clever."

He solved it. He had the name, but still no idea on how to finish the last movement. "I'm missing something; this title isn't complete. The note, she said the note had clues, too." He read it over and over... *'after you finish the score'*. "OH YES, YES, I SEE IT, I SEE IT!"

IT WASN'T MUCH of an interview. Danella was hired on the spot and immediately put to work. She had decided it was time to change her image; she had outgrown the last one. Her hair was still pulled back but she dressed fashionably, used a little makeup and had discarded her glasses for contact lenses. Jessica was impressed.

"Good thing you didn't include a photograph. None of the women would have voted for you," she teased.

Jessica had squeezed another desk, equipped with a computer and phone, into her office. Danella settled in. She asked all the right questions and Jessica, relieved, laughed, "Danella, you fill in the job description. We don't have the slightest idea how to handle all those media types or the most effective way to get our message out."

Danella took over and soon her phone was ringing and her computer buzzing. After a couple of days Jessica knew they had hired the right person. "I see you're going to need more room. I better call the carpenters."

Becky and Marcia paid a visit and welcomed Danella, dragging her off to meet any students who happened to be working.

The girls took her to lunch on her second day. With her quick wit and likable personality Danella fit right in and was happy and relaxed. Everybody was surprised and impressed by how much Danella knew about the foundation and electromagnetic energies. She had done her homework. She also revealed, cheerily, how much she knew about them personally.

"I couldn't wait to meet you, Jessica! I was captivated by you 'Zonies'. What a great book! When do I get to meet your sister?"

"Oh no, not before we do," cried Becky.

"Hey, what do you have on me?"
"Oh, not much, Beautiful Becky."
"WHAT?" That made them all laugh.

"I wish you had shown up earlier, Danella. We could have arranged for you to attend the premiere," lamented Jessica. "The seatings are all set; and hotel reservations are not available. Sorry."
"That is far more than I would have expected," said Danella with just a hint of disappointment, "I'll just hang here with the kids."

That problem resolved itself the next day.

"My youngest has come down with the chicken pox, Jess. I'm afraid I have to cancel," sadly reported Marcia. "Can Danella go in my place?"
Jessica immediately went to work and found that, with not much effort, she could make the switch if Danella really wanted to go.

After explaining to Danella what had happened, Jessica added, "I know this is really short notice - just two days before we leave. You need a gown and everything. Do you think you can manage?"
"Watch me!" she grinned.
"I thought so, never a doubt in my mind."

The day before they were to leave, the supercomputer was delivered. They stood in the operation room watching the technicians set up the huge device.

"Okay, all I need is to show Dr. McCleary how to program this thing. It may take a while."
"Ah, he's not here. Won't be back until Monday," reported Becky.

"Oh damn, we won't get back this way for a couple of weeks. I sent all the schematics to him. Does anybody here have experience with this type of machine? We could at least get you started and you might be able to work your way through with some phone support from us."

"Let me take a look at your setup program. I've worked on these guys before." They all turned and looked at Danella.
"You're kidding. I am really going to be pissed if you know how to run that thing. I'll put up with you and your good looks but not if any real brain goes with it!" threatened Becky.
"Don't worry, Becky, it's probably over my head," she laughed.

After about twenty minutes it was determined that the pre-programing was not over her head and she easily helped set it up.

"Great! I'll e-mail Dr. McCleary that Danella here can walk him through his schematics and you guys should be off and running. Here's my card, Danella; call me for support or if you want to change jobs."
"Oh, I love it, I love it," chortled Becky, "I can't wait for him to get that e-mail. The PR lady with the great body is going to train HIM.... How good is THAT!

THEY SAT IN a rundown motel room, blocks away from the Center, watching television.

"This is where we will be tomorrow night, Jorge, watching the Big Show on this wide screen TV. Those phony celebs haven't the slightest idea that their makeup is going to be ruined." He laughed so hard it made him cough. "One little phone call and this screen will go dead!" More laughing, more coughing.

"Shit, Enrico! Couldn't we just take *him* out?"

"NO, GOD DAMN IT! They want all of them to go POOF! And I won't make the call until that Zonie shit is front and center on the FUCKING STAGE!"

"Why do you hate him so much? You murdered his mother for Christ sakes. Did you think he was going to forget that?"

"SHE DESERVED IT! THAT BITCH DESERVED IT AND HE IS JUST LIKE HER!" Enrico bellowed. "Now her brat is going to join her IN HELL!" Jorge looked at his deranged brother in a strange way. Enrico never noticed.

Chapter 65: The Premiere

THEY WERE GATHERING in the hotel lobby preparing to hail cabs for a ride over to the Hall. Becky and Genevieve were waiting for Danella when Steve walked over. "Is A. J. still out of touch? I'm beginning to get worried."

"Hey Robo Cop. No, Jess talked to him this afternoon. She said he sounded tired and would be a little late. She had no idea what he's been up to."

"Hmmm. I was disappointed when he didn't show for the informal get together last night. I wanted him to meet Hannah."

"Yeah, we all want to know how the hell you talked that sweet thing into going out with you. She was the belle of the ball."

"Why, it was my gentlemanly charm. Ah, the premiere helped a little too."

"No shit."

"I saw the Hollywood gals and Jessica leaving earlier. Boy, were they pumped and looking gorgeous! As are you two ladies, I might add."

"Yeah, then how come you didn't invite me?" quipped Genevieve.

"Or me," chimed in Becky.

"Well, ah..."

He was saved by Danella who walked towards them.

"Isn't this your new friend, Beck? Oh, man."

"Yeah, it sure is. Oh man is right." It was the first time any of them had seen Danella with her hair down. She was stunning. Her wavy auburn hair flowed over her bare shoulders and down her exposed back, accenting her tight fitting golden gown as she glided over to them.

"Hi guys. Sorry I'm late. What? What's wrong?"

"Nothing, Danella. Absolutely nothing," croaked Steve.

The four of them had arrived early and were setting up the reception area. Wylie, Monica and some of the cast members would greet the guests. Rachel and Jessica tended to last minute details. It was a beautiful fall evening and lines were already forming out front.

Monica chatted with Patrice Harden. "When did our interview take place, Monica? About six or seven years ago?"

"Yes, something like that. I'm glad I could return the favor," she smiled. "Are you guys pretty much set up?"

"We are. And thanks for giving us the opportunity to cover this. When are you going to visit me in New York? I know you've got another even more astounding story to tell everybody. I mean you went from an unknown writer to a movie studio owner in just a few years!"

The crowd was filing in now, sipping cocktails and ooh-ing and ah-ing at the spectacular center. The museum and school were open displaying exhibits and photographs. The Hall was abuzz as the orchestra tuned up and people slowly found their seats.

"Skeet, I just got a strange call from Sean."

"Oh, where is he, Little Bit?"

"I'm not sure. He wants you to introduce him. He said he would be backstage with the Conductor."

"That *is* strange. He said he didn't want any special introduction. What do suppose is going on?"

"Beats me. He sounded... I don't know, not like himself."

The lights blinked on and off; in five minutes the program would start.

Papa Joe proudly escorted his date to the table up front in the raised pit as many of the celebrity savvy guests whispered, "Look, there's Papa Joe and Little Bit." Wylie and Monica had preceded them and were immediately recognized and acknowledged in the same way.

They were all in their seats as the MC introduced a local group to start the festivities with a classic Motown medley.

The orchestra, conducted by the first seat in the string section, played a beautiful Mozart Concerto. As the audience applauded the performance, stage hands wheeled out a concert piano and placed it directly center stage closing the curtain behind it, secluding the orchestra.

The MC waited for quiet and began:

"We invite everyone to stay after the showing of the movie to meet the cast. They will all be on stage. But now I want to introduce you to someone else:

She wrote the book. She wrote the screen play. She produced the movie. She owns the studio and is one of the main characters in the production. Her family addresses her by her Zonie name, Skeeter. We know this Detroit born artist by another name. Ladies and Gentleman, she's the reason we are all here tonight. Let me introduce... Ms. Monica Wilson."

Skeet briskly walked to the side steps and climbed the stairs carefully, holding her long gown away from her high heels as she did. The audience gave her a long standing ovation.

"Thank you, thank you..." She waited for the applause to diminish. "Thank you. The book, the movie - it's about my family. Not all of us were related by blood. We lived right here in the Zone." She nodded toward the piano, "The house we grew up in was located about where that piano sits. We called it Ma's house - you can visit its replica just down the road from here.

We didn't all survive, but in this very building, those who didn't are remembered: our three mothers, Nettie, Ma, and Meg, our uncle Billy and our sisters, M. J. and Sissy."

Monica glanced behind her. Standing off to the side where he couldn't be seen by the audience was A. J. Behind the curtain the conductor was frantically giving instructions to his percussionists, harp and flute musicians.

"There are four of us here tonight," Monica continued. "We are the survivors. My sister, Little Bit, is sitting in front of me and next to her is our beloved Papa Joe. You will recognize them in the movie, but I want you to see them and honor them now. Come on, stand up you two." They did and were greeted by a rousing ovation.

ENRICO WAS standing too. Holding his cell phone and glaring at the TV, he bellowed, "WHERE THE FUCK IS HE, JORGE? I DON'T SEE HIM. GOD DAMN IT!"

SWEEPING HER ARM, Monica added, "When you take in the wonder of this beautiful building, located amid plush landscaping and breathtaking gardens, It's hard to imagine what the Zone looked like when we lived and grew up here. Broken down houses, uncollected garbage, rats everywhere. The crime center of Detroit. But this was our home. And when you have a home full of love, you can block everything else out."

Many of them had read the book and they responded to Skeet's words with warm applause.

LISTENING TO HER every word, Enrico anxiously ran his thumb across the phone's call button and paced about. "WHERE IS HE? WHERE IS HE? Something is wrong. I KNOW IT!"

"Nothing's wrong, Enrico. Relax. She's probably going to introduce him."

"Block everything out, huh? WELL TRY BLOCKING OUT SATCHELS OF EXPLOSIVES, BITCH!" His eyes were blazing and he had turned bright red.

"Christ, Enrico! When you get like this you are fucking crazy. I'm stepping out for a smoke. Call me when he's on stage so I can watch you kill everybody." He left shaking his head.

Once outside, Jorge took a deep breath and let it out slowly. Reaching into his pocket he pulled out his cell phone, not his cigarettes.

FROM A. J.'s position, he could see the tables in front of Monica plus the first couple of rows but no one could see him standing back from the curtain in the darkness. Big George had stationed himself at the side stage. A. J. smiled as he watched Big George intently scan the crowd for possible trouble.

He observed his friends and family as they listened to Skeeter and felt a real joy seeing them all together. He didn't know Steve's date and didn't recognize the woman sitting next to Wylie. He assumed she was one of Wylie's movie star friends.

An unexpected chill came over him. And a sudden thought. Have we come full circle? Is this it? There is no more?

Don't be silly, we are just beginning. He knew better. His instincts were always right, "Something is wrong, I can feel it," he whispered.

Monica smiled at the audience, "This night is more than a premiere of a movie. It represents something much bigger. It's the manifestation of real social transformation." She paused and gestured toward the table where she had been sitting.

"You may have noticed that a certain member of our family is not sitting at our table. That's because he is backstage waiting to address you."

That sent a murmur through the audience. A. J.'s absence was noticed.

"I don't know what he is going to talk about but I suspect it will have something to do with this transformation. I know you want to hear what he has to say and so do I. Lets not keep him waiting."

She stepped back, turned and extended her hand towards the curtain, "He needs no introduction, my brother, Sean Ferrari..."

A. J. stepped out to a tremendous roar. He was an unexpected speaker; his name did not appear in the program. They were on their feet. He was the real star and everybody knew it.

"JORGE, GET IN HERE. THAT BASTARD IS ON STAGE! HURRY UP, GOD DAMN IT!" Enrico was now in an orgiastic frenzy, laughing and grunting like an animal.

"I'm coming. I'm coming. Give me a second, will ya. I got to take a piss and I don't want to miss this. Not that we'll see anything."

"No, but we will hear the BLAST! HURRY FUCKING UP!" Enrico panted.

Jorge delayed as long as he could, "Hey, look at him up there. Let's hear what he has to say."

"ARE YOU FUCKING CRAZY? NO SIR, IT'S SHOW TIME!" and he gleefully punched the call button.

Chapter 66: Love 5 Hate 4

A. J. HAD CARRIED the keyboard and M. J.'s composition book as he came on stage. He stopped by the piano and set the items on the polished surface.

The audience was still on their feet as he embraced Skeeter and escorted her to the stairs that lead to the orchestra pit. They were still applauding as he stood in front of the microphone. He looked at the tables where his family and friends were gathered. They were on their feet clapping and smiling. He grinned at Becky and Genevieve and looked at Hannah, cocking his head and smiling at Steve.

A special warm smile for Wylie, a look at Danella and then a second glance. He never forgot faces; he would try to place her later. Everyone else he acknowledged, including the professors, in the first row.

He felt a warm glow as he looked at his sisters and Papa Joe, extending his hand towards them. The audience picked up on that, setting off another round of applause. He looked to the side stage wanting to wave to Big George but Big George wasn't there. The alarms in A. J.'s head went off as he hurriedly scanned the crowd.

Too late. There's nothing I can do about it, he thought. Do what you have to do. He sensed danger, but never would he have believed the scene being played out just below his feet at that very moment.

"IT'S CALLING, MAN! It's CALLING! Come on, it shouldn't take that long. It's still FUCKING CALLING!"

Enrico suddenly became rigid, staring at the circling call indicator. His fox-like survival instincts kicked in.

"It's still calling... OH NO, son-of-a-bitch. LET'S GET OUT OF HERE!" They could hear the sirens. He fired the cell phone at the TV and bolted for the door. Jorge followed. A. J.'s image was still on the screen. He was smiling at the audience.

AS THE HALL quieted, he began. "Skeeter got it right as she usually does. This night is all about transformation. We were called Zonie rats, born and raised in a dangerous and hopeless environment. We never realized that as children because we were the beneficiaries of the best that any community could provide. My sisters and I had the finest teacher imaginable. We had a homemaker who provided us comfort and shelter, an angel of medicine who cared for our wounds, a man of law who protected us and a man of the cloth who gave us spiritual guidance. We lacked nothing that was important.

It would have been financially arrogant of me to transform the war-torn and rat infested Zone into what stands in it's place today merely to honor and memorialize our family. No. I wanted to build something that would illustrate what could be accomplished when people really care and love one another, no matter how trying and difficult their surroundings made their lives. I wanted the new Zone to exhibit, culture, education, and harmony, with only the old Zone's history as a reminder of what it once was."

ENRICO AND JORGE sprinted down the parking lot just as two patrol cars pulled in, one on each end. They were trapped.

Enrico, enraged, shouted, "YOU DID THIS, DIDN'T YOU?" pointing his drawn gun at Jorge. He didn't let Jorge answer and pumped two slugs into him, and then, screaming like the maniac he was, he charged the police who were waiting for him behind the protection of their car. Enrico fired off several rounds but hit nobody. He was cut to pieces by the returning automatic fire. The shot to his head is the one that killed him.

Jorge was lying in the parking lot and the police rushed up to him. He was barely conscious but managed to say, "Is Ferrari alive...? The others?"

"Who are you? Who do you work for?" demanded the police." Jorge grimaced; his eyes rolled back in his head and he died.

PAUSING, OBLIVIOUS to the dramatic shootout, A. J. smiled at his sisters and continued. "We, the children of the Zone, became successful writers, business executives, scientists and composers and we were able to do this because of our family and because of where we grew up, not in spite of it.

Yes, I said composer. Please allow me to share a story with you about my soulmate, M. J. This Hall is named for her because of her love for the arts. We all knew that she was talented but none of us knew how talented she was. Skeet's movie reveals M. J.'s love of classical music. What it doesn't mention, because none of us knew, is that she wrote a classical masterpiece. She started her composition when she was twelve years old and kept it in this book." He walked over to the piano picked up the dilapidated composition book and showed it to the audience.
"She shared this with no one." Skeet, Little Bit and Papa Joe, glanced at each other, astonished.

"M. J. was killed before she could complete her work; the final movement wasn't finished. She made me promise, just before her death, to complete her composition if something should happen to her.
I agreed, but knowing her intuitive abilities, I was alarmed.

M. J. died two months before her eighteenth birthday. After her death I sealed her composition in an envelope and kept it all these years. I never once looked at it, not a note. It was too painful. I had no idea of Its brilliance."

He went back to the piano and picked up the old keyboard. He and others laughed as he explained its history. Then he said,

"In the movie, you'll see how M. J. learned to play the piano and compose classical music by me playing this keyboard for her. There was no sound except for the CD recording that we were imitating. Neither of us ever played a real piano. I still haven't.

With the premiere coming up, I thought maybe it was the right time to look at M. J.'s composition. I was apprehensive and really didn't know what to expect, but I knew I had to open it. And last week, I did.

I am no expert in classical music but I've vicariously played hundreds of pieces for M. J. on this soundless keyboard. I can read music then play it in my head. After one movement, I knew this was special. It was written for the piano with harps, flutes, and percussion as accompaniment."

He paused, then continued, "I came here earlier than I had planned. I wanted the maestro of this great orchestra to look at the composition. He graciously did and confirmed its brilliance. I now had no choice. I had to complete it so it could be played for you tonight." A hum went through the Hall. The musically educated guests were now alerted that they were about to be treated to an unexpected performance that related directly to the film. Skeet, Little Bit and Papa Joe were dumbfounded.

"I spent two days and nights trying to understand her composition and finish it. I couldn't grasp the evolution of the events so dramatically and purposely being presented in the movements. I had to rethink it from a different perspective."

He then held up the note written in M. J.'s hand and read it to them. "A riddle," he said shaking his head. "We had played this game many times as children and now she was asking me to give a name to her composition by solving a riddle? She knew I couldn't resist the challenge and she couldn't resist challenging me," he grinned.

"Skeet and Little Bit are smiling," he said nodding at them, "They know all about M. J.'s love for riddles."

"Riddles. I should have gone there first; it would have saved me a lot of time. This was more than a kid's game. M. J. knew that I had to be completely and personally absorbed in the progression of the movements so I could finish her composition exactly as she would have done. Solving the riddle, she knew, would lead me to an understanding of those movements. And it did."

He paused and went on. "Hidden in each movement was a small anomaly, usually found in one of the notes. You had to look closely and stretch the imagination some, but there it was. By following the rules of our childhood game, I was able to determine that each movement was represented by a letter.

There were eight movements. Their letters in chronological order are: L - O - V - E - H - A - T - E ...she had just started to write the eighth, but never finished. Now I had the name of the composition but still couldn't understand its meaning.

It was clear that the movements were alternating from light to dark, but I didn't know why; nor did I understand their rhythm. Her note provided the final hint. She referred to 'the score' but she wasn't talking about music. She was talking about a contest where scores were kept: LOVE on one side, HATE on the other."

A. J.'s demeanor changed; he became more deliberate in his speech and the audience, sensing a shift in emotion, sat enraptured, still.

"Each movement was an episode of that contest. I saw it clearly - the timing, the type of instrument called for, its drama. M. J. was describing in each movement a contest, a battle, a scene. It was the story of her life, our lives in the Zone, played out in a classical composition from her birth to her death. She has portrayed in her musical composition what you are about to see in Skeet's film."

People murmured. They saw A. J. fighting to control his emotions.

His family and friends looked blankly at each other not knowing quite how to react.

A. J. went on, "I know this is not on the program so I will take you through the movements. When played, you'll be able to follow them easily. They're very distinctive." Then switching to a voice that acted out the drama, he continued:

"The first movement begins with a joyous blending of the harp, flute and piano, creating a fluttering sound. It announces the opening of children's eyes at birth then continues lightly on as they enjoy a happy childhood, a new sister, puppet shows, and parades: Love 1

The music is beautifully integrated and it rapidly moves into the second movement consisting of darkness with the sounds of heavy percussion and deep piano chords when innocence is lost to the tragedy of a fire: HATE 1

The light returns in the third movement as the children recover. They are being schooled, playing practical jokes on one another, going to baseball games: LOVE 2

The thundering kettle drums announce the transformation of the light back into darkness as the long fourth movement begins. The sounds of the piano are harsh and brooding. It is the darkest of times as their mentor and mother leaves them: HATE 2"

A. J. was clearly struggling as he personally relived this moment. There wasn't a sound to be heard in the Hall.

He paused, took a short breath and continued, "The piano slowly moves away from the sad heavy sounds as the harp and flutes help to bring the light back in the fifth movement. The children move into adolescence, a new sister is welcomed, they find romance and search out new and rich experiences: LOVE 3

The loss of two more loved ones sends the music spiraling back into darkness captured by the sixth movement: HATE 3

Then the flutes and harps return in the seventh movement as the children grow into young adults and express happiness about their decision to leave the Zone and plan new lives: LOVE 4

The seventh movement flows gently into the eighth and last movement. It is light and happy then It all comes crashing down. The drums beat heavier, the hard bass chords of the piano pounds, no harps or flutes are heard as a scene from hell emerges in the presence of the DRUG WAR!: HATE 4"

A. J. was sweating and taking short breaths. He looked out at the hushed audience and said, "M. J. wrote the light transition into the eighth movement; I wrote the rest. She couldn't finish it. The Drug War had killed her. I didn't think she wanted a tie score between the joyous times of our lives and the ugliness of hate so I wrote a short ninth movement."

The curtain opened and the orchestra prepared to play.

"I needed to hear the music and watch the pianist as he worked his way through the piece. I asked the maestro to have the orchestra play the composition for me. He had explained that his orchestra could perform on the flutes, harps and percussion instruments, but his pianist couldn't possibly be concert ready. I told him that he didn't have to be; M. J. had her own pianist.

I have never played a piano in my life but there is nobody more qualified to play her composition than I. We finally have a keyboard with sound." He sat at the concert piano and announced, "Ladies and Gentlemen: Love 5 Hate 4, composed by M. J. Munoz."

Thirty minutes later the audience was on their feet cheering and crying and applauding. Clamoring, "BRAVO, BRAVO!"

It had been a flawless performance. The orchestra had performed as if they had rehearsed for months.

A. J. had played with a passion that had taken the audience and himself back to the loving and violent days in the Zone. He re-entered the present drained and visibly shaken. He rose, gestured that he was all right to his family, leaned briefly on the piano for support and walked unsteadily off the stage.

Big George was waiting for him. "Come on, Boss. We have to go."

"Go? Go where?"

"To the morgue."

It was late. Steve and A. J. sat in A. J.'s hotel room.

"Sorry I called you away from the party, Steve. The cops were reluctant to give me any information."

"They were just following standard procedure when it comes to explosives. I made a few calls and they filled me in. Actually, their bomb squad did a hell of a job, A. J."

"Yeah, and so did Big George. He found that thing and the bomb guys were able to get right to it. I have to give him a raise."

"You should. If he hadn't located that package when he did … It was within minutes, A. J., and I'm not exaggerating. The call tipping the cops off came from Jorge's phone. How do you explain the mind of a criminal?
Once they disabled the detonator all they had to do was wait for the call, let it ring and trace the transmitting phone. Like I said, they did a hell of a job and got to those killers in a hurry."

"I had no problem identifying them, Steve. I guess I should have taken your warning more seriously."

"Well, I've got another one for you. That was a powerful and sophisticated bomb; it's never found in the hands of amateurs. They had professional help, A. J., and I don't think Enrico could have initiated the plot. It appears that you've got some dangerous enemies out there and it's possible that they were not just targeting you. They had us all together at one time and maybe saw an opportunity… I'm only speculating now. We need more information."

"Man! Steve, they could have killed all of us."

"Yeah, and hundreds more. Look, the investigation is going to Involve a lot of agencies, including us. Everybody is pretty much in agreement to keep a lid on this. Nobody wants a panic and publicity would hurt the investigation."

"I agree. It would do no good to frighten the others but I'm going to take some security measures, Steve. Anything you can do to help would be appreciated."

"Of course. You've got friends on the Hill and they would want to help. I'll coordinate it. Okay, get some rest, Rachmaninoff. And by the way, the film was outstanding. No wonder you love those girls so much."

"Yeah, yeah I do."

Steve gave A. J. a little hug as he left, noting the concern on his face.

They were all staying at the same hotel. A. J. had left a message for Skeet and Little Bit apologizing for his post performance absence from the party. He told them he had changed his departure time and would be leaving in the morning for Chicago on an early flight. He needed some time to sort things out.

He was about to turn in when he heard a light tapping on his door. A. J. wasn't prepared to see anybody and contemplated ignoring the intrusion but, feeling that it might be his concerned sisters, he opened it.

"Hi, I just thought you needed some company tonight."

"Well… I didn't think I did, but you always seem to change my mind, Wylie."

Chapter 67: Baby Girl

EVERYBODY WAS BACK at work Monday morning. The Hollywood contingency was reveling in the over-the-top reviews. "I've only seen one bad review, girls, just one!"
"Yeah, Rach, and that one came from the bitch who hates everything I'm in."

"Well, she's the only one, Wylie. Papa Joe went on and on about how much you looked and acted like M. J. and I kept saying, I know, I know, she was my sister! You were sensational and everyone asked me if you were going to get the leading role in Rinnistan. I just smiled and said that nobody else is even being considered."
"Why thank you, Ms. Skeet Studios. It's a good thing we have the same agent or I would have been surprised."

"Yeah, good thing," laughed Rachel, "and speaking of Rinnistan, I had a little chat with Genevieve. I didn't realize that she's been to Rinnistan and knows Dal. When I started to ask about Dal and Rinni's personal lives she became evasive, as did A. J. She suggested that a trip to Rinnistan and a interview with Dal would be helpful. A. J.'s memoir was written from an historical perspective but I've always sensed there was something missing. I don't know, maybe it's just my Hollywood flair for the dramatic creeping in."

"You know, I got that same feeling, Rachel, when I asked A. J. what Rinni was like. He seemed reluctant to talk about her. I pushed him a little saying that I needed to know more about Rinni if I was going to play her in the movie. He said sure and changed the subject."

"Okay, I'll ask him for more intimate details on the lives of both of them. If he knows," offered Monica.
"Good idea, but I think you better wait for a few days. I can't tell you how emotionally spent he was after that incredible performance he gave," sighed Wylie.

"So was I and everybody else! And to think he learned to play like that just by practicing with that broken down old soundless keyboard," said a still amazed Rachel.

"Yeah, I saw him play hundreds of classical numbers on that stupid thing. His performance was not a surprise to us smiled Monica.

THINGS WERE BACK to normal Monday morning at the foundation, too. The auditorium was filled with busy student assistants and the three women were in the operations room chatting with Marcia, filling her in about the premiere. A. J. was still upstairs working in his small office. No one had seen him since he left the stage Saturday night.

"When will the movie be released to the public? What was Wylie wearing? Did he really play the piano? Who's got pictures?"
"We all do," laughed Danella taking out her phone. "Here, you can look at mine first, Marcia."
Suddenly there was a burst of cheers coming from the auditorium.
"Uh, oh, Sean's entertaining them," explained Jessica.
"Come on, Danella, you're gonna love this."
"I'm coming. You do know that I've never met him," she smiled nervously.
"Oh my gosh, that's right, forgot about that."
A. J. sat at a desk on the stage working a computer.
Looking out over his excited students he said, "Okay, Bomber Squadron Number One, you guys are way behind; I'll give you another chance. Ready?"
"Fire away, Captain, we're short handed but we'll still kick their butts!"
"I don't think so 'Spotted Toad', you can't even find yours!"
"Okay, okay, pay attention now. Light travels faster than sound, this is why..."
Danella and Jessica walked into the room and stood behind the rows of students. "Do they all have goofy names?"
"Yeah, that's part of the fun. Look, someone's got the answer already."
"Uh, oh, let me see who's reporting in. It's Shabby Chic from the Roadrunners. Bad news if she gets it, Bombers. The riddle was: Light travels faster than sound. This is why...?"
'This is why some people appear bright until you hear them speak!' he read. "BINGO, she got it!" A. J. announced as the Roadrunners roared their approval.
"Ah, shit, they have more people than we do, A. J. You've got to even things up!" yelled a frustrated Bomber.
"Okay, Bombers, you do need some help. I see a couple of players who might be willing to step in and bail you out." He nodded in the direction of Jessica and Danella.
Everyone turned around and Surfer Boy from the Roadrunners shouted, "All right, it ain't going to help them anyway, but you can only have one of them!"
"Not me," said Jessica. "I'm lousy at word games."
Danella looked at the kids, shrugged and said, "Where do you want me?"
"Over here. Take Baby Girl's computer; she's home nursing a hangover."
Danella slid behind the vacated computer, logged in and said, "Fire away, Captain. Baby Girl is ready."
"YES! I think we got ourselves a player," cried the Bomber's Double Trouble. "What do you say, you Roadrunner wimps? Double or nothing?"
"Yeah, bring it on!"
"Okay," laughed A. J. "Double or nothing it is. Here's the riddle: I saw a woman wearing a sweat shirt with 'Guess' on it, so I said...

Oh, that was quick. The new kid filling in for Baby Girl is the first to report. So I said…" 'IMPLANTS'? he read. That made A. J. double over in laughter. Everybody else cracked up too, including Becky and Marcia who had joined them in the auditorium.

"Well, did she get it, Captain?" shouted a Bomber over the laughter.

"All I can say is her completion is better than mine," chortled A. J. "Double points for the Bombers! Back to work everyone."

The Bombers were on their feet cheering and giving 'Baby Girl' high fives. "Baby Girl, Baby Girl," they chanted as Danella made her way back to the operations room.

"Those kids are great," laughed Danella.

"Yeah, and it looks like they've found a new hero," quipped Becky.

A. J. walked in behind them and, looking at Danella and nodding toward the supercomputer, he said, "Well, Baby Girl, I understand you have some instructions for me."

"Oh yeah, ah, I'm sure you don't need them, I mean… Hi, I'm Danella," she blurted out putting on her best smile and extending her hand.

"I like Baby Girl better." He took her hand, "Oh, the lady in the red dress."

"What?" asked Danella, confused.

"And I really don't know a darn thing about this wonder machine. I never did get a chance to read the schematics. Come on, Baby Girl, show me what I need to know."

As he does with everyone, A. J. put Danella at ease as they worked together on the complicated supercomputer. He interrupted from time to time, waving Becky over to them, "Baby Girl, show Becky that sequence. Wait 'til you see this, Beck."

For the first time since she arrived, Danella felt like she was part of the team. And, surprising for a girl who hated to be recognized by a nickname, she didn't mind being called Baby Girl. She knew that it was going to be their special name for her.

THE SUPERCOMPUTER was exactly what they needed and their efficiency and response improved dramatically. A. J., working with Danella, was able to integrate all their computers with the supercomputer. They placed it on the opposite side of the room away from Becky, Jessica, and Marcia's stations. A. J. was going to move over and operate the large station but changed his mind.

A. J., as promised, hired a technician whose function was to keep all computers in both rooms running. His name was Wally Deakins and Becky naturally referred to him as 'Geekins'.

Geekins worked full time and had access to as many student 'Geeks' as he needed. He was a likable chap in his late twenties, knowledgeable and absolutely terrified of Becky.

“Do you plan on running both your computer and Big Huey?” Becky asked A. J.

“I was, but I think I’ve found someone more qualified to operate Huey. I can quarterback everything right where I am and send directions to Big Huey whose operator can correspond with you guys. We will only have to be in the operation room at the same time when we attempt to do a massive integration. That’s how we will conquer this thing. I will be more effective if I can see everything on the big screen up front without worrying about operating Huey.”

“Ah, have you talked to our PR person about this? She’s a little busy these days you know.”

“Nope, haven’t talked to Danella; that’s going to be Little Bit’s job. Like I said, we won’t all have to be in the room at the same time except when we have a complicated integration. We are all programmed into Huey and won’t need an operator full time until then. Baby Girl can handle both jobs for now, although I expect she’ll be spending more time with Huey as we move on.”

A somewhat skeptical Becky shrugged but figured A. J. knew what he was doing.

A. J. did know what he was doing but it had nothing to do with work efficiency. He was purposely trying to avoid everyone being at the lab at the same time.

That evening he was on the phone with Steve. “Thanks for the loan of the Cyberwar agent. Deakins is perfect. He’s all cop and he really knows computers.”

“Don’t mention it. I told you the guys owed you and it sure didn’t hurt that one of our secret projects somehow got miraculously funded. Not to mention that we have an interest in this, too, and besides, Deakins can do our work from anywhere. He doesn’t have to be in Langley.

Look, A. J. We have absolutely nothing on Enrico’s bomb plot. We’re working with everybody - FBI, Secret Service...

The quality of the bomb has everybody's attention. Its components came from all over the world; that’s how professionally built it was. We don’t like that kind of bomb expert flying beneath our radar. Knowing that their trail would go cold and untraceable, it allowed them to put the explosives into the hands of someone like Enrico. The big question is, why were you the target of people with contacts like that?”

“Yes, I certainly have my detractors but mass homicide? Frightening. Deakins has the lab locked down; I mean, the basement where he claims he is stashing inventory is a virtual snoop command post. He has cameras hidden everywhere and scopes them on his devices. No one is going to get in here without him knowing about it, day or night, and he is so good that none of my people suspect a thing. His biggest concern is Beautiful Becky; she scares the hell out of him. She calls him ‘Geekins’.”

"Oh, that's funny," laughed Steve. "I can't wait to bust his balls!"
"Well, not yet, I need him. I won't relax until we get a handle on this thing. I'm not worried about Skeet Studios, the Center, or Genevieve's operation, but I'm taking extra precautions here. I'll be sending my staff on business trips all over the world so all of us won't be vulnerable if somebody sneaks by Deakins."

"Great idea. Send Danella to Washington, I'll show her around."
"I bet you would. Oh, I almost forgot, Deakins wants to know when he's going to get 'Chip'. I think he's worried about someone walking in here laced with explosives."
"Yeah, that's really unlikely. This is not a terrorist operation, but it can't hurt. I'll check on it and get back to him."

GEEKINS WAS apologizing to everyone, "I'm sorry. He has to come to work with me or I have to quit. When I'm not at home he raises so much hell that my landlord is threatening to kick both of us out. Guys, this is 'Micro-Chip' but all his friends call him Chip."

Chipper was a seventy pound five-year-old blond Golden Lab and German Shepard mix. Besides being an incurable lap dog, he was a highly trained bomb sniffer.

"A. J. says it's up to you guys if he stays or not." Chipper already had his head in Becky's lap.
"I'll tell you what, Geekins, he stays and you go!" Becky was in love.
"Good boy," he said under his breath. "Good boy."

Chipper found more laps to nuzzle than he ever could have imagined. Everybody loved him, especially the students. They had to keep the reception room door open because whenever anybody came in from the outside, Chip had to be there to greet them. And he raised hell when he couldn't. Jessica had exclaimed, "Gosh, that dog thinks it's his job to greet and sniff everyone who comes through the door."

Geekins was always the first at work which meant so was Chip. He would race through the entire building sniffing everything out before any of the team walked in. No one questioned Geekin's early work habits and were delighted when the gregarious Chipper greeted them at the door.

"Ah, thanks Chip. You always start my day off on a positive note," laughed Jessica as she playfully scratched his ears. Chipper could always be found during the day curled up under Becky's feet or stretched out in Jessica's office. Lately he was hanging out nestled into Danella's couch in her newly constructed office adjacent to Jessica's. But he was always a short distance from the front door.

Danella and Big Huey were becoming best friends and she wore out the technician's phone support service in learning its secrets. She was also training everyone else on how to use it but all of them, including

A. J., deferred to Danella when there was a problem with any part of the system. It was apparent to everyone just how valuable Danella was becoming to the operation and, because she was so likable and modest, nobody resented her sudden rise to such an important position.

A. J. used Huey as an excuse for sending his staff all over the place. Marcia found herself spending time at Dr. Diane's or other clinics giving on the job training. He had Little Bit running errands that were never requested of her before. He would say, when they objected to losing valuable work time, that Huey was collecting everything and it was automatically being downloaded to their computers. He knew this was only a temporary solution because their presence was needed as they were getting more and more conclusive research forwarded to them. Only Danella had to stay put.

"Japan! Have you lost your fucking mind?" fumed Becky.

"Look, they are our most advanced partners and it's going to be critical that somebody else be able to do what we do," argued A. J.

"Why? Where are we going?"

"Nowhere. But I get real uncomfortable being the only game in town. Besides there is going to be a limit on how much we can handle. Wouldn't it be nice if we had operations like ours established throughout the world?"

"All right. I'll give you that, but what's the matter with live TV?"

"It's not the same, Beck, and I promise to get you back here as soon as possible. You train the Japanese, they send somebody to train the Russians, they in turn send somebody to train the French, and so on. It's too important. I don't trust the entrenched close minded scientific and medical community in our country." Not to mention, he thought to himself, those unidentified people that are trying to kill us.

"Okay, now here's what I didn't tell you. Genevieve is going with you. You're meeting Skeet and Wylie in L.A.; Tokyo is their stopover on the way to Rinnistan. They have a three day layover. You guys will really enjoy the Ginza."

"Well, why didn't you tell me that in the first place? When am I leaving?" said a suddenly happy Becky. "Man, three days in Tokyo with those guys."

"Shopping, food and drink, you ladies are so easy," grinned A. J.

BECKY WAS HEADING to say goodbye to Jessica when she heard the commotion. Danella was standing outside of Jessica's office holding her hand over her mouth.

"What's going on, Baby Girl?"

"Look, look at them!"

Jessica and A. J. were on the floor laughing and wrestling with each other. Chipper was jumping over them from side to side, excitedly barking. They were playing keep-away with a rag doll Chipper had claimed as his own.

"Oh, is that all? This happens about once a month only they've added Chipper to the mix. You remember that scene in the movie when those two were playing horsey?" Danella nodded her head yes, but still had her hand over her mouth.

"Well, there you go."

"This is too funny. They're famous people, Beck!" laughed Danella.

"Yeah, well you tell them."

Suddenly the doll came shooting out and hit Danella in the foot.

"Hey, give it to me, Baby Girl," exhorted A. J.

"Sure."

"I wouldn't do that if I were you."

Too late. Danella didn't heed Becky's warning and handed the beat up rag doll to A. J. In a nanosecond, she was on the bottom of the pile. A. J. threw the doll on top of her and all seventy pounds of Chipper landed squarely on her stomach. "OFFF!"

A. J. and Jessica were on their backs rolling with laughter. Becky was on her feet but laughing just as hard.

"Oh, so you want to play?" giggled Danella sitting up with her hair involuntarily summoned to her shoulders. "Here, catch, Beck," and she fired the doll at her. "Arghh," Becky instinctively caught the doll and a hand full of Chipper at the same time. "Oh gross, doggy spit!

I'm out of here. I'll send you bunch of juveniles a card from Tokyo! Shit, now I've got to wash my hands."

"See ya, Beautiful Becky, have a good time."

"Welcome to the family, Baby Girl," laughed LIttle Bit.

Danella, sitting in the middle of the arena, grinning, thought to herself: Okay, I'll settle for that.

Chapter 68: The Christmas Package

CANCER WAS NOT the only focus of their wide reaching research efforts. They were making their studies available to those who were experimenting with new treatments for diabetes and heart arrhythmia's. They were even helping in the treatment of spinal cord injuries. If the cure for these health problems was their goal, speed was their watchword. Time and time again A. J. would remind the team that every second counted.

Becky returned from her trip reporting that the Japanese were now capable of duplicating the foundation's work and would send their people to other countries to assist those nations. A. J. was delighted. The close call at the premiere had unnerved him. He wanted to be assured that their work would survive no matter what happened to him or the foundation.

More and more time was being spent in the operations room with all hands present. Under their system, they could pass huge amounts of information to each other, always looking for conclusive patterns to frequencies. They wanted to establish a bank of data to be made available to doctors and clinics all over the world. This information could lead to the identification of the type of cancer indicated by the patients' frequencies and immediately provide the right combination of impulses to recreate the healthy frequency patterns for transmission into the atmosphere.

This was still highly experimental and the processing of the thousands of bits of data now available to them was an enormous challenge. Deakin's security measures put A. J.'s mind at ease and he was a great help during operational times.

One of Marcia's student's computers went off line at a critical juncture and Geekins had her up and running in no time. Becky, without taking her eyes off her own computer, gave him a fist bump as he returned to his station. He smiled.

A. J. directed the content of information as he followed the efforts on the big screen but Danella controlled the flow of vital material with her expert use of Huey. She was developing an extraordinary ability to spot inaccurate feedback from any of the stations and would quickly hit the 'Red Alert' button. Whenever her alert flashed on the big screen, everybody came to a complete stop until the problem was identified. If they had been allowed to continue, their work would have taken them in a wrong direction. Sometimes it would take hours to regroup so every time the light came up, there was moaning and groaning. Amazingly, Danella was never wrong. Becky was her biggest fan.

After one typical day, full of stress and complications, A. J. noticed

Danella in her office hard at work on her computer. He wandered in and plopped down on her couch.
"Why don't you take a break, Baby Girl? We're all trying to kick back a little after the pressure we've been under lately. You're making me feel guilty."
"Oh, I'm not working, A. J. I'm fooling around with some architectural designs; it's been a hobby of mine since college."
Immediately interested, A. J. jumped off the couch.
"Really? Let me see."
"Oh, it's just an old Caribbean style home. I'm just playing around."
"Not bad, not bad. Did you know that I did most of the design work for the Center? I love to design things, but not build them," smiled A. J.
"Really? No, I didn't know that. You did a beautiful job."
"Well, I had lots of help on the interior. I much preferred designing the structure."
"That's interesting. I'm just the opposite. I like doing the interior but I have trouble figuring out where the rooms fit in relation to the building. Take a good look at these drawings and you'll see what I mean."
"You're right," he agreed. "Tell you what. Send me what you have and let me play with the structure; maybe between us we can design an island house?"
"I'd love it. Geez, that would be a lot of fun, A. J. Thanks."
And it was fun for both of them and for the next several weeks they exchanged e-mails in their down times. It proved to be a needed distraction. When she wasn't too busy, A. J. would pop into her office and they would play with their architectural project. The little Caribbean house was becoming larger and more elaborate in design.

THEIR INTERNATIONAL efforts were paying dividends as hundreds of lives were saved every day. Medical journals were reporting their successes and articles on the subject began to appear in magazines and the internet. It wasn't going to help the foundation's cause when one particular article went viral. It was titled, 'The Real Miracle'.
A. J. was awakened by a call from Genevieve at four in the morning.
"The office has been torched!"
"WHAT? WHEN?"
"It happened about an hour ago. The night watchman saw something thrown through the window; it turned out to be an incendiary bomb. No one was hurt, but it's a complete loss!" A. J.'s head was spinning. This was real trouble.
"Look, keep everybody away from the place and don't let anybody go back to work. Did you get today's business backed up?"
"Yes. I finished it while I was watching the late election returns. You'll

have it in the morning. Nothing is lost. Thank god we installed that system."

"Okay, you will be hearing from Steve... Sorry, Gen. Get some rest and we'll regroup tomorrow."

"Yeah, but I don't like forced vacations and I'm too upset to be pissed, but that's coming."

"You're going to have company on that front. Hey, who won?"

"Won what?"

"The election?"

"Senator Davis, god help us."

IT WAS AN ACT of arson committed on a privately owned building therefore a matter for the local police. However, this was D.C. and there would be cooperation between the police and the government's security people. Steve put the different agencies investigating the attempted bomb plot on notice that A. J., the principal target of the plot, was the recent victim of an arson. They immediately had their forensic experts on the scene looking for evidence that would connect the two events and possibly give them a lead.

A. J. decided to keep the investment company running but contracted out all the work that his in-house people were doing. The salaried accountants formed their own firm and A. J.'s investment company became their largest client. His on-floor traders easily found work elsewhere, being guaranteed A. J.'s business in their particular field of expertise. The staff personal were each given a full year's salary. His intentions were clear; he wanted to minimize his enemy's targets.

Genevieve, like the others, was not aware of the near tragic bomb episode and was dismayed at the breakup of the investment firm.

"Gen, The Center is up and running and we are not involved with the operation of it. Rinnistan is generating its own income and Omar is keeping them on budget. We will continue to make donations to them but we don't need a management team for that. Skeet's Studios is also humming along and Jeff has a real handle on the business. I'm personally in charge of the foundation and don't need any help there. What I'm saying is we don't have to have large investment returns; our passive income will be sufficient for our charitable contributions."

"Terrific. I'm back to practicing law which I hate," declared an unhappy Genevieve.

"Oh, no! You're not going anywhere. You will be keeping your finger on all our investments and following our selected foundation's activities. Also, you're going to investigate other foundations that could use our support. And I want you to manage my personal accounts and that means staying in touch with all our former employees. You can work out of your home. All you're going to need is a computer and your passport."

"Why do I feel that you're not telling me everything? Who the hell would want to burn us out, A. J.?"

"I don't know. Oh, you're also getting a substantial raise."

"Now I am suspicious."

Ignoring that, A. J. said, "And I want you to do some estate work for me."

"Why? You're not even thirty yet."

"Gen, you don't have to be old to have an estate."

"You're making me nervous, A. J!"

"Come on. I could get hit by a bus tomorrow, then who would take care of you?"

"Right A. J., right."

THE MOVIE, released in the second week of December, was an instant box office hit. All of them were becoming a source of immense public interest, none more than A. J. Danella had her hands full keeping the media at bay but with her personal skills she was managing it.

Rachel, too, was inundated with requests for information.

"I think Rinnistan will be a smash as soon as it's released," she commented to Wylie and Monica over lunch.

"But first we have to resolve how we want to handle Rinni's relationship with A. J.," added Wylie.

"Dal never violated his confidence but that photo of the four of them in combat spoke a thousand words. Wow, that was powerful. He never mentioned any of that to you, Monica?"

"No, not a word and, unless he consents, we are not going to make it a part of the movie. The same with his relationship with Rinni, whatever that was. I'll talk to him about it though.

Boy, was I surprised about Rinnistan. It was like a little oasis in a sea of sand surrounded by mountains. It had a cosmopolitan feeling with tea rooms and hotels. The streets were clean and traffic and parking was organized and orderly. Dal's police force was the most respected I've ever seen. With their expanded airport and new roads, that place is really impressive. As are Dal and Omar. They've given me a whole new perspective on how to produce this movie."

"Yeah, I was impressed too," added Wylie. "But I still want to know more about A. J. and Rinni. This is too juicy, Monica."

MOST OF THE students were off for Christmas break; everybody else was still working. However, things were slowing down in anticipation of the upcoming holiday.

A. J. insisted they have a small office Christmas party and surprised them all that morning when he arranged for a used grand piano to be delivered for the occasion. It was set up in the lobby in front of the auditorium and he was tinkering with it.

Jessica was manning the phones and Geekins was working on some disabled computers. There were a few students in the lab doing their homework on the computers. Chipper was stretched out on Danella's couch enjoying a nap. Marcia was home with her children leaving Danella and Becky in charge of the Christmas decorations.

"Baby Girl, I need you," A. J. yelled from underneath the piano. She walked over with a handful of garland, poked her head under the piano and said, "You called?"

"Your resume said that you could play the piano. I need you to play a few chords for me; play something sad and mellow."

"Okay, but I want a raise. I'm a member of the musician's union, you know."

"All right. You get a raise when I get one, but for now play those chords or no party for you!"

"Scrooge." She played a few sad chords from a dirge, "There. How's that?"

"I said sad not miserable!" he answered making her laugh.

"Thanks," he said as he slid out from underneath the piano. "That's all I needed. But you'll be earning your union dues because you're going to be the entertainer for our little party."

"Oh no, not me."

"Yes, you. Your resume said that you can also sing and we need somebody to lead us with the Christmas carols."

"Hey, he's right," chimed in Jessica as she joined them in the lobby. "I did see that on your resume."

"I just stated that I could sing; I didn't say I could sing well! And my piano playing is horrible - just ask him," she said pointing at A. J.

"She's right, but I'll make you a deal. I'll play the piano but you have to sing."

"Okay, it's a deal."

"Good, I've got some sheet music right here; lets practice a little." A. J. no longer needed to hear the sounds before playing the number.

They were having a great time and upon hearing the Christmas music, everybody came into the lobby to join in on the fun, including Chipper.

"I thought you said you couldn't sing well," said the piano player. "That was terrific."

"Yeah, Baby Girl, you're starting to piss me off again," exclaimed Becky. Danella smiled and shrugged, holding her palms up towards the ceiling.

"Okay. Lets try The Christmas Song." And as A. J. played the lead in, Chipper suddenly started barking furiously and bolted towards the front door.

"What's wrong with him?" asked Jessica.
The barking morphed into frightening snarls and growling.
"OH NO!" It was Deakins, and he tore into the front room, followed slowly by the others.
Deakins was staring at a Christmas package that someone had placed on the reception desk. Chipper was going crazy, jumping at the wrapped package, snapping and snarling. Deakins had to grab hold of him.
"A. J., GET EVERYBODY OUT OF HERE NOW!" he screamed. "MOVE, GODDAMN IT, MOVE!"
They hesitated for a moment but A. J. forcibly sent them out the door. They were all saying, "What's wrong? What's happening?" Everybody was now responding but Danella. She didn't know the problem but sensed the urgency and was running in the opposite direction.
"DANELLA, WHERE ARE YOU GOING?" yelled A. J.
"I WANT TO MAKE SURE ALL THE KIDS ARE OUT OF THE AUDITORIUM!" she shouted back.
Deakins tore past her heading for the basement. Chipper was now on top of the desk snarling and taking little nips at the package.
A. J. chased Danella, caught her, checked the auditorium, grabbed her hand and raced for the front door. Deakins had returned holding a black satchel and yelling into his cell phone. A. J. and Danella stopped and looked at him. He shoved Chip off the desk and ripped the satchel open, pulling out some tools. Seeing the two of them standing in the doorway, he yelled, "GET OUT OF HERE. TAKE THEM CLEAR ACROSS THE STREET. HELP IS ON THE WAY! GO!"
They bolted out the door and joined the others who were huddled in groups as they shivered on the sidewalk.
"NO! EVERYBODY GET ACROSS THE STREET," ordered A. J. They heard sirens and suddenly patrol cars were coming from every direction. A policeman ran into the building and within seconds he came running out yelling commands to his partners. They scattered and began knocking frantically on the doors of adjacent houses.
"SEAN, what's happening?" shrieked Little Bit.
"That Christmas package? It's loaded with explosives."
"WHAT? Oh my god! How? Who would do such a thing?" she gasped.
"A. J.! Geekins and Chip are here still in there!" cried Becky.
"They're government agents, Beck - both of them. They know what they're doing."
Silently they all stood by watching the frenzied activity.
Finally Deakins emerged from the building carrying their coats. He stopped and talked to the patrol officers then made his way across the street.
"I've disarmed it but that stuff is very volatile. The bomb disposal unit is on the way - here they are now. I better go help them and retrieve Chip.

They won't let you guys in the building until it's completely clean and they will need Chip's help." As he was leaving he yelled back, "Nice call, A. J."

"Come on," A. J. said quietly, "Lets go somewhere and I'll explain all of this to you."

Jessica's apartment was just around the corner and they crowded into her small living room.

"Okay, here's what's going on."

A. J. slowly and thoroughly revealed the close call the night of the premiere. "There was no time to evacuate everybody. I didn't even know what was happening and it was taking place right under my feet."

"Holy shit!" was all Becky could say. The others were speechless.

"I didn't want to alarm anybody; it would have accomplished nothing. The government wanted us to keep things quiet and I agreed. Knowing that we could possibly be at risk here at the lab, I brought in Deakins. He's a friend of Steve's and on loan from the CIA. He set it up so nobody could booby trap the place but asked for Chip in case a situation like this occurred."

"So that's what Deakins meant when he said 'nice call'; you had it figured right, A. J.," calmly stated Danella. "Who do we kiss first, you, Wally, or Chipper?"

"I think Chipper," smiled A. J.

"Okay brother, I know you. You're going to do something big, aren't you?"

"I won't put you guys or the kids at risk any longer, Little Bit. Look, we're not sure if the fire is related but somebody or some organization wants us out of business and they're willing to kill us to accomplish that. We're going to close the lab until we put *them* out of business."

Chapter 69: Only God Can Talk To The Dead

THE SLOWDOWN over the holiday season provided the perfect opportunity to affect an organized termination. A. J. targeted February 1 as the closure date. He was alone with Little Bit in his kitchen rehashing what had happened.

"I'm still in shock, Sean. I never dreamed that some crazies would want to kill all of us, and they almost did! And just look at who saved us, an ex-con and a dog!"

"Yeah, never thought of it that way." He smiled at Little Bit as she went on..."Boy, you sure find out about people in times like that. I mean look at Baby Girl; her first thought was for the kids - their safety - totally disregarding the danger to herself! Who does that remind you of?"

He said nothing.

"Sean, Skeet and the girls are still shaking."

"I know. She calls me every time she hangs up with you. I think she is the only one happy about our decision to shut the doors."

"*Your* decision. We've got some unhappy people around here, Sean. Don't get me wrong. We understand your legitimate concern but our fears are slowly turning into anger."

"It's not only us I'm worried about, Little Bit. If our enemies feel that they can't frighten us off, they might just start on our friends at the clinics and they are helpless to defend themselves. No, lets live to fight another day. That will give us *and* the authorities time to find these killers and keep everybody out of harm's way."

"Hmmm... Never thought about all our friends. You're right."

"Yes, and don't forget, depending on Steve's report, I still intend for us to go back to work, but maybe not as a team all located in the same spot."

Changing the subject, Sean added, "Have all the laptops come in? I'd like to have them for the gang when they're back from vacation. It will make it easier for me to tell them that we're closing shop. I don't want them to go back to work."

"Yes, they're in," sighed Little Bit.

A. J. WAS ON the phone with Steve. "We caught a break, A. J., our first lead. I say 'our' because we are now involved. There's a real suspicion of foreign involvement."

"That surprises me. Tell me about it."

"The forensic guys have come up with a substance found in both bomb crime scenes. Explosives using that particular substance have been found by Interpol investigating bombings in France."

"That's a clue as to where it's made, not to who used it," cautioned A. J.
"We know, but it's a start and those explosives entering our country has brought our agency into it."
"We don't think it's personal, A. J. They could have easily, at any time, picked you off or any of the others if they wanted to. We're beginning to suspect a cult ideology struggle here; this could be big."
"Oh man, that's all we need."
"Closing the lab is a good idea. If we're dealing with that kind of mindset, individual killings are murder to them and not war. They're after a demonstrative statement and destroying your lab and your whole team would do that for them. If that's the case, Monica, Jessica and the others shouldn't be individual targets."
"I guess that's comforting. Okay, we'll keep our heads down for now and wait to see what happens."
"The arson doesn't seem to be related, A. J. That's probably the work some fresh enemies. Remind me to never have dinner with you."
"Thanks a lot."
"Who else doesn't like you besides Zimmerman? We ruled him out; he's nasty but not violent."
"I don't know. The Government?"

THE NEXT FEW weeks were disheartening as they slowly executed the shutdown process. Jessica was busy utilizing her vast networking structure to inform their partners that the foundation was no longer processing all the information being forwarded to them. The clinics and individual doctors working with the foundation would be pretty much on their own. Dr. Diane and Ian were particularly upset; they were also losing a friend.

Marcia was the first to leave. With the students gone and the processing slowly being terminated, there wasn't much left for her to do. She was promised that she would be on the top of the list for recall whenever the foundation came back to life.

With the building under twenty-four hour surveillance by local police, Deakins was reassigned and so was Chip.
This was an emotional farewell. Everybody knew that they probably owed their lives to these two.

"Well, Mr. Wally Deakins, I rarely do this but here you are, and thank you." With that Becky hugged and kissed him. Turning her attention to Chipper who was sitting as close to her as he could get and playfully pawing at her leg, she knelt down and said, "You're my hero, you beautiful blond. I'm going to miss you." She surrendered to the doggy kisses he slobbered all over her.

Rising, she said to Wally, "When you guys retire him, put my name first

on the adoption list."
"Absolutely, Becky. The top of the list!"
Everybody else extended their gratitude and said their goodbyes. It was suddenly empty without the lovable Chipper around. Jessica would be retuning to Hollywood to work with Skeet, and Becky and Genevieve would reunite back in D.C. They didn't like being temporarily out of business but understood the reason behind it.
"You tell Robo-cop to get off his butt and collar those guys. We don't like this, A. J."
"Neither do I, Beck. You know I'll be searching for a way to get us up and running again."
"Yeah, I do."
That left Danella. She had found herself a home with them and didn't really have a life to return to. Jessica and Becky had become her closest friends and she was saddened more than the others. Jessica was A. J.'s sister and Becky was his partner; they would remain close to him but she would not.
Sensing her sadness, A. J. took her aside the day before everyone left and said, "Baby Girl, how would you like to do me a favor?"
"Sure, just name it."
"I need a baby sitter for Big Huey. Is your place large enough to make him feel at home?"
"Well, no," she laughed. "But it sure as hell would make me feel at home."
"Good, and don't forget, we have an island house to complete." Danella immediately brightened knowing that she was still part of the team and would stay connected.

THE LAB WAS closed and Big Huey moved but A. J. had no intention of terminating the foundation. He had accomplished his first goal of scattering everybody, now he set out to take the next step: wait for a period of time and find a safe house to work from. However, he thought that it would be impossible to fight an ideological cult movement if that's who his enemies were.
The country had a new president whose personal philosophy toward religion and science was not the same as A. J.'s. A. J. expected no help from the government. That was fair, he thought. The man was reflecting the beliefs of people who had put him in office. What A. J. didn't expect was the government's action triggered by an event in France.
There was an e-mail from Steve:

A. J., One of your research partners in Paris just had their lab blown up. Total loss, many dead. I'll give you more details when I get them. Steve

That was the one thing he feared most - innocent people attacked because of the scientific work he and the foundation were doing.

More information was coming in through the news media. An unnamed organization had taken credit for the bombing. They had made a statement through the internet that: “Only God can talk to the Dead!” A copy of the article, ‘The Real Miracle’, was attached to the statement.

A. J. was distraught. Those lost in the tragedy were his friends and he felt partially responsible for their deaths. All their accomplishments were being jeopardized by the fatal attack on the French clinic.

Steve phoned A. J. reporting the grim news.

“Fifteen dead and twice that many injured.”

“Oh my god!”

“There’s more. We just got a notice from the Justice Department; they want a full report on your ‘three incidents’. We have to cooperate. No telling what this Administration is up to.”

“Yeah, no telling. Thanks Steve.”

A. J. decided to put the building up for sale. He wanted his enemies to feel confident that they had scared him off. He didn’t want to endanger his team in any way. He would continue to live there until it sold.

A COPY OF a Justice Department’s directive was given to all pertinent government agencies; Steve forwarded it to A. J.

It was short and to the point:

There is a distinct probability that doctors, clinics, research facilities, and other medical centers engaged in the practice of transmitting electromagnetic frequencies into the atmosphere and retrieving them for reintroduction into their patients are being targeted by assassins.
This poses a danger not only to them but to the general public.

THEREFORE: It is hereby ordered under the powers given to this department by law, the following: Those who are engaging in the aforementioned activity shall cease and desist from such practice. The danger to the public from such attacks is too great to be ignored.

All pertinent security agencies are further directed to carry out the enforcement of this order.
From the office of: The Attorney General of The United States of America

It didn’t make the six o’clock news but it did send a buzz around D.C.

Genevieve had her ear closest to the ground when it came to politics. A. J. called her and asked that she put her snoop hat on and get back to him. She did.

“The word around town has it as a campaign payoff, A. J. He found a way to satisfy the extreme right of his base. It’s just politics. What are you going to do?”

“I’m not sure, Gen, but we won’t be setting up camp anytime soon, at least not in this country. This really changes things.”

Chapter 70: Fighting Back

A. J. WAS IN Washington conferring with Becky and Genevieve. He had some ideas on how they should proceed but wanted their personal input. He also had a meeting scheduled with Steve.

They met at a local pub and Steve was briefing him on the status of the investigation as they sipped cold ales.

"Whoever these killers are, they have a link to professional bomb makers. The explosives used at the French lab had the same characteristics as those intended for your demise. It's obvious that this is their weapon of choice."

"They weren't taking any chances, were they?" questioned A. J.

"Afraid not. Here's our profile. We suspect they wanted to get the world's attention and when they failed to take you out, they hit the French lab. They waited for a successful operation before they went public."

"You guys still feel there is some sort of cult at work here?"

"Yes, there's no doubt in our minds about it and we're quite sure that their demented philosophies are rooted in religious fundamentalism."

"Yes, I agree. That 'Real Miracle' article was so anti-God it would incite those types. It implied that our successes proved that no one ever died and we live on in the universe. That's preposterous. We've heard it before and tried to distance ourselves from that twisted logic. This guy took it to a new level by guaranteeing that in the near future, we could communicate with our deceased loved ones and it had nothing to do with an afterlife because they are still alive!"

"That's the way we see it too, A. J. You and your friends were gaining world acclaim and that was inspiring the anti-religious fanatics. I know that was not your intention, but nevertheless, the fundamentalists were threatened. And they might be Muslim, Christian, or something else. We don't know! But we think we *do* know their profile and we're working with Interpol on this one. The French are really pissed off."

"Well, at least the European governments didn't cut off the electromagnetic cancer treatments like our government did to us."

"I know you don't want to hear this, A. J., but the President might have a point here. Terrorists, religious or not, love to kill Americans. He had to do something! It just happened to coincide with his personal beliefs which made it easy for him."

"Well, I don't intend to make it easy for him."

"Uh, oh," sighed Steve.

A. J. WOULD HAVE been willing to sit on the sidelines for a while but when the Justice Department's order came down he decided to go back to work. It was now more important than ever that other research labs in foreign countries be trained to do the work that the foundation was doing. He dispatched a delighted Becky on an international quest to accomplish this. He, too, would be traveling the world doing the same thing, but first he needed a command center.

"Hey Baby Girl, you taking care of our big kid?"

"A. J.! I was hoping that blocked caller I.D. was you. Yeah, but he's bored stiff," she laughed.

"Tell me, do you still carry Canadian citizenship?"

"Yup, never gave it up and I still have my Irish citizenry too. Why do you ask?"

"How would you and Huey like to get back to work?"

"You're kidding! I am ready, Captain, just say the word!"

"It won't be interrupting your active social life now, would it?"

"Oh, that's funny. Huey is more exciting than the bozos I've been dating. What's this got to do with Canada?"

"Canada supports our work and is not concerned about assassins. Quebec City is particularly active and they are working directly with our European labs. They need to process the information faster. You and Huey interested?"

"Quebec City! That's home, A. J. Of course I'm interested! Wow, when are we leaving?"

"I've missed your enthusiasm, Danella," he grinned, "but you better hear it all first. There's a downside, Baby Girl. You will be working with clinics scattered all over the world so you'll be busy. Also, we are going to be extremely low profile - like underground. You know the danger. Still excited?"

"What danger? I'm already packing. Hear those boxes falling off the shelves?"

"See you in Quebec City, Baby Girl," he laughed.

"Genevieve will be calling with the details."

Danella would be doing roughly the same work in Quebec City that she had been doing at the foundation; taking in frequency information from around the globe, organizing it and forwarding it to the labs working on the resonation integrations. The difference in her Quebec assignment was that they wouldn't be doing any resonating themselves and people living in the U.S. would not be benefiting from the work.

Being a Canadian citizen and operating legally in that country, she would not be hassled by an unsympathetic government. A. J. still wanted her to keep a low profile so as not to attract the people who would do her harm.

DANELLA WAS AS happy as she had ever been in her life. She was back home, excited to reacquaint herself with many of her Canadian friends. Once again she was living in a French speaking community using her native language. She had forgotten how much she missed the bistros and boutiques.

Also, she was doing what she felt was important work and it kept her connected to Jessica, Becky and A. J.

Danella *was* the command center. Becky, Jessica, and A. J. communicated with her and each other through Huey. Jessica was staying in the loop. Huey now had Jessica's entire network downloaded and, through him, she was constantly sending updated progress reports from Canada to everyone logged into their system.

More important, using Huey, Jessica was notifying doctors and clinics in the U.S. where the resonating centers were located around the world and where to send their frequency information if they wanted to stay with the program. However, their patients would have to travel to those sites for treatment. She was working out of California using her own computer to talk to Huey. They were not breaking any U.S. laws. Two could play this game. They were fighting back.

Most of the U.S. doctors and clinics working with the foundation were as upset as A. J. with the ban on electromagnetic cancer treatments. They had seen first hand how effective the treatments could be. Many of their terminal cancer patients had walked out of their clinics completely cured of their cancers.

Some of them took matters into their own hands and set up clinics in Mexico and Canada to treat their very sick patients. The foundation's system was still operating effectively regardless of the formidable opposition. That fact was not lost on the President's advisors.

"What the hell do they expect me to do!" exploded President Davis in a meeting with members of his staff.
"I shut them down, damn it. Isn't that enough?"

"Clinics are opening up across both borders and it's pissing off a lot of our people," exclaimed Bud.

"Look, I closed them because of the physical danger to the public, not because of their unchristian practices! And besides, we don't control what those countries do. What? You want to start an International incident with our neighbors?"

"They're still exchanging information with other clinics stationed all over the world and they're doing it out of Canada for Christ sake!" persisted Bud.

"You guys are scaring me. Has all this power gone to your heads? Hasn't anybody in this room ever heard of the First Amendment?

It's not like they're pouring over the border. I mean, it's just an insignificant trickle and they're trying to SAVE THEIR OWN LIVES! If any of you guys were in that position with no other options, you would be like rabbits heading for the border!"

"It's going to get out of hand, Harry, you watch. He'll find some way where anybody can search the heavens for their lost frequencies. They won't need clinics!"

"We will look at it then if that happens, but in the meantime they are operating within the law."

"Okay, anything else?"

"Yeah, the U.N. opens up hearings on world health next month and they've invited McCleary to talk to some of their committees."

"What are you suggesting, we boycott the U.N.?"

"Of course not, Harry, but some people are. We have little control over those extremists and I think they've already done something stupid."

Chapter 71: A Misogynistic Little Worm

DANELLA FOUND A comfortable apartment above a shop in Lower Town, a trendy historic section of Old Quebec City. She could walk to everything but still remain somewhat secluded. She easily blended in with her environment and was enjoying her assignment.

It was a beautiful spring day. Danella and Big Huey were busy at work when the door knocker announced visitors. Who could that be? she asked herself. I wasn't expecting anybody.

Her old front door had been built decades before peepholes, so she was without a clue who her visitors might be when she opened it.

"A-HA... SURPRISE! We caught you with your hair down," said a grinning Becky.

"BECK, A. J. ...OHH!" Danella was completely surprised and almost knocked them over with hugs. "Why didn't you call? Come in, come in!"

"Hey, I like your digs, Baby Girl. Who's that big guy in the corner?"

"Never saw him before in my life, A. J., but he kept hitting on me so I invited him in," she laughed.

"What I want to know is how the hell did you get him up those stairs?" asked Becky.

"Ah, I think I had my hair down that day too; I had lots of help."

"No shit," chuckled Becky, "I bet you did."

"What are you guys doing here? Why didn't you warn me?"

"It was a spur of the moment thing. Gen had Becky and me scheduled into New York at the same time so we thought it would be the perfect opportunity to surprise you. Huey told us you would be here today."

"The snitch. I'm going to scramble his programs."

"What a cool place you have here, Baby Girl, and I sure do like this old section of town. You're going to have to show us around."

"Oh, I'd love to Beck. Where are you staying and how long are you guys going to be here?"

"We're at the Frontenac and we've set aside these next few days to play with you," smiled A. J.

"That's wonderful, not enough time, but great, great. I'm so excited."

The cozy bistro she took them to for dinner was the perfect choice to celebrate their reunion.

"This is really nice, Danella. Neither Becky nor I have ever been to this part of the world; I mean why go to Europe when you have this?"

"Yeah, I know. Thanks for the exile, A. J.," she chortled.

"What were you two doing in New York at the same time? I get dizzy trying to keep up with your itineraries."

"Yeah, so do we," said A. J. "Our surprise visit with you is directly related to our business in New York. We could have discussed things over the

phone but then we wouldn't be enjoying this wonderful evening together."
"No, we don't like phones; it's always better in person. As a matter of fact, I think I'll disconnect mine so I'll see more of you two," she grinned. "Okay, what's going on in The Big Apple? Are you going to send me there on a shopping spree?"
"Well, something like that," laughed A. J.
"I know your father was a diplomat for France in its dealings with the U.N. and you were often his date at their functions."
"Yes, that's right. It was really exciting for a young girl. I met some of the most powerful people in the world who were serving their countries."
"Do you suppose some of those people are still serving?" asked A. J.
"I know they are. Those are plum jobs and are not relinquished without a fight. Are you sending me to the U.N.?"
"Yes."
"What? I was kidding. You're kidding... you're not kidding."
"No, I'm not, Baby Girl. The U.N. is holding hearings on world health care in two weeks and I've been invited to appear in front of some of their committees. Becky and I will be there Monday for a week to prepare for it. We need to know what they want from us.
"Where do I fit in?"
"The following week we're scheduled to be elsewhere for the first few days and we need a presence in New York. The week before the hearings is when all the parties are held. We thought maybe you could reacquaint yourself with some of your father's friends and represent us at social functions. This is purely voluntary; if you don't want to go, it's all right. I'll ask Gen to cancel the Plaza reservations and Broadway tickets."
"A. Jaaay! ... Oh, all right, anything for the team," she giggled.
"I told you she would be a team player."
"Guess you were right, Beck."
"Okay, it's settled. Becky and I will have a number of contacts for you when you get there. Genevieve will start working on securing you invitations for the different dinners and parties."
"Geez, I'm going to need a lot of party dresses."
"Hey, you wanted to go on a shopping spree. You're still on an expense account. Go for it."
"Does he have any idea how dangerous that suggestion is, Beck?"
"No, he doesn't, but I don't think he cares."
"I don't, but here's what I do care about. Danella, this is going to give us an excellent opportunity to gain global support for what we are trying to do. You probably know better than I how effective the informal meetings are. We need someone to lay the groundwork for us; there's nobody better prepared or more qualified to do that than you."
"Thanks, A. J. Yeah, I can do this. My dad showed me how the game is played, and I think his friends will remember me. One thing, Huey can't

sit idle for too long; a lot of people are counting on him."

"We know. That's why you're going to have another visitor for the week. She's familiar with Huey and, with a little guidance from you, she will be able to temporarily hold the fort."

"JESS. You're sending me JESS!"

"Yup. Little Bit is more excited than you are. She wants you to call her as soon as you can."

"Like RIGHT NOW! We all can talk to her," insisted Danella as she punched out Jessica's number. "She can stay with me. Oh, are we going to have fun! JESS, it's me. WHEN ARE YOU COMING?"

A. J. and Becky were on an early flight back to New York.

"It was great last night, just the four of us. I think we all needed that."

"Yeah, we sure did. Beck, I'm beginning to feel a little guilty about Baby Girl. I think that maybe we're holding her back. She is beautiful, smart, and talented. She shouldn't be stuck behind a computer."

"That's where she wants to be."

"I know, but I keep thinking about what Rachel said to me, that Danella had everything it takes to make it big in Hollywood. And we are in such a good position to help her. No, she's got to have that chance and I'm going to make sure it happens."

DANELLA DID reconnect with some of her father's old colleagues and was representing the Brandon Foundation well. She received more dinner and luncheon invitations than she could handle. Their message was definitely getting out. She was surprised at how many people recognized A. J. by name but was dismayed at the misconceptions many had of the work he and the foundation were doing. She was trying diligently to correct that.

Danella enjoyed meeting with the diplomats from her birthplace, Ireland, and had made a point to attend the French Legation's luncheon to personally extend the foundation's condolences for those lost in the bombing of the research lab. It helped that she could speak their language. She had no idea what an important role the friends she made that day would soon play in all their lives.

Danella appeared to be everywhere as she took to her assignment like an experienced diplomat. Her picture even appeared in the New York society pages, posing with some U.N. middle east ambassadors.

The Brandon Foundation was acquiring a new face - a beautiful new face.

The United Nation's Economic and Social Council held a gala at the United Nations Hotel on the eve of the world health hearings. Many of the political emissaries from countries promoting world health were invited. Danella was a welcome guest to the party and she had a number of requests from men eager to be her escort. She politely turned them down, wanting to be free to roam about to make acquaintances with these influential world leaders in the health related fields. It was probably her most important engagement that week.

The event, held in one of the large hotel banquet rooms, was an informal affair designed to encourage the free exchange of ideas. There was an open bar with round dining tables filled with appetizers and chilled bottles of champagne. A jazz quartet played smooth sounds as the guests milled about.

Only one speaker, an important one, was scheduled to speak that evening: the Surgeon General of the United States. Members of the media were invited to record the event and reporters were circulating amongst the guests.

Over the clink of cocktail glasses and hum of conversation, Danella was chatting with some newly acquired friends when a nattily dressed middle eastern man approached her.

She recognized him. He was the assistant secretary to the Ambassador of Iran and one of the men who had asked her to be his date for the evening.

He interrupted Danella's conversation with her friends.

"Well, Ms. Fochett, I see you made it to our little affair, unescorted I presume. But there are plenty of men here. I'm sure you'll find an escort home." He said it loud enough that some of the people close to them stopped talking.

Danella bristled but said nothing, assuming that he was talking out of the champagne glass he was holding. She turned to walk away. He grabbed her by the arm, spinning her around and said,

"What's the matter? You save your special talents for that WHOREMONGER YOU WORK FOR?"

All conversation stopped.

Danella wrenched her arm away and with the Irish fury she rarely displayed she exhorted, "YOU MISOGYNISTIC LITTLE WORM!" and sent a close fisted punch on to a collision course with his prominent nose. Bright red blood spilled over his white dinner jacket as he howled in pain.

Danella became paralyzed by the havoc she had created as there was a flurry of activity together with the gasps and screams of frightened women. She felt herself being dragged by the arm away from the chaotic scene.

"This way, Danella. You have to get the hell out of here before those reporters are all over you!"

It didn't matter who the woman was. Danella ran alongside her as they tore out of the room, dashed down the hallway and exited the hotel by way of the rear door. They ran for a short distance, entered another hotel

and stepped into an elevator that took them skyward.
Safely in the elevator and out of breath, Danella looked at her rescuer and said, "I know you. You're, you're…"
"I'm Monica's friend, Patrice Harden. We met at the premiere of The Zone."
"Yes, I remember you. Where are we? Where are we going?"
"We're in the New York City Hotel and we are going up to my room. I was assigned to your little gathering with the Surgeon General tonight and it was more convenient for me and my crew to work out of here."
They rushed out of the elevator and walked to Patrice's suite. Once inside, away from all of the confusion, Danella suddenly became aware of the enormity of the situation and sat down heavily into a chair with her head in her hands.
"Oh, my god, I let him down. I let all of them down," she sobbed.
"Danella, I was right behind you. I heard everything that son-of-a-bitch said. No one can blame you for belting the bastard. He deserved it."
"You don't understand. I was supposed to make friends, not beat up important people! A. J. is going to fire me. After he kills me!"
"A. J. is not the kind of man to do that," laughed Patrice. "He'll understand."
"He might understand but the negative publicity can be so damaging to us. Some people are looking for a reason to attack us and I just gave them one."
"If you're worrying about that pompous Iranian, don't. My reporter's instincts led me to turn on my smart-phone. I recorded everything the idiot said. He won't give you any trouble."
"Patrice, I didn't see you next to me. Thank you."
"I had just walked up. I spotted you from across the room and was coming over to say hello."
"Well, I'm glad you did. I've got to call A. J. I'm in so much trouble."
A. J. immediately took her call and was forced to interrupt her rambling. "Whoa, whoa, slow down. You slugged who?"
She collected herself and told him everything in complete detail. He listened intently.
"I'm so sorry, A. J.," she sobbed.
"Put Patrice on."
"He wants to talk to you," she sniffled handing over the phone.
"It's Patrice, A. J. Look, she had every reason to…"
"I know, I know. Thanks Patrice. I owe you one, I won't forget. But I'm going to need more of your help."
"Sure, what can I do?"
"Keep Danella secluded until I can make arrangements to get her back to Canada. I might need your assistance on that too. Also could you e-mail me what you recorded on your phone? I'll get that into the hands of

friends who will end this thing in a hurry."
"Yeah, I'll be glad to do that. Anything else?"
"Yes, could you get a bucket of ice water?"
"Sure. What for?"
"If she hit somebody that hard, her hand has got to be swelling."
Patrice glanced at Danella's hand, "You're right, it is. I'll take care of it."
"Good, now put Rocky back on, and thanks again Patrice."
"Here, he wants to talk to Rocky," she snickered handing the phone back.
"Ohhh. I'll look him up and apologize, A. J. That might satisfy him."
"The hell you will! You saved all of us a lot of trouble, Baby Girl. Especially me. If you hadn't drilled that guy I would be the one looking him up and he would be suffering from more than a bloody nose!"
"Yikes! Patrice just stuck my hand in a bucket of ice water!"
"Good," he chuckled. "I don't want anything to happen to those lovely hands, and besides, I just sent you something on our island house. I think it needs a belvedere connected by a winding staircase. You've got to work on it. What do you think?"
"I think it's a great idea." She was smiling through the tears knowing what he was trying to do.
"Gen will phone you. We're getting you out of there. In the meantime stay with Patrice. We all love you, Baby Girl. Little Bit will be waiting for you."
She hung up, wiping away happy tears.
"You okay? You're smiling."
"He said he loved me." It drew a strange look from Patrice.
"Really?"
"Well, not quite. He said they all loved me."
"Close enough, Danella, close enough. See, I told you he would understand."

Chapter 72: The Reverend Mr. Cobb

THE FOUNDATION'S HOME in Evanston was sold and A. J. moved back to D.C. He leased a suite in a hotel close to the airport. Genevieve and Becky were his first two visitors and they were politely gagging down some very bad coffee A. J. had brewed as they sat comfortably in the lounging area of his quarters.

Genevieve gave her report. "All my research tells me that we can do it. I've received concurrence from some pretty high powered attorney friends of mine. It should be okay. That directive from the Justice Department does not apply to individual citizens. They would not be acting as a business or a profession where people congregate, therefore they wouldn't be posing any threat to the public's safety."

"So lets make sure I've got this legally correct. Patient resonation information can be sent over the internet to us. Then we route it to our programs and it doesn't violate any law."

"That's right, A. J. Just as you suspected."

Becky added, "All the patients have to do is let the doctors or clinics gather their information and send it on to Danella for processing. She assigns them an individual code number and forwards their data to labs scattered all over the world. They return the reconstructed resonating information to her. She checks for errors and downloads it into the patient's coded account where they can access it. Then the patients can follow the prompts set out in our transmitting and receiving programs and use their own computers to send their healthy frequencies out into the ionosphere.

Huey can handle it. Don't forget, he's not burdened by all that research material we were loading into him. Jessica will be helping Danella and Marcia is there if we need her."

"Oh boy, I wonder what fresh hell this is going to generate?" queried A. J.

"We're not charging anything, A. J. And we're doing this in the open with total disclosure, making no claims of a cure. We are treating this as experimental science and the patients are all volunteers. The ball will be back in their court," sighed Genevieve.

THE FRESH HELL would be coming from a meeting with the President and the United States senator from the President's home state of Alabama: Reverend Reggie L. Cobb.

"I told you, Harry, that he would figure out a way to get around your directive. Now we have to deal with the Reverend and he is *not* happy."

"What's new? He's never happy unless it's cocktail hour. Okay, go get

him, lets get this over with."
"Good morning, Senator, it's always a pleasure to see you."
"No, it's not, especially today. Lets get right to it."
"Of course. What's on your mind?"
"You know what's on my mind - that wacko scientist has gone right around your feeble order and is preparing to spread his lies to MILLIONS OF UNINFORMED PEOPLE!

He's claiming that he can cure cancer. He's practicing dangerous medicine and breaking every FDA regulation imaginable and you're not doing a FUCKING THING TO STOP HIM!"

"Don't come in here, Reverend, with your bullshit pulpit speeches. If you wanna talk to me you better have your facts straight. You obviously don't, so let me outline them for you:

One: Neither McCleary or his foundation nor anybody remotely connected to him has claimed that they can cure cancer.

Two: No one has ever died or become ill because of his treatments.

Three: He has disclosed everything about his science and has violated no FDA regulation. That would be like in ZERO. None!

Four: There have been thousands of certified cases where his treatment HAS cured cancers.

Now, what is it that you're really pissed off about, Reverend? Like I don't know. Come on, I want to hear it from you first hand."

"You don't get it, do you, Harry? I DON'T GIVE A DAMN IF HE IS OPERATING WITHIN THE LAW. HE IS NOT OPERATING WITHIN GOD'S LAW! You have to use your powers to stop him.

Don't you realize that millions of people will be storing their life's energy information in their computers and after they die, other people will send those frequencies out into space to contact them! If they're successful they will claim that there IS NO HEAVEN OR HELL and life goes on somewhere in the UNIVERSE. Can't you see the threat to the teachings of Christ!"

"McCleary is not making those statements, Reverend!"
"It doesn't matter. Somebody is and that bastard is providing the means for them to carry out their blasphemy!"

"I represent all the people of our country, Reverend, not just the extreme religious right!"

"Oh, so you want to talk politics. The off-year elections are coming up and, if you keep treating us like obsessive fools, we will support WHOEVER YOU DON'T SUPPORT, regardless of party. And if you think

that YOU have a chance to be re-elected without us, YOU ARE WRONG! I'm done talking to you, Mr. President, but we will be watching!"
And with that he stormed out of the Presidents office.

"Okay, Bud, get them in here. We can't let this get away from us." His circle of political advisors were assembled and the President outlined the problem for them and asked for options.

"Just let him and his extremist following go, Harry. We can't govern from that base."

"We lose their vote and we won't be governing at all," came a reply.

"Look, we will never satisfy him but we might be able to mollify him some and still keep our credibility with the rest of the electorate."

"How so, Louisa?" asked the President.

Louisa Lambros was the only woman in the President's inner circle.

"We don't back down on the directive. We let our global trade partners know that we would consider it interfering with our internal affairs if they allow people from their countries to download the objectionable frequency information and make it available to our citizens, either directly or indirectly. Severe trade sanctions should be the penalty."

"Okay. That would mollify the Reverend and his crowd, but what about the rest of the electorate and countries that don't agree with us?"

Louisa answered: "We let those countries know that we have no objections to that kind of treatment for cancer in their countries; we just don't want them to send it to us. Then we go on a lobbying campaign championing McCleary's right to do research on the subject. We make it clear, though, that we will not jeopardize the health of our citizens by sanctioning untested science. We will demand a ten year study on treatments using personal computer programs. The essence of the campaign is the protection of our citizens' health. And we will be out of office before the ten years are up."

"THAT'S IT, LOUISA! That's exactly how we should handle it. That's the way I've always wanted it. We won't need executive orders or legislation and there are no first amendment problems. Perfect! Okay, get the wheels going; we've got to stay in front of this thing!"

Countries around the world had no problem complying with the United State's demands. The electromagnetic cancer treatments would still be available to their citizens and the denial of the treatments to Americans was an American problem. It wasn't worth the risk of losing such an important trade partner.

Touché, Mr. President, touché.

Chapter 73: Wreckers Rocks

DANELLA HAD VISITORS - agents from Canada's Department of Commerce. They politely informed her that she and the foundation's services were welcome in their country but they could not export their work to the U.S. She knew they were coming and was not angry.

Becky had arrived that morning; together they would be training Quebec City lab researchers in the resonation procedures. Big Huey was sold to them and the foundation would soon be out of business in Canada.

"Well, Beck, nobody can say we weren't successful. This thing is taking off everywhere but in the U.S. You guys should feel proud. Look at all the lives you've saved and are saving every day."

"At first I was majorly pissed; but, you know, we did our part. We started this thing and someone else can go forward with it. Now there are research centers all over the world that know as much about this as we do. Besides, I need a change. How about you?"

"I love it here, Beck, but I'm restless. Jessica has invited me to visit her in Hollywood and I think I'll go. Monica wants me to do some screen tests. I used to act a lot in college, I enjoyed it. Well, I'll see what happens."

A. J. has already made it happen, Baby Girl, Becky thought to herself.

"Has A. J. said what he's going to do?"

"No, he hasn't, but he has been getting personally involved with Genevieve's operation and she says they're making barrels of money again. And he's taking flying lessons."

"Flying lessons. Why doesn't that surprise me?"

"He's not happy with the situation in our country. He had a long talk with Diane and I could tell that it really upset him. He won't quit, Danella, not him. Be ready; he might need us."

"Beck, I'd drop everything if he needs me."

"I know you would... so would I."

"OKAY, YOU'RE BOOKED one way into Quito and your appointment with Ecuador's international attorneys is set for the day after tomorrow. I've downloaded all the information concerning that pile of rocks off their coast that you're interested in. Have a good time and don't drink the water."

"Thanks, Gen," he smiled. "I'll keep you posted on my travels - and don't use my Power of Attorney to empty our accounts."

"Shit, I thought that you had forgotten about that."

He was in downtown Quito, the capital of Ecuador, sitting in the law office of the attorneys who handled state affairs for the country.

One of them was an old acquaintance from his Geneva days. "You still serving on the WTO, René?"
"No, A. J. They made me stay home. How about you? Still practicing law?"
"Occasionally, but usually representing myself, like now."
"Yes, so we were told. You're interested in purchasing some government property?"
"Maybe. There is a group of volcanic spires located about four hundred miles northwest off your coast in the middle of the Pacific. But it appears that both you and Columbia are laying claim to it. I'm not sure who I should be dealing with - you or them."
"You must be talking about 'Wreckers Rocks'. It's appropriately named - dangerous and worthless. Neither country wants it - too much liability - but we want the other to buy it so nothing gets done."
"I could be interested but only if it was ceded to me. Can you confer with Columbia and see if we can work something out? I'll pay a fair price but you're not selling a tropical paradise."
"No, that's for sure," he chuckled. "What are you going to do with it? Nobody has yet come up with a good idea."
"I'm not sure. Which brings me to my next question: I'm going to need the name of some construction engineers who know how to blast through rock. Their advice should help me decide if my ideas are feasible or not. Any suggestions?"
"Well, there are several. The National Excavation and Tunneling Engineers, 'Nettie', is well known and competent. The government gives them a lot of their work. They will tell you what you need to know but there are others."
"Nettie?"
"Yeah, that's how they refer to themselves. They're out of Guayaquil."
"Okay, I'll look them up. I like the name. Here's where I can be reached; maybe I can take Wreckers Rocks off of both your hands."
Guayaquil was a port city with a heavy industrial influence. A. J. located the excavation company and made an appointment to see Miguel Lopez, the head engineer. Their office complex was near the port. It was large and not particularly attractive. That's okay, thought A. J., they're engineers not architects.
He walked into the main office and introduced himself.
"Yes, Mr. McCleary. Mr. Lopez is expecting you. I'll tell him you're here."
"That was Maria. The American is up front," said Lopez taking the message from the receptionist. "You still want to see him alone?"
"Yes, Miguel, tell her to send him back."
A. J. followed Maria's directions and walked into the engineer's open office. He was greeted there by Carlos Marcos.
"Hello Sean, I thought it was you."

At first A. J. couldn't place him. He hadn't seen him since he was a kid. Carlos was one of the lucky ones who never seemed to age. A. J. remembered him.

"Carlos... I had no idea. I selected your Company because I liked the name. I might have guessed."

Carlos extended his hand.

"Yes, I have to admit I made the initials of my company's name fit as close as I could to the spelling of Nettie."

"I didn't know you were an engineer..."

"Yeah, my first profession. That's how I made enough money to get into my second profession. Hey, before I forget, you did a hell of a job with my property."

"You've seen it?"

"I was at the premiere, Sean. I stayed out of sight."

"Really. How fitting that you were there. You would have been welcome, Carlos."

"I'm not so sure. A lot of people think I started that war and I guess I did. I was trying to get rid of those guys, Sean. Yeah, for me personally, but I also hated that life. You did it right, Sean. I was in it for the money. Look, I stay connected. I heard about Enrico: that son-of-a-bitch would have taken me out too. I want to thank you for that; you cleaned up some unfinished business for me."

"Not me, Carlos. It was Big George. He found the bomb and that gave the police the ability and time to corner those guys. He was your man, Carlos, so in a strange way you took care of your own business."

"Okay, never thought about it like that, but, okay I feel better."

"Sean, or should I call you A. J.?"

"I prefer A. J. Sean's only for my sisters."

"All right, A. J. I really loved her, you know. She was the only woman I ever loved."

There was an uncomfortable silence, then A. J. said,

"I was only a kid, Carlos, but I'm sure she had strong feelings for you too."

"You... you've no idea how good that makes me feel. That was a nice thing to say."

"You did some nice things for us, too. Hey, your computer is at Ma's house."

"Yeah, I know. I saw it.

All right, you didn't come here to find *me*. What do you need, A. J.?"

"You ever hear of Wreckers Rocks?"

"Sure have! I'm quite familiar with them. Ah, some of my old acquaintances from Columbia had their eyes on it for their... shall we say nefarious enterprises? It's perfectly located for their activity - out of the way yet close enough to their base of operation. You going into the dope business, A. J.?"

"No, I'm not," he laughed, "but I *am* interested in purchasing those rocks. I take it your friends didn't settle there?"

"Hell, no. It was too dangerous even for them. Impossible place to build a sea base. They don't call it Wreckers Rocks for nothing. Here, let me show you. They commissioned me to do some preliminary surveying; I still have the drawings. Here they are."

He pulled some engineering plans out of a file cabinet and spread them on a drawing board.

"All of this was done with the benefit of satellite images. It even measured the depth of the water surrounding the rocks. They're not really rocks but the tops of volcanic spires; they rise hundreds of feet above sea level and run straight down into the water, perfectly smooth and impossible to scale."

"Yes, I was able to google some of that information. That's how I found them."

"From the air they look harmless enough because you see only the high tops of those mountains or spires, but in between those ranges are lower spires just below the water making all the surrounding area completely un-navigable.

Notice there are three separate ranges, all about a half mile long and maybe a couple hundred yards wide. They are perfectly straight, running north by north east and parallel each other. The waters running between them are both about seventy five yards wide. The center range is taller than the other two. It would make for a perfect port in the storm if you could sail into either one of those channels. But you can't, as I said. They're filled with the unseen tops of those lower spires. This place is totally uninhabitable and has no value."

"Let me ask you, Carlos, from an engineering perspective: is it possible to dam up one of those channels at both ends and pump out the water?"

"Yes, I suppose you could..."

"Would it also be possible to break up the rocks that block the other channel and dredge it, dumping the debris into the dammed up lane?"

"WHOA! I see where you're going. You could create a land base between two of those ranges and build a navigable port through the other! Jesus Christ, everybody's been thinking too small! That could work! Damn! We could blast a tunnel through the center range to connect everything by land!"

"Yeah, that's kinda how I saw it but wasn't sure if it was an engineering possibility."

"It sure as hell is. Look, the end of that northern channel has little coves running all through it. If we dam it properly and do some digging, we could build a basin that would trap all the rain water coming off those spires and make a lake! You would have all the drinking water you'd ever need. It rains barrels year around here. And if we place wind mills in between those jagged spires, we could have power! It would be beautiful - those coves are full of little grottos. That's why the green vegetation shows up on the photos!"

"You're more excited than I am, Carlos."

"Are you kidding? I love this kind of stuff. How did you see all this?"

"I don't know. Things like that sometimes just pop into my head."

"I'll tell you something else, A. J. It won't be as expensive to do as you might think. Dredging solves a very big and costly fill problem. We've got explosives today that we never had before which will also save a lot of money. We can easily reduce those lower spires into small particles and it'll be no trouble blasting a tunnel. That center range does have its narrow spots and we can use the tunnel to transfer the debris. The real work is building those dams to withstand seepage from the pounding of surf and from hurricanes. Hurricanes. That is always the drawback in ocean construction but your land mass will be protected on all sides. Unbelievable.

A. J., have you talked to the governments? Can you buy this collection of worthless rocks?"

"I think I will be able to deal with Ecuador; I don't know about Columbia. Those countries have a dispute going over ownership."

"Yeah, I found that out. If you have a problem with Columbia I may be of some service." A. J. raised his eyebrows but knew better than to ask.

"I do see one problem. My former friends would be drooling if they thought they could work out of the Wreckers. It could get dangerous."

"That's one of the things I would want to talk about with the Columbians. I suspect that their sea patrol police would be drooling also."

Carlos rubbed his hands together. "I'm really starting to love this. You would be building a little nation, A. J."

"That's what this is all about, Carlos."

"Hell, you don't fool around do you? Should I go to work and give you specifics and cost estimates?"

"Yes, the sooner the better."

"I'll give you every break I can. I love what you did for the Zone, Mr. McCleary. I wish I could have… had that kind of vision."

They shook hands warmly.

Chapter 74: Esperanza

COLUMBIA WAS THE PROBLEM. They were willing to sell their interest to Wreckers but not cede the property to A. J. Ecuador agreed to do both. Columbia wanted to maintain jurisdictional control which was objectionable to A. J. and a potential deal breaker. As an International attorney, A. J. knew that neither country could sustain a real legal claim to the area and he could file his own claim. The international waters were owned by no one. He let both sides know that that was an option open to him.

It was time to seek Carlos' help with the Columbians.

The three parties held another meeting. The Columbians spoke: "Mr. McCleary, we will only agree to cede our interest to you if you agree to build us a port for our small police fleet and enter into an agreement for our right to dock there at no charge and in perpetuity."

"I will agree to that if Columbia would extend its security protection to my property and my people. An International document can be drawn up at a future date. In the meantime, if I or my assigns don't perform as agreed to, then our contracts will become null and void and I will cede the property back to both countries."

The agreement was acceptable to all parties and A. J. became the owner of a pile of rocks located somewhere in the Pacific with no country having a claim to them. He never knew and never asked Carlos what he did to change the minds of the Columbians.

Carlos' land planners went to work on the design of the project. It would include elevated sites near the lake where buildings could be constructed. He immediately put his architects to work designing the foundation's new research lab according to A. J.'s specifications.

Two ports were planned: one for the Columbians and, on the opposite side in front of the tunnel, one for the foundation's use. The development included a hydrology system and sanitation facility. A powerful series of antennae would be installed high in the narrow mountainous spires. The plan also provided for an air strip big enough to handle a small Lear. Other improvements would be made as they progressed into the project. Construction was about to begin.

.

A. J. WAS TREATING Becky, Genevieve and Steve to dinner in a cozy Georgetown restaurant.

"What? Would you like to repeat that? I thought I heard you say you were going to declare your pile of rocks a nation! Did you ladies hear the same thing?"

"We did, but we're waiting for the punch line."

"Well, I don't think it's a punch line, but here it is: Carlos Marcos is going to convert those pile of rocks into a defined territory for me."
"That may not be a punch line but it's one of the funniest things I've ever heard," roared Steve.
"A. J.! You *did* drink the water," laughed Genevieve.
"We only know that Carlos guy through the movie; I thought Monica just made him up," added Becky.
"You're not going to think she made him up when I show you the plans for the new research lab he's having built for us, Beck."
"Holy shit, I think he's serious, guys. I'm getting nervous."
"Wait a minute, just a second. Seems to me I read in the case files somewhere that Marcos used to be an engineer... and he does live in Ecuador. You want to tell us about this, A. J.?" asked Steve.
After a brief recapitulation of the events, the three of them sat there dumbfounded.
"Aren't you supposed to have a government or an army or something to be a nation?" asked Genevieve.
"Not really. Anybody can declare themselves a country at any time. The hard part is to be taken seriously, like I'm finding out right now."
"Hold it, my disbelieving friends. I think I'm beginning to see a method to his madness," said a suddenly alert Becky. "As a nation our friend the President has no legal control over us. We can download our brains out over the internet and send it to the U.S. and there's not one thing he could do about it!"
"The thought did cross my mind," grinned A. J.
"That would be a start for serious consideration, don't you think? Also, I expect declarations of support from the countries we've been working with, which will give us recognition and credibility. Not to mention the treaties I'll be signing with Columbia and Ecuador. The only ones who would be interfering with the internal affairs of the U.S. is us and we don't give a damn about trade sanctions."
"Ah, he could declare war on you," said a half serious Steve.
"True, but I think many of our new brother nations might reverse those trade sanction threats. Huh? What do you think?"
"I think you're fucking crazy," hooted Becky. "But do I love it!"
"It might just work." Gen put down her wineglass and looked up at A. J. "It might just work!"
"It *will* work, Gen. Now I want you to get me an appointment to address my friends at The World Health Organization in Geneva. That's where we will introduce to the world the latest member of the family of nations."

"HERE. OVER HERE, A. J.!" She-lagh shouted as he left the gate area at the Geneva Airport.

A. J. spotted her and rushed over.
"Look at you! You're as gorgeous as I remembered," he said, nearly lifting her off of her feet with his exuberant embrace.

"Well, if you would visit me more often you wouldn't have to remember!" she snickered.
"Hurry. Go collect your things. I've got a great new place to take you for dinner. I can't wait to hear first hand about your adventures."
"Yes, and I can't wait to hear what's going on in your life, too. Can I drive?
"NO!"

It was a wonderful reunion, two old friends catching up on each other's lives. They were celebrating: A. J. drank a second glass of German beer while She-lagh quaffed a demi bottle of champagne. They were too busy enjoying each other's company to think about eating.

"I read Monica's book, A. J. and the movie finally got to Europe. I saw it last month in Paris. You must tell me now. Was all that true?"
"Every bit of it, She. Every bit of it."
"Damn. You weren't kidding about those scars, how awful," she sighed taking his hand.

They met for breakfast the following morning at their favorite place down by Geneva Bay, close to where A. J. used to live.
"So, you're going to make more headlines tomorrow at the World Health Organization."
"Well, we will see. Their Assembly meets every May to set up their agenda. I called in a few favors and asked if I could give a brief address to their members. They're interested and mostly support what we've been doing. I think they're curious about what we're going to do next."
"Yeah, well, you won't be disappointing them, that's for sure."

A. J. WAS A familiar face and the members gave him a warm reception.
"Thank you, and thanks for allowing me to address you here today." He smiled as he looked down at the assembled members.
"I see a lot of old friends out there. It's good to be back. Earlier I had the opportunity to talk to a few of you and it was comforting to know that you have been following the work of the Brandon Foundation.
We have our troubles. And I know you share in my sorrow for the lives lost in the bombing of the French electromagnetic research lab." He paused as the members murmured their acknowledgement.

"It's because of the tragedy and because of the resistance to our method of cancer treatment in my country, that I asked to address you today. I felt that The World Health Organization was the perfect forum for an announcement I wish to make."

He paused for several seconds and said:

"Members of this Assembly and all the people who share life on this planet, I wish to announce and declare that the Brandon Foundation has formed a new nation state."

That got their complete attention and they mumbled to each other.

"The Brandon Foundation shares the same health goals as those represented by this great assembly. But for us to carry out our research programs and treatments for cancer and other diseases and inflictions, we needed to find a new home - a place that would pose no unreasonable restrictions and would not endanger the lives of those working for us." There was a smattering of applause.

"Our new nation, appropriately named Esperanza, has been formed solely for the advancement of world-wide health."

He looked at his rapt audience:

"*Esperanza... Hope.* No other business will be conducted there. Esperanza will be governed by the Brandon Foundation through its directors and trustees.

This new micro-nation has a defined territory; it's all laid out for you on their web site. The territory will be complete with research buildings and living quarters for technicians and guests. It will have an airport and a navigable sea port. The country is located in the Pacific Ocean, about four hundred miles off the coast of South America. Title to this Pacific Island was ceded to our new nation by the countries of Columbia and Ecuador, and soon Esperanza will be entering into legal treaties with those two countries."

The members were beginning to grasp the reality of what they were hearing and many were nodding their heads in acknowledgement.

"Esperanza is unique because it is now the largest country in the world. You see, its citizens include every human being on this planet because that's who we represent in our quest to cure cancers and other diseases and we shall never stop in our efforts to do so. I will be sending official notices to all nations announcing the existence of our new country. We will be asking for recognition and support. Thank you for allowing us to start here. Our new nation would humbly accept your invitation for membership in the World Health Organization. Esperanza looks forward to the same fair and honest support you have given me in the past and I thank you again for allowing me to take up your valuable time. Good afternoon."

A. J. left the podium to a polite but energetic applause from the stunned members. They were not quite sure how to respond.

THE LEADERS ON Pennsylvania Avenue were not sure how to respond either.

"Well, Louisa, any suggestions?" asked the President.

"Yes, we should be the first to recognize Esperanza."
"What? Do you have any idea what the Reverend will do?" cried one of the advisors.
"Isn't anybody else as fed up with the Reverend as I am?" answered Louisa. "Who the hell is running this country anyway? Him or us?

The truth is, gentlemen, there is not a damn thing we can do, short of closing the internet to McCleary and that is in violation of everything this country stands for. Further, if we try to bully our friends for recognizing Esperanza, they will be sanctioning us! Those countries would have done nothing to interfere with our internal affairs. Let's show the world how gracious and democratic we are and let's be the first to recognize the new nation!"

The President had his hand over his eyes and was laughing.
"What the hell is so funny?" asked an annoyed Bud Adams.
"That guy has made us all look like fools. He formed his own country for Christ sakes! Who would have guessed *that*? I give up." And he laughed even harder.

"Check and checkmate, Dr. McCleary! Boy, would I like to meet this man. Louisa, we will not oppose him but we can't recognize their little nation either. We still have elections to win," he was still snickering.

ESPERANZA WAS receiving polite congratulations but no formal recognition from the important nation states. Most countries were waiting to see what the U.S. and their closest allies would do.

Columbia and Ecuador were not waiting. Now that Esperanza had declared themselves a nation, those two countries wanted to shore up their vested interest by entering into treaties with the new micro-nation. Columbia had a military interest and Ecuador wanted to provide the Galapagos with a place to harbor their ships during storms. That group of islands, owned by Ecuador, was only one hundred miles from Esperanza. Both countries also wanted health services that the foundation could provide.

Treaties were drawn up and signed and Esperanza became a recognized sovereign state in the family of nations. Their right to exist was legitimate and they could not be treated by foreign powers as a rogue state.

A. J., as chairman of the board of trustees of the Brandon Foundation, signed the documents as head of the de facto government of Esperanza. The protocol was now established and smaller states who had been receptive to the foundation's work in the past announced their recognition of the new nation.

In his first statement to all nations, A. J. thanked those countries that recognized Esperanza but made it clear that the new nation was not seeking a place in world government, membership in the U.N. or any other organization considered political. Their affairs would be limited to the betterment of world health. This won him more friends.

"GOOD MORNING, BABY GIRL. How's Hollywood's latest star?"
"Geez, a call from a president of a nation. Do I refer to you as Mr. President, His Excellency, or what?" she teased.
"Be careful or I'll send you to work with that under secretary of Iran!"
"You do that and Iran will have to declare war on Esperanza," she giggled.
"Oh no! We don't have any troops except for Becky, so I guess that will even the sides."
"Yup, that would."

"Okay, Skeet tells me that you tested out great and they want you to play the congresswoman, but you're dragging your feet. What's going on? Before you answer, I had nothing to do with Skeet's offer. I made it clear that we would give you the opportunity but you would have to make it on your own from there."

"Yes, and thanks A. J. You knew I wouldn't have it any other way; I really do appreciate it."
"But... but, I sense a but here."
"I like the work but not the lifestyle. Wylie has been introducing me to Hollywood. I love her and she means well... Her fans worship her, A. J., and the men... God, she can have anybody she wants! That's way too much distraction for me. The work has real substance but that glamour part is so shallow. I don't like it and I never did but it's a necessary part of the profession. I can't do it, A. J. Are you going to be taking applications when the new lab opens up?"

"Yours is already on file," he quipped, "but we are making plans. We never should have sold Big Huey."
"Oh, I want to help, A. J. Please."
"You know you're welcome anytime you want to come back, Danella. Think about it for a few days then we'll talk some more."
"It'll be a waste of time. Take me back now or I'll go to work as a car hop!"
"Car hop? Do they still have those?"
"No. See, now what am I going to do?"
He sighed and said, "You're going to come here to Washington, Baby Girl, but *you're* telling Skeet, not me."
"Oh, thank you, thank you, and yes I will tell her. It's the least I could do. Hey, I want to be Secretary of State!"

ESPERANZA'S FIRST cabinet meeting was held in A. J.'s hotel room.

Its ministers were squabbling over cabinet appointments. Becky dug in her heels; she wanted to be Secretary of Defense and was googling tanks. Genevieve refused to be Attorney General; she said she hated law. And so it went. Esperanza was off to a rough start.

"Okay," laughed A. J., "now that we have all cabinet positions settled, here's our first order of business: France wants to recognize us but they want to set up some form of diplomatic protocol first. Absurd, but that's what they want. So I'm sending our Secretary of State, Madam Secretary Baby Girl to Paris."

"What? A. J., I was only joking around. I don't know anything about those things."

"Sorry. You're the only one who speaks French. Find out what they have in mind and I'll join you for whatever formal ceremony they're planning. Seriously, I know a little about world politics and countries will be looking to see if they can use us to their advantage. We'll be fine as long as we stay clear of all politics. We want to be everybody's friend so we can do our work. A lot of people are terminally ill in our country and we must help them. We have to get that lab up and running as quickly as possible, so we will play whatever the game calls for to gain recognition and credibility."

DANELLA WAS dispatched to Paris on her first diplomatic assignment. She was as dazzling there as she had been in New York. The people of Paris knew of her French roots and accepted her as one of their own. She suspected that the French were using Esperanza to gain some sort of diplomatic advantage but it made no difference; it worked to their advantage also. For one with no experience, she skillfully maneuvered her way through the diplomatic channels and an immediate date was set for the formal recognition of Esperanza.

She was staying at a midsize Paris hotel and had already booked A. J. into a suite. He arrived on the late flight and left a message for her to meet him in the lobby in the morning.

Danella sat on one of the lobby's plush sofas checking her phone messages as she waited for A. J. It was early and, other than some delivery men going about their business, there were few people in the lobby. Many of the guests had checked out the day before. Seeing him approach, she stood up sliding her phone into her purse.

Smiling, he said, "Good morning, Madame Secretary." He suddenly came to an abrupt stop and his smile turned into a look of horror.

"I CAN HEAR IT... NO…!" He charged over and in one motion picked Danella up and slammed her onto the couch falling on top of her.

Their senses went dead. They neither heard nor saw nor felt anything. There was only darkness.

Chapter 75: The Lady In Red

THE BLAST WAS heard all over Paris. The shrieking of sirens pierced the ears of early rising Parisians. First responders stood numbly, looking at the pile of rubble that used to be the hotel entrance. The entire front of the building had disappeared; the rest of the three story structure remained standing.

An unmarked police car came screeching to a halt and a man not in uniform bolted out the door. In seconds he was barking out orders and excitedly talking into his cell phone. "I NEED HEAVY EQUIPMENT IN HERE! DOZERS AND CRANES AND TRUCKS. SEND ME ALL THE MEDICAL PEOPLE AVAILABLE. DO IT NOW AND I MEAN NOW!" The paralyzed men on the scene sprang into action.

A. J.'s head was buzzing, his ears were ringing and his breathing was irregular. His mind was whirling as he floated in and out of consciousness. He would become alert and coherent for the briefest of seconds and then spin out into a sea of jumbled thought.

He had lost all sense of time or awareness of the moment but his head was clearing. He struggled to bring his eyes into focus and rapidly blinked, trying to restore his vision. But it remained dark.

He couldn't see her or feel her, but he smelled her. And now he heard soft moaning sounds and then it all came racing back to him.

"Danella! Danella!" His speech was weak and he could barely hear himself speaking. She moaned again...

"Danella, Danella, can you hear me? Can you hear me?"

Her moaning stopped and he could hear her gasping for air. He felt her hair on his face as she turned her head slightly and then he felt her ear lightly pressed against his cheek. A. J.'s mind was now engaged and he realized that he was lying face down on top of her. Their heads were side by side and she lay on her back.

Danella faintly heard him call her name but couldn't answer. She tried to talk but nothing came out.

Automatically her head turned toward the sound of his voice. She couldn't get enough air and felt a heavy pressure on her chest. As Danella struggled to breathe, she heard the voice again.

"Danella, say something, say something. Speak to me!"

She was in a fog but knew the voice. Why is he calling me? Why...?

The fog was clearing. It was dark, so dark, and she didn't know where she was. Why couldn't she breathe? Then fear, terrifying and real...

"Danella... Danella!"

She heard him clearly now. He was close, really close, but she couldn't see him. She answered, "I hear you! Where, where are we? I'm frightened! A. J., where are you? What's happening?"

"Baby Girl, I'm right here next to you. Are you hurt?"
"I can't see anything! I can't breathe! What happened? Where are we? I... I'm so lost...so scared!"

"Listen to me, Danella. Listen. We are under thousands of pounds of rubble. I am lying right on top of you... my head is next to yours. Somehow we survived the blast... Do you understand what I'm saying?" He was talking in a half whisper being so close to her ear.

She heard the words but her mind was slow to comprehend. The darkness, her difficulty breathing... under rubble... the blast. She tried to put it all together.

"Oh, no," she gasped, as realization finally set in.

Hoping she was coherent enough to understand what he was saying, he urgently tried to explain, "There's a lot of weight on you, Danella. That's why you're having trouble breathing. You must take short shallow breaths and try not to struggle. They will find us."

She was quiet for several seconds as her mind took it all in. Then, speaking in a shaky and barely audible voice, she said,
"I won't panic, A. J. I won't."
"I know you won't. Danella, see if you can move your feet, your arms, your hands, anything."
She tried. "I can move everything except my body. I feel pinned down but I don't feel any pain. It's just hard for me to breathe. What... what about you? You don't sound right." she panted.

Ignoring the question, A. J. half whispered, "You *are* pinned down. Can you see anything? Any movement?"
"No, it's so dark, so dark."
"Don't just look up. Look down towards your feet, to your side. Look everywhere!" he implored.

"Okay. By my feet, I see... I see a different shade...ah, ah, a gray color. Yes, I'm not imagining it." Her eyes were beginning to adjust to the darkness.
"It's light creeping in from somewhere. Look carefully into that area. Is anything moving?"
"Yes, I can see particles floating. Yes, A. J. that's what they are, tiny particles!"

"Thank god. Air is coming in. There must be holes somewhere. We are not going to suffocate. Are you sure you're not in any pain?"
"No, no pain, just pressure on my chest. A. J., I can smell leather when I turn my head away from you. It's the couch. We're lying on the couch; it's cushioning us!"
"How close is that lighter shaded area to your feet? Is it on an angle?"
"It seems like it's just above my feet and yes, it's... slanting, like I'm looking through a crooked window!"

A chunk of concrete must have bridged the couch and created a pocket over us, he thought.

"A. J., can… can you raise yourself off me a little?"

Again ignoring her, he said, "Danella, can you feel where your purse is?"

"Yes, it's half underneath me but I think I can reach it."

"Good." he was speaking more slowly now. "See if you... can get into it … and find your cell phone."

It was a long stretch but she was able to tug on the strap enough to allow her to reach inside.

"I've got it, A. J. I've got it!"

"Can you bring it to your ear?"

"Yes, I think so. Yes, yes I can."

"Punch… Punch out the emergency code, Baby Girl. Tell whoever answers that we are alive and give them the location... of this couch... If you can get through... we'll keep the line open." His speech was getting weaker.

She was successful. They had provided a means for their own rescue.

"Danella, I'm numb from my neck down... no feeling... I can't move. Try to reach up and feel if there is anything on top of me." She ran her hand over his back and hit something solid.

"Oh my god! There's a block or something on the middle of your back! I can feel it but I can't move it. Oh no, oh no!"

"No, don't try to move it. I...I'm going to have to leave you for a while I must go... inside…" His voice trailed off.

"No, don't go! Don't go! A. J., talk to me, talk to me!"

He didn't respond. She was alone in the dark and terrified.

Trying desperately to avoid panicking she remembered the phone.

"Are you still there? Answer, please answer."

"Yes, I'm still here and we are coming for you. We've got excavation experts on site. They've started to dig. They need to go slowly; there are others to worry about. Are you still okay?"

"No, no, I think he's hurt badly. It's his back. He has no feeling. Hurry, hurry, please hurry!"

The cushioning of the couch was saving them. It released the compression of his body on hers and prevented him from being crushed from the top. She was in extreme discomfort from his weight but it was manageable. What was not manageable was the loss of his presence. She did not know what he meant by going inside and she was confused and frightened.

It seemed like an eternity but was actually only minutes.

"Danella, are you… you still with me?" he whispered.

"No, I stepped out for a drink." It was a joke generated by fear, anxiety, and concern for him.

"Of course I'm still here and don't leave me again. I'm scared, A. J.," she sobbed. "It's dark and I thought that you died and didn't take me with you! Where did you go?"

"I'm sorry, Danella. Tell them, tell them when they come, that… that the damage is in the cervical and lumbar region and that it's severe… and I'm losing fluids. I've slowed it down but it's a long-shot."

"What are you saying? What do you mean a long-shot? No, no, you're walking out of here with me and that's all there is to it."

"Danella…"

"No, don't argue with me," she sobbed. "You're not going to leave me, not now!"

Suddenly she was alert, "Listen. Did you hear that? Did you hear that noise?"

"Yes. Yes, I did. They're digging for us, Baby Girl. They're… They're right on top of us. They will have you out of here in no time."

"They will have *us* out of here in no time, A. J. *Us*!"

"Okay, *us*," he whispered.

"Listen to me for a second. There's something I want to tell you."

"I'm listening, just don't tell me something I don't want to hear."

"I don't think that I'm going make it… and even if I do… there won't be much left of me."

"NO. I told you not to tell me those things!"

"All right. But if I don't… I really didn't want to treat you as a sister. You were the lady in red… I knew, I just knew."

He was breathing heavily now and could barely whisper,

"I have to go back inside."

Chapter 76: Did You Say Lucky

THE PARAMEDICS WHEELED A. J. to the waiting medivac. He lay face down on the gurney. Danella walked briskly alongside. She was miraculously unhurt, not a scratch. She had lost a shoe - that was it. They placed him into the van; she jumped in back and they sped off with siren blaring.

There had been a banquet room directly above the lobby on the second level. The concrete floor of the third level dangled over the collapsed lower two levels. The rescue workers correctly assumed that the banquet room was empty of people and there was nobody buried above A. J. and Danella. It made their excavation work go much faster as Danella directed them to their precise location.

A huge part of the floor of the second level had indeed stayed intact and had come to rest on top of the back part of the couch. It had wedged itself between what remained of the wall behind the couch and the floor, creating a slanting protective tent over the two of them as the tons of rubble crashed down. However, a cinderblock-size chunk of concrete had preceded it and smashed into A. J. The tumbling protective tent had pinned it to his back. A. J.'s body had shielded Danella from any falling debris.

They were greeted at the emergency entrance by a flurry of activity. Medical personnel were rushing to help and the alerted members of the media swarmed about with their cameras and recorders.

"MS. FOCHETT, IS HE ALIVE? IS HE ALIVE?"

"DO YOU KNOW WHO'S RESPONSIBLE FOR THIS?"

"IS THIS CONNECTED TO THE OTHER BOMBING?"

She ignored them as they raced inside the ER. Security closed in and blocked the path of the throng of reporters. She was met by a man at the entrance to the O.R.

"Danella, I'm Jean - Pierre Simon, we met in New York at one of the U.N. functions. I was with the French legation. I'm chief of staff and administrator here."

"Yes, I remember. You're a neurologist. They said a team would be waiting!"

"I have them assembled. They're taking him directly to surgery. I will be assisting and I'll keep you apprised."

NERVOUSLY, SHE PACED about the surgical waiting room. Her phone was constantly ringing as word had spread fast on both sides of the Atlantic.

"Jess, I know very little. He was conscious when he went into surgery but was struggling to communicate with the surgeons. No... no, I'm fine, honest. Jess, he said some things when we were trapped that... that frightened me. You know how he is - he's never wrong. I'm scared, Jess. We should be prepared for something awful. Yes, I know, I know he can do miracles but this may be even beyond him. Look, everybody's calling. Can I just give you the updates and you notify the others? Thanks Jess."

Danella had just hung up with Jessica when a call from Steve came in.

"Steve, it's not good. I'm waiting for more information now. I just hung up with Jess. She's going to contact everybody for me but you can call anytime. I'm going to need some help, Steve."

"Danella, I just came out of a meeting with my bosses. Believe it or not, the President is involved. I think he underestimated A. J.'s popularity and is getting a lot of heat from many quarters. He's ordered complete protection for you two and is demanding our presence in France. I immediately volunteered and will be taking the red eye to Paris."

"Thank god. I'm no expert but I don't like the security around here - too many people roaming freely about. I need a friendly face, Steve. I'm not sure who to trust and I'm tired, nervous, and just plain scared."

"Can't imagine why! You've just spent hours buried in rubble for god's sake and now you're standing vigil! Look, I'll be there tomorrow morning. If you can, call me when you have more information. I know you won't do it but try to get some rest."

"Thanks Steve, I feel better already."

Dr. Simon walked solemnly into the waiting area. Danella was immediately on her feet.

"His injuries are horrendous. I don't know why he didn't go into cardiac arrest. It's amazing how stable his vitals are."

"Doctor, please..."

"Yes, of course. He was right. The damage to his spinal cord is in the cervical and the lumbar areas. They've been severed. It's complete."

"What does that mean? What are you saying?" she gasped.

"I'm sorry, Danella. Mr. McCleary is completely paralyzed from the neck down. There's nothing we can do; his condition will never change."

It was too horrible to contemplate. She turned away dazed, trembling, unbelieving.

The doctor droned on, "He has massive vertebrae fractures and bone fragments and splinters. That's what we are working on now, trying to stabilize the spine. He has survived but there are bound to be further complications."

It was like he was giving a battle report to a superior officer; there was no compassion in his voice. He would consider it professional behavior.

"I'm sorry. I will let you know when he's in recovery." He left her alone to deal with her shock and emotions.

She had no idea how long she had been sitting there. The events of the day had finally overwhelmed her. She knew that she should be calling people but couldn't bring herself to do it and only had a vague awareness of the people shuffling in and out of the room.

A young female aide walked slowly up to her.

"Ms. Fochett, I'm sorry to disturb you, but he is in the recovery room - awake and asking for you. Come, I'll show you the way."

At first the words didn't register but the aide stood patiently by waiting for her to respond. "Ms. Fochett, it's just down the hall. I'll take you there."

"What? Oh yes, yes of course, thank you."

A male nurse was tending to him as she entered the room. He recognized her and walked over.

"He's still a little drowsy but he's asking for you. We have him in a special harness. He won't be able to see you but he can hear. Please only a few minutes, Ms. Fochett. Dr. Simon is expecting you in his office. Once Mr. McCleary's settled into a room you will be free to visit."

A. J. lay face down in a special hospital bed. His head was straight and braced into a harness that extended over the bed. His elbows were against his sides with his forearms and hands placed alongside each shoulder.

Choking back tears and with as much strength as she could muster, Danella said, "Well, at least I can see you better. It's brighter in here."

Recognizing her voice he weakly responded. "Danella... did you make it out all right? Are you okay?"

"Thanks to you, yes." Tears streamed down her face. She was glad he couldn't see her.

"They... they said that you were... but I had to hear your voice."

"Listen, they want us to continue our talk up in your room so I'll see you there when you're settled in, okay?" She could barely keep her voice from quivering.

"Okay. Baby Girl... I think I liked it better when you were... underneath me.

"Oh. I know. So did I." She took his hand. He couldn't feel her touch or the tears trickling onto his arm.

She sat passively in Dr. Simon's office, numb, detached and drained.

"We have to keep him completely immobile. We can't take the chance of turning him. He must remain face down for some time. The cervical break occurred below the segments that control breathing; he got lucky there."

"Lucky? Did you say lucky?"

"I'm sorry, bad choice of words, I didn't mean it that way."

She glared at him.

"Look, we are doctors. Our prime concern now is keeping him alive. His condition makes him subject to strokes, deep vein thrombosis, respiratory failures, pneumonia, infections, well, just a lot of things. We can prevent most of that if we catch it early. He will be with us for quite a while. When he's stable, we will bring in the neural therapists, but there is really nothing that they can do. He won't have much of a life."

He had crossed the line. Danella slowly rose fighting to stay in control. "We'll see," she said coldly. "I'll be in his room; I'd appreciate an extra bed placed in there."

"Of course, Ms. Fochett. Of course."

Medical assistants were attending to A. J. and setting up his room when Danella got there. She walked to the visitor waiting area; it was empty and she sat down putting her head in her hands. She gathered herself, took out her cell phone and made the calls she dreaded.

SHE FOLLOWED the attendants as they wheeled an extra bed into A. J.'s private room, stopping at the nurses' station; they were expecting her.

"He's in the last room on the left, Mademoiselle. Here's a pass for you. You can come and go as you please at any time, day or night."

"Thank you."

"He'll be under a mild sedative for the night and he's sleeping now. He's in no pain. Oh, and here's a little cosmetic kit for you - toothbrush, soap, lotion and things like that. There's a private guest bathroom across the hall from Mr. McCleary's room; it has a shower. Just come to the desk for a key. The staff knows who you are and what you've done to help people… We are so sorry." Choking back tears, she came around the desk and gave Danella a hug, "Anything you need, just ask."

She accepted the genuine hug; it was just what she needed.

She hesitated before entering. There was no guard. The staff had completed their work and Danella was alone in the room with A. J. He remained face down in a position that she would see for months to come. His head was cradled in a harness that extended over the bed; it was designed to keep his neck stabilized. Thick padding encircled his entire face from forehead to chin, with an open space for his eyes, nose, and mouth. He could only look straight down. Except for his hair, A. J. was unrecognizable.

Danella stood over him and asked softly if he were awake. There was no response. She had no idea what time it was and only by looking out the window did she know it was late in the evening. The spare bed was positioned next to his and she sat on it for several minutes looking at him. Finally, she lay down on her side facing A. J. and fell asleep.

Chapter 77: The Antichrist

COMING OFF THE red eye, Steve headed straight for the hospital. He checked in at the desk and identified himself. The Agency had notified hospital security that he would be on the scene.

"Yes, Mr. Lowenstein, we have instructions for you to go to security upon your arrival. Their office is at the end of the hall."

He hurried down the hall, saw the police sign on their door and walked in. The head of security was there, apparently waiting for him. Steve introduced himself and could sense that they were not pleased with his presence.

"We can appreciate your country's concern for one of its citizens but we have everything under control and don't need any help," stated the annoyed commander.

Steve replied politely, "I'm not here to help. I've been instructed not to interfere but merely to report on what security precautions have been taken. We understand that you work independently of the police but they have the ultimate jurisdiction."

"Yes, that's correct. We call them if we need them but right now we don't need them," he said airily.

"Well, I'm sure you don't. Tell me, are those TV's close-circuited to Dr. McCleary's room?" He was looking up at the screens behind the officer's head.

"Of course they are. It's part of our security procedures." He was getting angry.

"Then why aren't they turned on?"

"What?" The commander wheeled around and looked at the blank screens. "I don't understand. They were on a minute ago."

"WHAT FLOOR IS HE ON?" demanded Steve.

"The third. But I'm sure he's all right, just some technical difficulty."

Steve tore out of the room. The stairs were at the end of the hall and he bounded up them taking two at a time.

Danella had just left the restroom and noticed that A. J.'s door was closed. She thought that was strange because all the nursing work had been completed earlier. Thinking that it was closed for privacy, she tip-toed in. A man stood at the foot of the bed with his back to her. He was reaching into a black bag and did not hear her approach. He pulled out an instrument and was attaching something to the end of it.

"What is that for?" asked Danella, concerned.

Startled, he quickly turned about to face her, still fiddling with the instrument. Then she saw what it was.

"YOU BASTARD!" she screamed.

Something clicked on the gun and the man swung the muzzle with the silencer attached towards her. She was on him before he could bring it completely around. Danella kicked him hard in the groin sending him to the floor crying out in agony. The gun flew into the air and landed behind him. Instinctively, she ran over and picked it up just as another man came racing into the room.

She was wide eyed and with her face contorted in anger she pointed the weapon at the attacker…

"NO, DANELLA, NO!"

The other man grabbed its barrel.

She was enraged and flailed at the man, kicking and biting him. He pulled the gun out of her hand just as the attacker was getting up. Steve hit him behind his ear with the butt of the gun and knocked him cold. Then the room was filled with uniformed security personal.

"Danella, Danella, what's happening?" It was A. J. struggling to speak louder.

Steve had her by the arm, "It's okay, it's okay. Go to A. J."

Still wide eyed and combative, she first looked at the man lying on the floor with his head bleeding, then to Steve, then to A. J., then back to Steve.

"STEVE, HE WAS GOING TO SHOOT A. J.!"

"I know. Tend to A. J."

She went to his bedside, "A. J., we had an… intruder. Steve's here, he removed him. It's all right."

"You could have been killed, Danella. I heard."

They were standing by the nurses' station. Steve was furious and on his cell phone talking to his counterpart in Interpol.

"Francois, they didn't even have a guard by the room, the incompetent bastards! The FUCKING GUY JUST WALKED RIGHT IN! Yes, I've got the weapon. They won't get their hands on it, but you better get the National Police over here right away before they LET THIS GUY JUST WALK RIGHT *OUT*! Call the locals. I don't want any trouble with them."

"That wasn't necessary, Mr. Lowenstein. We will take it from here and get the man into proper custody."

"Who the hell are you? And he won't be turned over to anybody except your National Police!"

"I'm Dr. Simon and I'm in charge here!"

"Nice to meet you doctor, now I know WHO TO BLAME FOR THIS INCREDIBLE STUPIDITY!"

The National Police arrived a few minutes later and took over the crime scene. They removed the assailant and professionally safeguarded the weapon for evidential purposes. The police assured Steve that they would fully cooperate with the U.S. investigating agencies.

A full time guard would now be posted and security would be handled by real police not the feeble hospital security force.

Satisfied, but still upset, Steve returned to A. J.'s room. Danella had pulled up a chair next to A. J.'s bed and was talking softly to him.

"Here's Steve, A. J. I know he's anxious to talk to you."

He knelt down next to Danella near A. J.'s head.

Steve took a deep breath, slowly exhaled and said, "Hey partner, what's with you and bombs, from Pakistan to Paris for Christ sakes."

"Well this time they got me." His voice was stronger and he was alert but still very weak. "At least I'm still breathing and talking. Thanks for collaring him, Steve. That was close."

"A. J.! Danella had him on the floor and was about to put a hole in him before I even got there!"

"Oh, you didn't tell me about that, Baby Girl. Steve, you gotta get her out of here..."

"Like hell. I'm not going anywhere. End of discussion."

"I don't think I would argue with her, A. J. I've got bumps all over my legs and I think I need a tetanus shot," he snickered looking at his bloody hand.

"Oh, oh, Steve, did I do that? Geez, I don't remember. It happened so fast... I was just reacting. I'm so sorry."

"Yeah, well I got off easy. I was right behind you. I saw how fast you put him down. Where did you get your combat training?"

"Okay, you two, you can fill me in later. I'm only good for short bursts but I will get stronger. I know what to do."

"Oh, sure. You get some rest but I'm going to get both of you out of here. In the meantime you will be under guard around the clock."

"Thanks, Steve." His voice trailed off... "Did she really bite you?"

A. J. HAD fallen asleep. Attendants came in and out continually checking his vitals and drip bags. "You've had a hell of a couple of days, Danella. You sure didn't need this morning's adventure. Are you going to be all right?"

"Are *YOU* going to be all right? Here, let me see that hand. Yikes!"

"All in the job. Come on, level with me: how are you? Honestly."

"I'll be fine, Steve. I don't know why but this morning's trauma hasn't upset me. It was almost cathartic. I can't explain. But I was sickened about what that creep was going to do. I'm worried, Steve."

"Me too. Tell me, how well do you know that Dr. Simon?"

"Not well, but I don't like him. I do know that he is a highly regarded neurologist, one of the best. We probably couldn't do any better so my personal opinion of him doesn't matter."

"Yes, it does. Look, I just got a call from my friends at Interpol. They really have something to work from now - a suspect in custody and a weapon. Also surveillance cameras caught some delivery guys leaving the hotel just before the blast. No employer recognized them. Do you remember seeing anyone in white uniforms?"

"Geez, Steve, I don't know. I wasn't paying much attention."

"Sure, don't think about it now. They also suspect our gunman is a followup - to finish the job. They didn't elaborate but they suggested that we move A. J. as soon as possible. That usually means that if his whereabouts is public knowledge, he is in danger and should be secluded."

"I don't think he's in any condition to move, Steve."

"Probably not. I'll have to talk to the good doctor and see what he says."

"Absolutely not!" is what the doctor said from behind his office desk. "Don't you understand that he is just two days from an extraordinary debilitative traumatic experience? His neurons leading to all body functions have been short circuited and he is having trouble controlling heart rate, blood pressure and body temperature. And other problems. He needs twenty-four hour care to help stabilize things. A sudden move now could kill him!"

"Look," countered Steve, "If he isn't given maximum protection that only seclusion can provide, something else is going to kill him."

"I understand your security concerns given our poor performance, but with the help of the National Police, we will be able to protect him from loose gunmen."

Not from planted bombs, Steve thought, but no need to raise that issue.

"And besides, he has another problem that must be treated here. He has a leak in spinal fluids that has not sealed itself. He needs special therapy that involves injections. I am an expert at that treatment and will handle the procedure myself. No, monsieur, you can't move him until he is stabilized."

Steve reported back to Danella: "He has made a strong non-rebuttable argument. A. J. is not leaving here, at least not in the near future."

"Not so bad, Steve. The staff here is excellent and they confirm that we've got the best in Dr. Simon."

"Yeah, I know, but there is just something about that guy…"

The two of them sat in chairs close to A. J. But for the circumstances, they were carrying on what would have been considered a normal conversation with him. A. J. was, of course, still weak but his voice was stronger and his head was clear.

"Danella, don't let any of the girls come over here. It's not safe."

"You try telling them! They're sitting still for now, but only on my promise for a telephone call. I bought us some time, saying that you're too weak to entertain visitors but should be able to talk by phone in a few days. They sensed your concern for them and I didn't tell them about the gunman. Steve is going to call them with some official reason for not coming but that won't stop them."

"Steve, any news on the investigations?"

"Yeah, here's what I got..." and he filled him in with the latest available information.

"Steve we've got to get out of here. It's too easy for... They could be nurses, orderlies, janitors..."

"I agree, but the doctors don't. You can't be moved, A. J., not yet."

A. J. was silent for a while then said, "Danella, I need to know exactly what they're giving me. It's compromising my own healing process and we have to eliminate a lot of what they're doing."

"Oh, that will stir him up."

"Who's *him*? I'm the patient and I'm in charge."

"Your neurologist, Dr. Simon."

"Yeah, he's smart and has some good suggestions and he has been keeping me informed. I do need help stopping that spinal leak and I will be reasonable and accept some assistance, but they will do it my way."

"Oh, this could get real interesting," chuckled Steve.

"One other thing - see if you can get their legal officer in here. I want to record my Power Of Attorney appointing Danella. I don't want them making medical decisions for me if I'm out of it."

"Man, you are feeling better."

"No, I just have too much time to think. I can't do anything else."

That brought a sniffle from Danella which she quickly suppressed.

"Baby Girl, I gotta talk to Becky, real soon."

"Sure, can I tell her why?"

"Yes. Tell Beck ... we're going to use our frequency methods to awaken dormant neurons... Then we will forge new nerve connections to paralyzed limbs and body parts. And we start working ... *now*."

She gasped. It was a race between the huge smile across her face and the tears rolling down it.

"I told that smug doctor that 'we would see.' I told *him*!"

Steve squeezed Danella's shoulder, "*ALL RIGHT*!"

ON THE FIFTH DAY of his hospitalization, A. J. had taken a turn for the worse.

"Steve, he was doing fine. Then, as you know, a couple of days ago he started to get weaker. Now, since morning, he's worse. The doctors say it was predictable, he had to much to overcome; but I'm not buying it. Something happened and they're not leveling with me."

"What is A. J. saying about it? He would know."

"He said he wants to talk to you."

"Okay, lets get in there."

"A. J., it's Steve. What's going on? Tell me."
Speaking without the strength in his voice that he had displayed earlier, he said, "Steve, it all started after taking those injections from Simon… I think he or someone is poisoning me."

"That son-of-a-bitch," and he started to get up off his knee.
"No, Steve. Listen to me. I suspected something was wrong but I didn't know for sure until after the injection this morning. I saw the impurity in my blood stream. It built up and I was able to detect it… Mom's gift."
"I can get him arrested for that, A. J. We just need to take your blood sample."
"Yes, but we're not sure he's the one. The serum is always delivered from the lab. Someone in there could be doing this."
"Right, good point."

"If it's Simon, he has to be making a switch in my room because the lab would be delivering untampered serum. He always closes the curtain when he gives me the injection. That's when he could be making the switch.

I'm betting it's him, Steve. Think about it. There was no guard at my room; Simon gives the orders around here and should have posted one. Any trained technician could be giving these injections but he insists on doing it. The lab provides the perfect cover for him. If poison is discovered in my body, the trail leads to the lab and not him.

My senses haven't been that dulled; I'm not being paranoid when I say that man doesn't like me."
"I feel the same way, A. J. He's creepy and rude," added Danella.
"I told you I didn't like him, Steve."

"I have my doubts about him, too. Copper's nose. I think you're right on target, A. J. I'll get him checked out with a full investigation."

"Good. Get someone in here today to take my blood sample and later, after a lab test, give me an antibiotic to offset the poison. Install a camera. He will never suspect it and we can nail him tomorrow morning *if* he's the one who's poisoning me."
"If we do or do not catch him on camera I'll crash his party before he injects you, and if he's made a switch, he'll be arrested."

"Steve, have your Interpol friends armed with search warrants for his house and office. Tell them that you're looking for the poison but I suspect you will find something else, too. There's got to be a reason for all this."

"When do I get to kill him?"
"After we get him on camera, Danella," countered Steve.

The undercover agent was a trained male nurse dressed for the part. He looked like a member of the staff going about his business. He simply pulled the curtain back to hide from the TV cameras and went to work drawing blood and installing a small camera on the inside of the curtain rod. The blood sample came back positive, identifying the poison. They had their evidence.

DR. SIMON FOLLOWED his morning routine. He stopped by the nurses' station, picked up the recently delivered serum and syringe and proceeded to A. J.'s room.

"Good morning, Dr. McCleary, Ms. Fochett, how are things today?"

"I think he's weaker, Doctor."

"The lab reports come in this afternoon. We will figure this thing out. Excuse us, Ms. Fochett, this won't take a second." He pulled the curtain back setting the tray on the bed.

The camera caught it all as he pulled a loaded disposable syringe from his medical jacket replacing it with the lab's syringe and then started the process.

A signal alerted Steve and he bolted out of the closet, ripped the curtain open and wrestled the astonished Simon into handcuffs. The cooperative joint operation with Interpol had their agents in the room collecting evidence and marshaling Simon to an awaiting detention vehicle. At the same moment, agents rushed into his office and house armed with search warrants. It was the perfect sting.

Dr. Simon's office turned up nothing, but the agents confiscated all his computers and forwarded them to their experts for screening. The house where he lived alone was also a dead end. A frustrated Francois was preparing to leave when his cell phone signaled. Hanging up, he said to his people, "Let's get back in there. They picked off a number from one of his computers and it's showing a non-listed receiver at this residence."

The search now took on a different flavor. Book cases and appliances were shoved about. They tapped on the paneling, the ceiling, the parquet floors.

And they found it - a trap door in the laundry room hidden under the dryer.

Even the most experienced espionage investigator would have been shocked: There were several rooms, including a massive electronics complex complete with computers, televisions, printers and high tech satellite equipment.

Its most astonishing feature was what could only be described as a propaganda room for the religious insane - hundreds of pictures and posters of Christ and religious artifacts of all kinds. Boxes and file cabinets were loaded with religious literature, tapes, CD's and DVD's. Books on Christ's teachings were piled everywhere.

And, in stark contrast but perfectly consistent, were thousands of articles written about the great sinners of the world: prostitutes, abortionists, homosexuals, idolators, atheists, and non-believers.

But by far the most frightening was a large room totally devoted to the Antichrist. Hundreds of posters and other printed material depicting the evils of the Antichrist were scattered about. Centered on the wall was a life size blown up photograph of a man dressed in robes with blood dripping from his hands. Underneath the photograph in large letters was printed, 'THE ANTICHRIST'.
His evil face was photoshopped but it was unmistakably the face of A. J. McCleary.

It didn't end there. 'SHE WILL HERALD THE ANTICHRIST' was the inscription on another life size photograph of a woman dressed in scarlet, riding a huge ferocious horse. The photoshopped sultry face was Danella's.

It could have been excused as the home of a depraved religious fanatic except for what was discovered in the rear of the cellar: a weapons room filled with automatic rifles and pistols, short to mid- range rocket launchers, and stacks of ammunition.

A. J. and Danella had inadvertently fallen into the jaws of their enemy.

More astounding information was discovered as they downloaded the computers. Hundreds of coded names appeared, followed by innocuous websites. These websites were regional; one had to live in a region to access its specific site. Most of the websites were European, but there were plenty in the U.S. How Simon had used these sites to pass information was a mystery. Clearly, they were dealing with a big coordinated army of fanatics whose goal was to purge the world of its sinners.

Interpol and the CIA now had a wealth of information and leads to work on. The long and arduous process of following those leads to disrupt and destroy this murderous cult had begun.

"A. J., TELL ME if you're getting tired and we'll continue tomorrow."

"No, I'm fine - just a little overwhelmed. But please go on. I know Danella wants to hear this, too."

"I do, but it can wait."

"No, I want to hear all of it."

"Okay. They're holding Simon on attempted murder and illegal possession of weapons charges. The gunman is now cooperating and Simon should eventually be charged for *that* attempted murder also. The bombing cases are moving forward and it's just a matter of time before they connect him to those crimes."

"How about that Antichrist business? I mean I do look good in red."

"Yeah, you do Danella," agreed A. J.

"So far those photographs haven't shown up anywhere except in his cellar. We're thinking that the whole bizarre display was something only for him and his deranged mind. His fascination with the Antichrist also helps to explain why he was obsessed with explosives. He wanted to disintegrate you guys.

It was just chance that you two landed in his hospital. He never expected you to survive the explosion. He couldn't very well bomb his own hospital so he must have been ecstatic to have the opportunity to personally take you out. To kill the Antichrist."

"Do you think he is the leader of this cult or just a loyal lieutenant?"

"That's the big unanswered question, A. J. We don't know. It'll be interesting when we start arresting his weapon suppliers. The gun has been traced and Interpol is about to act. We'll find out soon whether Simon is the top dog or not."

"Lets hope so. I want this to be over."

"Me too, Danella, which brings up the next problem. Rocket launchers. It's possible that those weapons could also be in the hands of other crazies and, if they are as determined as Simon was, you can't be defended here. We've got to move you, A. J., and it should be out of Europe. We know these fanatics could be anywhere, conducting their lives as responsible citizens like the good Doctor Simon. Your protector could be your killer. It will be months before we can break this thing. They just have to get within a mile of you with those rocket launchers. It's a real problem."

It was late the next morning before Steve got back to the hospital. He found Danella talking quietly with A. J.

"Good morning, Steve, any more interesting news?"

"Yes, Danella, there is. It appears that France sees the problem like we do. They want to offer the government's protection, up until the time that A. J. can be safely transported back to the U.S. Oh, *and* they have recognized Esperanza. Now you have diplomatic security on top of it. They're doing their part, A. J."

"I know they are, Steve, but Danella and I have come up with another plan. I'm still a little weak but feeling better. I'll let her tell you what we have in mind."

"Am I going to like this?"

"We think so," smiled Danella.

"The quicker we leave France the better it will be for everyone concerned. A. J. can travel, but not far. Simon was exaggerating the complications to keep him here where he could get at him. There are problems but nothing that a trained team of medical personnel can't handle. We're going to assemble that team, pay them big bucks and move A. J. within the week. He can't travel far because of the air pressure; we have to prevent more nerves from becoming dormant. We need your help."

"I *am* liking this, what can I do?"

"It's important that no one knows where he is. You've convinced us of that. We want you to figure a way to make it look like we're taking him back to America; but we will be going to another location."
"Right down my alley. I can do that. Ah, you will tell me where you're going. Right?"
"Of course, Agent Lowenstein, because you're going with us and you have to make the arrangements. I've been on the phone all morning and we have been made welcome. They are waiting to talk to you."
"Um, where did you say we're going?"
"I didn't, but A. J. and I have decided to go home."
"You just said you weren't going back to the U.S."
"We have another homeland, Steve. We're going to Ireland."

Chapter 78: Mirrors

DANELLA HAD MADE a bigger impression than she thought during her one week blitz of U.N. functions. Especially with her new friends from Ireland. They were enchanted by her and were proud of a native Irish lass representing a foundation that was doing such important work.

When she and A. J. determined to leave France, Danella contacted one of the Irish diplomats she had met and sought out his help. He was delighted to hear from her and after understanding the problem he put her in touch with an important minister in their Department of State.

The Minister listened politely then said: "We most certainly have heard of Dr. McCleary and you too, Ms. Fochett, I may add. Our U.N. delegation spoke quite highly of you. And we have been following your unfortunate affairs in France. But this is probably a matter for your State Department to be involved in."

Danella responded: "I don't mean to be impolite by disagreeing with you, Mr. Minister, but we don't think this is a matter for the U.S. State Department. You see, both Dr. McCleary and I are citizens of Ireland by birthright; that's why I'm coming directly to you for the protection we require."

He was silent for several seconds. "I did not know. Both of you Irish citizens, now that would be a-changing things! Yes Indeed, Ms. Fochett, Ireland will always protect its own and in your case we would be proud to do so. Have your security people contact me; you are welcome back here, Lass."

STEVE RUSHED INTO the room just as the medical team had completed A. J.'s preparation for the short hop to Ireland.

"A. J., Danella, we've got a problem!"

"What's wrong?" cried Danella.

"There's a woman downstairs confronting security! She says she's a friend of yours, A. J. Do you know her? She's dressed to the nines and standing on six inch stilettos. She's making a scene and insisting that she see you. Oh, she is absolutely stunning..."

"That would be She," chuckled A. J. "I was wondering where she's been. You better let her come up, Steve, she will anyway. Be sure to tell her what to expect in here; She-lagh can sometimes be a little unpredictable."

"Is that your model friend? I've been dying to meet her."

"Yeah, Danella, it is. You're in for a treat."

"Okay, I'll go get her and put everybody on hold. But we're on a tight schedule, A. J. Timing is important here," said Steve smiling.

"Actually, I kinda wanted to meet her too."

She-lagh burst into the room, hesitated, gasped, and went directly to the bedside kneeling on both knees placing her hand on A. J.'s head. Ignoring everybody else and speaking French she blurted out, "THOSE BASTARDS. THOSE SON-OF-A-BITCHING BASTARDS!"

"Hi She. You sound a little upset. What's wrong?" he joked.

"Oh, A. J., A. J., look what they did to you... I'LL KILL THEM! ... KILL THEM!"

"It's going to be okay, She. I want you to meet..."

"I've been on holiday and just heard. Look, here's what were going to do: you're coming back to Geneva with me. The girls will be with you twenty-four-seven; nobody will get by them. I've got great doctors. You know about Geneva's outstanding medical care."

"She..." all he could do was chuckle, "She, I've got my own girl; nobody gets by her either. This is Danella."

"Danella!" She was still on her knees and looked up for the first time since entering the room.

"You're the one who was buried with him?" Danella nodded yes.

She-lagh rose up and kissed her on each cheek. "Yeah, you'll do." She patted Danella on the shoulder then dropped to the floor crawled under the bed on her back and looked straight up into A. J.'s eyes.

"Damn, why didn't I think of that?" exhorted Danella.

"What do you think? Beats hell out of staring at floor tiles, huh tough guy?"

"Yeah, sure does, She, sure does."

"Look. Your security friend tells me I'm on limited time and he's taking you out of here. You call me when you get wherever you're going."

"I will, She."

"And you better be taking Danella with you!"

"I am."

"Good. I feel better. Hey, I've got a new sports car. I'll even let you drive it. Okay, let me slide out of here. And call me, damn it!"

She-lagh was standing next to the bed, "Mirrors, Danella, mirrors. It's an old modeling trick."

"Mirr... yes, YES, I get it. I GET IT. Thanks, geez."

"And *you*, cowboy, you better do a better job in protecting him!"

Steve threw up his hands in mock surrender, "Yes ma'am, I'll try to do my best."

"I love you, A. J." She leaned down and kissed him on the head and walked to the door. She stopped and added, "Danella, have you ever been a model?"

"Well, no."

"Do you want to be one?"

"I've got a job, She-lagh," she laughed.

"Just thought I'd ask." And she left.

"Man, I feel like I've just been electrocuted," shivered Steve. "Okay, lets get this show on the road."

"THEY'VE PICKED UP on our intentional leaks and are waiting out back with cameras. Remember not to look directly at them, Danella," advised Steve.

They wheeled A. J. out and carefully placed him in the waiting evac. Danella was all business and climbed in behind A. J. closing the doors to the click of cameras. They sped off to the airport.

A small U.S. military transport plane sat on the tarmac and the evac van pulled up to it. To the battery of cameramen stationed in the airport's viewing area, it appeared that Danella and Steve boarded the plane as the medical team wheeled A. J. up the plane's rear cargo ramp.

The paramedic closed the evac's doors, jumped in the drivers side and left the tarmac as the plane started its engines. It taxied onto the runway and prepared to take off.

"Man, that agent sure looked like you, Danella. How you doing, A. J.? It was crowded back there."

"Fine, Steve. Where are we heading now?"

"To a garage not far from here. The evac's going to have a makeover then we're off to a private airstrip."

The evac, now looking like a delivery truck, pulled into a hanger and parked next to a Lear jet. They made the transfer and in minutes the three of them, with their small medical team, were in the air heading for the Emerald Isle.

"When they get to Camp David, we will let a few designated photographers get some distance shots of your doubles getting into a military van. I hope her wig stays on straight; you don't look good as a blond, Danella," laughed Steve.

"You're good, Steve, you're good. Maybe we'll fly over Westport. I've never seen my birthplace from the air."

They did fly over her birthplace on the way to their remote new home near the North Atlantic coast.

Chapter 79: You Raise Me Up

A. J. HAD NEVER used his wealth for himself; now he had no choice. They leased a tax foreclosed millionaire's property, complete with airstrip, from the government. The estate was in a restricted private area and was large enough to house themselves, guests, and the small team of private medical personal. Separate quarters were provided for maintenance people and the security team stayed in bungalows on the property.

Steve finagled a reassignment to Europe and he coordinated all the security details. He would never be more than an hour away by air and stayed in close contact with Danella.

It took several days to set up. Danella was working on the last of the details. Nothing happened on the estate without her knowing about it.

"There. Do you prefer to see me full length or just from my head to my waist."

"I want both - the full length mirror and the one showing you at work by your desk with the computer."

"You got it." She made the adjustments and the intricate set of reflective mirrors had her placed perfectly. All A. J. had to do was move his eyes, up or to the side. When he looked down he was staring at a voice controlled computer. He was back with the living.

"She-lagh, I loooove you," sang Danella.

"Okay, lets do it again. Stand in front of the full length mirror and pose."

"Ah, A. J."

"Oh man, do you know how great it is to see you when we are talking?"

"I think so, and we better get to work real soon so I can see you too," she said softly.

"Look, your sisters are going crazy. Are you ready for our first Skype transmission?"

"I have never looked forward this much to anything in my life, Baby Girl. I only wish they could see me too, but they're going to like looking at you. I hope we got this thing set up right."

A. J. AND DANELLA had made good use of the previous owner's communication antennae and satellite dishes. With the help of government technicians, they were electronically up and running.

They hired an air service to deliver supplies and transport any needed medical specialists or passengers. The crew members were never allowed to leave the plane as Steve's privately hired security people professionally went about their work.

A. J. remained electronically connected with everyone but not on a daily basis; he didn't have the energy. Staying connected was another of

Danella's functions and she kept everybody in the loop including her new best friend, She-lagh. A. J. saved his energy for Becky. The two of them were devising theories and conducting electronic experiments. Jessica's talents were once again being utilized. Through her networks, she gathered the latest research data relating to spinal injuries. All information was forwarded to Danella who coordinated it before it was presented to A. J. Danella began to learn the extent of A. J.'s capabilities; he tired easily.

Electromagnetic research for the treatment of spinal cord injuries was being conducted around the world. However, there was nothing promising. Studies showed that they could stimulate neurons but not connect them to the nervous system. It was becoming clear that they would have to be the pioneers in this field of research, too.

Becky and A. J. were experimenting with the same electromagnetic techniques they had used in their fight against cancer. But in those earlier struggles, when outside energy came in, it had a highway to transmit the frequencies: the spinal cord. A. J.'s highway was disrupted at the top *and* the bottom. They needed to fix the highway before A. J. could direct the energies to his limbs and organs.

This was a different approach. They were not resonating organ frequencies but reconnecting nerve endings by using A. J.'s own brain waves to jump start the dormant neurons. This had never even been thought of before. A program had to be built that would initiate the process.

STEVE PAID ONE of his weekly visits and Danella greeted him as he stepped off the plane.

"How's he doing this week? Any progress?"

"No, afraid not, Steve. He spends a lot of time with Becky but both of them are frustrated. My room is across the hall and I hear him talking to his computer in the middle of the night. I'm starting to worry again. I know he refuses to sleep. He keeps working." They entered the house and went directly to A. J.'s room.

"Hey Steve, who's that good looking chick with you?"

Steve hesitated then laughed, "You get me every time with those mirrors, no sneaking up on you."

"I see they filed more charges on Simon."

"Yup. Interpol nailed him on both French bombings; it's murder this time. That's the good news; the bad news is that he didn't act alone. But they're popping little cells every week including some in the good ole U.S. of A. They're running scared, A. J., and making mistakes, but still a threat to you. You made a wise choice coming to Ireland. We don't think they're very active here, if at all, but we still haven't put them out of business."

"Simon still mute?"

"Yes, he does nothing but chant and pray. He hasn't spoken a word since we nabbed him and it's has been over a month now."

"Well, at least we're not front page news anymore. The reporters have even stopped harassing everybody back home."

"Yeah, that's right, and it appears that our little charade has worked. All the world, including the President, thinks you're at Camp David.

Okay, I'm going to go check the troops - talk to you in a little bit."

DR. H. STANLEY PECK was a faculty member at Trinity College of Medicine in Dublin. Recommended by one of Danella's friends in the government, he became A. J.'s primary doctor. Dr. Peck was young and didn't have a private practice. He was receptive to A. J.'s science but he also acknowledged the importance of modern medicine. Stanley was the perfect bridge between the two theories and made routine visits from Dublin to examine A. J. He knew that his principal responsibility was to keep A. J.'s internal organs functioning at an acceptable level, buying him the time to activate his dormant neurons.

Stanley had just finished his weekly examination of A. J. and was discussing his condition with Danella in the house's comfortable study.

"It's remarkable how he is functioning without the assistance of life support machines, antibiotics and other internal medicines that are normally used. But I'm beginning to see a decline, Danella. It's been almost three months now. Those brain messages are not getting through. He can't possibly keep this up no matter how he's doing it."

"Does he still have a fever?"

"Yes, but he did allow me to give him a mild antibiotic. I know that anything we give him interferes with what you're trying to do. And I think we can safely turn him now but you're right in resisting that. You shouldn't do anything to change the angle of the pathways."

"We're not even close, Stanley. I don't know what to do."

"Danella, we might be in for a race against time."

DANELLA HAD BECKY on Skype talking to A. J. on his computer.

"Becky, we're going to have to speed things up. We may have to use an electrical stimulator."

"What? We can't do that! It won't work. You know that we need your own brainwaves to stimulate your cerebral cortex to redirect all that incoming energy! We've got your brainwaves flying all over the planet. Everybody is helping to build the stimulation sequence. There are millions of impulses! We've got to make sure your brain recognizes its own waves and accepts them. Jess has fired up her network and saved our butts again!"

"Beck, I'm slipping… You better build that program now with what you've got or we have to go mechanical. We don't have to stimulate all the neurons, just some of them. The others will literally get the message."

A look of concern came over her face. "You wouldn't have said that if it wasn't getting serious. Okay. I'll get right on it."

"Build the program, Beck. We won't experiment, we will just activate it. You'll have to send it to Danella and she'll transmit it to me."

"A. J., that's dangerous. Without the experiments we won't have any way to determine the safe amount of voltage. She will have to manually make the adjustments! Once it's started she won't be able to leave her computer!"

"I know. God, I know. But we're running out of options."

DANELLA HAD BEEN at his side ever since they had been pulled out from under the rubble. Now, over four months later, the only part of A. J. she ever saw uncovered was the back of his head.

At first she was buoyed by his infectious optimism but as time dragged on she could see his decline. He was constantly battling fevers as he fought off infections and his heart rate was becoming erratic. His blood pressure would spike then stabilize as he directed his mind's energy into the blood flow bypassing the nervous system. He never whimpered or complained and pushed himself beyond his limits talking into his computer.

Danella was the caregiver, the nurse, the nurse's aide. She also ran the house, handled all computer messages and coordinated doctors' visits. When he couldn't sleep at night, neither could she. She was wearing down but drew her strength from him. She spent hours just sitting with him as he dozed off during the day. When he woke up, he'd go back to work and Danella would wearily gather herself together, put on her cheery face and work with him. As long as he was fighting, so would she.

Danella sat in the living area as A. J. was being attended to. She lay her head back on the chair and was absentmindedly humming to a song being played by one of the housekeepers.

"Oh, Danella, I didn't see you there. I'll turn this off if it is bothering you."

"No, not at all, the words are so haunting and… and poignant."

"When I am down and, oh my soul, so weary...hmm, hmm…
You raise me up so I can stand on mountains ...hmm…"

"Who's singing that? It's so beautiful."

"Ah, that be one of our own - the Celtic Women singing You Raise Me Up."

Moments later Stanley came in and joined her, "No, don't move, Danella, I'll sit right here."

"Danella, you've got to start the electromagnetic treatments soon, real soon. In a very short while he may be too weak to respond. The heart problems are getting serious. The spinal column is pretty much healed; you no longer have to wait."

"We're waiting for Becky. She is working day and night. The program crashed a few times but she's almost there." The tiredness in Danella's voice was obvious.

"I noticed you brought in some equipment, Stan. Are you going to forcibly hook him up?"

"No. They're life revivers, defibrillating and breathing apparatus."

He looked intently at Danella, adding, " ... electrolyte enhancers..." He paused. "Those kinds of machines."

"You think he's going to need those?"

"They're not just for him, Danella."

She stared blankly at him and said, "Oh Stan, I'm just a little tired, that's all."

"I'm a doctor, Danella. I know the signs. You're close to your breaking point. You've been constantly caring for him for five months now. You get no rest, no breaks, and you've lost a lot of weight. Look at you; you can barely keep your head up. I know what's going on, you are doing what no one else can. It's only you. The nurses can't help."

"I've got to be there for him...he never gives up. Can you imagine what it's like just lying there face down every second of the day for months on end? He can only move his eyes, Stan, and... and he only has a little feeling when you touch his head." She was sobbing now. "No, no, I promised myself I wouldn't do that. He should be crying, not me, but he never does. If he could see me now it would break his heart." She straightened her back, wiped her eyes and stood up.

"I must go back in there. He will wonder if there's anything wrong."

"Danella, your kind of fatigue is dangerous. Everything could shut down on you all at once! You've got to slow down!"

"I appreciate your concern, Stan, but I can't. I know what Becky's program is going to be like; I've been trained to work with those speeds. There's nobody else."

"Okay, but I'll stick around for a couple of days. I don't think you have the strength to work under this kind of pressure."

TWO DAYS LATER Steve flew in bringing one of the agency's technicians with him. They unloaded several computers and took them to

A. J.'s room setting them up at Danella's work desk next to A. J.'s bed. Steve was on the phone with Becky. "I think we're hooked up per your instructions, Beck: five computers and a large monitoring screen. Brad here says you can send your programs anytime. He's leaving in a few minutes but says there's nothing more for him to do."

"Okay, Steve. Thanks. Put Danella on. Make sure you're on speaker; I want A. J. to hear this."

"I'm here, Beck," answered Danella, "but tell me again what you want me to do." She's tired, thought Becky, she never would have asked that a few months ago.

"Sure. Go to my web site and download the program to all five computers. Go ahead, I will be able to see everything you do and I'll jump in to give you directions if you need it. Take your time." Danella went to work. "Done, Beck."

"Yeah, I see it. You're ready to go. Each computer has a different power amplifier. The voltage increases as you go from computer to computer. The lower output is in the left one and it increases from there, left to right. The voltage is marked on the top part of each screen. That's the best we could come up with on such short notice - crude but it should work."

"I understand. When I start transmitting, all I have to do is check the monitor and if it's too much or too little I just switch to the computer with the proper voltage. Hit a few keys and I'm off."

"You got it, Baby Girl. Just follow the program; it will tell you how to transmit. Each transmission contains millions of different sensory impulses all programed with A. J.'s brainwave frequencies. The signal will be electromagnetically directed to his brain receptors. But only *you* can make the adjustments. There will be a warning. Red means too much voltage, green too little. It will happen incredibly fast. You're the only one I'd trust to do this. Just pretend that they are five Baby Hueys. It should be a piece of cake for you."

"Yeah, where's Huey when I need him?" she sighed.

"Danella, Jess isn't here but she and I will be monitoring. If we're not getting the results we want we will change parts of the program on the fly; you don't have to worry about that. Danella, understand: once you start, you can't stop. It's a glitch we didn't have time to fix. We can slow it down but only for a few minutes."

"I understand. I stop transmitting when the program tells me to, right?"

"Right. It will mean one of two things. We were successful and he's been reconnected or it's a total failure. This has never been done before. Remember, we are only dealing with the cervical damage; the legs come later. We also have no idea how long this will take. We could lose millions of signals and will have to repeat - another glitch. We hate it but we just don't have time to correct the problems."

"You've given us a chance, Beck, that's all we can ask. We're ready."

"Okay, A. J. you there?"

"I am Becky. I got it all just as we discussed. Listen, everybody, I will be going inside, to do my part. I hate to leave you, Baby Girl, but someone has to direct traffic. Steve, I know what Danella will be going through. She's already dog tired. If you see her in trouble don't hesitate, pull her away from the computers. Stan will be close by. I need your word on that."

"You've got it."

"Now wait a minute..."

"Danella, I will not sacrifice you for me, but I promise if we fail, we try again. None of us like the odds, but we don't like the alternative either. Now - positive thoughts everybody.

Danella, you and I are going to be holding hands when this is all over."

There was nothing else said, but they all knew that there would be no second attempts.

"I'm starting transmission, Beck."

Chapter 80: I Love You Baby Girl

THE PROGRAM WAS designed to start slowly and it did. Danella was handling it easily as the green light flashed at long intervals. The commands picked up speed as the program read the brainwaves' feedback. Within thirty minutes the red and green warnings were flashing at an increasingly fast pace. Danella was not wavering.

Steve and Stan stood back anxiously observing. A. J. was silent and still. His computer was turned off.

After they had been in the process for over an hour both men were nervous. Danella was not; she remained composed as she fixated on the monitor. All that could be heard was the clicking of keys.

Suddenly she stopped and appeared to freeze. A calm voice came over the speakers: "Number three, Baby Girl, number three." It was Becky. Danella responded immediately; she had lost only a few seconds.

"Thanks, Becky, thanks. *Hmmm... You Raise Me Up..., hmm.*" Her hands were once again flying from computer to computer. Steve moved a few feet closer to Danella. He looked back at Stan who was shaking his head, no. She was on a short leash; both men were watching her every movement now. She continued on, humming the haunting melody of the song as she did.

Two hours in and there was still no indication that the process was coming to a close. "You're doing fine, Baby Girl, but we are going to slow the program a little. We don't like what we're seeing. You can take your hands off the keyboards. The commands will mean nothing for the next few minutes while we make a change."

She slumped back into her chair and her chin came to rest on her chest.

"Danella, are you all right?" asked Steve. It was the first time he or Stan had spoken since the transmissions started.

Danella didn't even look at him. She merely held up her hand gesturing that she was fine, but they both knew better.

He was about to bring her some water when Becky spoke,
"Sorry it was so short, but here we go." From working with her for so long, Danella knew Becky's M.O. Becky would make one more pass and, if unsuccessful, she would shut it down.

"Please, please," Danella pleaded as the warning lights began to blink furiously.

The next ten minutes seemed like hours to everybody. Suddenly the monitor was flashing. STOP. STOP.
She did. All computers quit simultaneously.
"No, no, tell me you didn't stop it, Beck, tell me."

An eerie silence that lasted for seconds was finally broken by the

sound of Becky's voice.
"It quit on its own, Baby Girl. We'll have to wait for A. J. We have no way of telling…"

Danella sat slumped in her chair, completely worn out. Stan pulled up a wheelchair that he had ready, anticipating her condition.

"Let's set her in this, Steve. I have a room waiting for her. They did. Danella was too exhausted to resist and didn't completely comprehend what was happening. As they were about to move her, she heard A. J. moan. "NO! Stop!" she yelled out, and tried to get out of the chair.
"It's okay, Danella, I'll take you to him," said Steve wheeling her the short distance to the bed.

A. J. had returned and feebly called out for her,
"Danella, are you here?"

She leaned her head close to his and with great effort said,
"Yes, I'm here."
"Danella, look. Look at my hand. Is it moving?"
"I'm looking at it, A. J. No, no it's not moving," she sobbed.
"Move, damn it, move!"

First his fingers twitched, then they started to spread apart.

She gasped. "A. J. A. J. … oh A. J.," and the tears fell.
"I feel it, I feel it, the wetness. Take my hand, Baby Girl, take my hand!"

She took his hand into both of hers, "I can feel your touch, I can feel your hand!" He also felt her tears on his hand and when he realized what they were, he cried too.

Stan rushed to the other side of the bed, "A. J., move your right hand if you can."

He struggled, but he made jerky movements with his fingers. He was moving his head also.
"Whoa, whoa, slow down, not all at once!" said Stan.

"Danella, touch my arm! Oh, I can feel it, I can feel it!"

She was trembling and her hands dropped to her side as she slumped forward. Steve grabbed her.
"A. J., she's hit the wall!" A. J. immediately knew the problem.
"STAN!"

"I've got her, A. J." and he wheeled her out of the room. She had collapsed into the chair.

Medical staff members were waiting for her in the emergency room Stan had set up. He had accurately predicted her collapse and his quick intervention probably saved her life. Her adrenal failure helped to trigger a ventricle fibrillation.

They hooked her up to the defibrillation machine and infused her with intravenous fluid. Her heart actually stopped at one point during the procedure.

Steve stood by her bed. "I need the full report, Stan, and in a hurry or you're going to have another emergency on your hands."

"Tell him she's stabilized and we're keeping her in a deep sleep; that's what she needs now more than anything else. It was close, Steve. Scared the hell out of me. How's *he* doing?"

"Christ, he's moving both arms and demanding to get out of the harness. You better get down there."

"I have a few more things to do here and I'll be right down. If I were a betting man I would have lost my shirt, Steve. Is there anything those people can't do?"

"Not much. My money was on them. Are you sure she is going to be all right?"

"She'll make it. That is one tough lady."

Steve's phone was ringing as he headed back to A. J.'s room. It was Skeet. "Yeah, he's got feeling from above the waist. Danella is stable; I just left her. Look, tell everybody that I'll send them the updates. I can't keep up with the calls. And Monica, call Becky for me. I told her I'd get back. Thanks."

Steve was reassuring A. J. when Stan walked in.

"She's under a twenty-four hour watch, A. J.," reported Stan "We're going to let her sleep for days if that's what her body tells us. We'll know if there's a problem and will deal with it. Now, how about you? I understand you would like to change positions?"

"Stan, I tried to slow her down but she wouldn't listen. You were right about her crashing; you were right about everything. Thanks, Dr. Peck."

"Yeah, it was a real juggling act. Now, I think I know this answer,but do you want me to bring in the picture guys? They've got portable machines."

"Not necessary, Stan, I saw it all. I just have to force myself to use my limbs. It seems that my muscles need to be retrained but they're getting the message. Go ahead and check the internals, but they responded first and are functioning."

"You know this is not supposed to happen."

"I know and it won't for anybody else, at least not as quickly. My mother's gift. But the reconnection process is valid; that's a real breakthrough. Now get me out of this thing, I want to sit up. Don't worry about the lumbar, I saw it and we won't be hurting anything."

THIRTY-SIX HOURS passed and Danella still slept. They periodically wheeled in A. J. and, with his drip bottles attached to his chair, he sat by her bedside. A complete role reversal. He was shaved and showered for the first time since the bombing. A. J. had retained the ability to direct the blood flow to his muscles and remarkably he had suffered little atrophy. However, there was substantial weight loss. He was slowly gaining strength in his arms and shoulders but for now he could only wheel his chair part way to his room.

Still paralyzed from the waist down, he needed help getting in and out of bed. He was awake when Stan walked in.

"Hey, just in time. Help me into the chair. I want to go see Danella."

"Sorry, I can't do that."

"What?"

"Yup, I've got orders not to."

"What do you mean? Who gave those orders?"

"Who do you think? She's coming to visit *you.*"

He sat there not sure he heard right, and then with a smile not seen by anybody for a long time, "She's awake, SHE'S AWAKE!"

"Yeah, last night. Just after you went to bed."

"Why didn't you wake me!"

"Not a chance, more orders. When she woke up, we took her off all the hookups and she was helped into the bathroom. When she didn't recognize the woman looking back at her in the mirror… well, I think her heart stopped again."

"I wouldn't have cared how she looked for god's sake!"

"You sure don't know women. No way she was going to wake you. She bombarded me with questions about your condition then sat in a chair for a while, got tired and went to bed. She's been up for about an hour this morning doing a makeover," he grinned.

"She's coming here? Jesus, Stan, *I* need a makeover!"

"Yeah," he laughed, "I can help you with that. Steve's with Danella. He'll walk her down when you're ready. A. J., I know you saw how thin she was, but she really is terribly underweight and has practically no color. She refuses to wear a lot of makeup, and oh, almost forgot, she wants to know if you want her hair up or down?"

"You're kidding… like I care? No, no wait. Down, I want it down."

"She was afraid you would say that."

He was in the room by himself waiting. His wheel chair was parked next to Danella's armless swivel chair. Smiling, he managed to push himself up and slipped into her chair.

There was a tap on the open door, "Hey, special delivery for one A. J. McCleary," announced Steve as he closed the door leaving the room.

She walked around the corner, stopped, and placed her hand on the wall for support. They looked at each other as if it were the first time they had ever met. In many ways it was. "You're sitting in my chair."

"Yeah, there's room for two," he smiled holding open his arms.

She smiled back, walked over and curled into his lap like a sleepy cat. Holding each other they rocked gently in the swivel chair.

"I love you, Baby Girl."

"Good thing," she purred, "I'd hate to be the only one in love here."

Chapter 81: One More Time

THEY USED THE next several weeks for rest and rehabilitation. Danella moved to a bigger room and set up her computer station. A. J. took over her old spot. He was wheeling himself everywhere and many times Danella would push him around the grounds. Released from all that life threatening pressure, they were rebounding.

Danella gained most of her weight back. Her color had returned and her hair once again had a luster to it. A. J. was still not able to digest solid food so he remained underweight but his strength was returning.

A. J. made it clear that he would not let the girls come over until he was out of his wheelchair. It was only recently that Danella and he had allowed themselves to be viewed on Skype. They looked amazingly fit for what they had been through as they sat side by side talking to friends and family.

"Little Bit, if you don't stop crying we're not going to call you again; you know what that does to me," he scolded as Danella handed him a tissue.
"Okay, okay," she promised, and then cried some more.

It was actually a joyous time as they found more reasons to love one another. They fired up their island house project and had it almost completed. A. J. found a picture of an old European castle and they decided that that would be their next project together - designing a castle of their own.

He was regularly corresponding with Carlos by e-mail, getting updates on the building of Esperanza. The difficult land development was completed and the construction of the Hall and out buildings was well underway.

There were no plans to work on A. J. He wouldn't hear of it until Danella was one-hundred percent recovered. He and Becky collaborated on a scientific report outlining the remarkable and successful procedure of his spinal reconnect. They published in medical journals and it was receiving international acclaim including in America.

Steve was coming that afternoon. It had been a couple of weeks since his last visit. Danella wheeled A. J. out to the air strip to greet him.

"Hey, look at you two," he called out as he bounded down the deployed stairs.
"You guys look great!" he shouted, giving A. J. a high five and Danella a kiss. "Drinking beer yet?"
"No, not yet," laughed A. J., "but Danella will have a glass of wine with you."

It was a beautiful clear day even on the North Atlantic Coast of Ireland and they were enjoying each other's company on the veranda.

Pointing to the south, Danella said, "You know, I was born not too many

miles from here. We'll have to visit Westport before we leave."
"Which brings up another reason for my visit," Steve said. "They've broken up what we're certain was the last remaining group of religious wackos in the U.S. Simon definitely had his hand in the attempted bombings in Detroit and Chicago. His contact in the U.S. had articles about you, A. J., dating back to your Geneva days. They came from Simon. His obsession with killing you and everybody around you has evidently been germinating for years."
"Then it was definitely him and this nightmare is over?"
"Yes, it was Simon and his followers, Danella, and they are out of business. You can safely go home now."
She stood behind A. J.'s chair, "Wow, I'm not sure how to take all this." He took both of her hands as she leaned down hugging him from behind.
"One more piece of good news! We sent the President a full report and he is going to lift the directive. The clinics can start up again."
"Oh, that may be the best news, Steve, just wonderful. Diane will be thrilled."
"Yeah, A. J. I think a couple of things have happened. There is no longer any danger to the public from those maniacs. Your report on the spinal reconnect is getting positive reviews from the medical establishment. And he's up for re-election next year."
"All that might be true, Steve, but you know something? I think that I will vote for the man."
"You're kidding."
"No, I'm not. True, his philosophies of life on all the social issues are totally different than mine, but you know exactly where you stand with him. He's honest. He loves our country and, as you pointed out before, there were dangerous lunatics out there who didn't care who they killed. He had to protect the people, and that came before politics. And when it came down to us, in the end he always did the right thing - like he's doing now. He never caved in to the extremists of his party. I really can't ask for more than that."
Steve looked at him shaking his head, "You're an amazing man, Mr. McCleary, an amazing man."
"So are you Mr. Lowenstein."

DECIDING NOT to risk it, A. J. and Danella remained in Ireland for the reconnect of his lower spine. They weren't certain what effect air pressure would have on dormant neurons.
Danella was back to full health now, but she would not be called upon to repeat her grueling performance.
Becky had cleaned up glitches in the software. The voltage control could now be handled by program commands and they would not drop

signals. However, Becky wanted the sequencing to be complete this time. She wouldn't rush this one and waited for Jessica's people to finish what they had started before.

It had been over two months since the first reconnect and although she didn't show it, Danella was getting nervous. She wasn't clear on the science but she knew that the longer they waited the more difficult it would be to awaken dormant neurons. A. J. *was* clear. He saw a threat developing, not in the reconnect but in the memory of the nerves in the muscles. He knew how difficult it was to retrain the muscles controlled by the cervical nerves, and the nerves in the legs were more complex. They couldn't wait much longer.

Becky's call was perfectly timed. "You two ready to go to work?"

They decided to do the procedure in A. J.'s room. It had been lucky for them before. Now they had a powerful computer specially designed to handle high end voltage and Danella was loading the program. A. J. sat in a slightly reclined Lay-Z-Boy directly in front of the computer. Stan was called in and the medical staff was on hand.

"We're ready, Beck. Tell me when you want us to transmit."

"You can go anytime, Baby Girl, same setup as before. Jess and I are monitoring and if we see something we don't like, we'll stop it. This is going to be so much easier. The program will do everything and we can shut it down with no danger to the procedure. We have a cellular audio connection with you and we can communicate at any time with each other."

"Anything you want to add, A. J.?"

"No. If you and I haven't covered everything by now, we aren't going to."

"No shit."

"We'll talk when I return, Beck."

"Ah, could you make it a little sooner this time?"

"I'll be up and alert for this one, Beck. You'll be the first to know," laughed Danella.

"One more time, guys. We will not have the drama as before. I'm convinced it's going to take a while to retrain my leg muscles. The important thing is the reconnect. I should be able to see it and Stan will confirm if the internals are cooperating as quickly as they did with the cervical. Okay, lets do this. I'm tired of chasing Danella around in a wheelchair; she runs too fast."

With that, A. J. left them and Danella commenced the transmission.

Everybody sat back silently watching the program as the red and green lights flashed on and off at steadily increasing rates.

"Wow, I'm glad I didn't have to deal with those speeds."

"Oh, that's funny, Baby Girl. Yours were much faster than that and you were dealing with five computers!" chimed in Becky. Danella looked at Stan who grinned and nodded his head.

Time dragged on. Danella couldn't sit still and was constantly checking the monitor and looking for any response from A. J. There was none. She wondered where he had gone to, what level of his mind... He had told her what to expect but his low heart rate was frightening to her and to Stan for that matter.

It was quicker this time - exactly one hour and nineteen minutes into the procedure the monitor was flashing. STOP. STOP.

"Beck?"

"I see it, Danella. It stopped on it's own."

A. J. hadn't moved for five minutes. Neither had Danella. His breathing rate increased, his eyes blinked, and he was back. They looked at each other. Her voice was silent but her eyes spoke. A slight smile, then: "We did it, Baby Girl, we did it."

They held on to each other, neither saying a word.

Stan was doing his job and Danella was talking to Becky who was talking to everybody else.

"Wow! They're alive and well; is that how you saw it?"

"Yeah, Stan, just like before; they jumped into action. It doesn't really take that much. There's a real lesson for you guys to learn here."

"Well, when you explain how you can see all that, I'll pass it on to my contemporaries."

"I don't know how I do it, Stan, and I guess I never will."

"Can you move the legs?"

"No. I expected this. They're connected but they don't want to move. This could take a while, quite a while."

In three days A. J. was totally free of all lines, tubes and bags. He was eating solid foods, controlling his lower body parts and showering on his own. He wasn't certain about one area of his lower body and was not ready to seek Danella's help, not just yet anyway. There was no movement in his legs. None.

Days passed with no improvement. If Danella was concerned she never showed it. She had complete faith that one day she would turn around and he would be standing in front of her. For now they were adjusting to his life in a wheelchair.

A. J. *was* concerned. He could see the neurons firing into his legs but the muscles were not getting the message. The pathways were open to receive the information, but his brain was not delivering. He would have to go deeper into the world only known to him and his mother.

Early one morning it came in the form of a leg cramp - the most welcome pain he had ever had. He tried to move his legs. It was difficult and took all his will power but he forced his legs and feet into action. It was hours before Danella expected him. He continued his forceful exercises...

The anticipation of that first step finally was too much to bear. He slid his legs over the side of the bed, rested his feet on the floor and tried to stand up. His knees buckled and he crashed in a heap. Unhurt and laughing to himself, he said, "This is going to take a little practice."

He decided to tell no one of his condition until he could literally stand on his own two feet. He knew what times Danella would be occupied, so for the next week he returned to his room during the day to 'practice'. At night he would train. He wasn't ready to run a marathon but he could walk the distance to Danella's room.

They were in her room sitting side by side as she worked on her computer, putting the final touches on their island house. A. J. was in his wheelchair.

"Hey, I forgot. I have something for you - left it in my room. I'll be right back."

"Okay, I'll be here."

He wheeled out the door, went a short distance, parked his chair,waited, then got up and walked into her room. Her back was to the door and she was looking at her computer screen.

"I'm back but you're going to have to give me a hand with this."

"Oh sure, A. J., sorry, I didn't hear you come in." She turned in her chair. Her eyes widened, she took in a short breath and held it. Slowly standing she took a step toward him still not breathing, not uttering a sound.

"Well, all right. I'll walk half way but you're going to have to do your part." He walked easily and steadily toward her and stopped several feet away. "Well?"

Danella took another step, then three quick steps. She stood in front of him raising her hands, trembling, not sure what to do next.

"You won't knock me over, Baby Girl." He took her into his arms.

It was the first time they had embraced and kissed, really kissed. The other part of his lower body was working just fine.

Chapter 82: The Wedding

THE NEXT FEW days were the most happy of their lives - magical days filled with the glow of intimacy. Danella found an antique walking stick for A. J. and they took long walks together exploring the estate and surrounding area. They Skyped every day with everyone, including Shelagh and promised that they would see them soon.

Sitting on the veranda, A. J. casually said, "I want to go to Esperanza after the wedding."

"What wedding? Who's getting married?"

"We are."

"Ah, A. J., I don't remember you asking for my hand. A girl likes to be asked, you know!"

"I did ask you!"

"When?"

"When you were lying in bed recovering."

"What? I was out of it. I don't remember that!"

"Well, you mumbled something that sounded like yes."

She stared at him for a moment and said, "How would you like to go back into that chair?"

"Oh, all right. If you don't remember, I'll ask you again." He was trying not to laugh. "But only for you." He knelt down and took her hand.

"Danella, will you marry me?" She paused: "I'll think about it." They both laughed falling into each others arms.

A few days later they were on one of their strolls, "You know when I was a little girl I used to walk up a path in my home town here in Ireland and look at a castle that was sitting on a hill. We had moved away but as I got older I used to fantasize about getting married in that old castle."

"Oh? Well, why don't you check it out. Maybe it's open to the public."

"I did. It's now owned by the City but they've opened it up as a tourist attraction. They've never held a wedding there but they do have a small prayer room that most castles had back then. It's tiny - a few benches and an altar - but they would rent it out. What do you think?"

"I think it would be perfect, and you did say you wanted to see your birth place before we left. Let's do it. That will be fun. Go ahead, make the arrangements."

"I did. We're getting married in three weeks."

"Danella! Now who's doing things without conferring? A man likes to help make the plans, you know."

"No, they don't."

"Ah, you're right. What else have you done?"

"Now that you've asked, Steve's coming in from the U.S. He's your best man and the town's priest has agreed to perform the service. That's it - just the four of us. And I told the girls already. We'll send them pictures and throw a giant reception party when we get back home."

"Wow, you have been busy. Is everybody okay with that? You know how women love weddings."

"They were disappointed at first but agreed that this would work out better for everybody. But they're all excited about the reception. Although Becky is concerned about who was going to stay with Chipper; she's like a new mother."

"Chipper. She's got Chipper?"

"Oh, in all this excitement, I forgot to tell you. Deakins helped arrange for Chip's early retirement. Becky was so happy."

"Let's send her a baby card."

"Good idea," laughed Danella.

THREE WEEKS WAS about right. It took them that long to close everything down at the estate. Danella's government friends cleared the way for them to pick up the license the day before the wedding.

They flew into Westport's little airport late that afternoon. Steve was meeting them. He waved to them as they stepped off the plane.

"Hey you guys, come on. Get into the car; we have just enough time to drive to the courthouse and pick up the papers."

"Whoa, you're taking your best man duties seriously."

"Well, hell yeah, A. J. Somebody has to. As soon as we grab the license we head over to the castle. The priest wants to make sure that we know all the rules. Then we hit the pubs. This is a great little town, Danella."

"Yeah, I can't wait to see it."

They could see the castle on the hill as they maneuvered the winding road leading up to it. They passed a shimmering lake and were enjoying the ride through the green valley.

"Wow, it's bigger than what I remember. Oh, A. J. it's beautiful."

Steve parked the car and they entered the castle through its huge front gate and were greeted by a caretaker. "Ah, yes, you must be the wedding party. The priest is in the small room at the end of the hall - the one with the double doors. Go on in; it's unlocked."

"This is just what I expected," said Danella, delighted by the high ceilings and old paintings on the walls of the gallery. "A real castle."

They found the door and Steve opened it for the bride and groom who walked in ahead of him. The room was dark.

"Here, I'll get the lights," said Steve flipping a switch. The room, instantly ablaze with bright lights exploded into a thunderous roar of cheers and applause. It was not a small room and was filled with people - all of them clapping, cheering, laughing and crying.

A. J. was stunned. He thought they were in the wrong room and turned to look at Steve and Danella. They too were clapping, cheering and enjoying every moment of his surprise. He turned back to the cheering crowd. They were all there, all of them. It was like seeing a documentary of his entire life as he began to recognize faces.

Little Bit could contain herself no longer and burst from the crowd, Skeet right behind her. A. J. was still shocked by the moment as he stood there holding them.

"You didn't believe that we would be willing to miss *this*, now did you?" laughed Little Bit.

"Not a chance," chimed in Skeet.

He was speechless.

A. J. released his sisters as the others moved up to greet him. Becky was at the front of the line; they had been through so much together.

"Well, it's about time you got off your butt. I was beginning to worry about you."

"I knew you would never let me stay down, Beautiful Becky." He hugged her and kissed her on the cheek.

"Whatever made me think that you guys wouldn't be here… "

"Genevieve, I see your hand all over this," he smiled as he put his arm around her. Rach, Wylie, Jeff, he hugged them all, kissing Wylie on the neck.

Marcia, Ian, and Diane were there, so were Brandon and his parents, and of course Stan and his staff. "How did everybody get here? When did…? Where are all you guys staying?"

When he saw the two of them, he was shocked: "Dal, Omar… you've come all this way… I, I don't know what to say." He embraced both of them. Dal wasn't concerned about this public display of affection.

A. J. kept looking back at them, smiling, as he moved to greet others. Carlos, Big George and Deakins stood together. 'Perfect' thought A. J. as he warmly greeted these special friends.

Dr. John, Dr. Hughes, Dr. Howe, and Wayne Stover were all there. A. J. thanked them, grasping them by the arms as he shook their hands.

"You saving the best for last?" He smiled and then held her tightly, "You'll always be first, She."

"Okay A. J., I need a picture."

"Patrice!" he exclaimed, happy that she was there. "Can I consider this repayment?"

"In spades, A. J., in spades."

The priest stood back from the crowd. A. J. found him; it brought a warm smile to his face.

His eyes glistened as he embraced the man he had known all his life. "Papa Joe, Papa Joe… of course you would be here. Now it's perfect."

There were others; many of the guests had brought wives, husbands, girlfriends and boyfriends. Danella's Irish diplomat friends were invited along with some of the French government officials who had been so helpful.

Refreshments and appetizers were carted in and the pre-wedding party began. There was a small stage off to the side, big enough for a piano. Two Irish fiddlers joined the piano player and the castle sprang to life with the sounds of rollicking traditional Irish pub songs.

He and Danella were gleefully visiting with everybody.

"Boy, A. J., you really were surprised," giggled Wylie.

"How did you pull it off, Danella?"

"Oh, easy! I just stepped back and let Gen do the work. All I had to do was keep my mouth shut," she laughed.

They moved through the crowd. A. J. had been fascinated by Dal and Omar's report on Rinnistan's phenomenal success story. The Hollywood girls now had them cornered and were taking the opportunity to gather more information for their movie.

"Look at Big George and Carlos," said A. J. nodding in their direction. "They're laughing and having more fun than anybody reliving their old adventures."

"Did you notice Patrice and Stan? They're really hitting it off. He gave her his card; she wondered what the H. stood for in his name. Dr. H. Stanley Peck."

"What does it stand for?" asked A. J. "I think he said Henry."

"Oh, here comes Steve with his new girl friend. She looks familiar."

"She does, A. J., and we're about to meet her."

"Hey, you two, I want you to meet Madison; you know her sister, Hannah."

"Oh yes..." They were interrupted by the clinking of glass.

Skeet announced, "I hope you are enjoying this little party, because, unfortunately, due to all the different travel plans that Gen had to deal with, there won't be a reception. At least not in Ireland. What do you say, everybody? A big thanks to Genevieve." Danella was clapping hardest. "Okay Steve, the Champagne glasses have been passed around. Do your job so we all can get back here by tomorrow morning."

THE IRISH LEPRECHAUNS did *their* job. It was a beautiful sunny day. Everybody had managed to squeeze into the room where the party was held. It had been converted into a church with benches brought in and an altar set up. The musicians were playing Irish love ballads as A. J., Steve and Papa Joe waited at the altar for the bride to make her appearance.

They were doing their best to blend in Irish traditions with an American ceremony. Danella had asked Becky and Jessica to be her maids of honor. She entered from the back of the room, walking to a fiddler's version of Vivaldi's Spring.

The bride was stunning in a peach colored dress open at the neck and cut just above her knees. Her beautiful auburn hair flowed over her shoulders as she gracefully glided down the aisle in open toed high heels. She was joined by Becky and Jessica as she neared the altar.

Papa Joe spoke to the guests before he began the service. "Danella has asked everyone to remain seated after the vows have been exchanged. There will be a special music presentation.

I know that everybody has either read Skeeter's book or has seen the movie. Skeet, Little Bit, Sean, and myself are family. I've known them since they were infants. In Sean's case I've known him not since the day he was born, but the second he was born. I baptized him as he was held in the arms of his saintly mother. Since that day I have performed many services where he was present. None of them were happy ones.

I never thought that I would ever have the opportunity to be with my family again and to preside over such a joyous event. Not only do I have the pleasure of performing my son's marriage ceremony but I am privileged to accept into our family a daughter, his beautiful bride. Welcome Danella, welcome."

The vows were exchanged and the happy couple turned towards the guests who were applauding and stomping and cheering. This was the Irish part of the service. Danella hugged Becky and Jess then proceeded to the musicians stage. She climbed the two stairs and picked up the microphone. A. J. had followed and stood a few feet from her.

The guests quieted as Danella began...

"What a wonderful wedding gift you all have given us by sharing this day. Thank you. I know how difficult it was for many of you on such short notice. I also know that Gen never takes 'NO' for an answer."

"You can say that again," someone yelled out as everybody laughed in agreement. Danella hesitated, lowered her head, looked up and continued. "The last several months... well, they haven't been easy. So many nights, as I tried to sleep, I lay there, weary, frightened, confused and heartbroken." Everybody became very still and were now listening intently to her every word.

"It was easy for me to feel sorry for myself and I would have except my suffering was nothing compared to what A. J. was going through. He couldn't move anything but his eyes for months, but he never gave up. He refused to let it beat him. His inspiration was what kept me going. I had nothing to give him in return except my love and devotion.

At the lowest point, a time just a few months ago, when I was allowing myself to think that maybe neither of us were going to survive, I heard this wonderful inspirational song. It described so much how I felt. With all due apologies to The Celtic Women, as a wedding present to my husband, I would like to sing this wonderful inspirational song to him. It's called 'You Raise Me Up'. And you did, A. J."

Accompanied by the piano and fiddles, she began the slow emotional song.

'When I am down and, oh my soul, so weary ...
You raise me up; to more than I can be...'

She sang it passionately, moving the audience to tears and when she finished, the applause came from their hearts.
Danella walked down the stairs. A. J. was waiting for her.

. . . .

Epilogue

AS THEY WERE cruising somewhere over the Atlantic on a flight to Quito, Danella leaned over and said to A. J.,

"Okay, when you get quiet like this I know something's bothering you. Want to tell me?"

He turned, smiled at his bride and picked up her hand.

"You know, I started all this because I was seeking an explanation to the gifts my mother passed on to me. I failed at that. I have no real idea how I can see into my body or how I learn languages like I do. It's still a mystery."

"A. J., it will be a hundred years or more before anyone figures that out. You have opened the door and laid the groundwork for those who will come after you. They will be studying everything that you did. Let someone else take over; you've done enough. Look at all the people who are alive today because of your quest. And now, there is real hope for those who are paralyzed from spinal injuries. You're going to have to be satisfied with that."

"You know something? You're pretty smart. Are you married?"

"Yes. Now, lets talk about something else. Tell me again why we still need our own country?"

"We are going to create a place where there can be a free exchange of ideas: scientific, business, sociological, doesn't matter. It will be open to anyone but they have to leave their politics at the gate. We're going to provide a forum for cutting edge research and technology without the interference of government or religion.

The Hall will be used for symposiums, conventions, or for just a place to meet. Esperanza will be a little island United Nations. We're going to have to build accommodations for our international guests and I have some ideas about that, too."

"Speaking of which, where are we going to stay? You were a little vague on that, A. J. I don't recall you mentioning anything about a Holiday Inn."

"Hey, we're going to a Pacific island. I thought we could camp on the beach down by the lake. It would be romantic, just the two of us."

"Yeah, that does sound like fun. Great idea!"

"Good, we'll do it. The crawly things shouldn't bother us too much."

"WHAT? What crawly things? I hate crawly things... A. J!"

"Oh, don't worry. They only come out at night."

"That's it. I'm not getting off the plane. NO CRAWLY THINGS!"

"Okay, okay, but there won't be any plane. We're going by boat. You can sleep on the boat."

"Boat? How far is it from Ecuador?"

"About four hundred miles. It will be a nice cruise."
"What kinda boat?"
"You'll see, you'll love it."
They took a cab from the airport and headed for the wharf.
"Boy, this place is busy. Look at all the boats."
"Yes it is. A lot of industrial shipping. Let's see if we can find our ship. There it is, right behind that fishing boat."
"Where? I don't see it."
"There. The one with the blue sides."
"THAT'S IT? A. J., it can't be more than fifteen feet long! I'm not going four hundred miles in that thing!"
"Man, you're picky. All right. Let's see if we can find another one." They walked further down the wharf and stopped.
"There, how about that one?"
"A. J., that's even smaller!"
"No, I mean the one it's tied up to."
"Oh yeah, that would be good," she giggled. "Wow, it must be some billionaire's yacht, what is it... about one hundred feet long?"
"Actually, one hundred and twenty-five."
"We can't take that..."
"Why not? Don't you like the name?"
She took a few steps closer to see around the smaller boat. "Oh my god!" she gasped. There - spelled out in big red letters - was the name:

THE BABY GIRL
WRECKERS ROCKS

"A. J., do you mean? Is this...?"
"Yes, and yes," he grinned. "Come on lets go aboard."
They were greeted at the ramp by uniformed sailors.
"Permission to come aboard, Captain."
"Permission granted Mr. and Mrs. McCleary," cheerily greeted the Captain. Here, let us give you a hand with those carry ons."
"A. J. ..." Danella stood open-mouthed, "This is ... such a ... I'm so... surprised!"
"I'm just getting even, that's all. I bought it from the Columbian government at a terrific price; they kinda confiscated it. Esperanza is the actual owner; it was in the budget."
"When did you get time to do this?"
"Ah, one phone call to Carlos. He knows everybody."
The captain took his time as the honeymooners enjoyed the salt air and gentle breezes. They were the only passengers.
"Do you think Beck will like her navy?"
"She'll hate it, no guns," laughed Danella.

"Hey! You can see the top of the mountain spires. We're not far now!"
As they closed on Esperanza, they were greeted by the Columbian sea police and escorted into the port.
Danella was excited and so was A. J.
"Look, A. J., I can see a little waterfall behind that high wall!"
"Oh yeah. That must be one of the runoffs from the pools filled with rainwater; they drain down into the lake."
They were about to enter the channel, "Geez, that wall is as high as a skyscraper! And it runs straight down into the water!"
"That is going to protect us from hurricanes, Baby Girl. All the development will be on the other side of this range."
"Look, A. J., there's a sculpture! Ships up on rocks. And check out the sign, 'WELCOME TO WRECKERS ROCKS'."
"Oh, nice touch, Carlos, nice touch."
The Columbian sea police on the docks waved to them as they entered the channel. They gave a hardy wave in return.
The Baby Girl pulled into dock on their side of the channel and the crew members jumped off and tied her down. They were parked directly in front of the tunnel. It was more like a wide arch only running for about twenty feet blasted right through the side of the mountain. Above the arch, chiseled into the rock, was the name of their little country.
They stood staring up at the carving, *ESPERANZA*, then made the walk through the tunnel. A. J. and Danella stood on the gravel path and looked around in awe.
"Look at all the vegetation, A. J., and those trees growing out of rocks. I thought you said it was desolate here."
"I thought it was. We're standing in the dredging from the other channel. I didn't realize how much sand and silt were deposited here.
Oh, I see it now. Carlos has sent the runoff from the lake down this little valley. Everything is growing because of the fresh water. He said things grew like crazy here. Was he right!"
A little farther down to their left was a cluster of small structures. Pointing to them he said, "That's where the workers lived. I had them convert those quarters into bungalows. It will be perfect for everybody when they come to visit or work. If they get island fever we'll fly them out or send them cruising on The Baby Girl.
Look to the right of the bungalows; there's the air strip. It looks like they will be able to taxi up close to this path. A perfect entrance."
They continued up the wide path and found the lake.
"Oh, it's bigger than I thought. Look, it curls behind those really high rocks. I can see the waterfalls, A. J., and there's more than one! Where does the lake go?"
"Into small coves full of grottos. Look at the tropical plants growing everywhere. I had no idea. Do you see those open areas in front of the

lake?"
"Yeah, I see them."
"I'm thinking about building a little village there with cottages scattered near the water. What do you think?"
"Now, there's our next project; lets work on it! Spectacular, A. J. I never expected this."
"Your right, it really is spectacular. People are going to love our little country. Lets continue up the path. The Hall should be just around this turn up ahead. Look at all the trees. What a surprise!"

The trail switched-back up and they had to climb a few stairs as they made the turn. There, stuck in the rocks in front of them, appeared the majestic Hall.

"Oh, it's enormous. And all that glass! Come on, A. J. Let's get up there!"

They stood on a small landing and A. J. leaned against a railing.

"Danella, look up behind me." He watched the look on her face as she peered over his head. "Oh, those waterfalls and the wild flowers. It is gorgeous!"
"It's pretty nice down below, too, Baby Girl."

Danella moved up to the railing and stood next to him looking down. She stared transfixed, with disbelief. She glanced at A. J. then looked back down.

"Is...is that...is that? Oh, IT IS, IT IS! A. J. OUR ISLAND HOUSE!"

"My wedding gift to you, Baby Girl. Let's go see our new home on the lake."

■ ■ ■ ■ ■ ■ ■ ■ ■ ■ ■ ■ ■ ■ ■ ■ ■ ■